IDA, *in Love* AND *in Trouble*

Veronica Chambers

LITTLE, BROWN AND COMPANY
New York Boston

This book is a work of historical fiction. In order to give a sense of the times, some names of real people or places have been included in the book. However, the events depicted in this book are imaginary, and the names of nonhistorical persons or events are the product of the author's imagination or are used fictitiously. Any resemblance of such nonhistorical persons or events to actual ones is purely coincidental.

Little, Brown and Company
Hachette Book Group
1290 Avenue of the Americas, New York, NY 10104
Visit us at LBYR.com

First Edition: September 2024

Little, Brown and Company is a division of Hachette Book Group, Inc. The Little, Brown name and logo are registered trademarks of Hachette Book Group, Inc.

The publisher is not responsible for websites (or their content) that are not owned by the publisher.

This book excerpts short quotes from *The Memphis Diary of Ida B. Wells* and *Crusade for Justice: The Autobiography of Ida B. Wells.* These appear as diary entries or in letters to Ida's little sister, Annie.

Quotes from *The Memphis Diary* can be found on pages 7, 44, 47–48, 52, 59–60, 62, 76, 90, 92, 103, 113, 116, 125–128, 132, 140, 157–158, 165, 168–169, 196–197, 210, 214, 217, 240, and 305.

Quotes from *Crusade for Justice* can be found on pages 16, 20, 23–24, 252, 281–282, 302, 350, and 375.

Little, Brown and Company books may be purchased in bulk for business, educational, or promotional use. For information, please contact your local bookseller or the Hachette Book Group Special Markets Department at special.markets@hbgusa.com.

Library of Congress Cataloging-in-Publication Data
Names: Chambers, Veronica, author.
Title: Ida, in love and in trouble / Veronica Chambers.
Description: First edition. | New York : Little, Brown and Company, 2024. | Includes bibliographical references. | Audience: Ages 14 & up | Summary: "A historical novel about Ida B. Wells, from her teen years up through becoming an investigative journalist and civil rights crusader without peer." —Provided by publisher.
Identifiers: LCCN 2023058950 | ISBN 9780316500166 (hardcover) | ISBN 9780316505789 (ebook)
Subjects: CYAC: Wells-Barnett, Ida B., 1862–1931—Fiction. | African American women—Fiction. | Investigative reporting—Fiction. | LCGFT: Novels. | Biographical fiction.
Classification: LCC PZ7.C3575 Id 2024 | DDC [Fic]—dc23
LC record available at https://lccn.loc.gov/2023058950

ISBNs: 978-0-316-50016-6 (hardcover), 978-0-316-50578-9 (ebook)

Printed in Indiana, USA

LSC-C

Printing 1, 2024

For Jason and Flora

&

For Paula Giddings,
whose brilliant scholarship and lively prose
continue to show so many of us
When and Where We Enter

PART ONE

Ida, in Love

1885–1887

Chapter One

The Mikado

February 1886

Ida perched languorously on the banister at the opera house, waiting for the curtain to rise. *The Mikado,* a new comic opera by Gilbert and Sullivan, had come to Memphis.

There were, officially, no segregated sections—only a tacit understanding that Black people and white people might attend the theater together if they kept mindfully to their places. But when the calcium limelights were dim, it was possible to move forward and get a better view—and when Ida could, she did. That night at *The Mikado* was no exception.

Ida had moved as far forward in the theater as she felt safe doing. The front of the mezzanine provided a much better view than the upper balcony.

Her friend Fanny said, "Ida, I think you might be the most courageous woman in all of Memphis."

Ida beamed, but her friend's words revealed the chasm that would always be between them. Fanny was amusing, but she was built to fit into society. Ida was fun, but she was always determined to go her own way.

Despite what her friend thought, Ida was not fearless. She was intimate with fear. It greeted her every morning before the sun rose. It sat heavy on her chest, a fat, lazy cat that refused to move, impervious to her pleas, in the name of all that was good and holy, for it to *shoo.*

But the opera house was not a place that required bravery of Ida. For her there was no corner of the opulent structure that did not delight the senses. If she could, she would enter the grand building early and wander the place, touching it all, from the cool marble to the thick velvet curtains to the ornate golden sculptures that curved up the walls on the orchestra level.

She wondered who had painted the gods and angels on the ceiling frescoes and if they had considered, even for a moment, giving one of the angels brown skin.

She longed to stand at the top of the elaborate staircase and descend as if she were a great diva with a four-octave range. Ida always dressed as if she were going to be seen, and on this particular occasion, she was wearing her favorite dress—a pale blue number with a candy-red underpinning. She had swept her tousle of curls into an elegant bun, and though no one could see her in the dark, she felt beautiful enough to be on the stage. Fanny, who was in all things more understated, wore a pretty pink dress with leaf-green embroidery. Ida would have loved to have a carte de visite of the two of them dressed for the opera. A memory to keep and hold for always.

Ida loved all kinds of live theater, but comic operas were among her favorites. She knew nothing about Japan before she saw *The Mikado,* and some would say she knew even less about what the country was really like after it. But the musical by

Gilbert and Sullivan had been an international hit, and the cast that night in Memphis seemed to delight in the broad, campy humor and the roller coaster of melody they were given to work with.

Ida could see that, beneath all the comedy, there was a great deal of craft. It wasn't just that there was an exquisite harmony between the tenors and altos, the sopranos and mezzo-sopranos. She felt lifted, as if on a hot-air balloon, by the way the singers bobbed and weaved between their chest voices and head voices.

Although some of the lyrics were purposefully nonsensical, Ida noted how the performers sang the staccato verses, making each word perfectly clear:

Three little maids who, all unwary,
Come from a ladies' seminary,
Freed from its genius tutelary.

She could gather the meaning from the context, but she vowed to look the word up—*tutelary.* Ida took elocution classes, because attending the theater in Memphis had taught her that diction was vital. She wanted her words to be understood, not just in her writing, but every time she spoke.

Ida was the daughter of parents who had been enslaved. When she was still just a girl, her parents died. Now there was no one to stand between her and all the pain the world had to offer an orphaned Black girl without connections or means. If fear was insistent on shackling itself to her side, then it had better be prepared to go all the places Ida intended to go.

Each day, her Lord made a decision; *He* decided whether she would live or die.

Each day, Ida had her own decision to make: to live—*really* live—or shrivel and rot in the husk of constraints society intended to assign her based solely on her gender and race. Ida intended to live. Really live. She came to the theater as much as she could. She got as close to the stage as she physically could because for her this was not merely entertainment. The drama onstage was a tonic, a tincture of bravery, a reminder of the boldness she needed to realize her dreams. This was what she was obliged to do with the days she had been given: take her life and put it center stage.

She was young and Black and free. A war had been fought for her liberty. A president had been assassinated for his commitment to justice. More than six hundred thousand men had laid down their lives in the bloodiest battles their nation had ever known.

As she set out in the world, Ida B. Wells did not have parents to warn her to tread lightly, that the Reconstruction South had many perils for Black people still. She had no family name to polish or protect. Day by day, scene by scene, she had to craft a life and cast herself at the center of it. Not as a bit player or a caricature of a hateful past but as a woman of tomorrow—a woman who did not ask or need permission. The blank page was her only dowry, and she intended to take that gift and make herself a writer.

She knew there were some of her race who thought that if they shrank themselves—their dress, their courage, their joy, and their ambition—their playing small would protect them from the whims and furies of the majority race. But Ida thought the notion that there was anything a colored person could do to truly armor themselves against any wrongdoing was a paper-thin folly, an ahistorical illusion.

When the gaslights of the theater dimmed and she was no longer fearful of being caught sitting outside the Black section, there was something else—something that captured her attention more than the singing and dancing and the madcap antics of the players on the stage who bumbled and lurched toward love.

Ida noticed that she and her fellow theatergoers laughed in unison and gasped with a single breath, as if they were musicians in an orchestra being directed by the same maestro. It was almost like a sociology experiment testing the theory that there really was only one race—the human race.

Later, in her diary, Ida would remark of *The Mikado*, "It is a delightful jumble of ridiculous and laughable; a comic combination of songs, speeches and actions, and dress." As the performance roared on, Ida continued to lean over the banister. And Fanny continued to feel what she always felt around Ida, a surge of admiration and just a smidgen of terror. What if they got caught?

Mark Twain called the period they lived in the Gilded Age. Ida had read that it was his belief that America, as it neared the end of the century, sparkled on the surface but was corrupt and lawless underneath.

He was not, of course, referring to the society of Black elites. Theirs was a world he did not know and could not imagine. If there was one thing that made Ida seethe, it was the cloak of invisibility that was constantly thrown over the best of their race—the hardworking, the moral, the educated, the prodigiously brilliant. If she ever met Mark Twain, she would bend his ear and let him know that among the darker hue of American society, there was no pass from the call for justice, no opting out of the quest for equality. As their sister Frances Ellen

Watkins Harper so passionately declared in 1866, "We are all bound up together in one great bundle of humanity."

Ida did not yet know how much Harper's vision for universal rights would become the blueprint for her own life's work. She knew only how deeply her head and her heart called out—*Amen!*—as she read Harper's words: "Society cannot trample on the weakest and feeblest of its members without receiving a curse in its own soul."

She had much to say and many worries, but that night, as Yum-Yum sang in her sweet soprano, "*The sun whose rays are all ablaze*," there was nothing to do but let the music wash over her and let the laughter of the audience lift her soul.

1885

Chapter Two

A New Life in Memphis

Six months before *The Mikado,* Ida had started a new career as a teacher in Memphis. She met the young men and women who would become her colleagues and friends at the New Central House, where the newly elected teachers of the Memphis school district first gathered. It was a bright September day, and the teachers, as well as members of the school board, had gathered for coffee, then a welcome lunch.

In Memphis, there were two classes of young and unmarried Black women. The vast majority worked as domestics and laundresses. Ida passed them in the street, these women holding bags of other people's dirty laundry who dressed up for work in fresh-pressed whites and grays to clean and serve.

Ida belonged to an upper class of men and women barely out of their teens. It was a club, an elite cadre of twenty Black schoolteachers. Only twenty. It was lucky, dream work.

She had come to Memphis alone from Holly Springs, Mississippi, her hometown. After her parents' death when she was sixteen, her brothers had moved in with family in rural parts of

Tennessee. Her aunt Fanny had moved to California in search of better job opportunities, taking her own daughter and Ida's little sisters Annie and Lily with her.

The afternoon had been organized by Tommie Moss, a young man who worked at the New Central House as a manager and who Ida liked immediately. She sat at the table between two women named Fanny: Fanny Thompson and Fannie Bradshaw.

"The sun in Memphis is punishing and exacting. Don't let it catch you without a dress that's pressed and clean," Fannie Bradshaw said, as if Ida needed to be reminded of something as pedestrian as looking sharp.

A stylish young woman who introduced herself as Virginia Broughton reminded her, "White gloves and a parasol are a must on Beale Street."

Fannie Bradshaw, who was quickly becoming Ida's least favorite of the Fannies, clucked, "You're a schoolteacher. Each year, you must be reelected to your post by the school board. I don't know what it was like in Mississippi, but a *Memphis* schoolteacher must be above reproach."

It had always seemed to Ida that, while it was a man's world, women were the wasps you had to watch. One whispered word at teatime and you could spend the whole year in a futile attempt at darning your reputation, with no guarantee that you'd be able to suture the wound.

Ida was taking it all in, the ladies' manual of teaching, when she noticed a young man staring at her. He was tall, almost as tall as her father had been, and he wore a dark gray morning coat and a perfectly pressed white shirt with a high, winged collar. He seemed to have noticed her upon first glance, and he smiled and waved as if greeting an old friend. While the members of the school board made their speeches, he never took his eyes off her.

All throughout the talk of rising above the clouds of ignorance, the ignominy of their enslaved past, and the importance of excellence in character as well as deed, his eyes seemed to be sending a steady message like the clicks of a telegraph: *Be mine. Be mine. Be mine.* When the formal addresses were at last finished and they were free to mingle and meet their fellow teachers, he approached her and said her name, not his: "Miss Ida B. Wells."

His name was Isaiah J. Graham, and he seemed to know all about her. She flushed to think that he had learned so much in such a little time.

They talked about books, Ida's favorite subject, and Ida was impressed that he had his own personal library. She knew by the way he talked about his parents and *their* educational pedigree that he was a member of what they called the Upper Tenth, the wealthiest Black Americans, many of whom were descended from generations of men and women who had been born free.

When he gave her his card and asked to call on her, she carefully put the card in her small shell-shaped purse and wished for the thousandth time that women's dresses had pockets.

Chapter Three

A Breath of Life

A few weeks later, Ida visited the Memphis Lyceum, a literary salon that was one of the most popular social activities in town. The room hushed as Fanny Thompson stepped onto the stage. She wore a chocolate-brown dress with a structured bodice. A lace bib overlay fell across her chest in a deep V; black lace adorned her sleeves and hung like an apron from her skirt.

She smiled at the room of two dozen who had come for the Friday night gathering. The gaslights around them were dimmed, and the room was awash in a saffron glow.

Fanny said plaintively, quoting a line from Ibsen's *A Doll's House* that Ida knew well, "'But our home has never been anything but a playroom. I've been your doll wife—just as I used to be Papa's doll child.'"

She turned to the front row of women, all Lyceum members, and whispered, "'And the children have been my dolls. I used to think it was fun when you came in and played with me, just as I think it's fun when I go in and play games with them.'"

Then, turning to the men, she said, "'That's all our marriage has been, Torvald.'"

The audience erupted into applause, and Ida clapped wildly too. As she brought her gloved hands together in ovation, she thought, *This is* possible. *This is something I can and, most certainly,* will *do.*

In the 1880s, lyceums and literary societies flourished in Black middle-class communities across the country. In Memphis, the Lyceum was run by the city's most prominent Black women, mostly teachers, and their Friday night gathering soon became Ida's favorite part of the week.

Susan B. Anthony and Elizabeth Cady Stanton had gained fame and no small degree of fortune by traveling in the postbellum lyceum circuit, but so had Black women such as Sojourner Truth, Maria W. Stewart, and Harriet Forten Purvis. Before coming to Memphis, Ida had heard these names, but she had not seen her female peers perform in front of an audience of enthralled men and women.

Ida had long heard men speak from pulpits, but at the Memphis Lyceum, women commanded the stage. The first night she attended, she took it all in, from the jeremiads calling for safety and opportunity to the dramatic and musical entertainments that brought the words of Tennyson and the music of Verdi into a community whose every action sought to be part of the lyric and melody in the masterful libretto of post-Reconstruction hope.

The Lyceum became the heartbeat of Ida's life in Memphis. In a letter to her sister, in California, she wrote:

Dear Annie,

Thank you for your last letter. I promise to visit you and L'il in Visalia before the year is over. Right now, Memphis holds me in its thrall. Teaching suits me as I thrill to the world of ideas. And there are suitors who court and send me love letters. (More about them later.) I have also found a community of women friends at the Memphis Lyceum, and it is there I have found what I did not know I was looking for—a breath of life.

The Lyceum is composed mainly of fellow teachers in the Memphis school district. They meet every Friday night in the Vance Street Church. The literary exercises consist of recitations, essays, and debates interspersed with music. It is pure joy to hear the words leap off the page, much the same way we loved Friday-afternoon oratorical speeches when we attended school. The exercises always close with the reading of the Evening Star*—a spicy journal prepared and read by the editor. There are news items, literary notes, criticisms of previous offerings on the program, a They Say column of pleasant personalities—and always some choice poetry.*

I cannot wait until I take to the stage to make my oratorical debut. Do not wish me luck, dear Annie. In the theater, the correct term is "break a leg."

Yours, as ever,
Ida

It was the first week of October, and Ida was still getting settled into her life in Memphis. She was thrilled to be teaching in a big city, not a rural country school, but the classrooms were crowded and the days were long. As she stood in front of the classroom, she wrote the day's schedule on the board:

9-12: PRAYER AND MORNING LESSONS
12-2: LUNCH
2-5: AFTERNOON LESSONS

"It is a fine day. Let us begin with a hymn," she said, smiling at the room crammed with nearly fifty students. It was a fourth-grade class, but the students ranged in age from eight to eleven.

"I'll call out your name, and you sing a verse," Ida continued. "By now, everyone should know the words."

She called on one of her favorite students, Patience Cullen. The girl had a voice like an angel. The girl stood up and began to sing:

All things bright and beautiful,
All creatures great and small,
All things wise and wonderful,
The Lord God made them all.

Henry Coleridge stood up next and began to sing in perfect pitch:

The rich man in his castle,
The poor man at his gate,
God made them, high or lowly,
And ordered their estate.

It inspired her. Their beautiful voices, and the fact that she could make a difference in their lives the way the teachers in her small town had done in hers.

That night, Ida went to the Lyceum filled with a sense of purpose. She felt her mood darken, though, when Lavinia Wormley, one of the Memphis teachers, walked up to her and asked, "Who are your people?"

The question was meant to sting, as it was about class. *Tell me who your parents are, did they go to college, were they born free, do you* belong*?*

Who are your people?

Ida tried not to wince. It was the ultimate Upper Tenth question. The subtext was: *Tell me your lineage, and I will decide just how much you matter.* If the power players in the Black community didn't know you, it was incumbent on you to show them why they should know you. The question brought with it a whole thunderstorm of emotion. Because the answer was neither straightforward nor likely to provoke the warmest response.

Ida was the proud daughter of Jim and Lizzie Wells. She was the oldest of five living children. Her parents and youngest brother had died of yellow fever in '78. Her sisters Annie and Lily were living with her aunt in California. Her brothers George and James, who was called A. J., were training to be carpenters, as their father had been. Her sister Eugenia had suffered from spinal tumors as a toddler and been paralyzed. After their parents' death, Eugenia was sent to an institution and died there. Ida tried not to think about her, the pain and agony of her short life, but Eugenia had been her people too.

Ida had been on her own since she was sixteen. As a child, she read voraciously, the Bible and newspapers and as many novels as she could get her hands on, but she had not been able to fulfill her dream of attending college.

She was a young woman alone in Memphis, and there were

times when this made her vulnerable at worst, suspect at best. Who were her people? For Ida, her people went beyond her family. She wanted to say, *Frederick Douglass is my people.*

Her people were Jane Eyre and every scrappy orphan that literature had to offer. Her people were the heroines of novels, like Meg, Jo, Beth, and Amy—women on a moral, spiritual, and, yes, romantic quest.

Would Lavinia Wormley blink if she named the indomitable Isabel Archer, who kept her company on long winter nights when she read Henry James by lamplight? Ida's people were the good Lord and His son, Jesus. She hoped. She was, she knew, far from pious. But she aspired to do right, and she hoped that if their God was as almighty as promised, He could see past her temper and indiscretions and into her heart.

She knew she had stood silent, staring at Lavinia for far too long. The woman had asked a simple question; only a simple answer was required.

"My people are the Wellses of Holly Springs."

Lavinia raised an eyebrow, pretending to search for a connection when she knew there was none. If the Wellses were Upper Tenth, the name would have shone with all the wattage of a skyful of fireworks on the Fourth of July. Still, politeness demanded that she pretend not to dismiss Ida as what was, in those days, known viciously as a "mulatto nobody."

Light-skinned enough for acceptance, too poor to penetrate the inner circles of the Black elite.

"I don't believe I know the name Wells," Lavinia said.

"That's okay. You will," Ida said with confidence. And then, as she walked away, she whispered to herself, "You certainly will."

She had been loved well and raised well for the first

two-thirds of her life—it was her intention to take what she had been given to craft a life that would make her parents proud. The Wells name would be synonymous with doing good for their people. She would see to that.

At the Lyceum, Ida noted that the skin tones of the women ranged from very fair—those who could nearly pass—to very dark. This made her feel the tent was bigger at the Lyceum than it was in other social circles. In the 1880s, the Black elite began to solidify their ranks—fair skin was often a critical requirement for entry into the most privileged circles. Many of the families could attribute their wealth and education to white fathers who granted them opportunities and sought, in some meaningful way, to acknowledge their paternity. So many of those Blacks who had an elevated status dating, in some cases, to decades before the Civil War shared a commonality of physical features—fair skin, straight hair, light-colored eyes, and aquiline noses—and this mark of privilege morphed into a preferred aesthetic. "Blue veins"—so called because they were Blacks who were light enough that you could see the veins beneath their skin—tightened their ranks lest they be lumped in with the formerly enslaved and bear the punishments that caste of Black people was still made to endure.

Ida knew all of this because her own father, Jim, was the son of a white enslaver. He had been both progeny and property. Yet her white grandfather had sought to do right by his son. It was he who saw to it that Jim trained as a master carpenter. It was because of the connections of his biological father that, in 1870, Jim had the money, $130, to purchase land and build a three-room house near the town square for his young family.

Jim had been light enough to gain entry into any room that the Black elite occupied. Ida's mother had been darker skinned. Ida and her siblings ranged in skin tone from the youngest,

Annie, who could pass for white, to the boys, who were somewhere in the middle, and to Ida and her sisters Lily and Eugenia, who were lighter than their mother but darker than the other children. When the census taker visited their home, he carefully noted that all the Wells children were "mulatto."

Ida was particularly aware that the issue of skin color was one of the ways in which men evaluated potential wives. The men of the Black elite, no matter how dark their own skin, almost always leaned toward whiter-looking wives, with the hopes of producing whiter-looking children. Blanche K. Bruce, the second Black man elected to the US Senate and a social climber of "unconquerable ambition," was said to have sealed his spot in the Upper Tenth with his marriage to Josephine Beall Willson, a woman often described as "fairer than many a Caucasian belle."

Ida saw nothing wanting in her own café au lait visage, but she was a keen observer of society's mores. While these upper-class Blacks did not want to pass for white, one only needed to take in the uniformity of their complexion when entering a room to know how much it mattered.

Two weeks after that "Who are your people?" question, Ida returned to make her stage debut at the Lyceum. She was to perform as Mary, Queen of Scots, opposite Virginia Broughton, who was to play Queen Elizabeth. The two women took to the stage to perform the story. Virginia, dressed in a bright tomato-red costume, played the virgin queen, who never married and ruled England for nearly fifty years. Ida played Mary, the cousin of Elizabeth, who ruled Scotland for twenty-five years and who many thought to be the true heir to the British throne. She dressed in a royal-blue overdress and black breeches, as it was known that Mary wore pants under her dresses to assist in riding horses as she went into battle against her cousin.

The scene Ida and Virginia performed took place after Mary's rebellion had failed and Elizabeth ordered that her cousin be imprisoned. Virginia appeared onstage, and Ida began the monologue she had rehearsed dozens of times: "'Is this Elizabeth, oh God, from out of these features speaks no heart.'"

Embodying Queen Elizabeth's icy chill with what Ida thought was considerable ease, Virginia stared at her haughtily. Ida continued: "'I turned to thee for aid and thou trampling on the rights of a nation and of hospitality hast cruelly treated me, abandoned me and finally exposed me to trial. But no more of the past. We are now face to face. Display thy heart. Tell me the crimes of which I am accused.'"

At the end of the performance, there were hoots and hollers and the clapping lasted so long that Ida felt flush. She and Virginia hugged each other and then, holding hands, took a bow.

The next day, a local correspondent for Cleveland's biggest newspaper gave the performance a rave, declaring it "the crowning literary event" of the night.

Chapter Four

The Evening Star

Right before the holidays, Virginia Broughton unexpectedly stepped down from her post as editor of the Lyceum's literary magazine, the *Evening Star*. The day of the election for the new editor, Ida went to the meeting eager to see who would be chosen to take Virginia's place. Fanny Thompson and fellow Memphis teachers Julia Hooks and Stella Butler were all natural choices. But as the meeting commenced, Julia stood up and announced, "We have chosen one of our newest members to be our new editor...."

Ida felt the room begin to spin around her. She did not actually hear her name, so Fanny had to push her to stand and take the stage. For once, Ida did not know what to say. Somehow, her new peers had seen to the core of her—her dedication to self-learning and the glimmer of raw talent that she knew she possessed. There was emotion, too, behind the flurry of reasoning her brain was engaged in. The election was a sign that despite Ida's sometimes prickly exterior, her peers had embraced her as one of their own.

Over the next few months, Ida poured every spare moment

into her work with the Lyceum and the *Evening Star.* She wrote to Annie that "to my great surprise, I was elected to fill the vacancy. I tried to make my offering as acceptable as hers had been and before long I found that I liked the work. The Lyceum attendance was increased by people who said they came to hear the *Evening Star* read."

It was a providential time for Ida to enter journalism. This was the heyday of the Black press, and readers supported hundreds of newspapers across the country. The *Evening Star* would become Ida's entry into a freelance journalism career that would, within a few years, have her work read nationwide. It was also during this period that she decided to use a pen name: Iola. A thoroughly Victorian single-name moniker that was a play on her first name. She could not remember how she had gotten the nickname. Ida was already a short name and easy to pronounce. But to her siblings, she was always Iola. So, to her readers, who she hoped to hold just as close, she would be the same.

In addition to her work on the *Evening Star,* Ida began to write letters that were increasingly accepted and published by Black weeklies in other cities. J. Dallas Bowser, the publisher of the *Gate City Press* in Missouri, was an Iola fan, as was Reverend L. J. Coppin, the editor of the wildly popular *AME Church Review.* Ida received a letter from Bishop Benjamin Tanner saying he would welcome a missive from "her brilliant pen" for his newspaper, the *Christian Recorder.* Each month, the post brought opportunities for Ida to write, but Ida would not partake in every one.

Miss Ida B. Wells
Memphis, Tennessee

You being one of the most powfull voices of our age and the Arkansas Little Rock Sun *being a new paper, it occurs to me that teaming up is surely the way to go.*

Will you start a branch of our paper in Memphis? You could keep 50 percent of every copy you sold—and of course, we'd feature your own writing, prominently, on a weekly basis.

Very truly yours,
Henry Fulton

Powfull? Ida scoffed; what was the use of writing for an editor who called her writing "powfull"?

As Ida began to organize her teaching clothes for the week, she considered the offer again. It was tempting, being the Memphis editor of a new paper, but having to sell the papers to make money—in addition to teaching and her own writing? That sounded like a losing scheme. She would have to write to him and tell him thank you for the offer, but no.

A few weeks later, Reverend Robert Countee, a pastor of one of the leading Baptist churches who also published a weekly called the *Living Way*, began publishing some of Ida's work from the *Evening Star* and invited her to contribute original essays to the paper on a regular basis. There was no pay, but the paper was highly respected and had readers throughout the country.

"All of this, although gratifying, surprised me very much," she wrote in her journal one evening after teaching school. "I had had no training except what the work on the *Evening Star* had given me, and no literary gifts and graces. But I had observed and thought much about conditions as I had seen them in the country schools and churches. I had an instinctive feeling that the people who had little or no school training should have something coming into their homes weekly which dealt with their problems in a simple, helpful way."

For the *Freeman*, Ida wrote an article called "Woman's Mission." The *Freeman* was the most prestigious Black paper in the nation, and its editor, T. Thomas Fortune, was a lauded member of the Upper Tenth. Ida was still a very young woman, just twenty-three, when she wrote the article asking the question "What is, or should be, a woman?"

Her answer was that a woman was "not merely a bundle of flesh and bones, nor a fashion plate, a frivolous inanity, a soulless doll, a heartless coquette—but a strong, bright presence, thoroughly imbued with a sense of her mission on earth and a desire to fill it."

In the early days, Ida often felt like her writing was rushed, squeezed into the late-night hours between her teaching work, the Lyceum, and the *Evening Star*. But the "Woman's Mission" essay shone with the confident thoughtfulness of an up-and-coming writer who had read widely and thought deeply about the world and her place in it. A new century was approaching, and Ida believed that the potential for women was "boundless." She boldly proclaimed that "only the ages of eternity will serve to show the results of woman's influence."

Thomas Fortune was so impressed that he gave the essay a prominent place in the paper and added a subtitle that introduced the piece as "A Beautiful Christmas Essay on the Duty of Woman in the World's Economy."

Ida slept with that edition of the *Freeman* by her bedside for months after Christmas had come and gone. Mr. Fortune would never fully understand the gift he had given her in championing her work in such a vibrant and unquestioning manner. She would continue to write, and she would teach herself to get better with every word she committed to the page.

At night, when she dimmed her gaslight, she imagined that the night sky, with its bejeweled coat of evening stars, was looking over her when she had no parents or family to do the job. These were the same bright lights that had guided Harriet Tubman, Sojourner Truth, and Frederick Douglass. She knew that in these years so close to and so far from the Civil War, there was a new world being made all around her, and she wanted to be part of it, the changing and the shaping of possibility for herself and her people. This new world for Black Americans would not build itself.

Chapter Five

Uplift the Race

It was a cold, wintry day, and Ida was teaching sonnets to her fourth graders. Booker T. Washington, the esteemed leader of the Tuskegee Institute, had said, "No race can prosper till it learns that there is as much dignity in tilling a field as in writing a poem." But Ida believed that, in troubled times, poetry had the ability to sustain a soul in a way that the pride of a well-tilled field never could. To that end, Ida had been trying to teach her students, who ranged in age from seven to thirteen, a sonnet by Shakespeare. She thought that if they could learn the poems by heart, that even if they eventually made their living tilling the fields, they would know that the soul-stirring power of verse was always within them, ready to be drawn up by the mere utterance of the words.

She watched her students hunch over their slates with pencils. They were supposed to bring their own cloths for cleaning the boards at the end of each day, but most did the job with spit and the sleeves of their shirts. Smiling at the room of forty-eight students, she asked, "Who can tell me what a sonnet is?"

Only two hands raised. Vincent Timrod and Madrenne Tibbs.

She called on Vincent.

"A sonnet is fourteen lines of verse," he said proudly.

Ida then turned to the girl, who looked disappointed that she hadn't been called on. "Madrenne, can you tell the class where the word *sonnet* comes from?"

Madrenne grinned, clearly pleased that she knew the answer. "*Sonnet* is derived from *sonneto*, which is the Italian word for 'little song.'"

"Very good," Ida said, pleased. The students did not know that she herself was enjoying memorizing the sonnets alongside them.

"I need to see more hands for the next part of the lesson, which is reading the sonnets aloud," she said sternly. "I know that more than two of you have memorized this magnificent verse." A dozen hands were raised, and she called on a boy sitting near the back. "Julian Phillips, rise when you recite so the whole room can hear you."

As Julian, a tall, thin boy in a shirt that was just a hair too small and pants that were almost comically big on him, stood up, his shoulders swooped down as if he were wearing a tremendously heavy overcoat. Ida did not admonish him to stand straight, though she longed to. She knew he was painfully shy and that raising his hand to recite the verse had taken all the courage that he had.

"Go ahead, Julian. You'll do fine," she said encouragingly.

"'My mistress' eyes are nothing like the sun....'"

"Very good, Julian," Ida said. "The next line, please."

"'Coral is...'"

"Yes."

"'Coral is far more red than her lips' red.'"

There was some snickering at the mention of "lips," but Ida gave the signal for the class to simmer down and they did. They continued reciting the poem in couplets until the triumphant end.

Bessie Daniels rose and read in a charming Southern drawl:

And yet, by heaven, I think my love as rare
As any she belied with false compare.

Ida enjoyed teaching sonnets because love was very much on her mind. Most of Ida's suitors lived in other cities. In particular, Nashville, where she had done summer studies at Fisk University, and Washington, DC, capital of the Black elite and where all those who aspired to join their ranks eventually went. Isaiah Graham had the advantage of being the only young man pursuing Ida who actually lived in Memphis.

Isaiah had dark skin and tightly coiled hair, and he was the son of a well-to-do family from Georgia. His father was a carpenter who had trained himself in the craft of architecture and used those skills to build up what was a profitable and well-regarded construction business (construction being a bull market in the age of Reconstruction).

Isaiah had a degree in classical literature from Atlanta University, one of the finest Black colleges in the land. Ida found his personal library to be even more dazzling than the man himself. She marveled at his limited-edition copies of novels by Charles Dickens. Ida felt overcome with emotion when he opened texts in Latin and Greek and translated them aloud to her. How could she not have great expectations of a man as learned as Isaiah?

She wrote about him in her diary constantly, referring to him alternately as G, Mr. G, I. J. G., and, when he disappointed her, a cool and distant Mr. Graham.

She went into town to have her picture taken at Greenlee's photo studio on Beale Street. Ida loved how, on Beale Street, one might encounter any of the Black men who were elected officers of the state. There was Lymus Wallace from the Board of Public Works. Then there were Thomas Cassels and Isaac Norris, just two of the fourteen men who held office in the Tennessee General Assembly. Ida saw them regularly coming to and from meetings at Zion Hall.

Beale Street hummed with opportunity. Building wealth was an essential component of the Reconstruction era for Black Americans. As she walked Beale Street, she imagined the greatness that might one day be her fortune. Just the other day, she had read the story of a tailor in Boston, one Mr. John X. Lewis, who not too long ago had been, as the paper described, "a ragged and barefoot slave," and who was now the picture of suited elegance with a business that was flourishing.

At the photography studio, Emile Greenlee was dressed impeccably as always, in a dress shirt, a bow tie, and light-colored pants. His studio featured a number of backdrops and tableaus. Ida felt like a theater star when she visited. One was a pastoral scene painted in a cloudlike hue of grays and whites; Ida always thought it looked like the pathway to heaven. Ida favored a backdrop with a lush lake and mountain behind it. Although Greenlee offered ornate posing chairs, she preferred to stand, as she thought it gave her petite frame a bit of a vertical lift.

The new cabinet photographs were larger than the old ones and were printed on a heavier card stock. You could choose different colors for the face and back of the cardboard mounts. Ida selected a violet hue and smiled as she thought about how smart her name would look typeset across the bottom—*Ida. B. Wells.* Ida advanced her relationship with Isaiah by sending him photographs of herself—a sign that she had deemed his attentions acceptable.

On the way home from Greenlee's, Ida ran into Tommie Moss coming out of his favorite Beale Street barbershop. Tommie wore freedom like it was a coat cut just for him. He wasn't arrogant, but confident. Tommie was part of the vanguard who were making Memphis anew—a member of the McLellan Guards. Tommie was going to be something in this world—even if, like Ida—he did not know exactly *what* that something was yet.

"Good day, Miss Wells," he said, greeting her warmly.

"It is a good day, Tommie," Ida said. "I am headed to the telegraph office next. Walk with me?"

"With pleasure," Tommie said.

They caught up on the latest talk about town; then the conversation turned from banter to dreams.

"I mean to open my own business," Tommie told Ida as they walked. "I was thirteen when I opened my first account in the Freedman's Bank. When the bank failed, I lost it all. Only a hundred dollars. But it was my hundred dollars, each painstakingly earned. But I know that won't be my last hundred. Opportunities are like streetcars in New York City. There's always another one coming."

Tommie was naturally good looking. But he was made even more handsome by the spark of imagination in his eyes and the joyful anticipation that punctuated his words. He was the kind of friend she had moved to Memphis to make.

"I've been dreaming, of late, of pursuing a position as a postal carrier," Tommie said.

Ida, who loved letters themselves more ardently than she did the people who had penned them, beamed.

"A federal appointment!" she cried out, encouragingly. "That would suit you well, Thomas Moss."

"I think it would, but there is a civil service exam and the business of the letter carrier's union. A few Black fellas have gotten in here and there, but it's exceedingly rare in this city."

Ida nodded solemnly. She had not known Thomas Moss long, but she knew he was one of those men who could make a way out of no way. "You'll figure it out, Tommie," she said. "It's the task of our generation—to see just how new the New South intends to be."

Later, Ida wondered why others took offense when *she* slipped on confidence like a string of pearls that slid on easily around her neck. As she walked home, she tried to think it through: *Hold your head high and people say you are uppity. Pick fault with yourself and others will call your bluff and raise you one more, belting out your faults like they were a poorly dealt hand of cards. And the women are worse critics of each other than the men.* And yet, she believed, the women who knew better should do better. They knew what it was like to be vulnerable—to have to play the waiting game for education, for love, for a place in good society. Ida was determined she would strike a different path to success and happiness, with no need to pass judgments on her fellow sisters along the way.

1886

Chapter Six

A Winter of Discontent

It was January 1886, a new year, and Ida was feeling the auld lang syne blues. One Saturday, she opened her mail, hoping for a love letter from Isaiah—who was a little boring but dependable—and got quite the opposite. A bill for ten dollars from her lawyer. Three years before, she'd brought a lawsuit against the railway company after she was thrown out of the ladies' car she'd boarded in Memphis, on her way back to Woodstock, Tennessee, where she had been working as a teacher.

It was common practice to sell Black women tickets to the ladies' car, but it was up to the conductor to decide if the women could stay. The smokers' car, where Black men and sometimes Black women were forced to sit, was known for more than its billowy waves of tobacco. There was often heavy drinking and gambling in those cars, and more than one woman of color had been assaulted in the smokers' car, with the white conductors offering no help or protection.

So, on September 15, 1883, when a white conductor looked at her first-class ticket and brown skin and told her to go to the smokers' car, Ida refused, insisting that "there were rough people in the front car. I have a seat and intend to keep it."

The conductor sized Ida up and said, "I will treat you like a lady. But you must go into the other car."

Ida, only twenty then and unafraid, replied, "If you wish to treat me like a lady, you will leave me alone."

He did not, and instead forcibly removed her from the train. Later, in Memphis, Ida hired a lawyer to bring a suit against the railway company. An attorney named James Greer took the case, and it was tried in the circuit court. Greer found a Black minister, G. H. Clowers, who testified: "I was on the train on 15th September 1883, when plaintiff was ejected from rear car; I was riding in the forward coach. There may have been 3 coaches, certainly not less than 2. The people in said forward coach where I was were rough, they were smoking, talking and drinking, very rough. It was no fit place for a lady. There were no white ladies."

The judge in the case, a white ex–Union soldier named Pierce, sided with Ida and awarded her $500 in damages, a staggering amount, worth almost a year's teaching salary. The headline in the *Memphis Avalanche* read, "A Darky Damsel Obtains a Verdict for Damages." The Chesapeake and Ohio Railway appealed the case to the Tennessee Supreme Court, so Ida didn't receive the damages the judge had awarded her. She paid her lawyer to continue the case, with the hope that she would triumph in the end.

Ida did not know where she would find the money to pay her lawyer as he appealed. It seemed like she could never catch up with her bills. She kept careful track of her spending in her diary. Her job as a teacher paid fifty dollars a month—more than any of the rural schools that she had taught in as a teenager after her parents' death. But the Memphis school board paid their teachers on an erratic quarterly schedule. Sometimes the December payment came in February, for example, or as late as April.

Having no husband, parents, or older siblings to help support her, Ida lived her life on credit. Her journal was the only safe place in which to confide her money woes: "Paid Mrs. Barclay $3 according to my promise on her rent yesterday. She wishes to raise my board, but I cannot do it."

She budgeted her modest check to the best of her ability. Rent was $15 a month. Her monthly streetcar fare added another $6.75. She loved clothing and knew that a pair of shoes cost $4 and the material to make a new dress would run her $15, as much as a month's rent. And, determined to rise in the ranks of the Black elite and augment her education as much as possible, she paid $2 a month for elocution lessons.

Ida and her fellow teachers at the time spent long days in drafty classrooms, not quite warmed by inefficient coal heaters. When public transportation was unavailable, she walked through the elements to work. As a result of these two factors, she suffered from head colds frequently. That year, her expenses included a hefty bill from a doctor for a painful and ongoing ear infection.

On cold winter nights, Ida read by the fireplace. Race was said to be the great divider, but literature illuminated the commonalities. She did not own the book, but she would never forget a searing scene from *Jane Eyre*. Jane, the orphan, has gone to live with her mother's family. She is the poor relation and treated as such. One day, she steals into the library and hides behind a curtain to read a book. Her cousin, John, an obnoxious creature, aged fourteen, finds her and questions: *What are you doing behind the curtain?* She tells him she is reading, and he demands to see her book. Ida remembered thinking that he cut her down for the same reason that enslaved people were forbidden to learn to read and write. Knowledge is always considered dangerous when the ignorant conspire to stay in charge.

Ida had memorized John's vicious words: *You have no money. Your father left you none. You ought to beg and not live here with gentlemen's children like us, and eat the same meals we do and wear clothes at our mama's expense.* Then the venom that will be followed by blows: *Now I'll teach you to rummage our bookshelves.* Even when she had nothing else, Ida could read, and there were books to be borrowed all over Memphis. As a teacher and a journalist, she needed to read, to develop her mind. But fiction was also the gift she gave to herself, it was how she parented herself, taking it all in—from the life lessons of the world to the frothy romances that were like a confectionary shop for her heart. She and the nation were growing up at the same time, deciding what they would become in the century ahead. It was an age of struggle, it was an age of countless questions, but for Ida it was not, by any means, an age of innocence.

Chapter Seven

An Indiscreet Request

February 22 was George Washington's birthday and, as such, a school holiday. Ida decided to spend the unusual free weekday writing, but what to write about? She thought constantly of the coming century. How would their lives be better and different? What invention might change their lives and the world? She spent the birthday of the nation's first president working on a short fiction piece she called "A Story of 1900." She worked until late afternoon, when Isaiah came by to invite her on a sunset stroll down Beale Street.

Most in their circle of teachers considered Ida and Isaiah to be a pair; even their names sounded like they belonged together. But Ida's closest female friends knew that he had not declared himself in a meaningful way, which meant she was still very much a single woman. Ida had told herself that she would promise herself to Isaiah if he asked. But he had not made the gesture yet.

Then she did something that a woman of her era ventured only at great peril to herself and her reputation: She brought money into their relationship.

Dear Isaiah,

It is with great trepidation that I write to ask if you might make a loan to me until our next payment from the Memphis school board.

If you are able to, I trust that you will handle this request with the utmost discretion. It is my solemn promise that this favor will be repaid with 10 percent interest.

Respectfully yours,
Ida B. Wells

Ida sent the note with a trembling hand. She knew Isaiah cared for her, and she believed that anyone who cared for her, to the depths that he claimed to, would not hesitate to help her if he could. His family had means—there was not the hint of shabbiness in his clothes or his living quarters. And then there was this, what Ida considered the greatest indication of Isaiah's wealth: A box of books arrived monthly, new hardcover books, including the latest translations from Europe, from a fine bookshop in New York City—and he never seemed to fret the bill.

She did not specify an amount, as anything he might have lent her would have been of help. She knew that she had crossed a line that elite society would never forgive, but as she wrote in her diary, it was a request she felt compelled to make because, as she confessed to her journal, she had found herself "reduced to such direful extremity." If word got out, her reputation would be ruined and her life in Memphis would be over before it started. She would not be elected by the school board the next year. No reputable landlady would rent her a room. Her only protection against scandal was in the hope that his discretion would match the levels of his declared affection.

The next Saturday, when Isaiah came to visit, he made no mention of Ida's letter or a loan. Rather, he pressed her to state her feelings and plans for their relationship explicitly. Ida watched him test her and thought, *He knows better.* Etiquette dictated that the man be the first to declare his intentions. Ida seethed and thought surely Isaiah was using her indiscreet request to make her flout the rules of propriety. When he left, it was all she could do not to shove him out the door. The loan would have been *helpful,* but she would make do until her next paycheck. More than the money itself, Isaiah failed to see that thwarting convention, loaning her a sum that would have been very easy for him to spare, would have convinced Ida that his feelings went deeper than furtive, stolen kisses and the florid prose that oozed from his pen. He would have shown himself to be a provider and a protector—which, for all her independence, was what Ida wanted most vehemently.

But the awkward exchange and the unresolved tension it created was the start of a dynamic that would color their entire relationship. Isaiah, awed by Ida's beauty and confidence, remained perpetually insecure about her affections and teased her when he sought to woo. And Ida, bothered by the idea that he had failed to rescue her with the loan, thought this was a bad portent for marriage. In the months ahead, she fell in and out of like with Isaiah. As for the request for the loan, neither of them ever spoke of it again.

Chapter Eight

Iola

A few weeks later, Ida rushed to her room in the boardinghouse. The *Living Way* had arrived, and in it was a published letter by Ida. She never got tired of it, seeing her name—her pen name, that is—Iola, in print. "On the page," she confided in her diary, "I have found her—the one I have searched for for so long—the real me."

It was common in those days for small-town weeklies to reprint articles from the bigger papers. Every month, Ida learned her work was appearing in dozens of papers nationwide. She had not come to Memphis to become a journalist, but she was proud of the way her words were winding through postbellum communities. She wrote in her diary: "It was not long before these articles were copied and commentated on by other Negro newspapers in the country and I received letters from other editors inviting me to write for them."

Off the page, Ida still searched for love and wondered what it might look like for a girl like her. With her writing now being read in Black papers all over, Iola was becoming increasingly well-known, and was often introduced, through letters, to eligible young men in cities like Washington, DC, and Nashville.

She believed she had enough beauty to entice an engagement: The letters from suitors in cities near and far that arrived every other day laid claim to it—sonnets that praised her golden-brown skin, her almond-shaped eyes, her slim waist, and the curve of her bosom.

"My new suitor is my very favorite," Ida confided to her friend Fanny as they walked home from school one day.

"Oh, tell me all about him," Fanny said, her eyes twinkling. Fanny wondered how Ida juggled Isaiah and the revolving cast of would-be lovers who corresponded with her from as far away as New York, Denver, and Washington, DC. "And is Isaiah terribly jealous?"

It was not her fault, Ida explained, if Louis M. Brown seemed to possess everything that Isaiah J. Graham lacked. Brown was originally from Memphis, but driven by his own ambition, he moved to Washington, DC. There, he worked for the Pension and Land office, where he also studied part-time toward a law degree at the venerable Howard University.

Like Ida, Louis Brown had journalistic aspirations. He was also a staff editor at and frequent contributor to the *Washington Bee*, which is how the two of them met.

He cleverly sought to woo Ida in print, writing in the *Bee* that Ida was "the brainiest of our female writers." But he did not stop there, Ida told Fanny as she carefully unfolded a newspaper clipping from her purse.

Brown had gone on in the same feature to declare that her

figure was fetching: "She is small in stature and tolerably well-proportioned." He also noted that *her* ambition was "unusual for a woman."

"He writes about you in a major newspaper! The intrigue!" Fanny said, knowing that most of the teachers in their Memphis circle would take to the fainting couch if they were even alluded to in the press. Nice Victorian girls didn't get talked about in public like this. But Ida was different, and that's what they all admired about her.

Ida had, in response, used her column in the *Living Way* to flirt back with Brown, writing that, "The *Bee* informs us that His Royal Highness of the 'Brown line of Kings' will visit the land of his birth soon. He will no doubt receive a warm welcome."

The following weekend, Brown took the train to Memphis, a considerable journey, with the express purpose of visiting Ida. Showing up at her door well after sunset, he invited Ida on a moonlit walk. Later, Ida's heart would beat wildly at the memory of what happened afterward. The two strolled downtown and found in a quiet corner of a park what Brown called "a trysting place." He kissed her, without asking, and the surprise of it, the *pleasure* of it, almost made her fall back with laughter. She'd waited her entire life to be kissed like *that.*

"Are you okay?" he asked when she could not stop giggling. "Did I do something wrong? Did you not care for the kiss?"

"Oh no," she assured him as she gathered her breath and her wits. "It was...perfection. Please do it again."

It took everything she had to pull herself away from the warmth of his embrace and ask him, finally, to walk her home. They were not promised to each other, and she could not be seen kissing a man for whom she had not been pinned. Still, despite the social danger of it all, she was in a daze. His kisses—*where* had he learned to kiss like that?—had filled her up like a hot-air balloon sailing an aerial ocean of desire and affection.

She thought of that first, unexpected kiss that evening, as she did many evenings following. If a felicitous marriage were her main concern, she would set her cap on Louis M. Brown and hope that he would ask for her hand in marriage. Marriage, though, was not Ida's endgame. She meant to become a writer of note before she became a wife. Only she knew that. It was not the kind of thing you could explain to other girls, much less to men who sent you valentines. But the intent to be a writer was pinned on Ida's heart more permanently than any suitor ever could be.

Valentine's Day had brought six furtive declarations of adoration to Ida's doorstep, though not all of them were equally impressive.

A suitor from Kansas City whom she knew only fleetingly, one Mr. Cyril Jones, sent what Ida thought was a letter of wooing words. But as she noted in her journal, "He uses chaste language, but his letters have not the easy and natural grace of a personal letter, rather, it has more of the essay in its makeup. Answered it only on Sunday and my answer was equally dry. I knew absolutely not what to say."

The next day, after school, she was pleased to find a letter from Preston Taylor, one of her most reliable correspondents. Preston was a minister and businessman in Nashville. He was not Ida's dream beau, but his undying affection for her kept him on her roster. His letters read as if he'd labored over them, and Ida appreciated the effort. Sitting on her bed, she held the letter and examined the handwriting. Careful, strong—his was a penmanship that had been practiced.

Dear Ida,

Distance is a devil and it seems another lifetime when you visited Nashville last. Only this page and our Lord know how I long to feel your head on my shoulder. What I would give to spend just one hour gazing into your dark, dancing eyes.

You are more alive than any girl I have ever known. Write to me as often as you can. Each letter embraces me, and I am nothing without your hugs.

Yours and devoted,
Preston Taylor

In her diary, Ida boasted, "There are three men in the city who, with the least encouragement, would make love to me. I have two correspondents in the same predicament."

It was not easy navigating the social maze of dating without a guardian's guidance or a chaperone to uphold her honor, but her growing renown as a journalist and an elocutionist underscored that she was a young woman of good conscience and merit. She was nobody's plaything.

Before she fell asleep that night, she took out her diary once more and wrote:

> I am enjoying existence very much just now. I don't wonder longer but will enjoy life as it comes. I am an anomaly to myself as well as others. I do not wish to be married but I do wish for the society of gentlemen.

She flushed knowing that the society of gentlemen that she frequented pined for her company too.

Chapter Nine

But Dear Me, Let Us Be Elegant or Die!

The first time Ida visited Menken's Palatial Emporium on the corner of Main and Gayoso, she went with her friend Fanny. The Emporium was a five-story building with two elevators, the likes of which had never been seen in Memphis.

They went on a bright April day, two weeks after the new Menken's had opened, when word had spread from one end of Beale Street to another that Black women were allowed to shop at the store unbothered. And moreover, J. S. Menken himself had told the *Memphis Appeal* that his store had no problem with good colored ladies who wanted to buy on credit. But it was only after the grand dames of Memphis's Upper Tenth—Mrs. Settle, Mrs. Graham, Mrs. Church, and Mrs. Love—had visited Menken's, returning with hats and parasols that looked like they came straight off the pages of *Harpers' Bazaar*, that Fanny and Ida made a plan to visit the sumptuous store themselves.

Once they arrived, the difference between the two friends'

temperaments became evident. Fanny was practical and efficient. She took the elevator to the fifth floor, bought a piece of pale blue paper to write her beloved, declared Menken's a marvel, and was ready to go.

Ida, on the other hand, discovered previously unimagined things of beauty and little luxuries to yearn for at the emporium. In the end, she was never sure if she had been born with a longing for sybaritic pleasures or if, in purveying its dazzling assortment of wares, Menken's had made her so.

She fought the impulse to let Fanny know just how annoyed she was that her friend was rushing her through the closest they might ever come to visiting New York or Paris. From the moment she stepped through the front door at Menken's, she felt like she'd gone through the looking glass to realms of modernity and luxury that she had not known enough of to imagine.

"Must be nice to Fanny," she told herself, fixing her face into what she hoped would pass for a smile and agreeing to leave. Life as a teacher, and life in the city, was undoable without female friends. Ida was a single woman who rented rooms in a boardinghouse. Fanny was patient and kind but also funny and forgiving. She needed friends like Fanny around her, especially when snobs like Fannie Bradshaw and Lavinia were always snipping about. It was vital that she not be called out as an orphan, or as a girl of unknowable, or perhaps even questionable, morals. Ida needed to be just another pretty girl in a long dress; a well-read, favorably employed teacher doing the Lord's work, shaping the next generation of Black leaders by day and partaking in only the most genteel of pleasures—tea, checkers, theater—by night.

As they exited Menken's, Fanny invited her to go home with her for the afternoon. They had spent all of fifteen minutes in the store. Fifteen minutes! Ida had noted the time on the giant clock on the first floor when they arrived and had to keep herself from wincing when she saw how little time had passed when Fanny suggested they leave.

She would return to Menken's alone—early on a Saturday when the store first opened, and if they let her, she would pass the whole morning, wandering and taking in each exquisite delight.

On Sunday, Louis Brown came over, and Ida suggested they pass the time by playing a game of checkers. It was one of her favorite entertainments, and over time, she had picked up a number of little strategies that she used to her advantage. One of them was that you should never be afraid to move your pieces to the center. You might sacrifice a playing piece, but you will never win by recoiling to the edges of the board.

As they sipped lemonade, Ida noted that Louis took his time with every move. Finally, an impatient Ida called him on it.

"Must you delay with every turn?" Ida said with a playful air.

"I must consider each move carefully, must I not?" Louis responded.

"Oh, I don't know," Ida said. "My father used to say, 'Study long, study wrong.'"

"With all respect to your father, that seems like a fallacy," Louis insisted. "The longer one studies, the wiser one is likely to become."

"I think what my father meant was that the longer one considers, the more self-doubt mounts."

"I disagree," Louis said, capturing one of Ida's pieces.

But in her next move, Ida claimed a king. Two moves after that, she was victorious.

"Now, sir, I declare the game is finished and I have beaten you," she said.

Louis Brown seemed so shocked by how quickly the game had been lost that Ida feared she had offended him with her skill.

"You are a fine player for a...," he began.

"A lady?" Ida offered.

"No," Louis said. "What I was going to say is that you are a fine player for a newly minted Tennessean."

And with that Ida's whole being softened. She had not done wrong by besting him so decisively.

After that, the week seemed to drag out as she waited for her return visit to Menken's. Tuesday brought a letter from a beau asking Ida to read up on *Othello* as his lyceum might need her to step into the role. On Wednesday, Ida had tea at the home of Mrs. Theodore W. Lott, one of the new generation of housewives in Memphis. Just two decades past Emancipation, it was rare and new for Black women not to have to work outside the home. But Ida did not envy the woman her privilege or position—and it seemed to her, later, that maybe Mrs. Lott knew it. She observed that Mrs. Lott was "good and kind and soft as a mouse." But as she added in her diary, "I like her immensely but can't say the feeling's returned."

As she waited for Saturday, there were articles in the paper about the new store that whet her appetite and imagination. As she was new to Memphis, she did not remember the old Menken's Dry Goods at 261 Main Street. But the local papers gave ample accounts of J. S. Menken, his humble beginnings, and his phoenixlike rise above the cotton-crop crash of 1882.

Ida learned that J. S. Menken had started his first dry goods store in Memphis in 1862. Three years later, his brothers, Nate and Jules, joined him, and the store became Menken Brothers. In 1878, Nate perished in the same yellow fever epidemic that had taken the lives of Ida's parents and her brother.

Menken Brothers thrived for two decades. Then one day in 1882, the employees showed up for work and found the doors to the store locked. There was a "crisis with the cotton crop," as the papers put it. Ida harrumphed. *I bet there was,* she thought. *You can't grow cotton at the same rates without an enslaved workforce.* She was impressed, however, that Menken found financing and paid his employees even when the first store went under, then began plans to rebuild.

The new Menken's at 371–379 Main Street was perhaps the largest department store the South had ever seen. Ida read that the two elevators alone had cost $10,000. The entire street-level front of the building was made not of brick, or brownstone, but of a fine, heavy-plated French glass. The store's entrance was palatial and measured twenty-five feet across, and a carpet welcomed shoppers to a grand vestibule with departments on either side. The stairways were made of the finest mahogany, and two sparkling European chandeliers held pride of place on each of the five floors.

Menken's was also the first store in the region to divide what had been previously sold together as "dry goods" into "departments." Another innovation of J. S. Menken was that he employed young women as "sales ladies" to help shoppers with their purchases.

Ida walked into Menken's the following Saturday dressed in her smartest day dress, a pale yellow-and-brown striped affair that she had sewn herself. She felt as if she belonged, and the elaborately patterned carpet felt as soft as lambswool underneath her feet. She looked up at the chandelier and smiled. In the Bible, the Lord had said, "Let there be light." But never in her days had she imagined that it could be as bright as a hundred suns inside.

The bustle was making a comeback in 1886, but Ida felt her own figure offered enough interest—coming and going—that there was no need to enhance it with extra fabric that made it difficult to move or sit.

She was particularly proud of the cuffed sleeves on her snug, fitted bodice. It had taken forever for her to even out the measurements, but now they lay smartly at the top of her gloves and the effort felt worthwhile. She glanced at the clock and was pleased to feel no worry. She had nowhere to be and she could take her time.

The lower floor of the emporium was dedicated to clothing—women's clothing, primarily—flannels, sateens, linsey-woolsey, matelassé cotton, and all manner of velvets. An exquisitely printed sign called shoppers to the center display with its promise of Silks! Silks! Silks!

This floor also had men's furnishings, and Ida pictured herself as a wife buying pattern and fabric to make her husband a new shirt for church. Another sign extolled that Menken's was the exclusive purveyor of Butterick patterns in the state.

Ida could imagine herself a wife, but she dared not tell a soul how little interest she had in being a mother. Her aunt Fanny wanted money for helping to raise her sisters. Her brothers George and A. J. were old enough to help, but they seemed to be in a constant state of struggle. George, sixteen, worked on and off as a stableman north of Memphis, in Millington, but couldn't seem to keep a job. A. J. was nineteen; he had recently taken to gambling, and his debts often fell at Ida's door.

But that was a worry for another day. Ida was at Menken's,

and there was no place for sorrow in the luxurious dreamland of Silks! Silks! Silks! The second floor was devoted to cloaks, shawls, and carpets. The third and fourth floors were dedicated to the wholesale business, and the fifth floor housed a millinery, an atelier, and a stationery shop, replete with a luxurious sitting area where ladies could take out their purchases and write letters while sipping tea from bone china cups.

William R. Moore, a former Tennessee congressman and a pro-Lincoln supporter, told a reporter at the *Appeal*:

> I consider Menken's one of the finest dry goods stores in the world. There are not a dozen finer stores on Earth. Stewarts is the only one in New York. Shillito, in Cincinnati, has more goods but is no more handsome inside and very little larger. Macy's, in New York, covers more ground but is a succession of old houses that were formerly residences and can't be compared to Menken's. London, with a population of four million, has not a dry goods store as this.

Ida had not been to New York or Chicago or London, but she took Moore at his word. And she had not met royalty, but no store had ever made her feel as close to royalty as Menken's. She decided to purchase a coat, on credit. She had spent the whole winter in a coat that her father had bought before his death. It was eight years old now, tight across the chest and cobweb thin.

She wandered the coats and considered every one within her price range. She felt like she could confidently spend a month's salary on a coat that would last for years and years. She challenged herself to be moved by practicality and not just beauty. A cherry-red coat was beautiful but would instantly be judged as too flashy. She longed for a deep-purple coat with a fur collar, but the price tag convinced her it was out of her range. It was far too dear. Finally, a salesgirl showed her a coat that had just recently gone on sale.

"This is the last of its kind," the girl said. "But I think it will fit you. Try it on."

Ida put it on, and while it was a little big in the shoulders, she thought this was actually an advantage.

She loved the color—the darkest navy with an exquisite black brocade trim.

The salesgirl wrapped it in a dark brown paper and tied the parcel with a thin floss of bright pink.

The following weekend, Ida wore her new coat to see *Dorothy*, a new comic opera at the Memphis Opera House. Accompanied by Isaiah and Fanny, she sat in the segregated section—not wanting to risk censure with a man in their company.

The musical was set in the English countryside, and Ida sat transfixed by how the characters of Dorothy and Lydia took control of their romantic future with both a lighthearted playfulness and a thoroughly modern daring.

On the way home, walking down Beale Street, Fanny and Ida locked arms and sang the giddy, silly, chorus from the third act—*Dancing is not what it used to be.* Isaiah looked alternately charmed and embarrassed. The streetlights glowed like faded yellow suns above them, and Ida was, without questioning or needing to add a postscript to the sentiment, happy. There was nothing like the spectacle of theater to cheer her. Song and dance and no requirement of her at all except that she open her heart and let the music pour in.

Chapter Ten

Letters from Mr. Charles S. Morris

Ida came home from school, the hem of her off-white dress a dusty brown from the streetcar ride. She took off her scarlet gloves, her compromise between the expectations of dress for a young woman in the burgeoning middle class and her own fanciful desires for bolder fashion statements.

She went to her room and began work on a piece that held a common theme in her early writing: the virtue of Black women and the importance of upholding Victorian ideals despite the slurs and indignities that remained from the days of enslavement.

She read the first few paragraphs over and, satisfied with the start, put her pen down. She would finish the piece that weekend and send it off to Thomas Fortune at the *Freeman*. She titled the piece "Our Women," and Thomas Fortune added the subtitle, "The Brilliant 'Iola' Defends Them."

If one needed proof that 1886 was not the same as 1876 or

even 1880, one need only look to this, a letter in *Lippincott's Monthly Magazine* that declared the Great American Novel would be written by a Black woman whose unique lens on the matters of race and gender would give her an unrivaled perspective on where the nation was and where it was going.

When Ida read these words, her whole body buzzed with possibility: Was this the sign she had searched for—the one that would call her from the waiting lounge of youth into the path of purpose and, perhaps, even prosperity?

Her love of literature was heightened by a new and lively correspondence with a Mr. Charles S. Morris of Louisville, Kentucky, whom Ida had met through the newspaper circuit. Like Isaiah, Charles came from a family of privilege and stature. He was a graduate of Howard University, and both his parents and grandparents were free-born Blacks. One fact that captured Ida's attention: Charles's maternal great-grandmother had been the half-sister of the founding First Lady of the United States, Martha Washington.

On Saturday, there was a letter from Charles. She held the letter in her hand and kissed it as if the man himself were in her arms and not a thousand miles away in Washington, DC. Then, lest anyone catch her in what she knew was a ditzy, girlish display, she retired to her room and threw herself on the bed. She kissed the letter three more times, sighing deeply after each peck. Finally, satisfied that she had extracted from the envelope all the magic it contained, she broke the seal and began to read.

Dear Ida,

You are a terrible distraction, and by "terrible," I mean "wonderful." I write you letters in my head all day, for there is not enough time or money or ink to capture all I'd like to say to you on the page.

Like you, I don't trust the man or woman who says, "I make friends wherever I go." There is so much fakery in society these days, I do not have the patience or temperament for it, and perhaps that will be my downfall.

Yet, just when I think I am lost, I come home to find a letter from you. Writing to you feels like talking to a dear and most treasured friend. And yet, we have never met—explain that riddle to me. That you answer my letters quickly is kind compensation for all I risk in baring myself to you.

When this letter is in the envelope and gone, I know I will feel a familiar loneliness. For I will not be sitting at my desk, talking to you with my pen. You are in Memphis, and the little closeness I feel is nothing more than an illusion. It is terrible. Also, blissful. The very best kind of deception. I bring it on myself and ask for more.

Yours with esteem,
Charles

"Found a letter from Mr. C. S. M. on my arrival home this afternoon instead of tomorrow as I expected," Ida wrote in her journal. "He understands and sympathizes with my position of almost complete isolation from my fellow being on account of lack of congeniality—and I think he does so more fully because his *own* experience coincides with mine."

Isaiah—with his love of Greek and Latin—had been

bookish to the point of being bungling and awkward. Charles, in comparison, was confident and quick-witted. He impressed Ida with his flirtatiousness and wordplay. She confided to her journal that she knew she could be fickle, but she wanted to give herself the space to follow her heart: "It seems I can establish no middle ground. It is either love or nothing."

To his great heartbreak, Isaiah was—at least for the time being—out; Louis Brown had been relegated to charming pen pal; and the charismatic and handsome suitor from Washington, DC, Charles Morris, was in.

The next day, Ida came home to find another letter from Charles. She put it in her room, deciding to save it for the end of the evening, when she could savor the words without distraction.

Mrs. Barclay asked if Ida would make supper, and Ida agreed.

"There's more than a few slices of beef left from Sunday supper, and I have made a fresh loaf of bread," the landlady explained.

"Certainly," Ida said.

She put Charles's letter on the small desk in her room and changed out of her teaching clothes into a simple white afternoon dress presentable enough if anyone came by but not meant to be worn outdoors.

In the kitchen, she cut the bread into thin slices and fried it in lard until it turned a satisfying shade of golden brown. Then she warmed the meat until it went from pink to well-done. She cut some fresh parsley and marveled that it smelled as green as it looked. Finally, she added a few shavings of fresh horseradish to a small side dish. She assembled the sandwiches carefully, cutting them into triangles, then piling them into a pyramid shape. There were fresh apples and grapes, and they would do for dessert.

After dinner, when the other girls had gone to bed and all the dishes were washed up, she went into her room and opened the letter.

Dearest Ida,

I am intrigued by the idea of you becoming a novelist like the Brontë sisters, because ours, I am sure of it, is the age of ambition.

I have never read a novel that captured the wild tales of families such as the ones I know. My parents and <u>their</u> parents were born free. My mother's grandmother was the half-sister of Martha Washington. Yet no one looks upon my kin and considers them founding mothers and fathers. No one has captured on the page the role they played in the building of this undeniably great nation.

If you should write a classical and representative work that elevates our world to the literary heights it deserves, then I do not doubt that you will find yourself, as you deserve, showered with love, respect, and honor.

Yours and devoted,
Charles S. Morris

Ida pressed the letter to her chest and then to her lips. Showered with Love. With Respect. With Honor. Was there anything else that a woman might desire? Dare she call him Charlie in her next missive? She smiled to herself—the thought of rewarding him with a pet name gave her no small amount of pleasure.

In the letter, there was a picture. She stared at it for a second. *Hmm,* she thought to herself. *He looks awfully young.*

She knew he was a divinity student, but as she gazed upon his visage, she couldn't help but think, *I thought him a man but this is the face of a mere boy.*

She wrote to him about his youth and inquired about his age. His response was sharp and reminded her that none of the men who corresponded with her could match Charles Morris for interest or intrigue.

Dear Ida,

You can be assured that I am no mere boy. It is the privilege, nay I say custom, of young men of our age to school themselves in the matters of the world before marriage. Do not count my years, but know that you can count on me being one who has arrived at manhood as a gentleman—and an adventurer.

Ever Yours,
Charles

His letter made Ida flush. This was, she was sure of it, how it felt to be spoken to as a woman, without having to pretend to have bandages over one's eyes. What had he learned as an adventurer? And what might he teach her if she was his true love? "Oh, Charlie," she whispered, using the nickname she dare not yet commit to the page. "How skillfully you navigate your epistolary bark to clear my shoals and quicksands."

The next day, Ida made an invitation to her favorite school friend, Fanny Thompson.

"Fanny, will you join me tomorrow for afternoon tea?"

"I would be delighted," Fanny said. "Jack Frost persists in his hold on us, and a warm cup of tea will do our weary bodies good."

"Splendid," Ida said. "I will make a raspberry tea cake. I've got a jar of preserved raspberries that I've been saving for just such an occasion."

Ida's mother had been lauded throughout their region of Mississippi as an extraordinary cook. Ida did not aspire to follow in her footsteps professionally, and yet it would have been impossible to spend sixteen years as Lizzie Wells's daughter and not learn the lessons that tumbled out of her pots and pans with the simple perfection of an unrestrained aria.

Ida enjoyed entertaining visitors. There was a great comfort in making a pot of coffee, pouring it into two cups decorated with a floral pattern, and slicing two hearty pieces of the homemade cake. She heard the knock at the door at the appointed hour and took a second to smooth her hair and wash her hands.

She and Fanny sat in the parlor room, and Ida revealed how Charles Morris had begun to permeate her every waking thought.

"I can hardly state the impression his letters have made upon me," Ida said dreamily.

"What do you like about him, not having yet met him in person?" asked Fanny.

"What don't I like?" Ida swooned. "Or more precisely, what does he not know? He woos me with literature, philosophy, and science. I think at last I have met the kind of highbrow being who can lead and direct my wavering footsteps in intellectual paths."

Sometimes Ida thought that she was profligate in her correspondence because it was something she could reach for. She still dreamed of university, of Fisk and the other schools that were offering opportunities for young women to improve their minds and lots in life. But there was also this. The feeling that she had made it to the lower middle class, to the land of the have-somes. She was welcome in any drawing room in Memphis's middle class, and her full mailbox was evidence that word of her—her beauty, her wit, her promise—was spreading. She would take what she had been given and alchemize it into something meaningful.

Dear Charlie,

I call you by the pet name that I use in my head. I hope that you do not find it forward. It is only that I can no longer hide behind the formality of proper names, when I am dizzy with your knowledge, starry eyed on the ideas that flow between us.

I wish you were here, or I were there, and that we could take long walks and discuss the books we have read and the ones we might write. I've read that the Library of Congress has more than 200,000 volumes in its holdings. It boggles the mind.

Have you ever visited it? I know that one of our own, Daniel Murray, is employed there. What a life that must be, to spend one's days surrounded by such portals of knowledge. I wouldn't need to take a single one off the shelves. I would just like to walk down the stacks and touch the spines if I could, take in the aromas. The scent of very old books is among my favorites.

I have endeavored to read Fool's Errand *by Tourgée, but it is slow going. I agree with him when he writes, "Reconstruction was a failure, so far as it attempted to unify the nation, to make one people in fact of what had been one only in name before the convulsion of Civil War. It was a failure, too, so far as it attempted to fix and secure the position and rights of the colored race." But I think the novel itself is a failure; it trembles along the tightropes of political propaganda and melodrama and topples at the chasm in between. It leaves me neither with optimism for the nation nor the least concern for the main characters—Eliza and Michael.*

Tonight, there is much to prepare for. There is an inauguration for a training school of manual labor at the LeMoyne Institute. There will be a mixed reception of Black and white teachers. Colonel J. M. Keating, the editor of the Memphis Appeal*, will make an address, as will Rabbi Max Samfield, who heads the synagogue on Poplar Street. It is for this, nights wild with new ideas, that I came to Memphis.*

Ever yours,
Ida

After the disappointment of *Fool's Errand*, Ida had turned to reading *Ivanhoe* by Sir Walter Scott. She was twenty-four years old and had read, by her count, more than two hundred books. But she had still never read a novel by a Black author, and never one by a Black woman like herself. Could she do it? Could she craft characters and scenes that brought her own people to life on the page? She wanted to, and surely there was some inspiration to be found in the pages of Scott's Saxon romance. Ida sat on the bed in her room and read aloud her favorite passage from the novel: "'I have heard men talk about the blessings of freedom. But I wish any wise man would teach me—what use to make of it now that I have it?'"

Ida closed the book and considered how it seemed like all the very good questions were buried in books. *What use to make of freedom* now*?* Certainly, that question, and the urgency of it, was a dilemma for her people too.

Chapter Eleven

Honey for Friends, Stings for Enemies

The presidency of Grover Cleveland had not set Ida's mind at ease. While some supposed that it was worth it to give a New York Democrat a chance, Ida felt that it was foolish for Black Americans to pledge party allegiance to either the Republicans or Democrats.

She wrote a searing condemnation of the limited choices to Black voters that was published in the *Freeman*:

> I am not a Democrat because the Democrats considered me a chattel and possibly might have always so considered me, because their record from the beginning has been inimical to my interests; because they had become notorious in their hatred of the Negro as a man, have refused him the ballot, have murdered, beaten and outraged him and refused him his rights.

In the same editorial, she let it be clear that she had little trust for the party of Lincoln, the Republicans:

> **I am not a Republican, because, after they—as a party measure and an inevitable result of the war—had "given the Negro his freedom" and the ballot box following...**

She paused then and read her words aloud, feeling the weight of them and wondering if they captured all her rage and ire. "'All through their reign,'" she said, "'while supposedly advocating the doctrine of the Federal Government's right of protecting her citizens—they suffered the crimes against the Negro, that have made the South notorious, to go unpunished and almost unnoticed.'"

Black people had been, she believed, the backbone of the American south. And yet for all their toil and fealty, they remained more prey than peers. But that was right: The crimes against her people went unpunished and almost unnoticed. There was a new wave of restrictions and subsequent repercussions that were making the lives of the Black middle class harder to navigate.

That week, a woman named Belinda Shelby had come to Memphis to visit family friends for the Easter holiday. Ida could hardly believe it when news spread around town that Shelby had been forcibly removed and manhandled by two police officers for wandering into what was often referred to but was not publicly demarcated as "the white park." Learning to read between the racial lines was so essential, but not simple at all. Ida felt it was her duty to write about the world in "a simple, helpful way." She would go on to explain, "I wrote in a plain common-sense way on the things which concerned our people. I never used a word of two syllables where one would serve the purpose."

Blacks could not count on Republicans for protection, as they had in the past. For context, she wrote, one need only look to the events of the last ten years.

> In consideration of the fact of the unjust treatment of the Negro in the South; of the outrages and discriminations to which he has been a victim... do you really and candidly believe your assertion that if appealed to in honesty the white people of the South "could not and would not refuse us justice?" I don't believe it, because they have been notably deaf to our calls of justice heretofore.

Ida longed to sign her own name to the damning words, but she signed, instead, Iola. Everyone who mattered knew who she was.

One Friday evening at the Lyceum, Robert Countee, the editor of the *Living Way*, took to the stage and began to give an extemporaneous lecture on the origins of the fraternities and their growing influence in Black communities. There were more than a hundred men and women in the audience—members of the church, the press, and the Lyceum, as well as the secret societies.

In Memphis, fraternities such as the Odd Fellows and the Masons were increasingly popular in the 1880s. They took their place in Black society, alongside postwar secret societies such as the Sons and Daughters of Ham, who had agitated, underground, for civil rights and protections during the turbulent years of Reconstruction when the paths to political clout were anything but clear.

Ida had seen firsthand that in cities like Memphis where

there were very few Black elected officials, the fraternities, with their growing power and coffers, could exert influence on behalf of citizens when necessary. But Black ministers loudly and vehemently railed against both the time and money that these new social clubs drew away from their churches.

Ida occupied an interesting place on the spectrum of these debates. Many of the weekly publications she wrote for were funded by the churches. For her, the press and its backers were a necessary choice—if not on the question of morality, then on the question of her burgeoning journalism career.

"Do we know who we mean when we talk about the Masons?" Countee asked as he began his lecture at the Lyceum. "George Washington was a Mason, as were nine of the men who signed the Declaration of Independence. Every time we use the name John Hancock as a euphemism for our signature, we are, in fact, keeping the lore of a beloved Mason alive."

The crowd began to whisper among themselves. You did not discuss the Masons in loud tones, in polite society, and you never bellowed about them from any stage. Ida herself wondered, *What is Countee playing at?*

Taking the crowd's murmurings as encouragement, Countee smiled and continued. "But what are the tenets of an organization like the Masons? They believe in self-government and free enterprise. They believe God does not bother with the deeds of man as long as he abides by the laws of nature in this world that the Almighty has created."

The whispers had turned from a low-level hum to a persistent chatter.

"What did this mean?" many wondered. "Were the Masons atheists, or Christians who sought a way to circumvent spiritual laws?"

"There are rituals and emblems when one belongs to the Masons," Countee said—bravely, Ida thought. "You've no doubt heard of the secret handshakes, but did you know there are costumes? Some might say it is not my role to speak of an organization with which I am neither affiliated nor in conflict with. But as a man of the press, I believe that it is my job to hold the powerful accountable. So let's talk about the rituals and secrets."

He opened a memorandum notebook, and just as he was about to reveal what many of the crowd had longed to know, a melee ensued. Ida did not know who knocked Countee on his back. But within seconds, there was a tussle of ministers and fraternity men throwing blows, and every woman except Ida in the establishment headed for the door.

Ida rushed to the stage, looking frantically on the floor for the editor's notebook. She searched in vain but was determined to continue when she felt a tug on her arm. It was her friend Tommie Moss.

"Come on, Ida," he said, grabbing her away from the tumbling circle of men in suits who were flailing and fighting wildly. "These men are swinging so hard and fast that they can't tell their enemies from a woman or a tree for that matter. You'd better get out of here before you get hurt."

When he'd seen her out of the Lyceum to a circle of waiting women, she thanked him for his chivalry.

"Very kind of you," she said, smiling.

"What were you doing? When all the other women went toward the door, you went right toward the fight," Tommie said, incredulous.

Ida looked down at her shoes, just a little embarrassed. "I was looking for Countee's notebook."

Tommie laughed, a big belly laugh that sounded like a

whole table of happy folks gathered around a dinner table for Sunday supper on a bright summer day. "Only Ida B. Wells," he said. "Only our Ida."

She smiled. Tommie saw her, really saw her—and he appreciated her for being exactly who she was.

The next morning brought even more shocking news. That night, Robert Countee was visited in the night by a gunman who assaulted him and threatened to do worse if he ever again threatened to reveal fraternity secrets.

Ida was infuriated. Like the cowards they were, the fraternity had sent an armed man to a good man's house in the dead of night, caught him sleeping, and sought to silence him with fear.

Unafraid of the potential retaliation that might await her, she quickly penned an editorial.

> To the history of an enormous amount of money paid into their treasuries with nothing to show for it in the way of real estate, parks or even a multitude of widows and children cared for—let us add the union of the mob and we have the history of what fraternities have done for the elevation of society in general, complete up to today.

"I couldn't care less about their costumes and the rituals of their secret societies," Ida told Fanny at school the next day. "They have means and influence. What good are they doing for the sake of our people who sorely need it?"

"If they went after a well-known man in his own home, aren't you afraid of what they'd do to an itty-bitty thing like you?" Fanny asked.

"My oath," Ida said, "is to truth, not fear. Besides, I think, I hope, that these fraternity men have enough gentlemanlike mores in their souls not to come after the likes of me."

Countee, grateful for the support, published Ida's piece in the *Living Way* that Saturday. The next week, she received a note from Thomas Fortune in New York.

Miss Ida B. Wells
Memphis, Tennessee
My esteemed Miss Wells,

We at the New York Freeman have been following the drama around our journalistic colleague, Mr. Countee, the secret societies and fraternities of Memphis, and their growing rivalry with the churches.

Your editorial encapsulates the issues at hand so powerfully. I dare say, I think this is your fiercest and finest letter yet. We'd like to publish it in the Freeman, which you know has a national subscriber base that numbers in the thousands.

Very Truly Yours,
T. Thomas Fortune

The fraternities piece in the *Freeman* brought more letters and more requests for the words of Iola. She came home from school one afternoon to find a copy of the *Freeman* with her latest editorial about the negligible differences between the Democrats and Republicans. The paper came with a letter from Fortune praising her for her "clear and forcible" insight.

Not everyone loved Ida's being clear and forcible. One of her detractors was Calvin Chase, the editor of the *Washington Bee*. He'd had enough of Ida's friendship with men he admired like Thomas Fortune and his own editor, Louis Brown. He was friends with Blanche Bruce and did not appreciate Ida's digs at the powerful man. He thought the "Woman's Mission" essay was overrated, and he let it be known that he had little regard for "Iola," whom he referred to as "the star-eyed goddess of the Memphis *Living Way*."

He called her out as part of a coterie of would-be journalists who had "the mania to scribble for the press" and "the desire to see their maiden efforts in print." It was clear, Chase insisted, that Iola had written nothing worthy of publishing in the major presses, and he urged readers to look closely at Ida's grammatical and typographical errors as proof of her amateurish prose. Lest there be any doubt of how deeply he intended to wound the young journalist, he titled his screed "Honey for Friends, Stings for Enemies."

Chapter Twelve

Important Nothings

In Memphis, the members of the Black middle class spent their weekends and evenings making social calls. Some saw the obligation of calling upon friends and neighbors as a chore, but for Ida, there was a great deal of amusement in making these visits. She did not come to Memphis alone to keep to herself.

One Sunday afternoon, she went to call on Fanny Thompson. Fanny seemed to be always busy with embroidery. Ida liked to sew dresses, but she didn't embroider—the dainty handiwork for the sake of dainty handiwork. Domestic pointillism was not her métier.

"You should try it," Fanny said.

"I am all thumbs," Ida said, looking down at her hands, which she could honestly say had a tendency to swell in the heat.

"I'd never be as good as you," Ida said diplomatically.

Ida was never going to be a master of the domestic arts, but she set herself goals each month. She aimed to read as widely as possible—both fiction and nonfiction as well as plays and poetry for her work with the Lyceum. It was challenging, though. Some days she was so tired from teaching and writing letters to editors about publishing her work that, when she'd gotten only a few pages into a book she had assigned herself, she would scold herself in her diary: "Made small progress in books last week & hoped to have done better this week but I seem to find such little time to do anything in."

That Saturday, she put the finishing touches on her first attempt at fiction, "The Story of 1900." It was the tale of a young Black teacher, much like Ida herself, who nobly endeavors to train her students for life in the new century, where she believes the opportunities for them will be limitless. In the story, she declares that her aim is to "lay a foundation for a noble character that would convince the world that worth and not color made the man."

Satisfied with her efforts, that Monday after school she sent it off to the *Fisk Herald*, where a young W. E. B. Du Bois was an editor. They published it just a few weeks later in their April issue.

Louis Brown was coming to town, and Ida had a hundred things to do before his arrival. He was older, sophisticated, and Ida could see him as a potential husband—both of them becoming journalists of note.

That Friday, after school was dismissed, Ida tidied her classroom. Too many students and too few desks and supplies meant the room was generally a mess by the end of the day. She knew that it would be a terrible start to the next week if she walked into the classroom on Monday and found desks facing every which way, chairs overturned, and papers scattered across the floor.

She heard a knock on the door and turned to see Isaiah

Graham. He looked sharp in a navy-blue suit and a white shirt that complemented his dark-brown skin.

"Good afternoon, Mr. Graham," she said. It was the habit of the teachers to use honorifics on school grounds—both out of respect and to set an example for their students.

"A very good afternoon to you, Miss Wells," he said. "May I help you tidy up?"

She nodded her head. "That would be wonderful."

"I was wondering if it would be okay if I called tomorrow?" Isaiah asked. "It's Saturday."

Ida grinned. "I know the days of the week, Mr. Graham."

"Then would you be open to receiving me?"

"I'm afraid not," she said cheerfully. "I have company visiting from out of town."

Isaiah shook his head. "Louis Brown."

"He is a friend," Ida said coyly.

"A friend who would like to be more than a friend," Isaiah muttered grumpily.

"Mr. Graham, may I see you outside, please?"

"Yes, let me walk you to the trolley."

They walked in silence for ten minutes, and when they were a safe distance from the school, Ida let him have it.

"Isaiah, how could you?"

"How could I what?"

"How could you imply that my behavior with Louis Brown, or any man for that matter, was anything but respectable?"

"Gosh, Ida. Must you let me know your disappointments at every turn?" Isaiah huffed. "He's the one who wrote about kissing you in the pages of a major newspaper!"

He then recited the words aloud, his southern drawl dripping with what Ida read as a kind of venom:

Some say, that when you kiss her, do so without force
And you will avoid all scuffles.
That we know there is something sweet
In this style of osculation.
That if her ruffles you have rumpled,
And put her in a fluster.
That you do not mind that, as you can fix it,
If you are a re-adjuster.

"There is no mention of me in that paper," Ida said primly. Louis Brown had sent her the clipping, letting her know—as if she hadn't already guessed—that his pen name was Elembee (a phonetic spelling of his initials) and that he had sought to capture his infatuation with her through poetry, which the paper had agreed to publish. Ida knew all of this but also knew that none of it was Isaiah Graham's business. She stared at him blankly, since innocence was beyond her acting abilities.

Isaiah kept pushing. "Come on, Ida. *Everyone* knows it's you."

"There is nothing that 'everyone' in Memphis knows except for the lies and aspersions that you cast on my good name."

She was worked up then, careening back and forth between fury and sadness. The two emotions were such pillars in her life that there were moments, moments like this one, when she could hardly separate anger from anguish.

"You say you care for me," she said, making every effort not to spill the tears that Isaiah Graham did not deserve to see.

"You know that I do."

"Then pray act like it," she said finally.

"I'll ride with you on the trolley," he said. "Make sure you get home safe."

“No thank you, Mr. Graham,” she said. “My safety, like my reputation, is none of your concern.”

When she got home, she thought, *He knows better. He* knows. *The problems of our people. All the traps that await a single woman should she be perceived to make a misstep. And still he chose to provoke me.*

Isaiah was as deceitful as he was weak. He claimed to care for her but made no move to solidify their relationship. Perhaps, Ida thought, that was for the best. What kind of marriage would they have, bickering at every turn?

Chapter Thirteen

Quadrille

Ida slipped into her one evening gown, a black silk number she had sewn herself, with many weeks of work put into the effort. She would soon be off to her first Memphis ball. It calmed her that it was not a function of the Black elite of Memphis. It was a celebration of May Day and was to be a gathering of the teachers and shopkeepers, the day laborers and homeowners, who made Memphis hum.

As she got dressed, she thought of a clipping that one of her correspondents, H. H. Avant, had sent her. It was an editorial from the *New York Times* that declared that "Blacks were overeager for their rights, walking around with chips on their shoulders while whites felt powerless and outnumbered."

As she applied fragrance to her wrists, she thought, *Can we just live? Why is it wrong to want to* live *when just living has been denied to us for so long?* She had borrowed "diamonds" from Fanny—an elaborate necklace of fake stones strung on a black velvet ribbon. She loved the weight of it as it hung on her neck.

Finally, she smoothed her curly hair into an updo, securing it with a double-pronged hairpin topped with shiny clear stones that had belonged to her mother. *Oh, Mama,* she thought, as she tucked in an errant lock of hair. *The things you never lived to see. What I would give to see you and Papa waltzing across the room tonight.* It seemed to her that every joyous moment in her life was like a photo negative—all that was gone and missing glowed spookily around it.

Mrs. Barclay kept a looking glass in the hallway outside the bathroom, and Ida stood in front of it for a long time, admiring her appearance. She particularly liked the way the fabric draped, like the costume of an opera singer, subtly showing off the smooth skin of her décolletage.

When she arrived at the ball, she greeted her fellow teachers: Fanny and Fannie, along with Virginia Broughton and Lavinia Wormley. The main central ballroom was flanked by two sitting rooms: one in which the men smoked cigars, and the other in which the women reclined and spoke in hushed tones about all the goings-on of the event.

The Fannies and Virginia complimented Ida on her dress, and Ida complimented their looks as well. Lavinia assessed Ida with a cool eye: "I can never wear black. It makes me look like the old lady who lived in a shoe. But you somehow pull it off." Ida smiled even though inside she was steaming. It was her first ball. She would somehow rise above.

Fanny Thompson hooked her elbow into Ida's and said, "Come, let us go and have some punch."

Virginia Broughton cautioned against it: "I wouldn't if I were you. It has pineapple rum in it. My advice is to stick to sweet tea."

Ida nodded politely and followed Fanny to the refreshment

table. She had every intention of trying the punch. She could have sweet tea any old time.

"I've never had pineapple rum before," she said, her eyes dancing with curiosity.

"Then you must try it," Fanny said cheerfully. "It is delightfully exotic like a breeze from the Caribbean Sea washing over you."

Ida took a small sip and then another. It was sweet and delicious and unlike anything she'd ever imbibed before. "Oh my stars," she said appreciatively.

"Be careful," Fanny said. "It's stronger than it tastes. Too much and you'll be flat on your back. They call it 'punch' for a reason." She offered Ida an elbow. "Let's take a stroll around the room."

Ida promenaded with her friend as the musicians played one merry romp after another. She was happy not to be sitting in a corner. Her stroll with Fanny gave her the opportunity to take it all in. The women all in their long gowns, the men in their immaculate formal suits—all of them shades of brown and tan. None of the dancers seemed to have a hair out of place or a visible drop of sweat, even as the twelve-piece orchestra teasingly ramped up the pace of Strauss's *Sorgenbrecher.*

"Isn't it marvelous?" Fanny cooed.

"Oh, it is."

"I should like to have a photograph to capture the moment so I shan't forget the splendor."

Ida thought some about this. A photograph would be lovely. A painting would be even better. Benjamin Tanner, the publisher, had mentioned in his last letter to Ida that his son, Henry, was saving money to travel abroad and study painting in Paris. Looking around the room, Ida wanted to write and tell him,

Forget Paris. Come to Memphis, Henry. Come and paint us *in the manner of Sargent. A Black woman draped in diamantés and silks would cause far more scandal—and, I imagine, bring more sales—than the portraits of Madame X.*

Ida smiled and let her senses take in all the finely dressed couples dancing. She marveled at how the women knew just when to join their movements—matching them step by step, pushing them forward, then pulling them back. The dancers seemed to capture how she felt when she was writing. She endeavored to move the words on the page as the dancers moved their arms and legs; her pen was both call and response, sending a message and relaying everything she'd heard and learned.

She loved, too, how her peers seemed to add their own layers to the traditional ballroom moves. Their motions unraveled something rich and new in their collective souls, the distinctly Black and Southern rhythms harmonizing with the old European notes of classical music. Ida watched them dance and imagined that, all across the country, young people were choreographing new moves for a new era, from Memphis to New York, from Chicago to San Francisco.

"Do you enjoy the choreography?" Therese Settle asked.

"I do, I do," Ida said.

The walkaround started, and Ida watched with admiration as the dance leader with his top hat puffed out his chest, a smirk on his face as he strutted around the room. It reminded her of her father and the way he would grab his mother's arm and dance her proudly around the wood-burning stove in their home.

She knew the ballroom wasn't the fanciest. But it was evening, and the room glowed like a theater set and everything seemed just a little more magical than it perhaps was. She suspected that the first bright rays of morning light would show that the curtains were faded, that the gilded chairs and chandeliers were secondhand, maybe purchased at a good price from some southern manor that had fallen on appropriately hard times. The walls were lath and plaster, not marble. The moldings were simple, not ornate. But it was all more wonderful than she could have imagined, never having previously been to any sort of ball at all.

Ida watched as Fanny and the other teachers danced the quadrille. She'd seen them practicing in the schoolyard after school. The way they moved without missing a step showed that the effort had been worth it. The top-hatted leader and his partner walked all the other dancers in a circle around the ballroom; then they separated. The men sauntered gallantly to the right; the women stepped gracefully to the left. They circled each other, first with the men on the inside and once again with the women on the outside. Then, as the music crescendoed into a fast waltz, they reversed the circle, with the women on the inside and the men on the outside.

"Ida, it's your turn," Fanny said, her voice floating across the dance floor like a melody. "Join us for the handkerchief dance."

"But I don't know how to do it. I haven't been practicing like everyone else."

"Nonsense," Fanny said. "You don't have to be perfect. You just have to have fun."

Ida blinked and let the words wash over her. Not worry about appearances and missteps? Not feel shame for her shortcomings and all that she lacked? If only she could. Maybe just for tonight.

Fanny handed her a handkerchief and said, "Take this and just follow my lead. It'll be me, you, Stella, and Eliza."

The women gathered in the center of the room, facing the crowd. They playfully shook their handkerchiefs at the group of men that approached them—Patrick Guignon, John Bruce, Randolph Peterson, and Isaiah.

The men stepped in sync around the women, in a circle, as the women shook their handkerchiefs flirtatiously. Isaiah winked at Ida. She raised an eyebrow at him.

Fanny whispered, "Okay, Ida, on my count, throw your handkerchief, and the gentleman who catches it will be your partner for the next dance."

Ida nodded.

Fanny smiled and whispered, "One, two, and... three!" Ida threw her handkerchief in the air with playful delight. Isaiah moved to catch it, but at the last moment, John Bruce edged in front of him and caught it.

"I believe the next dance is mine," he said.

Ida nodded.

Isaiah glowered and picked up Stella's handkerchief from the floor where it had fallen. He bowed to his second-choice dance partner, not quite gallantly, and they all began to dance.

John Bruce and Ida glided around the dance floor to a waltz by Chopin. Ida recognized it from her piano classes, although she'd never been able to play it the way the orchestra did.

She did not want to be courted by him, but she enjoyed dancing with John. In his arms, she felt both rest and a quickening of the heart. She loved how much of the evening felt like play. How there was the unexpected switching of partners and the opportunity to flirt without it being construed as misconduct. If only there were a ball every weekend, she thought, she'd never feel so blue again, knowing that there was always a tonic of symphony and movement awaiting her.

The last dance was a game in which participants exchanged partners every third turn around the ballroom. Ida danced with Jerome Copeland, Isaiah, Patrick, and Thomas Turner, a local teacher and editor of the *Memphis Watchman*, whom she didn't know well.

Isaiah chattered the whole three times around the room.

"Ida, did you know there is now a National Colored Baseball League?" Isaiah said.

"I did not."

"There are eight teams. The Cincinnati Browns, the Louisville Fall City, the New York Gorhams, the Boston Resolutes…"

Ida placed an arm on his shoulder and leaned into him.

"Isaiah," Ida said softly. "Please. I cannot hear the music."

He spoke no further then and simply tightened his grip around her waist while twirling her in time to the music.

It was well past midnight when Fanny said, "I think we should go. We don't want to be caught out too late, like Memphis Cinderellas."

Ida agreed.

On her way out the door, Isaiah pressed a note into her hand. "You were the most beautiful girl here tonight," he said.

"That is untrue, but very sweet of you to say," she said, giving his hand a friendly squeeze.

When she got home, she read the note. It was full of typical Isaiah florid prose. Something about loving her. Another inevitable thing about wanting to kiss her perfect lips.

She balled the note in her hand and threw it away. *Enough*, she thought. For all the encouragement she had given him, he had never sought to bind their relationship—even into anything resembling an engagement. “He is a child,” she said to herself. “I don’t and cannot feel that I belong to him.”

Yet even the uncertainty about her love life could not tamp down the joy Ida felt about the ball. She lay her body down in the bed, but her mind and heart were still doing circles around the ballroom. So often she felt like the work she did went unseen. But the dancing, especially the dancing games, gave her a sense of belonging and connection that it seemed she was always yearning for. For a few hours, at least, she could close her heart to the worries of the world, grab the hands of her friends, and pass under the graceful arbor of music, laughter, and community.

Chapter Fourteen

A Matter of Reputation

The school year was almost over, and Ida was counting the days until the first week of June, when she could stop teaching and devote herself fully, for the summer at least, to her writing.

Mrs. Barclay came in and handed her a stack of mail. "I don't know how you keep up with the letter writing, Ida," she said. "Only so much daylight on any given day."

Ida smiled. "Oh, don't you worry about me. I manage just fine."

"Take some advice from an older woman," her landlady said. "Mind your eyesight, child. You're going to need it."

Ida went into the parlor and made herself comfortable in one of the two ladies' chairs. The room was simple but well appointed. There were two upholstered gentlemen's chairs and two tufted chairs for the women, a draped center table, wood-paneled walls, and a plaster swag above the fireplace.

"Luck be a slim envelope with a gentleman's handwriting

on it," she whispered to herself as she sifted through that day's post.

She decided to open the letter from Nashville first. A caller? Or a publisher?

"Ah," she said as she scanned the letter. "A potential publisher."

Miss Ida B. Wells
Memphis, Tennessee
My dear Madam,

The student editors and staff at Fisk University have read your work in the Living Way and the Freeman with great interest and appreciation. And we were honored to publish your piece "A Story of 1900."

I write to encourage you to write for us again and soon. It is our wish to reprint any letters you care to share with our community of future leaders, young men and young women of your age, in the Fisk Herald.

Write to me and you can be assured of a prompt and enthusiastic reply.

Very faithfully,
W. E. B. Du Bois

Ida had longed to go to Fisk, but a summer of classes was all she had been able to manage. It would be an honor to write more often for the *Fisk Herald.*

Despite his lack of commitment, Ida continued to date Isaiah. He was erudite and well-placed, intellectual and good-looking, albeit a little staid. One night she allowed him to kiss her, and that led to a steamier make-out session. After such a show of passion, Ida expected Isaiah to follow up with a declaration of love. That he did not do so was an insult to Ida, and she made no attempt to hide her ire.

She was embarrassed and angry. Writing in her diary, she admitted:

> I blush to think I allowed him to caress me, that he would dare take such liberties and yet not make a declaration.
>
> I believe he loves me, but he is certainly enigmatical in his behavior.
>
> He seems not to have confidence in my actions and was he to plead with me on his knees now, for no consideration would I consider his proposition. He had his opportunity and lost it thro' fear of being deceived and other timidity and it shall not occur again.

The next day, she waited all day for Louis Brown to arrive as he had promised in a recent letter. He did not darken her door until nearly dinnertime.

"Louis, how lovely to see you."

In these moments, she wished she had somebody she could ask about what was the difference between what was natural and what was villainy. What *exactly* was the feeling aroused by a man that you should marry without hesitation, and how could you tell the difference between that virtuous ardor and the palpitations caused by the type of man who was so treacherous, you should run in the other direction.

Ida didn't think that Louis Brown was the most handsome man she'd ever met. It was more that he was the most charismatic. Everything about the way he moved seemed designed to draw her in.

"We could go to see a show. *The Royal Middy* is playing at the Opera House."

"Oh no," he said. "The theater bores me."

She let the remark pass, although it was, she was sure of it, the first real flaw in Louis Brown's character.

"Let's take a walk," he said, then whispered, "to our favorite place."

Ida knew that Louis liked to walk toward the Bluffs, past the river pathways where the proper folks promenaded. Once, she had let him walk her out there, to a bridge where he could kiss her on the lips. But just because he had done it before did not mean that she would allow it again. She insisted that they go to a restaurant on Beale Street for tea and something sweet, and the expression on his face the entire night was anything but.

A few days later, she received a plaintive letter from him.

"Oh, Ida," he wrote. "I could understand you better in another way."

Another way? Did he not know the danger of his words?

Ida was sure from the way his lips and hands sought her out that she knew his meaning well. She did not know what upset her more—that Isaiah was right about Louis or that she would be forced to draw the line lest she be ruined before the life she was trying to create for herself had even begun.

She hated that this—the protection of her virtue—rested solely on her shoulders, but these were the times she lived in.

"I don't know what construction to put on it," she wrote in her diary of Louis Brown's attempts at seduction. "Lest I should be charged with the wrong one, I make none."

Walking to Odd Fellows Hall for coffee one afternoon after school, Ida opened up to Fanny.

"What would you do—if a man were to make suggestions?"

"Men don't make lewd suggestions to women they see as potential wives, Ida."

"Forget I asked," Ida fumed.

Fanny paused, remembering perhaps that Ida B. Wells was not one for confessions or showing insecurity. There was convention. And then there was Ida.

"Well, Ida," Fanny said lightly, "I think it's true that men sometimes need reminding of their better angels. A firm rebuke should set your courtship on the right course again."

"Thank you, Fanny," Ida said, then did a rare thing and embraced her friend. Ida hated feeling that she owed anyone anything. But she was grateful for the advice and being able to speak out loud some of the words that resided primarily in her head.

When she got home that night, she wrote to him.

Dear Louis,

I will speak frankly, as I hope that you are gentleman enough to keep our conversations and our letters private. Your attempts at seduction crossed the line. I am a lady, but your behavior showed no understanding of that fact. You think that I am a creature whose chastity is an artifice for a twisted and hidden guile. I am writing to assure you, dear sir, that this is not the case. Mine is not a contrived purity, and because I have no father or older brothers to stand guard around me, you thought it your lordly pleasure to make suggestions that would not stand the test of polite society.

I accepted your apologies in the moment and my forgiveness stands. But you must know that I will certainly cease all correspondence if you ever again consider it necessary to inform me of the fiery depths of your affections.

With sincere regard,
Ida B. Wells

The whole next day at school, Ida felt a flush. She had done nothing wrong. She had handled the manner to the best of her ability. She *liked* Louis Brown, but she also felt it was imperative that when she did turn her attention to marriage that she be able to offer her husband a blank page. Any rumor to the contrary was as dangerous to her reputation as a sullied truth. The set they were part of—the teachers, the journalists, the business owners, and the lawyers—was so small. She hoped that Louis Brown would understand that she herself was not without affections, but when it came down to a choice between prudence and passion, she was beholden to choose prudence every time.

A week later, a letter from Louis Brown arrived.

Dear Miss Wells,

I received your letter and I think I would rather keep your friendship than risk it. We are fellow scribes, intellectual helpmeets, and race people.

Let us rewrite our story from what was in favor of all that might yet be. What say you if I regard myself as your big brother and approached you with only admiration and affection as my (singularly talented) little sister.

Yours always,
Louis

Ida read his letter twice. She shook her head. Big brother? Singularly talented little sister? That man. Kisses like pecan pie. Poetry like Coleridge. There was only one word that could describe Louis Brown in all his good-looking, clever-lad complexity. *Slippery.* Louis Brown was nothing if not slippery.

Chapter Fifteen

A Strange and Hazy Freedom

Ida stood in front of her classroom, seeing in the long and dangly limbs of her oldest students her own teenage self. There were only two more weeks of school left, and the students were as impatient for summer as she was. What could she give them? How could she guide them through the unprecedented age they lived in? Politics were never part of her simple lesson plans, but she felt it important to arm her students with an understanding of the world they would soon be entering.

She smoothed down the skirt of her simple brown-and-white plaid dress. The school board did not like the teachers to "dress like magpies," so she alternated between this dress and a trio of simple solid frocks—navy and brown wool for the fall and winter, two white cotton ones for the warmer months.

"We are building a new political path," Ida explained.

It had been almost ten years since the Compromise of '77. In order to secure the presidency for Rutherford Hayes, Republicans agreed to withdraw all federal troops from the South. States could make laws regarding the treatment and rights of Black people as they wished, a broad freedom that ushered in a new era of restrictions, oppression, and, eventually, violent suppression of civil rights.

"So, if Reconstruction is over, Miss Wells, what do you call this era?" Silas Purvis, one of Ida's favorite students, asked.

"I don't know," Ida said honestly. "I don't know."

It was, Ida thought, a strange and hazy time when freedom—the feeling of it, the knowing of it—was as changeable as the weather. There were days when she sat in the theater and felt like she was not just watching a show but watching the curtain raise on a new era of possibility, not only in Memphis but in all of America and the whole world. And there were days when she strolled down Beale Street in her favorite violet velvet-trimmed dress, with her like-new parasol from Menken's, and thought, *This is the kind of life my parents only dreamed of.*

But then she'd hear of a case like the Mississippi courthouse murders, where mobs appointed themselves judge and jury, then murdered and mutilated the bodies of Black men accused of crimes, with no fear of retribution from their government or their God. Every instance of so-called lynch law she read about made her feel as if she'd been sucked back in time, as if the days of enslavement were a tornado blowing back through the nation, leaving everything they had fought for in its wake.

The dichotomy of a tremulous present and a very present past sat uncomfortably, side by side, in her heart, and she thought, *Was this what Dickens meant when he said it was the best of and the worst of, at the very same time?*

Miss Ida B. Wells
Memphis, Tennessee
My dear Miss Wells,

I write to you from the fair city of Detroit. My brother Benjamin and I are the founders and editors of what we believe to be the finest Black newspaper in the region, the Detroit Plaindealer.

We read your letter "A Woman's Mission" in the New York Herald and would like to reprint it in our newspaper. We mean to support the women journalists of our hue who, as you write, have the ability—through their wisdom and discernment—to lead men to a higher moral ground.

Our elder sister, Meta Pelham, is a staff reporter on our paper. Your writing, we believe, would find powerful companionship with hers in our humble pages.

We await your response.

With kindest regards to you,
I remain,
Robert Pelham Jr.

Ida decided she would write an essay for the *Detroit Plaindealer* at her earliest convenience, and perhaps, if she continued to contribute, they would send train fare for her to visit their city. Ida knew few women journalists, and Meta Pelham sounded like someone she'd very much like to meet.

That evening, after supper, she took out a copy of *Harper's*

Magazine that Isaiah had lent her. She crawled under the blankets, propped her pillow so she could sit up comfortably, and began to flip the pages. Suddenly, she felt her throat catch. There was an etching of a painting by Winslow Homer.

It was called *A Visit from the Old Mistress.* In it, a family of formerly enslaved people inhabit one half of the image. On the other side, "the old mistress"—their onetime enslaver—stands beseechingly as if she expects to be invited to supper. It is clear from the family's expressions that they have not forgotten the horrors they endured, perhaps at her behest.

It brought to mind stories Ida's parents had told her of their enslaved years. Her mother told tales of how she had been beaten mercilessly on the plantation. She grew up knowing that the brutality of enslavement was a recent memory for her parents, not an ancient history. When Ida was young, her paternal grandmother came to see them in Holly Springs once a year. When Ida was twelve, her grandmother came and casually mentioned that first night, "Jim, Miss Polly wants you to come visit and bring the children."

Ida remembered her father's face. She'd never seen such a mélange of fury and fear before.

"She wants to meet your children," her grandmother said, as if "Miss Polly" was an old family friend.

Her father took a deep breath, put his fork down, and clasped her mother's hand as if reaching for strength he wasn't sure he had. "Mother," he said softly. "I never want to see that old woman again for as long as I live. I'll never forget how she had you stripped and whipped the day after the old man died, and I am never going to see her."

Her grandmother shuddered at the memory and looked furtively at Ida, who was the oldest and the only child who seemed to be paying close attention to the conversation. "The good Lord teaches us forgiveness, Jim," she said. "I taught you to forgive. Hate will never make us whole."

Her father shook his head. "I've made my peace with my god, Mother. And I guess it's all right for you to take care of her and forgive her for what she did to you, but she could have starved to death if I'd had my say-so. She certainly would have, if it hadn't been for your kindness and generosity after the war ended and she had nothing."

Later, when Ida was a little older, her mother explained that the situation with Miss Polly was more complex than she had previously understood. The woman was not only a former enslaver. Miss Polly's husband had been her father's father and Ida's grandfather. For all intents and purposes, Miss Polly had been Jim's stepmother, and she'd had Jim's mother stripped and whipped out of some misguided sense of jealousy and spite and an abundance of cruelty.

Ida stared at the Winslow Homer painting for a long time. When the tears finally came, as she knew they would, she closed the magazine, dimmed her lamp, and laid her head on her pillow. Slavery was twenty years over, but its tangled web of secrets and lies would be with the nation, Ida suspected, for a very long time. The truth is that she didn't know a single Black person who was not related in some shape or form to white families who had been enslavers. Yet the way that racism played out in the South with so much hate and violence almost seemed like some wildly irrational attempt at cover. It wasn't just that, underneath, Blacks and whites were more alike than not. It was just that as God was their witness, Black and white Americans were again and again, across a bloodied family tree, the very definition of kin.

Chapter Sixteen

Charles, Again

It was the end of May, and Ida was still waiting on the April paycheck from the school board. Money was tight, and Ida, being low on funds, was out of stationery. Having just enough to write one letter, she wrote to her beloved Charles.

It did not help that Charles, who had once sent her *thirty* letters in quick succession, had not written for weeks.

Dear Charles,

I understand that you are busy and that the work that keeps you is far from frivolous. Yours is the effort that will uplift and advance the souls and the future of our people.

But if I may, I'd like to speak plainly. I depend on your letters for both emotional and intellectual sustenance. Your dexterity with language is unmatched, and as greedy as it may seem, my deepest longing is for your words to fly to me, in black and white, every day that God has gifted us.

Your obliged and affectionate friend,
Ida

The next weekend, Ida went for her elocution lesson and spent that Saturday working on Lady Macbeth's soliloquy. When she got home, Mrs. Barclay said, "Letter for you. Mr. Charles S. Morris of Washington, DC. Haven't seen that name in a good while."

Ida held it at arm's distance. Just his name on the envelope seemed to beat with a kind of energy like no other.

Ida opened it, and the words disappointed her.

Dear Ida,

I misplaced your letter and so you must forgive my delay in answering it. I moved, and the move has thrown all the carefully ordered elements of my life asunder.

It was my understanding that it was my devotion to books, my studies, and the advancement of my career and the development of my mind that drew you to me. Yet your last letter seems to scold me for applying myself to my work and not to my correspondence.

If you have not patience with me, then I do not wish to be the means of displacing you from the stations of peace and a warm, constant affection.

Your happiness is dear to me and you only need say the word and I will quit these missives. You are a woman of formidable intelligence and beauty. I will accept it bravely if it turns out that

I am inadequate to the task of being the bringer of your joy.

Devotedly Your Own,
Charles S. Morris

Ida liked the idea that Charlie cared enough to counter her letter with such emotion. Having borrowed some writing paper from Fanny, she spent that Sunday evening carefully crafting a note to him. Perhaps he might be impressed if she showed how much Shakespeare she knew?

Dear Charlie,

I have set myself the task of learning the part of Lady Macbeth. Do you know this passage?

"Shake my fell purpose, nor keep peace between
Th' effect and it! . . . Come, thick night,
And pall thee in the dunnest smoke of hell,
That my keen knife see not the wound it makes,
Nor heaven peep through the blanket of the dark,
To cry 'Hold, hold!' "

Can you imagine me saying those lines? Scandal! And I cannot wait.

Now and always your own,
Ida

Louisa May Alcott had written, "Take some books and read; that's an immense help; books are always good company if you have the right sort." That Saturday, being low on funds and the energy to do much else than lie in bed, she curled up with *Vashti*, a novel by Augusta Jane Evans. The book was pedantic, and yet Ida found herself to be drawn in by the popular writer's charms. "From reading the books, I should like to know something of the authoress," she confessed to her journal. "I should judge her to be an exquisitely refined creature, passionately devoted to music, art, literature, flowers, with all the panoply and luxury money can provide. She could hardly be otherwise than pure who writes so purely and she must possess a mighty intellect." Reading the book, imagining the adventurous life that the author surely led, cheered her up.

But then another letter from Charles Morris arrived and it was not what Ida expected:

Dear Ida,

I was surprised to receive your last letter and taken aback with the seeming delight with which you quote Shakespeare and a play in which he seems to laud cold-blooded murderers and paints the demonic figures of witches as soothsayers to be believed.

I am someone who believes in the freedom of women. My own mother, as you well know, is a graduate of Oberlin College. But the freedom of the fairer sex must be tempered with prudence, don't you think? Is it circumspect for an eligible young woman like yourself who is courting the best of young men to take to the stage and recite the words of a lunatic who begs—not to God, I am sure of it—that he unsex her so she might find the courage to commit evil without hesitation.

I have said my piece and now I must end this letter, even though it is shorter than I would like.

Booker T. Washington, the illustrious founder of Tuskegee University, comes to the divinity school to give a lecture tonight. I have been lucky enough to be invited to dine with him afterward. I look forward to sharing with you all that I learn.

Your devoted,
Charles S. Morris

Ida read the letter twice through, put it down, and picked it up to read it again. Why would Charles criticize her for reading Shakespeare? Shakespeare! It could not possibly get more respectable and acceptable than the great British playwright. She wondered if his pique was a sign of his cooling affection. Surely she had not made a serious misstep? But perhaps this was the invisible line that stood between her and the more elite young women of her circle. She could not claim as Charles and his ilk could that her parents and grandparents had been born free. She herself had been born enslaved, had come into the world as property—the Emancipation Proclamation had been signed six months after her birth, and she could not help but feel at times that she carried the memories of being enslaved beneath her skin, haunting memories that pulsated through her blood and were carried in and out of her heart and brain. He had said she was marriage material and that the best of men sought to court her. Then he'd all but called her a demon worshipper who lacked judgment and strong moral fiber. She felt at times that all that was required of her was that she be "good"—the rub was that the one word was a placeholder for thousands, an endless traverse of quicksand which every day she was forced to navigate anew.

Ida went to bed feeling desolate and cheerless. Waking

up the next day, determined to shake off her blues, she took a calling card to Julia Hooks, who agreed to receive her that afternoon.

They discussed the next meeting of the Lyceum, and Ida talked about how she had been tussling with Lady Macbeth and how scandalized Charles S. Morris had been by a play that was written two hundred and fifty years before.

"The Queen of England has no problem with the Lady, I can assure you," Ida said, although as she said the words, she wasn't entirely sure they were true.

"He'll get over it," Julia assured her. "I am preparing the Habanera from Bizet's *Carmen*, so if you go down in scandal, I will accompany you."

Ida felt warmed by Julia's words. Maybe it was her own melancholy that sometimes set her apart from the other teachers, rather than any real rejection of her by her peers.

"This will cheer you. I heard the funniest story," Julia said as she poured Ida a cup of tea. Ida preferred coffee, but the pleasure of Julia's company was treat enough.

Julia had also made a plate of cucumber sandwiches that Ida nibbled on while eagerly waiting to hear the story.

"Apparently Lavinia Wormsley ran into Ada Coleridge on Beale Street. And according to Lavinia, Ada cut her dead in the street."

Ida raised an eyebrow. "That doesn't sound like Ada Coleridge."

"Exactly," Julia said. "But Lavinia has been busy telling everyone in town that Ada slighted her in the most outrageous fashion. In fact, she's gone so far as to say she will not speak to Ada again unless Ada issues her a formal apology."

Ida grinned. The drama of it all.

"Well, last night, I was having dinner at the Settles'. Lavinia was there, as were Ada and Victor Coleridge. Therese started to tell a story about how a horse on Beale Street seemed to have just gone crazy—he took off down the street with the carriage door wide open and with no seeming discernment between the street and the sidewalk."

Ida nodded. "Oh, I heard about that crazy horse."

"But this is the thing: Upon hearing the story, Ada Coleridge said, 'If I had seen that horse take off like that, I would have gone running.' Then her husband said, 'Oh, dear Ada, you wouldn't have seen anything at all. You are so short-sighted that the horse would have trampled you.'"

Julia began to giggle and could not stop. "Ada didn't 'cut her dead.' She never saw her!"

"What did Lavinia say?" Ida asked, laughing so hard, she almost spilled her tea.

"She didn't say a word," Julia said. "But then Therese, who is a woman not to be trifled with, turned to her and said, 'My dear Lavinia, I'm not read in on the matter entirely, but I think you may owe our Ada an apology.'"

Ida slammed her hand on the table. She was laughing so hard, she felt the need to steady herself. "No!"

Julia nodded. "Yes! It was a sight to see."

Ida said, "Oh, I am sorry to have missed it. But I do love it when a gossip gets a good comeuppance."

Walking home from Julia's home, Ida felt a warmth in her chest. She would keep up her correspondence with her suitors, apply herself to her writing, and push ahead even when it was hard. Things were going well, and they were going to get better.

Chapter Seventeen

Picnic

Ida loved much about Memphis, but no quarter held the sway of the riverside parks. The cobblestone landing on Riverside Drive between Beale Street and Jefferson was a cacophony of sights and smells, with markets for everything from cotton to mules. Ida liked watching Mississippi riverboats that called at the port.

A bit farther down the drive, it was tranquil. The rains had finally stopped, the days were warm without being unbearably hot, and on the occasion of it being the end of the school year, the teachers had decided to organize a picnic.

They gathered that first Saturday in June, and to Ida, the whole scene felt like a page out of nature's picture book. Thomas Cassels, an Oberlin-educated attorney whose wife taught in the Memphis school district, found the most beautiful section of the park, a shade garden wild with azaleas and dogwood. They sat on a great flat rock, and the sun warmed their faces.

Tommie and Betty Moss had brought blankets. Ida helped lay them out, and as she sat, she turned to admire a bed of plush violet flowers. "These hydrangeas are as fat as a baby's head," she said.

"Oh, Ida," Stella Butler said, laughing. "You always say the most controversial things."

"I hear we are to have a surprise guest," Randolph Peterson said, winking at Ida.

Ida wondered who.

"A gentleman from Louisville."

Out from behind a tree stepped the fine figure of Charles Morris. She recognized him from the photographs he had sent, since they had not yet met in person.

Ida beamed and stood up to clasp his hand.

"You are pleased to see me," he said softly.

"More than I can respectfully show," she said.

He took his jacket off and sat down next to Ida on the blanket. She was happy she had worn her new pink-and-white plaid walking suit. She had made it herself and was especially proud of the bib of black lace that she'd used as a festoon around the collar.

Fanny Thompson and Ida had made a platter of sandwiches. Lavinia Wormley had brought a tray of pickled oysters. Thomas Turner had brought a tin of chocolate nougats that he'd purchased during his last trip to Washington, DC. Minutes turned into hours as they feasted on each course. And just when they all declared they were so full they couldn't eat another bite, another basket was opened and there was more to dine on: a sumptuous spread of cold fried chicken, cut into dainty pieces, slices of cold ham, and freshly made biscuits, cakes, and buns.

Some of the men lay back to nap in the sun, while others in the party began to play checkers.

Charles took a jar of cold sweet tea and asked Ida if she would take a walk with him. She followed him down the river path and marveled that he seemed to be able to name every one of God's creations that they encountered, "You can see it here," he said, placing her hand on a giant leaf. "This is the frilly frond of a fern. It's different from this, the smooth surface of a hosta leaf."

"I feel so at peace here," Ida said.

"It's only natural," Charles said. "We're human. We're meant to move in harmony with nature. Her pace and patience are meant to guide our actions as creatures of God on Earth."

"Spoken like a true divinity student," Ida said, quick with the comeback. Then she added, "But I like what you said. When you speak, it sounds more like poetry than a sermon. I promise."

"The Earth was never meant to be ripped and ransacked for every resource," Charles said. "We were never meant to be beaten and broken to do that work. Slavery was an abomination, not just to humanity but to all of this, the natural world."

Ida sighed contentedly and thought of the words of Louisa May Alcott. Perhaps it was true what Alcott had written: "You don't need scores of suitors. You need only one, if he's the right one."

When they rejoined the group, Julia Hooks asked Ida, "Are you going to attend the National Education Association meeting in Topeka next month?"

"I would very much like to go," Ida said. She loved to travel, and this was going to be a mixed-race conference, with both Black and white teachers in attendance.

Thomas took out an article from the *Cleveland Gazette.* "Read this, Ida," he said. "This is a letter from one of the organizers."

> We, as colored teachers, are usually conspicuous in our absence from educational associations. The

> way to destroy ignorance and prejudice is for Blacks and whites to meet in common council, to cross swords in friendly, intellectual combat, to exchange views, to test each other's methods, etc.

"My cousin told me that there is a network of Black Topekans who have organized inexpensive accommodations for teachers like us all over the city."

"Cheers to that," Fanny cried.

"It's a new day!"

The new days are starting to feel too much like the old days, Ida thought, reflecting on how while the Black Codes that limited where they could go and how they could gather had been repealed, they still seemed to be very much in effect. *But,* she thought, *it is our job to keep moving the nation forward.*

Before he left for the train station, Charles handed Ida a bouquet of flowers tied with sisal twine. "I picked them myself," he said. "The lavender ones are asters. You can tell because of the bright yellow buttons in the middle. The fuchsia ones are called bee balm."

Ida smiled. Their exotic colors brought to mind hot, faraway lands like the Caribbean and India.

"I found some Virginia bluebells, and—come closer, smell these—they're called Sweet White Trillium."

That night, as Ida dressed for bed, her little room filled with the intoxicating scent of the flowers. No man had ever wooed her the way Charles Morris had. But he lived in Washington, DC, and they had only ever met in person once. Keeping up a hearty correspondence with a string of suitors had taught Ida that for some men, writing passionate love letters was a kind of sport that they played right up until the moment they decided to marry a young woman that you had never known existed. But she and Charles were what the minister at her church had called "equally yoked." No man she had met before him so suited her in intellect, ambition, and temperament. Maybe their fairy-tale romance would develop a life beyond the written page. In the meantime, it had been a truly spectacular, one-of-a-kind, picnic and day.

Chapter Eighteen

An Invitation Wrapped in Roses (but Mind the Thorns!)

The next weekend, Ida found herself busier than she expected. The school board had sent—in June!—the paycheck for April. Ida paid twenty dollars to settle her bill at Menken's and fifteen dollars to Mrs. Barclay. She spent twenty cents for a pair of new gloves and mailed ten dollars to the lawyer working on her railroad case.

Ida had big plans for the upcoming summer. She hoped to travel with her fellow teachers to Topeka for the National Education Association conference, with a stop in Kansas City, then to carry on from Topeka to Denver, and from there on to San Francisco, ending with a stay at her aunt's place in Visalia. "If I am going to make this trip happen, I must start economizing," she told Fanny Thompson. "But it is so challenging for me to do without."

In anticipation of her summer journey, she purchased silk

to finish a dress, material for the lining, and needles and thread to replenish her supply. The whole lot cost $15.80. Eighty cents more than her monthly rent. She longed for a parasol to promenade when suitors came calling but held back. Dressing well was always a priority for Ida. It meant a lot to her and reminded her of her childhood, when her mother took such loving care with Ida's hair and clothes. Their church friends had always commented that Lizzie Wells's girls were the best dressed in all of Holly Springs. It made her hold her head up high that despite her limited means, she often received compliments on her clothes in Memphis. But it came at a cost. As she confessed in her diary, "My expenses are transcending my income. I must stop. It seems as if I should never be out of debt."

To her point, that Saturday night, she went with Fanny Thompson and Julia Hooks to see Lotta Crabtree, a onetime child actor who was called the San Francisco Favorite, in *Mam'zelle Nitouche.* Walking back downtown on Beale Street, arm in arm with Fanny and Julia, she marveled, "Lotta is a bundle of fun, nonsense, and comicalities."

Julia agreed. "Did you see how she kicked up her heels and commanded the stage?"

Ida nodded. "I read that she is near forty, but for all the world looks precisely like a girl of ten, full of gaiety and innocence."

Fanny said, "It is the feminine ideal—that kind of guilelessness."

As Ida got ready for bed that night, she thought that this is what she loved about Memphis—the social life that gave her some of the joy and innocence that she longed for when she felt isolated and on her own.

The next day, Isaiah picked an argument with Ida, something

about Ida trying to hide their connection in the hopes of encouraging even more correspondents to write to her. Then he did the unthinkable—he grabbed Ida's hat and dashed off in the rain.

Ida walked home miserable—an umbrella kept her dry, but she felt exposed without her hat. *What did Isaiah intend to prove with such an antic?* she wondered.

The next day, Ida arrived at school to find Isaiah waiting with her hat, which had been ruined in the rain.

Ida took her hat—it was a dead thing, beyond repair, but she vowed to dispose of it in the privacy of her own home.

"We should stop playing around," Isaiah said—as if the matter of the hat and Ida having to walk bareheaded in the rain was a game that she had initiated or consented to. She fixed him with a withering glare but did not say a word.

For two days, every time they crossed paths, she pretended to look through him as if he were an invisible man.

On the third day, he came to see her after school—shifting, nervously, from foot to foot like a man on the firing line.

"Do you have something to say, Mr. Graham?" Ida asked impatiently.

"Do you?"

"I did not come to your home, Mr. Graham."

"I ah-pah-lo-gize," he said, with what Ida could only read as sarcasm.

Ida would have rather been reading or thinking about her novel, or doing anything but wasting breath on a man who was increasingly more bother than fun.

"You apologize for what?" Ida asked, refusing to let him off the hook.

"For being childish and unchivalrous," Isaiah said. "For ruining your hat and letting you walk bareheaded in the rain."

"Better," Ida said.

"Come on, Ida," he said, making himself comfortable on a chair. "Do you care for me at all?"

"Time for you to go, Isaiah."

That night, Ida turned to her truest friends, her books. What was to be made of Isaiah Graham? Was their jousting a story they would tell their future kids someday, or was she wasting her time with a man who would never be a true partner and her intellectual match? It didn't help that there was always a bit of a class balance dangling between them. She could forgive his awkwardness, the fact that he was not as witty and quick as other men. But his arrogance and the way he wielded it was harder to overlook. It was, as Jane Austen had written so many years before, "I could easily forgive his pride, if he had not mortified mine."

She was challenged by courtship on fronts other than Isaiah too. For a young woman, courting was a minefield of ambition, deference, discretion, and the management of delicate male egos. For Ida, this was always a hefty task. But perhaps no man proved more challenging than Mr. Paul Jones, an attorney from Kansas City, to whom Ida had been introduced by a mutual friend through correspondence.

Paul's first letters were browbeating diatribes about the politics of the day. Ida described them in her diary as "long homilies about the requirements of the race." She let him know, as gently as she could, that he need not be so "stiff" in his tone and that she needed no entreaty about uplifting the race—it was her deepest mission in life.

A response from Paul arrived within a matter of days.

Dear Ida,

I've been thinking of you all day. Your cabinet photograph sits in my jacket pocket, and it is as if you are planting little kisses on my heart.

Yet I wonder if I am right to feel all that I do. Is it true that you are pinned to a fellow teacher in Memphis? If your heart belongs to another, then I shall make the best of it. But I pray you do not ask me to return the photo card. It is the stuff that dreams are made of. And dreams are always innocent and harmless, are they not?

Write to me as soon as you can. The words from your pen cheer a fellow so.

With sincere regard,
Paul Jones

Ida, in response, was coy. "I told him," she stated proudly in her diary, that "I had no objection to cultivating the acquaintance of the cultured and thinking men of the race."

When Ida wrote to say she would be stopping in Kansas City on her way to Topeka, Jones's missives came so quickly that Ida half wondered if he was delivering them by horseback himself.

Dear Ida,

Please allow me to be your host when you come to Kansas City. I will meet you at the train station and arrange accommodations for both you and your friend, Miss Bradshaw.

Please confirm that this arrangement suits you.

Yours in service,
Paul

Ida received the letter and was unsure what to do with it. He was a bachelor, after all, and her reputation was everything. Jane Austen also wrote, "I hate to hear you talk about all women as if they were fine ladies instead of rational creatures. None of us want to be in calm waters all our lives." Ida, at times, longed for the calm waters of being considered a fine lady. But the combination of having a public voice and being single and of marrying age meant she *had to* tread carefully.

Dear Paul,

It is a kind offer, but I think Fannie and I should stay where the other teachers have deemed suitable. We are so kind to have a friend such as yourself, willing to make such arrangements for us. Although we must decline the offer, we look forward to meeting you in Kansas City, where, we are certain, a fine time will be had by all.

Thank you again,
Ida B. Wells

Paul wrote back immediately.

Dear Ida,

You don't know me well, but it is my hope that my character and person will be familiar to you before too long.

The rector of my church has endorsed my choice of your accommodations.

Please, dear Ida, leave it to me.

Yours in service,
Paul

Chapter Nineteen

Etiquette

That evening, Ida dined with the Settles, who she was just getting to know. Therese had been one of the first Black women to attend Salem College, and her husband, Josiah, was the leading Black attorney in town. The very epitome of a Memphis belle, she had a ballet dancer's poise and most days wore her hair in a simple, shiny chignon.

After dinner, as they settled in for a cup of tea by the fireplace, Therese tried to warn Ida that even church-approved accommodation would not be enough to protect her reputation.

"Letters are one thing, Ida," Mrs. Settle said. "But you don't know this man. People will interrogate his intentions in trying to secure a location for you to stay and will question your judgment for letting a man who is not your kin arrange your lodgings."

Black women held the standards of etiquette. The train cars and opera houses did not give them the consideration of being ladies. But they were determined to continue to earn that moniker in their own quarters and communities until white

America recognized that they, too, possessed every virtue of womanhood.

For more than two hundred years they had been property—rape and sexual assault had been a constant, and they had been powerless against the terrors rained down on their family and flesh. It was two decades past Emancipation, and the weapons they had to prove their moral fiber were thousands of corsets and gloves, hundreds of thousands of hearts hoping for equality, millions of tiny exhales each day when the sun set and they and those they loved were safe and sound. Twenty years to overcome two hundred years of subjugation. That was, Ida knew, a nearly impossible number to square, and yet they had no choice but to try. And keep trying.

The past could not be undone. The present, however, was under their control. So they policed themselves and each other, because they believed—deeply—that their lives depended on it. The discipline they contorted themselves to maintain would be a blessing to their daughters, and their daughters' daughters, going forward, for generations to come.

Ida sighed. She did not want to hear that her every move reflected on the collective, but she knew that it was so. Mrs. Settle was a doyenne of the Black elite: renowned for her beauty and her quick mind. Ida found her friendship and mentoring flattering.

"You are right, of course," Ida demurred. "I am grateful for your counsel. It's helpful to have a lady of your stature tell me the things I ought to know."

Therese Settle smiled. "You know, I read your columns. I never miss a chance to catch up on the noteworthy musings of the great Iola."

Ida turned her face toward the fire, surprised by her own

modesty. She talked about her writing so rarely that she imagined Iola was another person entirely—a woman who lived in her own house and had her own bed. Iola, in those halcyon days of her writing career, seemed a being so separate from herself that Ida might well run into her one day at Odd Fellows Hall or the Opera House.

"You are so confident on the page," Therese said. "Trust in your heart—that's all any of us can do." She asked, "Do you wish to be married, Ida?"

Ida considered the question. The thought of romance thrilled her unequivocally. But the institution of marriage, as so many seemed to define it, put women in a box that was frightfully small. Ida wanted a mighty love, but not if the price was too high. Still, she paused before she spoke. She did not think this was the answer to give someone who had shown her such kindness.

"Yes, I would like to be married," she said softly. "Very much so."

Therese looked pleased with the response and offered, "Then you must mind the rules of courtship carefully. Our power as women is built on the foundation of how we control our interactions with potential suitors from the very start. You must set the stage, and only men of quality will follow your course."

That night, Ida wrote Paul a letter declining the offer but made the decision to go see Fannie Bradshaw before she mailed it.

Dear Paul,

I pride myself on being decisive, but this matter—you being a bachelor, me being a teacher with a name to uphold is... how should I put it? Delicate.

Thank you for your kind offer of church-approved housing.

I am grateful, but must, respectfully, decline.

Sincerely,

Ida

The next day, Ida went to see Fannie Bradshaw. Ida did not care much for her fellow teacher but had agreed to travel with her because it was better received and safer when two single women traveled together. Ida envied the house she lived in. Fannie's aunt, Agnes Bradshaw, had come from Jamaica, and the house was a blend of British-influenced island styles. There was a wide, wraparound veranda and a majestic staircase at the center of the house. The walls of the parlor were painted a bright bluish green, and the kitchen was a sunny yellow.

Ida approached Fannie with trepidation. The back and forth with Paul Jones was unsettling. She wished for a swift and definitive conclusion and tried to explain to Fannie that she had passed on the invitation.

"I am on a budget, Ida," Fannie said. "Your gentleman friend has kindly offered to sort arrangements."

"I must also be careful with my spending if what I've saved is to last me the entire summer. But there is the question of reputation."

Fannie shrugged. "You worry too much about these things, Ida. The Black community in Kansas City is like Memphis, small and tight-knit. If there were cause to be concerned about Mr. Jones, we would've heard it by now. Let us not turn down his kindness out of misplaced suspicion."

Ida sighed, but eventually agreed.

She tore up the letter she had written to Paul, sad that she'd wasted good paper and ink, and wrote him a new letter, accepting his offer.

He wrote back, the picture of patience.

Dear Ida,

Say no more. Your arrival in Kansas City is everything my heart desires. Your intelligence is evident in your writing. Your beauty will no doubt live up to the compliments that precede you. And if you are half as lively in person as you are on the page, then we shall find no shortage of entertainment as I introduce you to our fine city and the community of the Upper Tenth that calls this fine place home.

A carriage will meet you at the station. I await the opportunity to make your fine acquaintance, with all the patience I can muster.

Your obedient servant,
Paul Jones

Chapter Twenty

Black Swan

A rainstorm pummeled the city, with fourteen inches falling to the ground, bringing all locomotion to a halt. She had to walk to school for a meeting of teachers, taking the long way, via Main Street, with the hope that that street would be just a little less flooded. She was due at school at eight but did not arrive until after ten. Wet. Exhausted.

Isaiah had been in a mood all week, and Ida could hardly think what she had done to rile him up. He asked to walk her home after the teachers' meeting, and when they had arrived at her lodging, she invited him in.

"Ida," he began.

"I do not know what I have done," she said sincerely. "I desire always to do right, and I surely must fail sometimes, but you can be assured of my *intention* to do right. That is unwavering."

"Well," Isaiah said as he paced the room, "it is precisely your intentions that I have come to question."

Ida felt afraid. It was as if she were back in Holly Springs and the rumor mill had her in its clutch once more.

"Someone has told our circle of gentlemen friends that you were heard to say it is a privilege to go out with you."

"Who is that someone?" Ida demanded. "I would never say such a thing."

"The identity of this person must be protected," Isaiah declared, his voice rich with condescension.

"Do you know who it is?" Ida asked. "Do you know and won't say?"

Isaiah did not answer her but went on to say, "This same someone also let it be known that your stores of self-confidence are matched only by your lack of discretion. Any fellow who dares even exchange a friendly greeting with you is sure to hear tales of it on Beale Street before too long."

Ida was glad she was sitting, because she was sure she could not stand. Rage seethed in her and she prayed for a cooler head. Sitting in the parlor room of Mrs. Barclay's home, she wanted to smash the vase of dried flowers and break every dainty piece of bric-a-brac that she could get her hands on.

She was done with Graham. Graham, who had not declared his love for her, but buzzed about her malignantly if any other suitor swayed her attention. If he loved her, he would defend her honor against such cock-and-bull rumors. If he loved her, he would not assault her with anonymous slurs against her very good name.

Ida would not let him see how devastated she was by his words. She could not give him the satisfaction of knowing his mission had been successful.

She looked away, counted to ten, and prayed for her Lord and Savior to shape the words that were taking form in her mouth.

"My words and intentions have been severely misrepresented," she said, as simply and calmly as she could. "I need solitude and space to unravel this assault on my character."

"As will I," Isaiah said, meaning what, she did not know.

She walked him to the door and pulled away when he attempted to put a reassuring hand on her shoulder.

"Good day, sir," she said.

"I have only shared what I heard because it's my hope that you might try and love me," he responded. "When you go to your room to think, think on *that*. Could you love me?"

The next morning, she went to her room and wrote him a letter: "Do you speak in earnest when you ask if there is any chance of my love?"

He wrote back immediately: "Indeed, I am entirely and honestly besotted."

Ida responded, "All right, let us try."

That night, in her diary, she fumed:

> I know it is unchristian-like to burn for revenge as I do but a demon is tempting me to lead him on and fool him at last. When I think of how I could & can fool him and of his weak imaginings to the contrary, petty evidence of spite work, and he has been safe hitherto because I would not stoop to deceit—I grow wild and almost determined to pay him back.

She paused to consider. Anger and pride were such familiar companions. She had vowed to rein them in, but how could one expect her to tolerate such mistreatment? Because she was a woman and society required her to display a certain temperament, was it necessary that she ignore the screaming in her heart when she knew injustice and misdeeds were afoot? She kept writing, in the hopes that the feeling of her ink pen on the smooth paper might also smooth the tempest within her:

> But I will do the right as I know it—because it is right. I have never stooped to underhand measures to accomplish any end and I will not begin at this late day by doing that that my soul abhors: sugaring men, weak, deceitful creatures, with flattery to retain them as escorts or to gratify a revenge, & I earnestly pray My Father to show me the right & give me the strength to do it, because it is right, despite temptations.

Could she do it? Pretend to love him, then throw him over the minute he proposed marriage? Making it clear to all of Memphis that he had pined for her and it was she who had found him wanting. "Such premeditated and deliberate insults! My blood boils at the tame submission to them," she confessed to the tear-soaked pages.

She wanted to punish him. He had *earned* the thrashing. But her own inner compass would not allow it. She had been brought up by two God-fearing parents who had never done wrong when the right thing was so evident. They had left the earthly plane, but she could not dishonor them by abandoning the faith they had held to with pride. If only God could quell the fury and anger that raged within her.

Instead, she turned to her diary, writing not only her observations and her dreams, but her prayers too: "I shall pray for Mr. G & all others who have formed themselves in a league against a defenseless girl, that they may see the light & injustice done me and that I may bear it meekly, patiently."

Revenge would have to wait, however, as there was much to do before her departure. On Wednesday morning, Ida ironed her clothes. There was no avoiding sad iron day, and Ida spent the next three hours pressing her clothes with the ten pounds of solid cast iron that was the only weapon for the job.

She went to town and emptied her bank account, and when each bill was paid in full, she tucked away the remaining eighty-five dollars, which was to be her purse for the summer.

Her twenty-fourth birthday was fast approaching, and at the post office, there was the most marvelous surprise from Nashville—an early birthday gift from her admirer Preston Taylor. His note said that the necklace of stones was an "acrostic" piece of jewelry and that the first letter of the name of each stone was a letter in the word. The necklace was diamanté, with a green gem to symbolize emerald, a purple stone for amethyst, a red stone for ruby, another green stone for emerald, a dark blue stone for sapphire, and a light blue stone for turquoise. The necklace, Preston wrote proudly, symbolized that she and she alone was his DEAREST. Ida loved the necklace, and only wished that she felt something like love for Preston Taylor.

That afternoon, Ida went to Phillipa Blanc's to drop off a book. When she returned home, Mrs. Barclay told her, "Mr. Graham came by to visit. He said he'd be back in an hour."

Ida sat in the parlor for three hours, but there was no sign of Isaiah.

Annoyed, she ate her supper, then went to her room and changed out of her day dress. That night, in her diary, she wrote, "Mr. Graham came while I was away and did not return that night. He left me without a farewell & I thought he would return but he did not. I don't know how to take him. He is either afraid to trust me, or does not care for me at all. I am too proud to beg but I must be loved with more warmth than *that*."

On Saturday, Louis Brown came over to invite Ida for a carriage ride. She dressed carefully for the occasion and felt her heart leap as he helped her into the carriage. As the horses carried them down Beale Street toward the Mississippi Riverbanks, Ida took in the view of the city that she had come to love and think of as home.

In the privacy of the carriage, Louis had boldly taken her hand and did not let go. The feeling of him holding her gloved hand made her feel safe and secure in a way that she rarely felt.

Louis said, "Ida, you have no father or big brother to advise you, so I wish to speak frankly to you."

Ida's heart sank. So here it was.

"I should always prefer you speak frankly to me."

"Men who are of courting age must divide the women they meet into two camps."

"Is that so?"

"There are the women they find endearing and the women they find entertaining."

Ida shook her head. "These distinctions are so boring—and outdated."

Louis laughed. "Only you would say so."

Ida shook her head. "Every woman who longs to *really* live her life would say so. Can't a woman be both endearing and entertaining?"

Louis paused for a second and then gave her that familiar sideways flirting glance. "If any woman might, you could," he said. "But our lives are not our own, Ida. We must build a free world for generations of Black people to come. It is serious business. Tough times are upon us, and harder times are coming."

Ida thought of how divided the states of America remained. "I know that," she said solemnly.

"Men of my generation must make the distinction between women with whom they can build and those with whom they may be drawn to but could never marry. You don't easily fit into either category, but any man will wonder, do you want a husband or a career? Will home life ever be enough for you?"

Ida was quiet then because it was a question that she asked herself often—about a home life—and whether it would be enough.

"Everybody wants a home," Ida said finally. "But what 'home life' means is different for every woman."

Louis Brown smiled. "I think not every woman, Ida. But different for you, certainly."

It was a Friday night in June, and both Ida and Julia Hooks were to perform at the Lyceum. Whenever she heard Julia Hooks sing, it was, Ida thought, as if she were the new Black Swan. Elizabeth Taylor Greenfield, a woman Ida's grandmothers' age, had been the first woman to bear that sobriquet. Greenfield was America's answer to Jenny Lind, who was known the world over as the Swedish Nightingale.

Ida had read that Greenfield's extraordinary octave range and dizzying operatic repertoire were a powerful blow to racial misconceptions in the years leading up to and after the Civil War.

The *Cleveland Plain Dealer* wrote, "It was amusing to behold the utter surprise and intense pleasure which were depicted on the faces of her listeners. They seemed to express: 'Why, we see the face of a Black woman, but hear the voice of an angel, what does it mean?' "

Ida had grown up hearing about Elizabeth Greenfield, "the Black Swan," the great opera singer who even as slavery ruled the nation had traveled to London and performed for the Queen of England. Ida did not know anyone who had ever been to Europe, but she only had to close her eyes to imagine Elizabeth Greenfield sailing across the Atlantic, wearing the most sumptuous gowns and jewels as she hobnobbed with British royalty. Elizabeth had long been a legend their parents spoke of, proudly, to remind them to arc unceasingly toward progress. But on this new day, in the great city of Memphis, they had Julia Hooks, whose voice seemed able to travel down any compositional pathway. She wore a simply cut, but elegant, dress in a raspberry hue that bewitched like a kiss blown from the stage. She smiled and said, "Tonight, I will sing for you 'Porgi Amor,' from the opera *The Marriage of Figaro*."

There was a gentle murmur in the crowd, and Ida was excited, as this was neither an aria nor an opera that she knew.

"To set the scene," Julia continued, "the countess is married to the Count Almaviva. She knows that he is unfaithful to her. She is heartbroken that her love is not enough for her husband, whom she loves deeply. So she pours her lamentation into song."

Ida did not speak Italian, but as Julia sang, her voice seemed to encircle them with the countess's grief and despair. At the same time, her effortless mastery of the lyrics and the sheer musicality was like a flame that drew them closer and promised to keep them warm. When she was done, Ida was not alone in reaching for her handkerchief to dab away the tears.

As she approached the stage, she hugged her friend and

said, "When you sing, even the angels cannot hold back their tears. Bravo, Julia!"

Ida was next on the evening's program and had prepared two selections for recitation. The first was from *Macbeth* when Lady Macbeth reads aloud her husband's letter about the meeting with the witches. Ida relished playing the lady, pouring into her all the ire and cold calculating that a proper girl in the Victorian era could never express.

She held a piece of paper onto which she'd copied the script in her best handwriting. She'd even dyed the page with tea to give it the look of a Shakespearean-era artifact. She glanced at it occasionally, but that, too, was an act; she'd memorized the whole thing.

The audience seemed to be taking her words in. The story of the tragic hero was a world away from their own, but the temptation of ambition and the slide into darkness that it caused tugged at their own hearts. Ida knew that, on the surface, they shared a collective desire to uplift the race in these decades after the evils of slavery. But at the same time, it was likely some misdeed did reside in and among them. It was what made them human.

"They met me in the day of success," she began sotto voce, making eye contact with each person in the front row. "And I have learned by the perfect'st report that they have more in them than mortal knowledge."

Then she walked to the back of the small, makeshift stage and glanced over her shoulder, lifting her head as if Shakespeare himself had crafted the words for her and her alone to speak.

"When I burned in desire to question them further, they turned air!"

Ida waved her hand overhead, deliberately, as if she were a

ballet dancer and her fingers could dissipate the stars across the night sky.

"Into which they vanished."

The applause when she was done was thunderous, and Ida smiled. The immediate gratification of theater was unlike any other. But then when she tried out a new piece—the sleepwalking scene from *Macbeth*—the audience responded with soporific indifference.

It was a sad note to end her last public performance on before her trip, made bleaker still by the fact that she ran into Louis Brown afterward, and he treated her neither as lover nor sibling, but with deliberate indifference.

That night, in her diary, she wrote, "Mr. B. seemed very cold & contrary and I wondered where the glamor of his presence was."

Chapter Twenty-One

Off to Kansas City

July Fourth arrived at last, and Ida and her friends celebrated the 110th anniversary of the nation with their first ride on a sleeper car. They boarded at 4 PM for the nearly five-hundred-mile journey to Kansas City. The overnight portion of the ride was a marvel, and Ida felt like a baby being rocked to sleep by the big hulking metal arms of the train chugging along the track.

In the morning, the issue of Black women not belonging in the "ladies' car" was raised again, and they were put into a third-class car despite the tickets they had purchased. As she scribbled in her diary, the move was a step down, "a dingy old car that was very unpleasant."

The women needed the intervention of a gentleman, and help arrived in the form of Dr. Albert Sydney J. Burchett, a well-dressed physician friend. The doctor got them more suitable accommodations in the second-class car, and Ida was reminded that her own court case was still pending.

Ida and Fannie Bradshaw got off the train in Kansas City

with a coterie of fellow teachers: Fanny Thompson, John Bruce, Phillipa Blanc, and Benjamin Sampson, the principal of Ida's school, among them.

Ida and Fannie walked down the row of waiting carriages, asking each if they had been sent by Mr. Paul Jones. But neither Jones nor the carriage he promised was anywhere to be found.

Rescue came again in the form of another gentleman. While wandering around the station, Ida ran into J. Dallas Bowser, the editor of the *Gate City Press.* Bowser and his wife, Dora, upon hearing of the young women's predicament, invited Ida and Fannie to stay at their home.

"This is outrageous," J. Bowser said. "You must stay with us."

Joining them in the carriage, Ida wanted to pinch Fannie for insisting they accept the offer from Paul Jones, and she wanted to pinch herself for not listening to the sage counsel of Therese Settle.

At the house, she trembled as she learned that the "accommodations" Jones had arranged for was a house where men and women dallied without regard to the constraints of marriage or reverence for the will of the Good Lord.

Moreover, Bowser, after making some inquiries after the fact, discovered that, while Jones was a lawyer, he was also known as a heavy drinker.

Ida was embarrassed that she had almost entered into the offer of accommodations that most certainly was meant to be a bribe upon her affections. "Be not concerned," Mrs. Bowser said. "Tomorrow I will give a reception in your honor, and you will be cheered, and all the peril that may have fallen you will have been forgotten."

Over the next few days, Ida quickly filled her calendar with socials, carriage rides, and literary debates. Her diary would list the names of nineteen "new acquaintances" she made during her nine days in Kansas City.

After church on Sunday, Ida was greeted by a schoolteacher friend, Mercer McGee. The very one who had introduced her, by letter, to Paul Jones.

Mercer was a teacher but built like an athlete. He had a big smile and he greeted Ida with a brotherly embrace. "Ida, you come to my town and don't call on your friends?"

Ida kept her arms at her side and eyed him with an icy gaze. "What kind of friend are you?" Ida asked. "Do you know the situation you nearly put me in?"

Mercer shrugged. "Believe me, I did not take him to be a cad. Accept my apology."

Ida shook her head. "I'll consider it."

Mercer grinned, "Come on, Ida. You know you can't stay mad at me. Let me walk you into the reception."

At the church reception, Ida was approached by another well-dressed gentleman. He had small teeth and a big smile. From the moment she glanced at him, Ida didn't trust him.

"Ida B. Wells," he said, extending a hand. "My name is Hank Leary. I'm a friend of Paul Jones. Pleased to make your acquaintance."

"A friend of Paul Jones is no friend of mine," Ida said bluntly.

"He would like to invite both you and Miss Bradshaw to go riding tomorrow."

Ida wanted to laugh. "Go riding with that louse? I refuse."

Julia Evans, a school principal in Kansas City, hosted a night of games at her home. It reminded Ida of a little cathedral with its arches and windows with diamond-shaped panes. After a tasty dinner of mutton cutlets with strawberries and homemade ice cream for dessert, they retired to the parlor. They played a card game called Logomachy that Ida had never heard of before but could not wait to play again. And many rounds of Parcheesi brought them to the midnight hour and beyond. But just as they were getting ready to leave, Julia stood at the door and said, "This party will not be complete without a lark of some sort. So, I propose a contest."

The hostess handed out cards and pencils. "The rules are this—you will have ten minutes to write the best joke or amusing anecdote you have ever heard. At the end we will read the cards out loud and the applause will decide the winner."

Ida smiled. She loved games of this sort, and she knew many jokes but hesitated until Julia called out, "Last three minutes!" to write something down.

They took turns reading their amusements, and the room filled with the sounds of merriment.

Phillipa stood and read her card: "Marriage is an institution intended to keep women out of mischief... and get them into trouble."

The room dissolved into laughter.

Fanny was next, and she read her offering with the kind of theatrical flair that made the Memphis Lyceum members proud. "See here, old chap," she said in a pitch-perfect British accent. "I've found a button in my salad."

Then she read her own response, in a droll American accent: "That's all right, sir. It's part of the dressing."

Robert Coles was next: "Why is a dog like a tree?"

The gathered group responded, "We don't know, Robert. Tell us why!"

"Because they both lose their bark when they die."

Finally, it was Ida's turn, and she stood and explained, "A man said to a preacher, 'That was an excellent sermon, but I'm afraid it was not the *least* bit original.' The preacher was taken aback. He had written the sermon himself the night before and had not copied a bit of it from any other source than his own mind. The man said he had a book at home that contained every word the preacher used."

The guests looked at each other and Ida quizzically.

Ida smiled and said, "The next day, the man brought the preacher a dictionary."

The applause was immediate, and Ida sat down, pleased that she had put on a good show.

Julia Evans said, "I'll be right back."

She returned with a small box and handed it to Ida. "Well, Miss Wells," she said. "Your story takes the cake, quite literally."

Ida opened the box, and inside was a beautiful golden cake with boiled white icing. She thanked her hostess and went back to the Bowsers', eager to share the cake with them the next day at teatime.

It wasn't until five days after her arrival that she actually met Paul Jones face to face. She came out of a photographers' studio on Steptoe, where she had just had new cabinet photographs taken, and there was Paul Jones. She recognized him from the photos he had sent her.

"Ida B. Wells," he said. "We meet at last."

She turned to walk away from him, and he put an arm on her shoulder.

"Let me give you a carriage ride," he said. "The driver is waiting."

He pointed to a lavish black carriage that was parked across the street.

She turned and kept walking. "Don't speak to me, Paul Jones," she said. "Touch my shoulder again and you will regret it."

He turned from entreatment to enmity in a flash. His face contorted and his words came out in an angry tumble: "I, a lawyer and a gentleman, offered you a carriage ride in my city, and you dare humiliate me in public. You are not the lady you pretended to be in our previous correspondences."

"It is precisely because I am a lady that I must demur."

"You think too highly of yourself, Ida Wells."

"If that is the case, and I do not believe it is," she said, begging her voice not to crack, "it is only because I must elevate myself from the depths in which you attempted to cast me with your disregard for my reputation and character upon my arrival."

That afternoon, a scathing letter arrived.

> *Miss Wells,*
>
> *I leave out the "dear" because nothing in your behavior recommends it. You have insulted me publicly, and I regret ever making your acquaintance.*

You and me both, Ida thought. She continued reading:

> *I had heard that you were mercurial, bad-tempered, and profligate with both your affection and your rage. I did not believe any of it. But now I must stand with your detractors, and trust me when I say that our number is many.*
>
> *With no regard for you at all,*
> *Paul Jones*

That night, after dinner, Ida asked to have a word with Mr. Bowser, who had shown her such kindness.

"You are a good, sensible man," Ida began, moderating her voice so that she might sound the same.

Mr. Bowser smiled at her benevolently, and she remembered what it was like to be sixteen and to see the kindness in her father's eyes whenever she went to him with a challenge or vexation.

"You know well the deceptions and improprieties Paul Jones employed to bring me to Kansas City under the guise of being my bachelor host."

"I am read in on the matter," Mr. Bowser said.

"Since our arrival in your gracious home, I have refused his every invitation, and now he considers himself humiliated and has written me the most vile, threatening letter—full of rumors and reprobation against my character."

"Tread lightly, Ida," her host said, as gently as he could. "A woman has little recourse once a man has set his mind to ruining her name. Write to him and tell him that in such a whirlwind trip you are sorry you did not have time to visit, but you wish him well."

"I shall," Ida said.

As she walked back to the room she was sharing with Fannie, she shook her head at the inanity of it. She should write to him? Why should she apologize? For what reason could she possibly be sorry? Her thoughts ran as they so often did to revenge—and knowing that none was possible, she switched to rage.

As they got ready for bed that night, Fannie carped that "your Mr. Jones proved to be unreliable in every way. I wonder how you could have encouraged him without fully understanding his character and his standing in society."

The words stung, especially as it was Fannie who had pressed her to accept the not-so-gentle man's invitation.

"Oh, Fannie," Ida said. "Your silence at this moment would be an extraordinary gift."

Fannie made a sour face. "Don't snap at me because you made a bad choice in a beau."

Once Fannie was asleep, Ida took to her diary, wanting to not forget the force of her feelings. "I was so angry," she wrote. "I foamed at the mouth, bit my lips, and then realized my impotence—ended in a fit of crying."

Chapter Twenty-Two

Topeka, Denver, and Salt Lake City

But Kansas City was just the beginning of the journey. Ida and the group of educators from Memphis traveled on to Topeka, where the National Education Association was having its first interracial conference. Thousands of educators from around the country were gathering, and the community of Black Topekans had grown in less than two decades from 473 in 1870 to almost ten times that number. The community boasted six Black newspapers, and any number of Black clubs and cultural organizations.

Ida, who thrilled to the world of ideas, spent a busy week meeting teachers from around the country and attending panels and lectures.

She wrote to Robert Countee, editor of the *Living Way*:

Dear Mr. Countee,

I write to you from a historic multi-racial gathering of teachers at the National Education

Association in Topeka, Kansas. It is to be a momentous gathering of six thousand–plus teachers. Train travel is opening new worlds to our people. If you are amenable, I would like to write an exclusive travelogue of the famous sites one might see from Topeka to Denver to California, where I will end my journey. My aim will be no less than to capture, for your readers, the varied carols our nation now sings.

Respectfully,
Iola

Countee wrote back right away saying a travelog from Iola would be a summer treat for his readers and could she send all material for publication no later than August 1?

On the last night, Ida and Fanny Thompson joined a group of seventy-five educators at the Music Hall.

The curtains parted and an older gentleman said, "Ladies and gentlemen, we have an extraordinary treat for you tonight. All the way from Nashville, Tennessee, we have the Fisk Jubilee Singers!"

Ida turned and squeezed Fanny's hand. She had attended a summer session at Fisk, had longed to attend the university but could not afford it. "I have long heard of these singers," she said. "But I have never seen them sing."

"Oh, it's been my dream to hear them ever since I read about them in the *Memphis Free Speech*," Fanny said.

Five women and five men walked onto the stage. The men were dressed in light khaki suits and crisp white shirts, and the women wore fashionable navy dresses with just a touch of shine to the material.

These were the young men and women with angelic voices who had toured America and then sailed on triumphantly to Britain and Europe. They had performed "Steal Away Jesus" and "Go Down Moses" for Queen Victoria, and now Ida was their audience.

As they began singing the first spiritual, "My Lord's Writing All the Time," Ida felt as if they were singing right to *her.*

The songs reminded her of her parents, of sunny Sabbath days when they rose early to dress for church, and sunsets when her father would sit with her mother, just swaying as her mother sang spirituals in her soft, sweet voice.

The choir sang for more than an hour, and when they were done, Ida jumped to her feet, clapping. The entire room was on their feet, and the singers began to sing again.

Still, when it was over and they gathered in the Music Hall lobby for refreshments, Ida said, "It was too short. It was just too short."

Fanny took her hand and said, "Oh, Ida, I have never seen a finer display of beauty, dignity, and nobility."

"It makes me proud to be a Black woman," Ida said.

"The pride they are making the world bestow in our people is their gift to all of us," Fanny said solemnly.

Ida had been able to take advantage of a special fare for journalists and planned to travel all the way to California to visit her aunt and her sisters. She knew that her aunt hoped she might stay in California, but once she arrived, she would explain to Aunt Fanny why Memphis was her home.

Ida had planned stops along the way to California based on writing assignments she'd lined up and friends of friends who had promised her lodging. In Topeka, Ida parted ways with her dear friend Fanny and traveled on to Denver.

In the lobby of the Inter-Ocean Hotel, Ida was greeted by Eliza Jane Brown. The story of Eliza Jane and her mother, Clara Brown, was the stuff of legend. Clara had been freed before Emancipation and became the first Black woman to move to Denver. During the Gold Rush, she established a successful laundry business. She worked side jobs as a cook and self-taught nurse and midwife. A tall, elegant woman with a mind for business, she carefully collected the gold dust she found in miners' pockets as she cleaned their laundry, and over time her fortune became so great that she was able to fund the construction of one of the first Black churches in Denver, St. James Methodist. She expanded her business by buying homes and lots throughout the state. In the growing Black community in Denver, she was known as Aunt Clara, and her home was a refuge for those who were newly arrived and in need. She helped so many people that the citizens there began to refer to her as the Angel of the Rockies.

She spent decades searching for her daughter, who had been sold away from her when the girl was just a teen. After many years of writing letters, she found Eliza Jane in Iowa and brought her back to Denver. Clara died in '85, the year before Ida arrived in Denver. But her story was so well-known that everyone said, "When you arrive, find Eliza Jane Brown." So Ida did.

The two women sat and sipped coffee in the hotel lobby. Eliza Jane, who at that time was a still-striking, statuesque woman in her fifties, said, "Your reputation precedes you, Iola.

Many say you are set to become the finest journalist of your generation, woman or man."

Ida bowed her head shyly. She worked hard at her writings, but she knew she could do better—and God willing, with the right editors and guidance, she would.

"And you are single?" Eliza Jane said.

"I am," Ida said.

"Come to my house for supper tomorrow. There is someone I would like you to meet."

The next day, Ida arrived promptly at the appointed hour at the home of Eliza Jane Brown. She had never seen a house like it. It was a gorgeous deep cerulean blue, the kind that made Ida think of sailboats and the Mississippi and the sky right before sunset. An Italianate masterpiece, it featured bracketed cornices, dentil molding, and a portico.

Ida walked into the dining room, and the walls were a bluish gray that made it seem like the long mahogany dining table was floating amid the clouds. A butler, Black, dressed in a formal black suit with a crisp white shirt, showed her to her seat, where her name was written in calligraphy. The table was set for eight, and soon the other guests poured in. In all, the party, was made up of Ida, three married couples, and one excruciatingly handsome young man.

Eliza Jane looked pleased as she watched Ida and the young man glance furtively at each other. Then she introduced them.

"Edwin Hackley, may I present . . . ," Eliza began.

But Edwin took Ida's gloved hand, bowed in an old-fashioned but completely effortless manner, and said, "Miss Ida B. Wells, you need no introduction."

Eliza said, "Edwin Hackley is the first Black American to pass the bar in Colorado. He is the future of our people, as are you. I expect you will have much to talk about."

Edwin took the seat opposite Ida, and as the butler served the courses, they got to know each other.

"Two thousand Black Americans now call Denver home, and we aim to have many more," Edwin said.

Eliza, who sat to Ida's right, whispered, "Because Denver's Black community is primarily young men, a young woman like yourself could have the pick of gentlemen."

When Edwin offered to show Ida around his city, she accepted gladly.

The next day, Edwin began his city tour with statistics. "Denver is projected to be the twenty-fifth largest city in the country in just four years," Edwin said proudly.

"And what is Memphis? Surely we are in the top twenty-five too." Ida was always bullish on her hometown.

"Hmm," Edwin said. "In the last census, Memphis ranked forty-fifth or forty-sixth."

"It can't be true," she said incredulously.

"It's okay," Edwin said, smiling playfully. "Small cities have their own charms, and some say that Memphis belles are the prettiest of them all."

Ida nodded and took the compliment in. Edwin Hackley was a charmer. "So where are you taking me?"

"A friend of mine works at the Tabor Grand Opera House. What would you think of a backstage tour?"

Ida beamed. There were few things she loved more than an opera house.

"Some say this is the finest building ever built in Denver,"

Edwin said. "It is named after the mining millionaire Horace Tabor."

Ida walked around the building in wonder. The building was a behemoth; she thought it gave the mountains in the distance a run for their money in its breadth and width.

"It cost a million dollars to build."

The opera house was clad in red brick and white limestone, and as she walked around the outside of it, the stone and brick seemed to coalesce into what felt like a shimmering wave. Ida thought of her father, Jim, and how he built their home with his own hands. How she wished she could wire him in Holly Springs and say, "Dad, here's the money. Take the next train to Denver, because there's something you've got to see."

At the stage door, Edwin and Ida were met by Edwin's friend Harry Hampton. Harry was tall and muscular but with a boyish smile that bordered on shyness. He and Edwin greeted each other as if they were brothers, and Ida felt a surge of pride—they were not just men on the move, they were men who were kind.

The inside of the opera house was just as astonishing as the exterior.

"The stairs are marble," Harry said, pointing to the grand staircase that looked like it belonged in a castle, not an opera house. Walking into the main auditorium, he explained, "The theater seats fifteen hundred people."

Edwin said, "Harry is one of the ten stagehands who manage the sets and costumes and everything backstage."

Ida took it all in, trying to imagine what it would be like to attend performances in this grand place. "It is everything you say and more. It's the finest opera house I've ever seen."

Edwin placed a gentle hand on her shoulder and softly said, "Look up, Ida."

When he spoke, he leaned in so close that Ida thought she almost felt his lips brush her neck.

She followed his instructions, and the ceiling, a fresco painted in the vibrant colors of a Colorado sunset, was unlike anything she'd ever seen.

After he showed them backstage, Harry walked them out into an elegant vestibule. "Now, you'd think this is where our tour would end, but old Horace is nothing if not ambitious."

"Up there," he said, pointing to the second floor. "Those are office spaces. Down the hall, there's a drama school. Follow me. There's more."

Ida followed Harry and Edwin down a hallway, and at the first door, Harry stopped and reached into his pocket for a key. After jiggling the lock, he flung the door open. "Take a look at this, Ida."

She was almost as taken by what she saw in the room as she had been by the fresco in the opera house. "What in the world?" she sputtered.

It was a barbershop, but one unlike any she'd ever seen before. On either side of the room, there were four walnut chairs, with leather seats and back. The floor was a luxurious checkerboard tile, and above it all, there was a small chandelier.

"It's as if the chandelier in the opera house had a baby and they put it in here." Ida giggled. "Who would think to put a chandelier in a barbershop?"

"And who would think to put a barbershop in an opera house?" Edwin said, equally incredulous.

"Horace Tabor, that's who," Harry said, as proudly as if he'd built the place himself. "A gentleman always keeps his whiskers trimmed."

Edwin nodded. "It's not a bad idea. Barbershops are social centers for men. A lot of business takes place in these kinds of chairs."

Ida took note. Of both Edwin's insight and his unmistakable good looks. "Well, thank you both for the tour," she said. "This has been the highlight of my trip to Denver."

"But the tour's not over yet, Ida," Harry said. "I've got one more room to show you."

She laughed and said, "One more surprise like this, Harry, and I may need a fainting couch."

He smiled and said, "Follow me."

He led them down the same hallway and pulled out another key, but this one opened up a dramatic set of double doors. Ida wouldn't have believed it if she hadn't seen it herself. Inside the most beautiful opera house she had ever seen, there was a bona fide saloon.

"May I offer you something to wet your whistle?" Harry asked.

"Just water, please," Ida said.

He poured her a glass, and the three of them took a seat at a wooden table with beautifully carved chairs.

"This place is a wonder," she said.

"I knew that the opera house is usually closed on Monday, so I thought you might enjoy poking around," Edwin said. "Lucky for me, Harry was free to play tour guide."

"I thank you both," Ida said. "I have enjoyed myself thoroughly."

"Then my task is complete," Edwin said.

That night, Ida confided in her diary, "Edwin Hackley must be one of the finest young men I've had the good fortune to meet."

On her next to last day in Denver, Ida woke up before sunrise to take a carriage out to Colorado Springs. She didn't want to do it. She'd been up late at dinner with Edwin, and her bed was warm and comfy. But she had been assigned to write travel pieces for both the *Living Way* and the *Gate City Press,* so off on the carriage she went.

Hours later, as the carriage rolled down the dusty road, the most enormous red rock formations came into view. Ida was in a carriage with five other tourists, and she could hear them all sigh with wonder as they got closer to the extraordinary peaks.

"Now I can see why they called it the Garden of the Gods," Ida said.

As they walked around each formation, Ida scribbled in her notebook. The guide, a casually dressed gentleman in his forties, said, "The West is both the past and the future for Black Americans. Nearly sixty years before the silver boom, James Beckwourth, a Black trader and trapper, joined the William Henry Ashley fur trapping expedition. A legend of the Old West, Beckwourth was known from Colorado to New Mexico to California for more than four decades."

He led them on a walk along a trail, and Ida found herself at Manitou Springs. The guide said, "This particular fountain is called Twin Springs, and some say it's the sweetest water in all the land."

Ida reached down, cupped her hands, and sipped. It was cold and sweet. "I wish I could take some of this water with me," she said.

The guide laughed. "You and every other visitor to the springs."

She'd had less than a week in Denver, and before she knew it, Eliza Jane's carriage was dropping her off in front of Union Station.

Walking into the grand Beaux Arts hall, Ida knew that she could not *live* in a train station, but staring up at the 180-foot clock tower and the gleaming Italian tile and terrazzo floors, Ida felt like the building was more palace than depot.

Edwin Hackley approached her with a smile that was bigger than Christmas. "People say that stepping into the station is like stepping right into a grand hall in Paris."

Ida outstretched her gloved hand. "I was just imagining that it must be. It's good to see you, Mr. Hackley."

He looked over her ticket and took her bags from her. "Let me handle this for you," he said gallantly.

For Ida, there were no sweeter words. She exalted in the care and company of chivalrous men. He walked her to the track where her train was scheduled to arrive, and they made light chitchat as they waited.

But when the train pulled in, he lifted her face to his and gazed into her eyes. "Promise me you will not let my letterbox sit empty and forlorn."

Ida shook her head. "Your letters will be the first to which I reply, Mr. Hackley."

Edwin looked disappointed. "First means there are more than one. Am I to understand that I am joining a queue of suitors?"

Ida smiled sweetly and said, "For the right gentleman, there is no competition."

When he helped her get her bag on the train, he stood on

the steps, kissed her hand, and did a dramatic bow. "Until next time, Ida B. Wells of Memphis," and the handful of men on the platform whooped and clapped.

She boarded the train and sat in a window seat. Edwin Hackley's warm, handsome face beamed at her from the platform, and Ida waved until she could see him no more. Never before had she felt so much like Juliet.

It was forty-one hours by train from Denver to Salt Lake City. Plenty of time to think and reflect. That past winter, she had thought everything in her life was a mess—her career, her finances, her love life. But summer brought sunshine, opportunity, and something that felt a lot like hope. She had two assignments for major publications. She'd had a wretched encounter with that terrible Paul Jones in Kansas City, but the men who sought her company in Topeka and Denver were proof that she was not without charms. She'd paid down some of her biggest debts and had a little money in her purse. And there was this—she was going *West* west. She was more than an average schoolteacher. She was a journalist and an explorer.

She traveled through the Rocky Mountains' great Continental Divide, and in Salt Lake City, she slipped into a service at the awe-inducing Mormon Tabernacle. But as she only had one day in the city, she could not even stay for the entire sermon.

A few days later, Ida took a ferry from Oakland to San Francisco. There it was! The city, the Golden Gate strait, and the dazzling Pacific Ocean beyond it. The city was enchanting, a Babel of languages and ethnicities. Ida walked through Chinatown and felt like she'd been transported to Asia, surrounded by a people and culture she'd never seen.

That afternoon, Ida visited the offices of the *Elevator*, a local newspaper. She was greeted by the editor, Philip Alexander Bell, a distinguished older gentleman. Ida guessed that he was at least seventy years old. He was fair enough that he might have passed for white, but he had spent his entire life working for civil rights. He had been born in New York and worked for many years as an abolitionist. In the years after Reconstruction, he had turned his focus to voting rights and initiatives that would create opportunities for young Black people in the Bay area.

As Ida sat in the small office on the second floor of an office building in the Fillmore District, he explained, "Most white Californians oppose integration. But this is where journalism can play an important role. At the *Elevator*, we report the facts without a tinge of personal supplication or subjectivity. Our authoritative, impersonal tone has had the greatest impact in persuading those who might oppose us to our cause."

Ida found this interesting, as the majority of her own work consisted of personal letters and essays to the editors that held forth on her opinion.

"Do you think, then, that the letters of Iola do not rise to the standards of your journalism?" she asked.

He shook his head. "Not at all. You are gaining a voice among our people. In many cities, such as Memphis, Detroit, Kansas City, and Washington, DC, the Black press plays an important role in informing and inspiring our people. But in California, we are but a small minority. The majority of my readers are whites who view the *Elevator* as a window into a community that they do not know and cannot access."

Ida thought this was wise. She had not considered the role the Black press might play in providing an impartial, informed point of view into the Black community that many white readers might not otherwise receive.

"Thank you, Mr. Bell," she said, clasping the older gentleman's hand in hers. "I have gained much from our conversation."

He smiled at her. "It gives me hope to meet one of the next generation of journalists. You must remain steadfast in your efforts. Honesty and bravery will power the cause forward faster and more effectively than emotion and literary artifice.

"You know, Ida," he continued. "You remind me of a correspondent we had at the *Elevator*. Her name was Jennie Carter."

Ida nodded. "The name is familiar."

The editor continued, "She was based in Nevada. She wrote under the pen names Ann J. Trask and Semper Fidelis."

Warmth filled Ida's heart as she said softly, "Always Faithful."

Bell said, "Yes. She passed away a few years back, but I have compiled some of her clippings for you to take with you."

He handed Ida a sheaf of papers.

"Such a gift," she said. "I regret I have no gift for you."

He shook his head. "Nonsense. Our conversation has been its own reward. And someday, when you write a book—because surely you will write one—send a copy to me, and I will drop everything and read it from cover to cover."

Ida flushed at his confidence in her. *Let it be so,* she thought. *Oh, let it be so.*

Bell stood and said, "You'll read it in her clippings, but I want to urge you to carry forth some advice that Jennie Carter once gave me that has stood me in great stead. She told me that the secret to a good and satisfying long life could be found in three things: The first is to keep your head cool and calm. The second is to keep your feet dry and warm."

She nodded, and the older man continued: "The third, of course, is the hardest but, I daresay, the most valuable of them all—keep your heart free from anger."

Ida, who knew that her temper was her greatest weakness, promised him she would try.

Chapter Twenty-Three

Oh, California

Visalia was far away from the South, but Ida knew it had been pro-Confederacy during the war. What had started as a trading post for miners had missed the brass-ring chance at being a new city when the Southern Pacific Railroad main branch bypassed it in the seventies.

The city was hoping to reinvent itself as an agricultural center, but the schools were poor and the financial prospects were dim. A few years before Ida arrived, a fundraising campaign for the whites-only public school had ended with the lynching of a Black man—a day of celebrations at first, but then women, men, and children gathered to gawk at the body of a man hanging from the Court Street Bridge over Mill Creek. It was a story every Black person in Visalia told visitors and newly arrived residents, a warning of all the hate that was hidden under the bright California sunshine.

The carriage ride into Visalia left her hot, dusty, and tired, but when her aunt Fanny opened the front door, it was like the sun had been locked inside that little home. She had not seen her little sisters in a year, and she hardly recognized them. Lily was eleven, no longer a little moppet but barreling toward her teenage years with a newfound grace and poise. Annie was fourteen, almost as old as Ida had been when their parents died.

Annie held Ida tightly. "My dearest sister, a published writer, a teacher! You are doing it all, and *nothing* and *no one* is holding you back!"

Fanny's daughter Ida looked to be Annie's twin, and the two girls sat together, elbows interlocked and eyes dancing.

Aunt Fanny seemed older too—but also more tired and lonely. "Good to see you, Ida Bell," she said, using the middle name that only family ever did.

Ida embraced her again and felt the outline of her mother in her arms.

After a "welcome home" dinner of chicken croquettes and sweet-potato pie, her aunt Fanny whispered, "It would be so nice if you could stay. Teach at the colored school—just for a year."

After a week of Fanny's needling, Ida sold her return ticket to Memphis. But the joy of being with her family soon gave way to the realization that the world outside her auntie's door offered few pleasures for a single Black woman. Visalia had no lyceum, no dances for its Black residents, no paper for Ida to write for, no theater or concerts for her to attend. There were no baseball games on the weekends or elegant dinner parties followed by lively games of Parcheesi or checkers to while the night away.

She wrote in her journal a week after her arrival, "Not a dozen colored families lived there, and although there was plenty of work, it was very dull and lonely for my aunt and the five youngsters in the family. There was good work and good wages for my aunt, and better health than back in Memphis, but no companionship."

Moreover, Visalia was not safe for a young Black woman to explore on her own. Her aunt reminded her daily, "Ida, you must never go out without an escort." Fanny had a friend from church, Lutie, who escorted Ida in town. But Lutie was rarely available. In her diary, Ida wrote, "I've no books, no companionship & even an embargo is laid on my riding out with the only one who can take me." It had been a long time since she'd felt so lonely, so far away from the life she wanted to live and the woman she hoped to become.

The US Postal Service had meant many things to Ida over the course of her young life. It was the matchmaker who transported love letters between her and the society of "cultured gentlemen" she longed to know. Letters had also been the building blocks of her burgeoning journalism career—letters from Iola that were published in the biggest newspapers of the Black press.

In Visalia, letters became something else entirely—a compendium of confectionery, something vitally sweet at the end of the long, hot, and wearing days. She received a letter from Fanny Thompson telling her that her brother George, now in his early twenties, was soon to be married. She wrote to him and wished him well. She was not close to her own brothers. They had been twelve and eight when her parents had died, and as they'd been sent to live with other relatives, she came to think of them more as distant cousins than as siblings.

Other letters brought less emotionally complicated news. The first week, there was a bonbon from Therese Settle, a chatty missive about the goings-on in Memphis.

Dear Ida,

We had the pleasure of hosting Mr. Cyrus Field Adams, a professor of the German language at Kentucky State University. He and his brother also, for a time, managed a newspaper in Louisville called the Bulletin*. He is, as you might expect, a fan of the irrepressible Iola.*

He is moving to Washington, DC, where he will certainly cut a fine figure among the Upper Tenth, if for no other reason than his sharp wit and rapier-like insight. I shall give you an example. At dinner on Sunday night, he poked fun at his own blue eyes and pale skin. While others might be boastful of their ability to pass for white, Mr. Adams told the dinner table—not him. "My trouble," he said, pouting, "is that all my life I have been trying to pass for colored."

You can only imagine the cackles and laughter around the table.

Your sincere friend,
Therese

She welcomed unexpected letters from new friends from her time in Kansas City.

Dear Ida,

You were a lively and welcome interruption to our Kansas City summer. It would be a delight if you came back. What might I tell you about our fair city that might entice you to return? There are now more than 20,000 of us living in the city, many residing in a neighborhood I don't think you had the opportunity to visit, Rattlebone Hollow. More and more of our families arrive from Canada each year. I do wonder what life must be like up north and how it compares with life in the city.

You mentioned an interest in horse riding. Next time you are in town, you should meet Tom Bass. He is a trainer of fine show horses and an accomplished rider. A few years ago, he married Angie Jewell, who is, I'm proud to say, a cousin of mine on my father's side. Tom Bass is the first colored rider to ride in the American Royal Horse Show, and word of his talents has spread so wide that he has been invited to ride in the Royal Horse show in England. Can you imagine?

Write to me when you can and know that I will respond promptly.

Your new but dear friend,
Eliza Grey

And there was a letter from Isaiah, ever faithful, if a little dull.

Dear Ida,

Oh, what delight your last letter brought me. I am always encouraged to learn what you are reading. The Gwendolen you describe in the Eliot novel seems to me like the most reckless sort. What kind of woman plays roulette and pawns the family jewels when few are so lucky to have such treasures? Who would allow it?

Ours is a long ladder, but books as you describe make me joyful that we do not live as people in novels do!

Your obedient and humble
servant,
Isaiah

Ida meant to be done with Isaiah, but her loneliness gave his shortcomings a veneer of awkward charm that they lacked when the two lived in the same city.

Dear Isaiah,

Your last letter baffled me, especially as I had understood you to be a lover of books, like myself. What does it mean to be glad that "we do not live as people in novels do"?

It is my desire to love extravagantly, travel widely, and be a force for change in every way that my abilities will allow. I am afraid that my heart arcs in a different direction from yours, for I very much want to live as people in novels do.

For what it is worth, I never gamble and have no interest in roulette.

Your assured friend,
Ida

A flirty letter arrived from Louis M. Brown.

Dear Ida,

My law degree is secured, and I thank you for your letter congratulating me. It is one of the many things we share—a passion for education and betterment.

This one particular crest scaled, I now find myself freer than ever to think of more sublime pursuits. In that category, you occupy no small amount of my thoughts. I am curious about how you are finding California.

My thoughts, too, are drifting west. I have been thinking about trying to pass the bar in Colorado, where I hear a man like me dare not be afraid to express a mountainous ambition.

Have you heard of the Ensleys? Newell Houston Ensley is a professor of theology and Latin at Howard. He graduated as the only one of our race in his class from Newton Theological Seminary in Massachusetts. Few men possess his mix of charisma and intellectual rigor.

You would love his wife, Elizabeth Piper Ensley. She also teaches at Howard. Mrs. Ensley has traveled extensively through Europe and has many tales to tell about the fight for women's suffrage in England. Of course, it's a sign of Newton Ensley's progressive nature that he supports his wife's suffrage pursuits.

The couple have been talking about a move to Denver. The population there may be sparse, but the social circle that is developing in that city is of the highest quality.

Yours always,
Louis

Ida closed her eyes and imagined herself Mrs. Louis Brown of Denver. Having been to that city, she could picture it now—the two of them in a big, sprawling home done in the new Shingle style, with a gabled roof, exposed rafters, and a big, generous porch for games and reading books and sipping sweet tea.

There'd be no need for her to teach with a lawyer's income. She could dedicate herself to writing full-time. What a thing.

Ida opened her diary and let herself dream of Louis with the full abandon of her twenty-four-year-old heart. Louis, she had no doubt, would be a success in anything he set his mind to. Ida believed that, if Louis applied himself to winning her love, she would in turn "help him prove to the world what love in its purity can accomplish."

But for all her suppositions about how grandly she might love her future husband, her heart did not yet beat for Louis alone. Hoping to bait Charles Morris into making a declaration, she told him she was considering marriage and wondered what it would be like to raise her children in California. As she sealed the envelope, she told herself, "I know he will be surprised at the tone of that letter."

Despite the fine time they'd spent in Denver, she had not received any correspondence from Edwin, which was disappointing. To pass the time, she decided to apply her August days—the precious free time on a teacher's schedule—to her writing. She worked on an article that she called "Our Young Men" and sent it to the prestigious *AME Church Review.*

"It is one thing," she explained to Annie, "to be published, but I need an editor."

"What's an editor do?" Annie wondered aloud.

"An editor corrects your writing and helps you make it smarter, more powerful."

Annie smiled. "You're the smartest woman I know."

Ida wrapped her arms around her sister. She didn't say that Annie was probably right and that was, at least in part, because Annie didn't know many educated women. She just let her sister's admiration sit on her skin like a beam of sunshine on a perfectly balmy day.

"Thanks, kid," Ida said, tugging on Annie's braid.

"No, seriously," Annie said, smoothing her braid back into place. "You should be an editor. You should be in charge of the biggest and best newspaper in the country."

"Oh, Annie." Ida sighed. "If I could get the world to see me with your eyes, I could do anything at all."

Ida appreciated the compliments, but her ambition was not driven by ego alone. It was a critical time for her people. Just that week, all the Black newspapers in the country had led with the news of the hanging of Eliza Woods, a Black woman in Jackson, Tennessee. Woods was a cook and had been accused of poisoning the white woman she worked for. The dead woman had been found to have been poisoned with arsenic, and a box of the stuff called "Rough on Rats" had been found in Eliza Woods's home. Woods was taken to jail, but before she could stand trial, a crowd of more than a thousand people had dragged her from the jailhouse, taunting her as a Black "she-devil" who murdered an "esteemed Christian lady."

The case haunted Ida. The woman shared the same first name as her mother, who had also been a cook. Ida turned to her journal to capture her thoughts and to find some degree of comfort. Woods, she wrote, "was stripped naked and hung up in the courthouse yard. Her body was riddled with bullets and left exposed to view! O my God! Can such things be and no justice for it?"

Indignant, she fired off an article and sent it to the *Gate City Press.* She tried to keep in mind the words of Philip Bell about the power of impartial words to persuade, but she was so filled with emotion, she could not keep her pen from the pitch of indignation. She sent the article off, knowing that it was an epistle of fury and frustration. "It may be unwise to express myself so strongly," she wrote in her journal. "But I cannot help it, and I know not if capital may not be made of it against me but I trust in God."

In the weeks ahead, she would wonder how to make her writing stronger, what it would take to work at the level she aspired. She knew she had her critics, but she did not think that they understood her effort, her aim, and her intent. "I think sometimes that I can write a readable article, and, then again, I wonder how I could have been so mistaken in myself," she wrote, feeling her body weary with exhaustion. "A glance at all my 'brilliant?' productions palls on my understanding; they all savor dreary sameness, however varied the subject, and the style is monotonous. I find a paucity of ideas that makes it a labor to write freely and yet—what is it that keeps urging me to write notwithstanding all?"

Chapter Twenty-Four

Spillikins

Summer was coming to an end, and Ida could no longer ignore the decision she had come to weeks before. She could not stay in Visalia. Every day that passed, she feared that the San Joaquin Valley would swallow her whole like those plants that turned carnivorous, snapping insects like tigers with their seemingly innocuous green and pink stems.

She waited until Saturday, when Annie, Ida, and Lily were going out to the park to play the game of graces with their friends.

Ida sat on the back porch of her aunt's house, shelling beans for supper.

"Aunt Fanny," she said, "this time in Visalia has meant more to me than you could ever know. I can't thank you enough for caring for my sisters. My parents, God rest their souls, would be so grateful."

Aunt Fanny sucked her teeth and looked sideways, "Thank you for the roses, niece. But let's get to it—what thorns have you for me today?"

Ida sighed. "I have to go back to Memphis."

"Why?" Fanny asked.

"Because I'm lonely," Ida said softly.

Her aunt harrumphed. "I'm a widow with nothing but these children for company and conversation. You don't think I'm lonely, child?"

"But it is worse for me!" Ida pleaded. "I'm a young woman, and I'm just beginning to live. I have my whole life ahead of me."

The words came out before she could reel them back in, and she could see that her aunt was wounded by them.

"Don't measure me for a wooden box yet, Ida," she said.

"I'm sorry, Auntie," Ida said.

"Save it," Fanny said. "Take your sorry with you. But I hope you have a plan to step up to your responsibilities, because if you go, you've got to take your sisters with you."

This was not possible, and Fanny knew it.

"I don't make enough money to take care of Annie and Lily," Ida said.

"Well, you best figure it out. You're young. Well-educated. And like you said, you've got your whole life ahead of you."

That night, after her sisters, cousin, and aunt had gone to sleep, Ida took out her diary and wrote, "I regret more and more every day that I sold my ticket." The moment called for sacrifice. As Ida wrote, "I feel more and more that my first duty is to my sisters and to my aunt who has helped me when I had no other helpers. I will stay this year, at whatever personal cost to myself."

Ida's career and life increasingly resembled a game of spillikins. All she could do was throw up every stick she had and see what she might pick up in the process.

Another unexpected stick was thrown into her hand. Louis

Brown wrote to say he was not moving to Denver after all. He was going to Kansas City to practice law there.

Ida hardly knew what to do with herself. She needed to leave California. She sat down and pondered her options in her diary:

> I thought long over the matter, then wrote a letter to Mr. Robert Church of Memphis, Tennessee, asking for the loan of $150 with which to return. I told him the circumstances of my condition—although he did not know me he could find out by reference to the Board of Education that I was a teacher in the public schools and would thus be able to repay the money. I told him that I wrote to him because he was the only man of my race that I knew who could lend me that much money and wait for me to repay it. I also told him not to send the money unless I had been reelected, as otherwise there would be no need for me to come back to Memphis.

Ida's aunt, meanwhile, was determined to keep her in Visalia.

"I've got news for you," her aunt said. "I've secured a position for you in the Visalia school district," her aunt said. "They'll pay you eighty dollars a month—that's more than you made in Memphis."

Ida's heart sank.

"You've got almost fifty children crammed into your classes in Memphis, am I right?"

Ida nodded. Everything in her was screaming *no, no, no, no, no,* a thousand times, *no.* But she stayed silent.

"You'll have eighteen children in your classroom here. That's got to be better."

Ida knew that her aunt must have pulled every string at her disposal to get her a position at this late date. She also knew that the math more than made sense. In Memphis, she wouldn't receive her first term payment until December. It was the Memphis practice of paying the teachers at irregular intervals that kept Ida in debt. By contrast, she could save $300 after a year teaching in Visalia. Knowing that she could not afford to turn the offer down, she wrote in her diary, "I shed bitter tears of disappointment."

The day before she began classes, she received a letter from Louis Brown. Inside was a clipping from the *Washington, DC, Advocate* that read, "Ida B. Wells has decamped for the West and Louis Brown is headed to Kansas City. May the couple live long and prosper."

Escape from Visalia was her only thought. If it came by way of marriage, to the right man, of course, that would be okay too. Ida felt stifled in the home with her aunt, sisters, and cousin. There was no quiet place to read or write or think. And if her aunt saw her "sitting idle," she quickly assigned her a domestic task.

Visitors were rare, so Ida was thrilled when she received word that Professor W. W. Yates, one of her new friends from Kansas City, was coming to California and would make a detour in Visalia with the express purpose of visiting her.

She received him in her aunt's kitchen, and, thankfully, her aunt generously took the girls out to the park.

She poured her professor friend a cup of freshly made sweet tea and poured one for herself.

"I hope my friends back east won't forget me," she said wistfully.

"You're not pleased with the arrangements in Visalia," he said.

"I will apply myself to my duties," Ida said. "But as for the development of my mind and the condition of my heart, there is nothing here for me. I am so far from everyone and everything I have come to know and cherish."

"You are aware that, in Kansas City, there are many fans of your writing," he said. "Your visit this summer only solidified what a delight it would be to have you as a member of our community. Would you consider teaching in Kansas City?"

Ida said she would, but wondered, "Isn't it too late for such an appointment? Hasn't the school board already offered all the available teaching contracts?"

Yates smiled and stood. "Come now, surely I don't need to tell the great Iola that the wheels of change are always turning? I must take my leave, but let us stay in touch."

Ida's spirits were lifted by his visit, but she felt resigned to spending a long, miserable year in Visalia. She knew the school schedule well. California schools opened the first week of September. In Kansas City, classes commenced the second week, and Memphis schools began the week after that.

On the first day of school, Ida reported to work and found that eighteen Black students awaited her—the entire population of Black children in the city. "What is going on?" she asked the school principal.

The principal explained that as it was such a small school district, all the students were usually taught together, but the Black parents had asked for Ida to teach their children separately.

They didn't want their kids in a classroom with Mexican, white, and American Indian students for fear that their children would be treated as second or third or fourth class. They preferred segregation over what they feared would be a year of degradation and slights.

"Are you kidding me?" Ida asked. "Do they have no regard for the liberties and equality we have been fighting for in this country since the retreat of the Republicans in '77? Did they sleep through the Civil War?"

"Are you telling me or asking me, Miss Wells?" The principal sighed wearily. "We've set up a makeshift classroom in an abandoned storeroom down the street. They used to trade saddles there. It still smells of leather and polish. It's kind of a lovely scent if you ask me. I'll get Miss Fisher to show you the way."

Ida taught that day as if in a daze.

"Am I really meant to perpetuate segregation?" she asked her aunt at dinner that night.

"Look," her aunt said, unbothered, "if they were paying me eighty dollars a month, I'd segregate those children any which way they told me to."

On Tuesday, the spillikin sticks were jumbled again when Ida received a telegram from Missouri:

> YOU WERE ELECTED TO TEACH IN THE KANSAS CITY SCHOOLS LAST NIGHT. WIRE WHEN TO EXPECT YOU.
> W. W. YATES

Ida's aunt, upon hearing word of the telegram, begged her not to leave Visalia. To back her up, she enlisted the help of Ezekiel Ward, a lawyer, and one of the pillars of Visalia's Black community. He was a tall man with a bellowing voice that recalled the most fearsome preachers at the pulpit.

"You are young, but you should know that the abandoning of a lucrative, highly desired teaching position will be a stain on your reputation from which you will never recover," he said threateningly. "I have connections throughout Missouri and Tennessee, and on the East Coast as well. I will see to it that the stunt that Miss Ida B. Wells pulled on the good people of Visalia is an object lesson that is known and never forgotten. Even if I have to personally write a letter to every single Black press in the country."

Ida cowered underneath the threat. She was trapped. Her good name was her most valuable possession. The reputation she was building—as a woman of her word, with a gift for words, was the foundation of her future. She could not fight this fight and win—and she knew it.

"I will send the telegram tomorrow," she said softly.

Before school the next day, she went to the telegram office and sent the following message:

> THANK YOU FRIENDS FOR THIS INCREDIBLE OPPORTUNITY. I MUST RESPECTFULLY DECLINE.

On Wednesday, Ida arrived at school to find there were no supplies allotted for the Black students—and no word on when even the basic pencils and notebooks might arrive.

She smiled at the students and told them she would return shortly. She stood outside in the California sun, felt the warmth of it cover her face and her closed eyes, like a laying on of hands. "Give me strength, dear Lord," she whispered to herself. "Give me the wherewithal to see this through. Give me... *strength.*"

On Thursday after school, Ida came home to a stack of

letters. There were seven pages of treacle from a still-smitten Isaiah Graham. There was a flirty mash note from Robert Cook in Kansas City. Preston Taylor, in Nashville, wanted Ida to know that he was still very much in love and wished he could come and see her in California. There was a chatty Memphis dispatch from Fannie Bradshaw. But the last letter had handwriting that Ida did not recognize.

When she opened it, she was surprised to see it was a letter from Robert B. Church. He wanted Ida to know that he had it on good authority that she had been reelected to her teaching post in Memphis, and he was more than happy to make the loan she requested. Inside the envelope was a draft for $150, almost half a year's salary.

Ida could hardly believe it. She was desired as a teacher in the finest schools of color in the land. And the money meant she was free. Free to go and live and work wherever she might choose.

The next morning, she sent a telegram to W. W. Yates:

> **LEAVING TONIGHT. IF TOO LATE TO SECURE THE POSITION YOU OFFERED, WILL GO ON TO MEMPHIS.**
> **IDA B. WELLS.**

She taught the day at school and then went to the bank to cash her draft. As she entered her aunt's house, she girded herself for the battle to come.

For the better part of two hours, her aunt hurled insults and harangued:

Ida, I didn't think you would try it on.

Your parents must be turning over in their graves the way you have thrown over family for your own frivolous pursuits.

You underestimate the influence of Mr. Ward. He will bury you. I wouldn't be surprised if you never get another teaching job again.

When her aunt paused to take a sip of water, Ida sighed and said quietly, "Auntie, I do not have the strength to fight with you. I am leaving on the next train and taking my sisters with me."

Annie, to Ida's surprise, wanted to stay in Visalia with Fanny and her daughter.

"You go, Ida," Annie said. "Maybe someday I'll fly off to the big city too. But for now, I'm happy for this to be my home."

That night, Ida left for Kansas City with her sister Lily in tow.

Chapter Twenty-Five

There Shall Be Confusion

Ida and Lily arrived in Kansas City on the Tuesday after school began. After she sent her first telegram, a local teacher, Callie Jordan, had been elected to her post. Upon receipt of the second telegram, the school board—which was clear in its desire to hire more experienced Black teachers, who were in short supply in '86—dismissed Miss Jordan and rehired Ida.

The next morning, Ida went straight to school and found her fourth-grade class waiting for her. But the principal and a good many teachers were longtime friends of Callie Jordan and her family. They made it clear to Ida that their sympathies were with her, and throughout the day, they showed Ida—in word and deed—that she was not welcome.

"There will be no warmth for you in or outside these school walls in Kansas City," the principal warned.

Ida was shocked and saddened that she was not being given

a chance to prove herself a worthy colleague and friend. But she also knew that the frankness of her new peers was a sign to be believed. Her year in Memphis had taught her that your fellow teachers were the most important people with whom you spent your days. They made up the core of any single woman's social circle. If they were hostile and resentful as she walked the grounds of the school, then she could be sure that there would be no invitations to dinner, dances, concerts, or socials. She would be a social pariah—and that would make life in Kansas City not a hair better than it had been in Visalia.

She dismissed her class and only smiled when the students called out, "See you in the morrow, Miss Wells!" When the last of them had left with an enthusiastic wave, she sat at the desk and wrote out her resignation. It was the second such letter she'd written in the span of a week. She walked into the principal's office and let him know that he was free to hire Callie Jordan once again.

By the time she had gotten to her new home, word of her resignation had spread throughout the community. Mr. Yates and Mr. Coles arrived first and tried, unsuccessfully, to convince Ida that the icy reception she had received upon her arrival would soon thaw as people got to know her and appreciate what a gem they had in their midst.

When J. Dallas Bowser, her kind interlocutor from the summer, arrived he was elegant, well-dressed, and furious. He had been Ida's savior when Paul Jones had threatened to besmirch her reputation, and now, he believed, she had let him and Kansas City down.

As Ida watched him pace the parlor floor in his navy suit, with its slim lapels, and the finest pale blue shirt and tie, Ida felt like it was a sequel to the row she'd had with her aunt and

Ezekiel Ward just days before. He said, "I've already sent an announcement in type that the *brilliant* Iola will be an associate editor at my newspaper, in addition to sharing her gifts as a teacher in the Kansas City schools. I will tell you now that the choice you are making is not representative of the *brilliance* for which you had previously been known."

"But—" Ida began.

"I am not finished speaking," he said, cutting her off sharply. "This is the next logical step for you. You move forward. You keep growing as a journalist, as a teacher, as a person. Why in the world, at a time when our people are looking ahead, are you insisting on going backward?"

His argument was convincing. But Ida had made her mind up to return to Memphis. Even at the age of twenty-four, with all the uncertainty that swirled through her life, when she was decided, she was resolute.

"I am sorry to seem ungrateful," she told the circle of powerful men. "I am appreciative of all you have done for me. And it's my hope that one day you will once again hold me in high regard. But I do not wish to start a new life, in a new city, on the back foot. All day, I have felt that I have—through no fault of my own—found myself with more enemies than friends in Kansas City. My position in Memphis is waiting for me. I shall leave at once."

Ida and Lily boarded the night train to Memphis. And on Saturday, she walked into the teachers' meeting that had been scheduled to prepare for the opening of school on Monday.

Captain Collier, the schools' superintendent, said, "Miss Ida B. Wells—I'm surprised to see you. I'd heard word from Superintendent Greenwood of Kansas City that you were to join *their* ranks."

Ida smiled and said, "Rumors and conjecture, Cap. Those were just rumors and conjecture. I am here for my assignment."

After all the grades were assigned, the teachers were treated to a luncheon at Odd Fellows Hall. After dining on platters of sandwiches, followed by tea cakes and other sweets, there were reflections and toasts to the new year. Ida, who felt like she'd spent most of the summer like Jonah, unsure if she'd ever make it out of the belly of the whale, rose to speak. She smiled at the long table of her colleagues. Isaiah winked at her, and she had to admit, after the summer she'd had in California, seeing him made her feel stronger pangs of affection than she had felt for a good long while.

She thought then of the words of Ben Franklin and decided to put her own spin on his ambitions for their then still new country. She lifted her glass of sweet tea and, paraphrasing the inventor, said, "To the educators of our people, may your lessons, like the sun its meridian, spread a luster throughout the school year that enlightens our people, so our students may, in turn, enlighten the nation and the world."

When the luncheon was over, Ida and her favorite Fanny took a long walk along the waterfront. Ida regaled her friend with the tales of her summer—all that had happened since they parted ways in Kansas City just two months before. When Ida had finished recounting the adventures she had packed into only the first eighteen days of September, Fanny said, "So you have already taught in California and Missouri, and now you will begin in Tennessee? You are a time traveler of the highest order, Ida."

Ida smiled and said, "Someday, I'll tell my children about it—in the year 1886, I managed to teach in three states in the course of a single month. Four days in Visalia. One day in

Kansas City, and an entire school year, the good Lord willing, in Memphis."

"Never a dull moment around you, Ida B. Wells," Fanny said, embracing her friend. "It's good to have you home."

Ida returned the embrace and looked out on the riverboats idling down the Mississippi. "Fanny, you have no idea just how good it is to *be* home."

Chapter Twenty-Six

Meet Mr. Albert Alexander

Ida was determined to make deeper inroads into the inner circles of the Memphis Black elite. This effort got a grand boost when she and her sister Lily found a room to let with Therese and Josiah Settle on Lauderdale Street, one of the most fashionable addresses in town.

Although Ida had dined with the Settles before, seeing the house in full and knowing she would live there was still a little astounding. Both Ida and her sister's eyes widened at the mahogany wainscoting and the way their shoes slipped, almost like they were dancing, across the wide-board oak flooring. The piano in the drawing room was finer than any Ida had ever seen in a church, and the library overflowed with volumes, some of which Ida was confident were valuable limited editions. A kitchen with ivory-painted cupboards was to the rear. The outside of the house was marked by a giant porch with hand-carved spindle work and swings that faced each other. To Ida, the Victorian house looked like something out of a fairy tale.

Technically the Settle home wasn't open to renters. It was a sign of Ida's growing stature in the community that the couple had decided to let a room to her and Lily. In conversation, Ida was used to taking the lead, but she reminded herself that it was important to show deference to her host, now her landlady. Ida noted that her much wealthier friend had a gorgeous wardrobe of colorful bodices and overskirts, some of which featured a peplum waist, the latest style.

The palette of her dresses confirmed that she was a woman of means. Ida's eyes had greedily taken in how they ranged from the palest lavenders to the reddest reds to sapphire blue and peridot green. Ida, who loved clothes but was constantly bested by her budget, opted for navy and brown dresses for winter and bleachable white dresses, with a pale yellow alternate, for summer.

Their first night on Lauderdale Street, as they settled into their twin beds, Ida confessed to Lily that she thought Therese Settle might well be "the sweetest, quietest, and most ladylike creature it has ever been my good fortune to meet."

The Wells sisters settled nicely into the home—helping to prepare meals on the weekend and joining the family in board games, like Parcheesi, in the evening.

One evening, Ida was helping Therese clean up the kitchen when the older woman smiled coyly at her. "I have a present for you."

Ida beamed. She had been at the Settles' for a month and

longed for her host to pass on some discarded hand-me-down—a tea dress that she had tired of, a pair of gloves whose tea stains would not come out, a battered but brightly hued parasol. Really, she'd have taken anything.

"What is it?" Ida asked, keeping her voice as light as a meringue.

Therese's eyes flashed. "Not what, my dear, but who."

Ida put the pan she had been drying down. She had been without a proper beau for too long. Correspondence with eligible men in far-off cities kept her mailbox full, but her Friday nights were startingly empty. Meeting Therese's gaze, Ida pretended she was on the stage at the Lyceum and that she was not poor, near penniless Ida Bell from Holly Springs. She straightened her carriage as if she were a bored royal on a continent on the other side of the sea. It would behoove her, she thought, to behave as if the matter of her own betrothal were not a question of if but when.

She felt fairly certain that she was as pretty as any other Black girl in Memphis. She knew for sure that she was smarter than the lot of them. She believed herself to be a catch and intended to comport herself accordingly.

"Okay, who?" she asked, languidly.

"You'll see tomorrow," Therese said. "He's coming for Sunday supper. . . . And I suggest you don't wear the brown dress."

The next morning, Therese gave Ida a flamingo-pink overskirt—silk taffeta with velvet ribbons. As Ida felt the weight of it in her outstretched arms, she knew it was the single most luxurious thing she had ever owned.

"It's got a tear in it I'll never mend," Therese said, clearly fibbing. "But you're such a whiz with the needle, I'm sure you can make it work."

Ida thought to wear it with a simple white blouse and her best navy bodice. But when she showed the combination to Therese, she shook her head no.

Standing up and heading to the staircase, Therese said, "You should take the matching bodice—a gift for helping me around the house."

In their bedroom, Lily watched Ida slip into the pink outfit.

"You look like a proper lady," Lily said. She admired her older sister. It was why she had chosen to accompany Ida back to Memphis after a year out west. California's sun was no match for Ida's shine.

Ida smiled at her own reflection in the small, heavy mirror that hung in their room.

"You could even be a princess in that dress," Lily continued.

Ida made a shooing motion with her right hand. "Now you stop," she said, clearly flattered.

"Promise you'll pass that dress on to me when I get to courting age?" Lily asked. Her two braids and simple cotton dress made her look even younger than her eleven years.

"Promise," Ida said, looking her sister directly in the eye. She hoped that when the time came, she'd have more to offer her little sisters than hand-me-down dresses.

The Settles had a girl who helped them with the cooking and cleaning during the week. But on Sundays, Therese Settle did it all herself. Ida came down to find a feast laid out on the table in the formal dining room—baked country ham, corn pone and crispy biscuits, sweet potato casserole, and hot buttered beets. For dessert, Therese informed her, there were brandied peaches and homemade ice cream.

The surprise guest, Albert Alexander, was as handsome as a stage actor, with a chiseled jaw and black, wavy hair. As Ida settled into her seat opposite the dashing young man, who had been newly appointed as a teacher in a nearby school district, she could not help but congratulate herself. She had been orphaned at sixteen and left with no one to look out for her or help her make her way. But here she was, less than ten years later, living in one of the finest homes in Memphis, a respectable teacher, a writer on the come up, and suitors knocking on her door.

After dinner, while L'il and Mr. Settle listened to Therese play piano, Ida and Albert made their way to the porch. Respectfully, they each took a seat on one of the two porch swings that faced each other.

"Well, that was a fine supper," Albert began. "So, Miss Ida Bell Wells, tell me what's good."

Ida flushed that he used her middle name. She liked a man who had done his research.

"Well, I read in the newspaper that scientists are learning new things about the planet Mars every day."

He smiled at her. It seemed to be true what they said about her—that she was beautiful but maybe too smart for her own good.

"Did you now?" he said, looking up at the sky. "I have to admit I'm not sure that this Mars planet even exists."

"You can't see the new discoveries with the naked eye, silly," she said. "You would need a telescope."

"Well, I may need to find a telescope," he countered. "You know you can't believe everything you read in the papers."

She nodded. "That may be true. But the twentieth century is coming, and I think we're going to see a whole lot of things we never even imagined were possible. I believe that with my whole head and heart."

"I have a question about the more immediate future," Albert said. "Would you consider being my date for the Odd Fellows dance next weekend?"

Ida shot him down in an instant. "Oh, Mr. Alexander," she said, her voice a honey pot of rejection and sweetness. "I don't think so."

Albert Alexander looked confused, and Ida was pleased. He knew himself to be a suitor of high merit. Therese Settle had promised that she would smooth the way for him to get to know the Wells girl, since she had no kin to speak of. He did not understand the quick rebuff.

"And why not?" he asked. "Have I done or said something to offend you so early in the game?"

Ida smiled. She liked that he recognized that this—from their first hello, to the way they passed biscuits across the dinner table, to this conversation on the porch—was all a game.

"On the contrary, Mr. Alexander," she said. "I have witnessed that, for all of your training, well-educated men—such as yourself—seem to struggle to follow the commands of the dance floor. I myself am a very fine dancer, so it won't do for you to embarrass me in public."

Albert grinned and shook his head. "Well-educated men, you say?" he challenged. "Would you really lump us all together and dismiss us as a class, the way whites group and dismiss all Blacks?"

Ida tilted her head and appraised him without reservation. He was far too good a catch to let dangle on the line for too long, but she would let him work for it just a little bit longer.

"May I speak plainly?" Ida asked.

"I would prefer it."

She let her elocution slip then, deliberately and melodically. "Can you jook, Mr. Albert Alexander? Because when I step into a dance in Memphis, I need my partner to be smoooooth."

Albert laughed then, the laugh of a man who had learned to claim every room he entered as his own, as if tradition, hierarchy, and racism were not his problems.

"I'll make you a vow." Albert said, thinking on his feet. "If you go to the dance with me, I promise you cake *and* a cakewalk."

His bon mot amused her, and she acquiesced with glee.

"I will hold you to your word, Mr. Alexander."

1887

Chapter Twenty-Seven

We Are Illuminated

Albert Alexander was as good a dancer as he promised, and he and Ida began seeing each other. He invited her to come to a demonstration of electrical lighting on Beale Street by the famous Lewis Latimer. For the occasion, Ida had washed and pressed her favorite dress, a wisteria-colored number with steel-gray satin ruffles along the bodice and satin cuffs at the wrists.

"You look as sweet as cherry wine," Albert said when he picked her up.

"You know what Jonathan Swift said about flattery, don't you?" Ida asked.

Alexander shook his head. "I do not."

"Well, he said, 'Flattery is the food of fools.' "

Alexander laughed. "Miss Ida B. Wells, if you are not the most well-read mind on this side of the Mississippi."

Ida waved a finger at him and brightly said, "Oh look. Even more flattery."

They walked toward Beale Street, not holding hands but

close enough that their hands brushed occasionally. Albert was kind and entertaining, and Ida enjoyed his company.

"Did you know that Memphis was named for the great African city Memphis, in Egypt?" he said. "Which sits on the banks of the majestic Nile River?"

Ida did know but didn't see a need to tell him. "Oh, I'd like to go to Egypt, see the pyramids and the Great Sphinx."

He laughed. "Ida B. Wells, *you* are a sphinx."

"I could not possibly know what you mean."

"You court in riddles and no man yet has solved them, though it is rumored that many have tried."

It was true. She was now one of just two female teachers at the school who were unmarried. But this did not bother her. Marriage, as it was, had never been the point. If the bond of holy matrimony had been the only summit she sought to scale, she would have done the deed ages ago, but it was not.

As they walked, Ida told Alexander all that she had learned about Lewis Latimer.

Ida had read all about him in the papers. She took out a folded clip of Thomas Fortune's paper, formerly the *Freeman*, now called *The New York Age*:

> **Lewis's parents, Rebecca and George, had escaped from enslavement in Virginia and fled to Boston in the early 1840's. On their first day in the northern city, a Southern slaveholder had recognized George and within weeks, he'd been arrested. But George's case caught the national attention and got right to the heart of one of the most pressing questions of the day—could**

> a person who made his way to a free state be captured and returned to captivity in the South? George Latimer was defended in court by none other than Frederick Douglass and William Lloyd Garrison. His son was sixteen when he joined the navy. A year later, having earned an honorable discharge, he obtained a position as an office boy with a patent law firm. There, he showed an aptitude for using drafting tools and a gift for sketching patent drawings. He eventually became head draftsman at the white-owned firm.

All of this was enough to earn Ida's admiration and respect, but it was what Lewis Latimer did next that filled her—and the world—with wonder.

"Did you know, he was only twenty-six when he earned his first patent for a more evolved toilet system for railroad cars than had existed before?" Ida asked.

Albert laughed. "That's impressive."

"He was only twenty-eight when Alexander Graham Bell hired him to do the patent drawings for Bell's telephone."

"Is that so?"

"Then he joined the US Electric Lighting Company."

Ida went on to explain that the firm was owned by Hiram Maxim, who was Thomas Edison's rival in the race to patent the best electrical lightbulb. It was there that Lewis invented a more efficient carbon filament that laid the groundwork for the giant leaps in electricity that were coming.

Three years after his historic invention, Edison hired him away from US Electric. And as the *New York Age* raved, "Lewis

Latimer not only works side by side with the Wizard of Menlo Park, he also helps translate Edison's data into German and French so that a global team of scientists can innovate together in an unprecedented fashion."

Alexander said, "I'm going to have to keep my eye on this boy genius and make sure he doesn't steal my best girl."

Ida laughed at the suggestion but secretly thrilled to the fact that a suitor as prominent and dashing as Alexander had called her his "best girl." She could not imagine how the evening could get better.

When they arrived at Beale Street, she quickly found their friends Fanny and Julia, who were standing with Tommie and Betty Moss. The streets were filled with neighbors and friends waiting to see the demonstration.

Ida looked around and said, "Has anyone seen Mr. Latimer? I should like to interview him for the *Living Way*."

Fanny pointed to a tall, slim man dressed in a finely cut suit, with a slight mustache and spectacles. "He's that handsome one, over there."

Betty Moss said, "I like a man in spectacles. It makes him look worldly."

Tommie tapped Albert on the shoulder and joked, "Maybe we should leave the women to fawn over the boy genius."

Betty Moss kissed her husband on the cheek. "You're the only genius I'll ever need."

Ida remembered how in church that past Sunday, the minister had talked about the importance of finding a partner who was equally yoked—someone who was your match in both talent and temperament. She thought to herself, *Tommie and Betty are the embodiment of that ideal.* She hoped that someday she would find that kind of match.

A limelight flashed, and Lewis Latimer spoke. He did have a baby face, but his voice was as powerful as Frederick Douglass's at the podium. "I see that I have got your attention. Light will do that. Which is why I have dedicated all of my days and many of my nights to this work.

"But as I stand here on Beale Street," he continued, "I want to make a particular statement about the importance of invention in this place and time."

Ida took a notebook and pencil from her sack and began to scribble his words down.

"Most of us had parents who were born into slavery," Latimer said earnestly. "Even those among us who were born into freed families are closely acquainted with the dehumanizing effect of slavery. We live in a time where there are many who seek to use the judicial system to deny us our full rights as American citizens."

"Preach," Ida whispered to herself, writing as fast as she could.

"I work for a man named Thomas Alva Edison, and I've come here today to demonstrate the electric lighting system our team has patented. But I will also say that you do not have to be an inventor or an engineer to find ways to transform dark to light."

His words were like a melody, inspiring and uplifting, floating through the pitch black of the Tennessee night. "There are teachers in this crowd," Latimer said. "Architects and artisans. Journalists and lawmakers. Barbers and construction workers. My father owned a barbershop. Together, he and I hung wallpaper at night. We need you all to work on the business of inventing possibility, opportunity, and excellence, every day. My boss likes to say that genius is one percent inspiration and ninety-nine percent perspiration. I don't know a Black person who couldn't tell you all about that ninety-nine percent of blood, sweat, and tears."

The crowd cheered loudly.

"So I urge you to not forget, in all of your honorable toil, about the one percent inspiration. Gentlemen. Ladies. Let there be light."

With the flip of the switch, Beale Street, which had been dark as night, was awash with so much light, it was as if they'd all fallen asleep for an instant and woke to the brightest dawn.

Ida—shocked by the pure power of the electricity—dropped her pencil and bent to pick it up.

When she stood again, she saw that her friends were silent. Fanny, Julia, Alexander, Tommie, and Betty were transfixed by the magnitude of what they saw before them. Electric light surrounded them, and Ida thought that they might well have been transported to a fairy land.

Both hope and fear lived in her heart, and Latimer, with his electric lights, lit them up like fireworks blazing across the night sky. There was hope, the feeling that she was living in the midst of a vibrant, extraordinary time in history. And if she could step ahead into the future and just read about the times she was living in, she would enjoy it very much.

But she was also living with the steady hum of fear. The South was clawing back its power—Ida saw mounting evidence of this every week. Black people had a long road ahead of them. But Latimer and his lights, Ida was convinced, were more than a miraculous advance of the industrial age. Watching the baby-faced boy genius surrounded by admirers on Beale Street, Ida felt like the electric lights gave the inventor a kind of angelic glow. Was he a prophet? A messenger sent from their God to assure them that they would never again be plunged into the complete and utter darkness of bondage? The electric lights were a symbol of the great human capability to push back against the night. The Civil War had not settled their freedom once and for all. But they were moving forward, and no matter what was coming, there was no way the South could unring the bell.

Chapter Twenty-Eight

Justice Deferred

In April 1887, after two long years of legal challenges with the railroad, Ida received a letter from her lawyer, James Greer. There would be no more bills from him because the Tennessee Supreme Court overturned the ruling in Ida's case against the rail company. They had taken away her sex, noting that she was a "mulatto passenger," not a lady. As the court documents read, "We think it is evident that the purpose of the defendant was to harass with a view to this suit and that her persistence was not in good faith to obtain a comfortable seat for the short ride."

Furthermore, the ruling underscored that, while a Black woman could purchase a first-class seat and the railroad was well within its rights to collect the higher fare, the ladies' car was de facto "whites only" since white women were the only women who could be considered "ladies."

As Ida wrote in her diary, "I felt so disappointed because I had hoped for such great things from my suit for my people generally. I have firmly believed all along that the law was on our side and would, when we appealed to it, give us justice. I feel shorn of that belief and utterly discouraged. And just now, if it were possible. I would gather my race in my arms and fly away with them."

Ida thought there were only two paths ahead for Black Americans—progress and the unrelenting push toward equality or a kind of shadow slavery in which their people would be divided into two swaths: the oppressed and the oppressed who are offered a mere modicum of freedom. She wasn't sure why it was that there was always a sliver of Black people who were offered a little bit more access and opportunity than the rest. Was it because hope was the succor that the downtrodden needed to survive?

Was it because by the act of liberating a few, the majority could fool themselves into believing their humanity was intact? If a few Black people lived in mansions, danced at balls, visited the White House even, then was it meant to imply that those who were propagating violence in the post-Reconstruction South weren't monsters? Were they really to believe that the republic only meted out to its darker-hued citizens what each caste deserved?

Chapter Twenty-Nine

There Isn't Much

Ida walked past the home of Robert and Anne Church on Lauderdale Street. Fanny had lent her a novel by Henry James that she wanted to read. She slowed her pace until she was not moving at all. Robert Church had saved her from Visalia with the loan that had allowed her to return to Memphis. But she and he were not social peers. She had never been invited inside the Church home. But she knew, as did her friends and fellow teachers, some of what lay behind the awe-inspiring facade. The mansion—really, that was the only term for it—was three stories high. The style, Ida had learned, was called Queen Anne, and it was the first home in Memphis to feature the architectural design.

The front of the home featured a tower with an octagonal room, placed on the right front corner. A covered veranda wrapped around the left side of the house, and on the right side of the house, there were tall, vertical windows with stained-glass borders. From story to story, the materials shifted from shingle to brick to clapboard. On the top floor, there were large bay windows. Ida had heard that each of those windows featured upholstered built-in benches where you could sit and see right out to the Mississippi River. Ida could imagine herself on a window seat of the Church home, reading, writing, and dreaming through those bay windows.

Ida had heard that the Church home had fourteen rooms, six of which were bedrooms. Behind the house, there were stables for horses and separate quarters for servants. The frescoes in the parlor had been hand-painted by artists from Italy. And the carpets in the living room had traveled by ship from Europe to the States, then by riverboat from New York to Memphis, and thus had traveled farther than most of the guests who would walk over them.

Ida had little patience for the Black aristocrats who sought only to enrich themselves at the expense of the struggling masses. But Robert Church was different. He was what they called a "race man," dedicated to the uplifting of their people, like her father. And he had a daughter Ida's age: Mary Church, whom everyone called Mollie. She was a student at Oberlin College. Ida felt the old familiar feeling of envy wrapping like a scarf that was tied too tight around her throat. When it came down to it, Ida couldn't care less for fancy houses or servants or bay windows and Italian frescoes. As many books as she had read, as many articles she had published to increasing acclaim, she felt there ever hung above her a doorway that would take her to even greater heights of intellectual acumen and, like the round tower of Robert Church's home, that was a fairy-tale realm that she would never enter.

She looked up at Robert Church's house once more. A young woman looked at her from the tower.

Ida knew then that it was time to go. She had stared at the Church home long enough. Having picked up the good-as-new copy of *Washington Square* by Henry James from Fanny, Ida now had nothing to do but sit in the sun and read.

It had been her plan to sit in the backyard and read, but when she got back to the house, Therese Settle wasn't smiling. She sat at the dining table, dressed in a heavy black moiré dress.

"Ida," Therese said. "You are in serious arrears in your obligations to us."

She held a piece of paper. "You paid no rent in November and December. Only ten dollars in January and five dollars in February, nothing in March, and five dollars in April. That brings the total due to almost seventy-five dollars."

Ida looked at the piece of paper and blinked. "This can't be right. I've paid more than this. You know how erratic the school board is about paying us."

"I know, but I also understand that you were at Menken's just yesterday."

She held up a bag.

"Did you search my room?"

"Your room?" Therese scoffed. "This is my house."

Ida was flustered. "I've paid much more than this. I'm sure that I paid November, December, and January rent in full."

"Where is the record of it?" Therese asked. "Do you keep a budget book?"

Ida did not. She wrote her sums in her journal, but she could not show Therese her journal. It was full of the ire she held for people, including fellow teachers and the young man she had kissed when things seemed to be cooling with Albert Alexander.

But the truth was that her records of her financial doings were sketchy—driven as much by feeling as anything else. When she had written in January, "It is a new year and I am debt free," had that been accurate? Was the sentence merely a *reflection* of her determination not to owe anyone or anything ever again? Had she really been caught up, or was it that she had paid just enough to the Settles that she thought they would be satisfied until her train case settlement came through? Then the case had been settled against her after two long years and countless payments to the lawyer.

She looked at Therese Settle. It hurt to see the features of the woman's face hardened, the expression of disdain and contempt that seemed to say, *We are not equals. How foolish of you to think we ever were.*

"I apologize for the discrepancy," Ida said, looking the woman in the eye. "I will catch up by the end of summer. I will take on a summer teaching job. In the meantime, L'il can help keep the house clean and run errands as you need her to. I can also cook. Whenever you want. Whatever you want."

Therese, softening just a bit, said, "I do love how you prepare duck, and your spinach in a cream sauce would be nice too."

Ida nodded. "You shall have it."

As Ida went into the kitchen to do the washing up, she thought of what those who praised her would think of "Iola" given over to such domesticity. She had believed she had avoided this: the servitude. She had become, against the odds, a teacher. She had dedicated herself to journalism; she wanted to be a voice, a pair of hands carrying a lamp of learning to those who would lead their people. Everyone said she was becoming one of the finest journalists of her generation—a distinction that included few women. But the writing barely paid, and for all she worked—teaching, writing, running the Lyceum, making a home for L'il, sending money to Aunt Fanny—she had so little to show for it.

She finished the dishes in the kitchen and went up to her

room, her pride in tatters, her mind sick with worry about the debt. Ida did not know where the money went. She was paid her winter wages in April, and no sooner had she received the lump sum than it was gone.

The week dragged on in slow agony. Therese barely nodded in her direction when she greeted her in the morning. Josiah said nothing at all. After school and on the weekends, Ida exhorted L'il to dutifully take on the tasks Therese set out for her as if their lives depended on it, because the roof above their heads did.

When she got to the Lyceum on Friday, the room was abuzz. As she entered, the members all turned to her and applauded.

"I mean, I never turn down praise," Ida said. "But I don't understand what this is about."

"Have you not seen the *Journalist*?" Fanny asked, handing her the broadsheet.

Ida laid out the paper Fanny handed her and read:

> **Ida B. Wells is the journalist who struck the hardest blows at the wrongs and weaknesses of the race. She is also one of the few who is read and revered as widely among the men as the women. There is no doubt that Miss Wells is the undisputed Princess of the Press.**

Chapter Thirty

An Evening of Excellence

When the post arrived and Therese Settle handed her a heavy white envelope, Ida had no idea of what to expect. The heavy white stock was wrapped in a bright red ribbon. *A wedding invitation, maybe?* she thought. But nobody she knew had that kind of money to spend on paper when there was a whole wedding to pay for.

She opened it and read:

THE BOARD AND MEMBERS
OF THE LIVE OAK CLUB
HAVE THE GREAT PLEASURE OF INVITING
MISS IDA B. WELLS
TO CELEBRATE AN
EVENING OF EXCELLENCE IN COMMERCE AND THE ARTS
SATURDAY, JUNE 25, 1887
NATATORIUM HALL

Reception at 8.

Dancing at 9.

Refreshments at 11.

She had heard about the event. It was the talk of all of Beale Street. But she did not ever imagine getting an invitation. She recalled Lavinia Wormsley's haughty interrogation when they first met: *Who are your people?* Ida's answer had confirmed that she lacked wealth and familial connections. She was a teacher. She was pretty enough. She might marry any one of the up-from-their-bootstraps young men who were flooding the colleges and universities after Reconstruction. But it was very hard, if not impossible, for a young woman to scale the heights and find her place among the aristocrats of color. A young man of humble origin might—there were always errant or auxiliary daughters with no need for fortune who were in want of husbands. But men in search of brides were a far more calculating lot. As Ida considered the matter, she thought it was a good thing that she had no interest in scaling the ladders of society as a wife. She would marry for love. She would make her living with her pen, and if, on occasion, she was invited to dine and dance on top of the pyramid of privilege, she would not turn it down. She was fond of entertainment, and the Live Oak ball, with its bright white invitation, wrapped in a silk ribbon, promised to be a night unlike she'd ever seen.

In the end, it turned out only three teachers at the school had been invited: Ida, Julia Hooks, and Virginia Broughton. The next day, Ida went to Menken's to buy material to begin a dress. The fabric she chose cost twenty dollars. Almost half a month's salary for the loveliest swath of silk she'd ever seen—a blue the color of summer skies and jewels, that seemed to catch hints of ultramarine when the light hit it just so. She bought a pair of steel-gray gloves and a hat to match, and put it all on credit.

Walking home with the bag of her purchases in hand, she tried not to scold herself for once again spending beyond her means and going deeper into debt. It was, she believed, a necessity. Members of the school board would be at the dinner, and she would need to be reelected to secure her teaching job for the next year. Beyond work, she could possibly meet her future husband at such an event, and if so, she wanted to make an impression he would never forget. But apart from either of those scenarios, the charges at Menken's could be chalked up to the simple fact that for Ida, this invite to dine and dance among the Upper Tenth was the Memphis equivalent of being invited to the White House. Her life had been anything but a fairy tale, but on this night, it was her intention to sparkle.

The night of the ball, Julia Hooks had arranged a carriage for the event and offered Ida and Virginia a ride.

"Good evening, Ida," Julia said.

"Good evening, Julia," Ida greeted her warmly. "Your dress may be the most beautiful thing I've ever seen."

It was. The most exquisite shade of marigold with tulle that draped around the bodice and a fitted whalebone corset that made a V into the body of her skirt. The palest print of giant roses could be seen in the body of the skirt.

Definitely store-bought, Ida thought. *Not made by hand at all.*

"You are a vision," Ida said.

"Can you believe it's a hand-me-down?" Julia said proudly. "A cousin of mine is a seamstress in New Orleans. All of the rich ladies bring these dresses back from Paris for her to copy. Sometimes when they tire of them, they give the couture dresses to her to help pay down their bills."

Ida sighed. "A dress from Paris. I couldn't imagine it."

The carriage stopped, and Virginia Broughton stepped in.

"Good evening, ladies," Virginia said. "Did somebody say 'Paris'?"

Virginia's dress was a fiery red, also store-bought, Ida soon learned. An extraordinary damask with embroidered sleeves that fell like bells just past her elbows.

The carriage pulled up to Natatorium Hall. There was an elaborate carpet leading from the street into the hall.

"So no one drags mud inside," Julia whispered, answering the questions in Ida's dazzled eyes.

When they entered the hall, the orchestra softened its playing to a decrescendo, and a tall man in an immaculately pressed tux announced, with what seemed to Ida like the faintest of British accents:

Miss Julia Hooks!

Miss Virginia Broughton!

Miss Ida B. Wells!

The men in the room did the slightest bow, and the women tilted their heads in greeting.

"Wow, they sure do things differently in the Upper Tenth," Ida said softly. Then, when they were out of earshot, "And what was that accent? British?"

"Caribbean," Virginia said expertly. "All the smart set are hiring their butlers from the islands these days. Speaking of smart set, I must greet Nettie Langston Napier."

Julia walked Ida around the room and pointed out all the swank folks that Ida did not yet know.

"By the window, the tall man with the woman in the purple dress. The Honorable Samuel McElwee and his wife, Lavinia."

Ida had read about him in the papers. McElwee was the

most influential legislator in the Tennessee General Assembly. "Born enslaved, attended the Freedmen's Bureau Schools," Ida said, pitching her voice at a discreet decibel. "Attended Oberlin. Fluent in Latin and German. Head of the Tennessee Republican Convention and delegate to the Republican National Convention in Chicago in '84."

Julia laughed. "Ida, are you sure you're not wasting your skills writing trifles like 'The Woman's Mission'? It seems to me that the way your brain works, you are more Sherlock Holmes than William Lloyd Garrison."

Ida's cheeks pinkened. She had yet to get her hands on a copy of *A Study in Scarlet*, but she had read all about the adventures of the brilliant consulting detective in *Lippincott's Magazine*.

Ida greeted Isaac Norris and his wife, Stella. Isaac owned a thriving coal and wood business. Stella was a distant cousin of Ida's, on the side of her aunt in California.

Julia pointed out Robert Church and his wife, Anna Wright.

"Our first Black millionaire," Ida said, trying not to stare at the man whose wealth had made him a figure of national interest. She did not mention that it was Church's largesse that had brought her back to Memphis.

"Yes, but best we not approach him ourselves, as that may be seen as bad manners. But I will say that is wife number three," Julia revealed, steering Ida in an arc away from the Churches.

"A two-time widow?" Ida asked, her voice tinged with sadness.

"A two-time divorcé!" Julia giggled.

Dancing was a more staid affair than Ida had hoped. No handkerchief games or cakewalk, but they did a beautiful arbor dance where they linked arms and made an arch that each couple took turns passing through.

Ida found as she studied the room that, in between the dances, pieces of society came together like a jigsaw puzzle. There were Alexis Peterson and Olivia Rustin, dancing so closely that their every turn confirmed the whispers of their love match and the rumored soon-to-be-announced engagement. There were John Boyd, the esteemed lawyer and magistrate of Tipton County, and Thomas Sykes, a four-time elect of the North Carolina legislature, clearly plotting something bigger than the punch bowl over which they lingered.

For Ida, the event provided an unexpected pleasure, the thrill of observing people unguarded, as if the ballroom were a stage and she were seated in the best box of the opera house. She noticed, right away, that there was a slight adjustment to the rules of comportment that were sacrosanct outside of such events. At a dance, it seemed, men and women could touch each other freely, with no real worry of gossip or scandal.

Dinner was served by waiters who came around with large silver tureens of each course—first okra soup, then oysters, then ham, then potatoes, then whole roasted turkeys—golden with crispy, aromatic skin—the size of which Ida had never seen in her entire life. For dessert, there were platters of fruit and bowls of freshly made peach ice cream. Ladies were served thimble-size glasses of wine, but Ida did not mind. She was not used to it, and even just a few sips of the claret-colored amrita made her feel shy and giggly.

Ida found herself in the arms of dance partners so frequently that there was hardly a moment to sit and sleuth. A man in a suit and tails played the piano accompanied by—Ida counted them—six violins and two trombones. At the earliest opportunity, she snuck away to a low tufted chair almost hidden behind a heavy red-velvet curtain. She sat there and cast her eyes skyward. There were garlands of fresh flowers draped on every wall. Ida wondered if anyone would notice if she snipped a handful of irises and scorpion weed and took them home. She laughed at the thought, and noted as well that she did not have a pair of scissors. Even if she did, there'd be no end to the gossip if she tried to purloin a few buds and the whole arrangement came crashing to the floor.

It seemed to Ida when she started dancing again that time slowed down and the music faded to a low and lovely hum, like a gifted soprano singing under her breath so that she alone might hear. She saw Julia and Virginia being twirled around the room, but they were moving so languidly that she could see them and really take it in—the delicate curves of their jawlines, the elegant rustle of their gowns, the bright light in their dark brown eyes and the sunbeam wattage of their smiles.

There was her own dance partner, Temple Barkley, a freshly minted master's student from Oberlin College, off to begin his first teaching job at the Tuskegee Institute. He was not a prospect, but he could dance like a dream, and Ida wished she could capture in a cabinet photograph how fetching a pair the two of them must have made on the dance floor.

In her mind, she had been fully in the moment, so she enjoyed the last two songs languorously and luxuriously. She appreciated them all the more because before she knew it, the ball was over. Carriages awaited them and spirited them away to their homes. Ida slept in her gown that night, unwilling to take the dress off and willing herself to keep dancing in her dreams. Despite her meager circumstances, her debt, and her missteps, she had been able to go to a truly grand—*spectacular*, even—ball.

The next day, the *Memphis Watchman* ran a report that

declared the banquet to be "the most successful occasion that Memphis has witnessed in Colored Society." They also noted that, among the younger roster of New City guests, there was musical prodigy Miss Julia Hooks, who wore a saffron gown, "a couture confection, straight from Paris," and the teacher and journalist Miss Ida B. Wells, who wore a "striking blue surah lace overdress."

Three weeks later, Ida turned twenty-five. In her diary she wrote:

> This morning I stand face to face with twenty-five years of life, that 'ere the day is gone and will have passed by me forever. The experiences of a quarter of a century of life are my own, beginning with this, for me, a new year.
>
> Already I stand upon one fourth of the extreme limit (100 years.) When I turn to sum up my own accomplishments, I am not so well pleased. I have not used the opportunities I had to the best advantage and find myself intellectually lacking. And excepting my regret that I am not so good a Christian as the goodness of my Father demands, there is nothing for which I lament the wasted opportunities as I do my neglect to pick up the crumbs of knowledge that were within my reach.
>
> Thou knowest I hunger & thirst after righteousness & knowledge. O, give me the steadiness of purpose, the will to acquire both. Twenty-five years old today! May another 10 years find me increased in honesty & purity of purpose & motive.

Chapter Thirty-One

A Perfect Instrument

Ida spent the summer of 1887 working on her writing.

She still had aspirations of writing a novel and hoped that Charles Morris, with his dazzling prose, might help her with it. She wrote to him about the literary partnership of the philosopher John Stuart Mill, hoping it might inspire him.

Dear Charles,

I think often about writing the great Black American novel we discussed and hope that you might guide and advise me. Have you read John Stuart Mill, the British philosopher? He believed in the equality between men and women and credited his wife, Harriette Mill, with elevating all his best work.

In the "Subjection of Women," he wrote, "The subordination of one sex to the other was wrong in itself and is now one of the chief hindrances of human improvement. It ought to be replaced by a principle of perfect equality admitting no power or privilege on the one side or disability on the other."

When he spoke of his wife, he called her mind "a perfect instrument." I cannot imagine a finer compliment that any man has paid a woman whom he loves. I am borrowing every book that friends will lend me with the express purpose of developing my mind in just such a way.

Ever, my dear,
Ida

A week later, there was a letter from Charles Morris, and the bolt fell.

Dear Ida,

There is much talk of Memphis being the New City, but I hope your time there does not mean you espouse all of its ideals. Some say that we must not expect us as young people to uphold the old traditions, but I disagree.

We are the first generation of colored people who have the freedom to fully glorify the femininity of Black women. For centuries, she has been misused and trodden on as chattel. It is our job, as men, to restore her to the pedestal of noble womanhood to which she belongs.

I would not mind a wife who wrote novels, as that falls within the realms of feminine creativity. As you and I have discussed, from Austen to Alcott, some of the finest novels have been written by women. These women authors, I might add, had the honor of being called ladies in every room they entered.

But journalism is a sticky wicket, as it is an intramural sport that plays with politics. Politics, you cannot deny, is a sodden, bespattered business. I've heard it said that "Iola" is the true princess of the press. But I long for a wife who sees our home as the only kingdom over which she might reign. A delicate creature who will look to me as her protector and pathfinder in the world outside our front door.

In return, I will aspire to achieve a level of success that will bring comfort, recognition, and respectability in good society to my future wife and the children we will one day have.

Please do not misunderstand my words. It is not my intention to elicit promises. I speak in the abstract about ideals and expectations. But I must admit, I am curious. Are we aligned on the lives we might lead as we leave our wandering youth behind and look toward winning the prize of love?

Yours, still sincerely,
Charles S. Morris

There were a few more letters where Charles carped on about how modern women were good at so many things but very few of them seemed to seek excellence in the domestic arts. In particular, he seemed to find the housekeeping skills of the residences he visited in Washington, DC, to be lacking. Ida thought to herself, *He has not the courage to end this romance, so he pushes me away with more and more talk about his need for a traditional wife who will exalt, above all else, matters of housekeeping, when he knows that could not possibly be me.*

Talking it over with Fanny, she lamented, "I do not think I am the woman of his dreams, which saddens me so because he is, in so many ways, the man of mine."

Charles Morris had not formally ended it, but Ida knew that as they lived so far apart, his letters would dwindle until they stopped altogether. She admired him so much, so enjoyed his quick wit and charming conversation. She hoped that they could stay on good terms. To that end, Ida sent him a letter, begging that the end of their courtship not be the end of their acquaintance. In her journal she wrote of Charles, "I hope we might have a lasting friendship, increasing over the years, such as I read about, see very rarely, and have experienced never."

In a sign of respect, she returned all his letters to him. She cried as she sent the box of letters by post and consoled herself that weekend by taking to her bed early and rereading *Jane Eyre.*

Ida knew that, at twenty-five, she was expected to be married. And it was true that she was now the only schoolteacher at her school who wasn't engaged or betrothed. But Charlotte Brontë had gotten it right when she wrote in *Jane Eyre,* "I can live alone, if self-respect, and circumstances require me to do so. I need not sell my soul to buy bliss. I have an inward treasure born with me, which can keep me alive if all extraneous delights should be withheld, or offered only at a price I cannot afford to give."

Ida believed that she had an inward treasure in her writing—that the pen name Iola had come to mean something across the country was no small feat. And yet she thought she was only starting to become the journalist she aspired to be. There was a long ladder ahead, and while she ached for love, she could not rest on the lower rungs and wait for it.

Although they had never lived in the same city, the days seemed long and lonely without enchanting thoughts of Charles S. Morris to fill her head and the sweet anticipation of waiting for his letters. She began reading *Middlemarch*, and as she tried to settle herself with the idea that Charles would not court her any longer, she found herself rushing home each day after school to curl up by the fire and read. She did not need supper, just coffee and bread and time with her book. The characters in Eliot's novel, she noted, aspired to make the world better, but their idealism felt futile. It was a luxury that her race did not have, Ida thought, when she found herself only halfway through the 880-page tome.

Reading had always been, for her, a way of exploring the gospel of possibility, a telescope into secret worlds and private lives. So what was she to make of the marriage in *Middlemarch*? Ida found the marriage between Dorothea and Casaubon to be an object lesson in taking one's time in courtship. As she explained to Fanny, "Dorothea thought she would find the life of the mind by marrying a great scholar. Casaubon assumed an educated wife would elevate his own intellectual pursuits. But in the end, he resented her for seeing his shortcomings so clearly. And she came to see that he was neither adroit nor affectionate."

Fanny, who had not read the book, still took great interest in the conversation. "I think this is one of the most challenging questions that we face. Most men will *say* that an educated woman is highly desirable. But still, they respond most favorably when a woman does a kind of play acting. It's best if they are the ones who teach you what ideas to embrace, what politicians to support, even what jokes are the most humorous."

"The notion that the average woman can help elect any man to office is a cipher," Ida said. "We cannot vote."

"There are those who say we influence the vote through persuasion, the influence we have on our husbands, fathers, and brothers," Fanny said.

"I would rather have the ballot than blandishment," Ida said sternly.

"One day, we will," Fanny said resolutely.

Ida smiled at her friend. "Yes, one day, we will vote."

Chapter Thirty-Two

Finding Her Voice

September rolled into Memphis with its welcome cool breezes and reprieve from the summer heat. While Ida's teaching career remained challenging and stagnant, her writing career continued to grow. She journaled, "Although I had made a reputation in school for thoroughness and discipline in the primary grades, I was never promoted above the fourth grade in all my years as a teacher. The confinement and monotony of the primary work began to grow distasteful. The correspondence I had built up in newspaper work gave me an outlet through which to express the real 'me' and I enjoyed my work to the utmost."

While many of the nation's "woman's columns" focused on domestic life and the more genteel elements of community life, from her earliest writing, Ida wrote boldly about the Black upper class with a particularly withering eye toward those who took advantage of Gilded Age opportunities with little regard for the less privileged members of the race who were struggling without the protections of Reconstruction.

Ida had ambition and longed to be part of an exceptional and vocal Black community of writers and thinkers. But the point of all that opportunity had to be at least, in part, dedicated to the greater good. She worried that too many in the Reconstruction Era were enriching themselves at the expense of the community, and she particularly abhorred when the Black press published sycophantic softballs to the aristocrats of color. After reading one such "celebration of who's who in the Black community" in the *Detroit Plaindealer*, Ida stormed to her desk and penned a fiery response:

> I cannot call to mind a single one of [these men] who has expended or laid out any of his capital for the purpose of opening business establishments...for the young colored men and women who have been educated [and cannot] find employment.

Ida wrote witheringly about men who sought political office only to enrich themselves with little regard for the people and promises that landed them in office.

She was working on a new essay skewering the Upper Tenth when Therese knocked on the door of the room that Ida and Lily shared. "Ida, you have a caller."

Waiting in the sitting room was a tall, well-dressed man, whose broad shoulders and substantial height made him a daunting figure. He was wearing a dark gray suit of the finest material Ida had ever seen, a matching vest and pants, and a crisp white shirt. Ida made a mental note to write in her journal about his "volubly thick mustache"—surely she might be able to use that detail in her novel one day. It was a warm day, but he had the air of a man who always kept his cool.

"I'm the Reverend William J. Simmons."

"Pleased to meet you, sir."

"I'm the publisher of the *American Baptist* and president of the National Colored Press Association."

Ida sat up a little straighter.

"Forgive my unannounced visit. I was passing through Memphis, and I could not depart your fine city without completing the task with which I was charged."

"And what is that?"

"The *American Baptist* would like to engage you to be our first-ever female correspondent."

Ida smiled. "It would be an honor, sir."

"I will pay you the fee of one dollar a week for your letters."

Ida sighed. It was the first time in four years anyone had offered to pay for her writing. Sitting back in her chair, she felt flooded with emotions, like a character from a Brontë novel. *I have to remind myself to breathe*, she thought, quoting the beloved line from *Wuthering Heights. Almost to remind my heart to beat.*

Ida learned that Simmons had escaped from slavery with his mother and two sisters. He'd gone on to earn a degree from Howard University and had served as president of the State University of Louisville.

His praise and invitation to become a correspondent was both a boon for her writing aspirations and a welcome source of additional income. The column proved to be a productive outlet for Ida to try out all the ideas that had been building within her—what did it mean to be Black? What did it mean to be a woman? And most importantly, what would it take for people of her hue and gender to truly belong? Could this country be reconstructed into a land that treated Blacks as equal citizens? As Ida wrote in one of her early columns, "We are Negroes, but we are also Americans."

One reason for Ida's growing popularity was her willingness to skewer not only injustices by whites, but what she perceived as those who fell short in the Black community as well. One of her favorite targets was Blanche K. Bruce. In one editorial aimed directly at the senator, Ida wrote, "Tell me, what benefit is a 'leader' if he does not devote his time, talent and wealth to the alleviation of the poverty and misery and elevation of his people." And as protection against anyone missing her intention to skewer the powerful, she titled the piece, "The Functions of Leadership: Iola States Some Facts About Leadership Which May Make Somebody Wince."

Chapter Thirty-Three

Snow Day

The knock on Ida's door came just as she was willing herself out of bed. It was November—*How, already?* Ida thought—and it was hard to get up when the fire had died down hours before and the frost had slipped into every crack and crevice in the home.

Therese peered in and said, "Isaiah Graham is at the front door for you."

Ida sat up in the bed, sure she had misunderstood her landlady's words. "You can't be serious."

"I am."

"But it's not even seven AM."

"You get out of bed and tell him, because I don't think the man can read his own watch."

Ida swung her legs over the side of the bed and stood, smoothing down the wrinkled heavy cotton nightgown. She had made it herself and was proud of the cap sleeves and the ivory satin ribbons she'd sewn down the front, from the neckline to the hem. It was beautiful, but it was never meant to be seen, especially by a man who was courting her.

She could hardly imagine the scandal that would surely ensue when word got out that she'd greeted a gentleman in her nightclothes. Still, it couldn't be helped. She didn't have time to change. Isaiah would not be fool enough to beat the rooster to her front door unless something was really wrong.

Ida walked into the parlor and said softly, "Good morning, Isaiah."

He was fully dressed and looked august, handsome even. The glow of the early morning sun suited him. He must have felt the same of her, because he said, "She wakes a vision. How many maidens can make that claim?"

She walked into the parlor and took a seat, gesturing for him to take the chair opposite her.

"I take it by your silly talk that nobody has died," she said.

"Nobody has died," he confirmed. "I came to tell you that school is closed today. There was a snowstorm last night, and the snow is still coming."

"Untrue. They never close school because of the weather."

"They do when there's sixteen inches on the ground. I didn't want you to start walking to work and miss the notice. I know how easily you catch a cold."

Ida flushed. He could be so aggravating, but he did care about her. "That's very kind of you, Isaiah," she said.

Therese came in and offered them both a cup of coffee. "No school. How lucky for you. Do you plan on posting up in my parlor all day, Isaiah?"

Ida took a sip of her coffee and inspiration struck. "Therese, what would you think if we hosted an afternoon at home? Just teachers. All respectable folk."

Therese considered and then agreed. "Does that mean you'll make supper for the house too?"

"Gladly," Ida said.

"Then permission granted," the older woman said, departing the room.

Ida smiled. "Okay, Isaiah, since you're dressed, will you spread the word? Storm party. Teachers. Husbands and wives. Invite Tommie Moss and his wife, Betty, too. Tell them all to bring an instrument or bring a plate, but don't come up in here empty-handed."

"I will," Isaiah said. "For the record, I don't cook and I'm not musical, so how about I bring you a novel I've just acquired. You can borrow it. It's called *The Scarlet Letter* by a fellow named Hawthorne."

"Never heard of it."

"It's about a woman fighting for her good name in Massachusetts. I think you'll like it."

"I am intrigued," Ida posited. "Thank you for coming by, Isaiah."

"Thank you for being beautiful. I'll see you at three."

Ida watched him walk out the door. It was nice being reminded of why she had fallen for him in the first place. She wasn't a fool, as she sometimes feared she was when he was being brattish and obstinate. There was something, some spark, that drew her to him.

She dressed and marveled at the gift of a full, unplanned day ahead of her. She made herself another cup of coffee and thought through what she might make with the bounty that the Settles' pantry offered.

There was leftover chicken from the Sunday supper, so she decided immediately that she would make chicken croquettes.

Ida boiled the meat, removed all the gristle, then chopped it until it was minced. She didn't need to measure, because her hands knew the recipe better than her mind. Milk, flour, butter, some finely chopped onion, and then the minced meat. She seasoned the mixture with salt and pepper, and shaped them into small, bite-sized rolls. When it was closer to the appointed hour, she would dip them in an egg wash, batter them with breadcrumbs from day-old bread, then cook them in lard until they were crispy and serve them hot.

There was a large container of macaroni in her pantry, and Ida knew that would serve a crowd well, mixed in a Dutch oven with cheese and stewpan butter and covered with breadcrumbs. She set about that, happy to be cooking in a warm kitchen on a snowy day. Finally, she would make a chocolatey shoofly pie, using the flour and molasses that the family always kept on hand.

At three sharp, people began to arrive. First at the door was Isaiah with the promised novel. Then came Julia Hooks: "I couldn't bring my piano, but Silas has a violin and I thought we might perform a piece from Gilbert and Sullivan's *Pirates of Penzance*."

Ida was proud of the spread, along with the tea and coffee and lemonade. There were buns and a loaf of freshly made bread. Tommie and Betty Moss brought a platter of salt-cured ham that drew oohs and aahs from the crowd.

"Ida, surely the head of the Lyceum will offer us an entertainment on this magical snowbound day."

Ida humbly said, "Honestly, I've been so busy cooking, I haven't prepared anything."

"The food is good," Thomas Turner said. "But a reading would be better."

Fanny squeezed her friend's shoulder, "Certainly you can share something that has captured your imagination as of late."

Ida thought for a moment and then remembered a piece she'd been trying to learn by heart. "I can," she said. "I won't be more than a moment."

She went to her room and returned with a sheet of paper. On it, there was a poem she'd copied from a book at school.

"I'll read a bit of this," she said. "It's a poem called 'Christabel' by Samuel Taylor Coleridge."

Alas, they had been friends in youth:
But whispering tongues can poison truth;
And constancy lives in realms above;
And life is thorny and youth is vain;
And to be wroth with one we love,
Doth work like madness in the brain.

The room fell silent, except for the crackle of the fireplace. Ida could tell the other teachers felt it too. How the poem that had been written more than seventy years before seemed to speak exactly to this moment in their lives. They were the "friends in youth," and they knew well how thorny life could be and how whispering tongues could poison the truth.

She continued:

They stood aloof, the scars remaining.
Like cliffs which had been rent asunder.
A dreary sea now flows between.
But neither heat, nor frost, nor thunder.

The teachers had tightened the circle around her as she read. Some were holding hands, some tilted their heads upon stronger shoulders. This was a moment that was bound, by nature, to be fleeting. Some of them would move. Some of them would marry. New teachers would join the school and others would leave. Each of them would have to make a decision about how they could best contribute in their shared quest to blaze a trail into the twentieth century for Black Americans. It was 1887, and the 1900s were closer to them than the world and the war they had been born into.

"And now, to end with Byron," she said.

Ida delivered her last lines slowly, pausing to make eye contact with each of her guests:

Fare thee well! and if for ever,
Still forever, fare thee well:
Even though unforgiving, never
'Gainst thee shall my heart rebel.

When she was finished, she nodded and the room filled with cheers and bursts of applause. Ida felt transported from the carpet of the parlor floor to the mainstage of a grand opera house. She hugged her women friends and shook hands with the men.

"Only Ida B. Wells could give a reading like that," Tommie Moss said.

"Another cheer for the pride of Holly Springs," Thomas Turner said, and the clapping began anew.

So often she felt out of step and barely able to manage the pulls and responsibilities of her life. It never occurred to her that feeling unskilled was a tenet of youth and that the unknowing was a bramble of being in one's twenties that few, if any, managed to evade. Ida knew she was inclined to feel alone and lonely. But she hoped she would never forget this party and this day. She needed to remember, on the low days, the way her friends followed her words around the bends and curves of her gestures and intentions. The way a poem had carried them out of a simple room onto the seas and cliffs of the world out there. She could not sing, despite the monthly music lessons that cost her two dollars a go. But she could bring music to her words when she recited.

"We should go out in the snow," she said.

"A snowball fight?" Preston offered.

"Not a chance," Thomas Turner said. "But I get Ida. We should see it up close, feel it too."

"Only Ida wants to go out in the snow."

"We may never see a snow like this in our lives again."

"I sure won't," Virginia said. "This kind of weather makes me want to move to Florida."

Ida made another pot of coffee as they put on their coats.

They stepped out onto the front porch to take in the scene together. As the snowflakes gently tumbled down, they began holding one another close, in silence.

With only the falling snow to accompany her, Julia Hooks began to sing from Schubert's "Ave Maria." As she sang, she looked at each woman in the crowd, from Ida to Fanny to Virginia to Betty. She sang the lines in Latin, then in English, then in Latin again.

> Dominus tecum. Benedicta tu in mulieribus.
> *The Lord is with thee. Blessed art thou among women.*
> Dominus tecum.
> *The Lord is with thee.*

PART TWO

Ida, in Trouble and in Love

1888–1895

1888

Chapter Thirty-Four

Meeting Mollie

Ida had, by the age of twenty-six, received many fine invitations. She had been invited to dinners, dances, and even balls with some of the most elite members of Memphis society. Yet none of the invitations had, before today, been personally delivered by a young, tall man dressed in the finest gray linen vestments. He looked like a footman from a fairy tale, and if after he handed Ida the large white envelope embossed with the bloodred seal he had pointed her toward a pumpkin that turned into a carriage, she would not have been surprised. But he did not. He only said, "May I return in one hour's time for your reply?" She said he could. Although she did not know what the envelope contained, she could only imagine that her answer would be yes.

She sat down at the desk in her room and studied the handwriting on the front. It said: *Mlle Ida B. Wells.* She had seen that salutation before, but only in books—Mlle, short for Mademoiselle. The French intrigued her but also deepened the mystery: Who would write to her in French?

She opened the envelope.

My dear Miss Wells,

We have not yet met but your reputation as a journalist and orator at the Lyceum travels far beyond the reaches of Memphis. Will you favor me with your company for afternoon tea on Tuesday next at my father's home?

It will be a simple affair, but as I am only in Memphis for a few short weeks, I will take no denial.

Believe me to be, yours sincerely,
Mollie Church
Lauderdale Street, Memphis

Ida took out a piece of her favorite stationery and wrote carefully:

My dear Miss Church,

I hasten to reply to your kind invitation, which reached me this morning. I feel most happy in accepting your thoughtful appeal and will see you, Tuesday next, promptly at four.

I remain, yours truly,
Ida B. Wells

The servant returned at the top of the next hour, and Ida handed him the letter.

On the day before her appointed meeting with Mollie, Ida ran into Tommie Moss downtown.

"Ida," he said, taking her by the hand and twirling her as if the sidewalk were a ballroom. "I have front-page news."

"And what is that, Tommie?"

"My wife has had our baby. Late last night."

"Oh, Tommie, congratulations," Ida said. "And look at you, out and about, looking spry as ever after such a night."

"Well, I didn't do the hard part," Tommie said.

"Boy or girl?"

"Girl," Tommie said. "And there is more."

"Tell me," Ida said, beaming.

"Our little girl. Her name is Maurine. We would like you to be the godmother."

Ida couldn't believe it. Her eyes filled with tears quicker than she could stop them.

"Tommie, you can't mean it," she said softly.

"Now don't tell me that we've done made *the* Ida B. Wells cry."

"I'm not crying," Ida said, with a sly smile. "It's just Tennessee dirt kicking up in my eyes."

"Uh-huh," Tommie said. "Betty and I are so proud of the work you do, Ida. You put equality and justice before everything—even your own comfort sometimes. That's what's going to make this a better world for our baby girl to live in. That's why we chose you for her godmother."

"Thank you, Tommie, I am so honored."

"Now we are more than friends," Tommie said. "We're family."

Ida let the words sink in and kept herself from tearing up again. She took a deep breath and gave him a respectably quick embrace.

"I'll be around with a basket as soon as Betty and that baby are ready for visitors. Send her my love."

"She will be glad to hear it," Tommie said.

The next day, Ida arrived at Mollie's dressed in a lavender and gray windowpane-plaid dress. She thought she looked smart enough for the occasion.

Mollie wore a navy dress with golden embroidered flowers and a narrow bustle with an *en coeur* neckline. She was tall and elegantly dressed with a mischievous eye. She invited Ida into the formal sitting room. The walls were of the brightest blue with just a hint of a pale apple green that popped when the sun hit it just so. The white molding seemed to Ida like edible pieces of marzipan. As did the medallion moldings on the ceilings.

Ida looked down at the rugs, which had a beautiful floral pattern that reminded Ida of a painting by Mary Cassatt that Ida had seen in a copy of the *Saturday Evening Post* she'd borrowed from the Lyceum.

Mollie caught Ida taking it all in and said, "The rugs are Aubusson. They're from France, as are the chandeliers. I swear Father's furnishings have traveled more of the world than the average Memphian."

"Really," Ida said, staring up at the shiny, sparkling globes above her.

"Come have a seat on the *canapé*," Mollie said.

Ida was confused.

Mollie giggled. "I'm being pretentious. That's just French for a couch." Ida sat down and folded her hands on her lap. Then Molly smiled and said, "Where shall we begin, as I have a hundred questions to ask you? Tell me, how is it that you came to be the great Ida B. Wells?"

It was a different question than Ida was used to. It wasn't

"Where were you born?" or "Where were you educated?" or the dreaded "Who are your people?"

So Ida told her about her parents, her mentors, and her travels.

"Oh, Ida, you will have me join the ranks of journalists yet as your stories prompt me to ask so many questions."

Ida flushed. "Allow me, then, to ask you a question," she said.

"Anything."

"What was Oberlin like? Tell me everything."

Mollie smiled. "Well, did you know they called my major, classics, a 'gentleman's course'?"

"Why on earth?"

"Because the program centered on an emphasis on Latin and Greek."

"You are a wonder to study those ancient languages," Ida responded.

"Well, I excelled at my course, so much so that when Matthew Arnold, the great English poet and champion of the classics, visited Oberlin, I was selected out of more than two dozen students to recite for him."

Ida was so impressed, and although it had not been her accomplishment, she felt a burst of pride. There was no subject a Black woman could not master given the right training and opportunities.

"If only old Lincoln had lived to see what his proclamation had wrought," Ida whispered, enthralled by the elegant creature who sat before her.

"Do you know what happened next?" Mollie asked, sotto voce.

Ida did not.

"The man led a standing ovation and then asked to be introduced to me after the event."

"No!" Ida said.

"He took my hand and said, 'My dear Miss Church, I did not expect to hear such fine Greek spoken at an American university, but I find myself doubly impressed by your recitation.'"

"Why is that?" Ida asked, bracing herself for what might come next. "What did he say then?"

"He said, 'I was surprised to learn that a person of your race could speak Greek so fluently when I was led to believe that the tongues of Africans are so thick it is hard for them to pronounce the more refined romance languages.'"

Ida gasped. "He did not!"

"You know he did."

"How did you respond?" Ida said. "I would have stuck my tongue out at him."

"Well, I said, 'I agnoia kai i vlakeia dystychos mastizoun stin Europi.'"

"And what does that mean?"

"It means, 'Sadly, ignorance and stupidity plague Europe.'"

"Well done!" Ida said, beaming.

A young girl arrived with an entire strawberry shortcake and a silver pot of tea. Ida thought it looked like something out of a children's book. Mollie murmured a soft *merci*, and the girl nodded and disappeared.

"Cake?" Mollie asked.

"Oh yes, I love strawberries," Ida said.

"Me too," Mollie said. "Father always makes sure that cook is down at the river to get the freshest supply from the riverboats when I am in town."

The cake tasted as good as it looked, and Ida wondered what was in the cream that made it taste so rich.

Mollie seemed able to read her mind. "It's clotted cream," she said. "Cook makes it in the English fashion; it's got a higher fat percentage, and so it's silkier."

Then she said, "I hear you also had an incident, in the ladies' car on the rails."

Ida nodded. It still hurt that the case she had won had been overturned.

Mollie shook her head. "I fought off a brakeman with my parasol when he tried to force me out of the ladies' car. Anything would be preferable to being subjected to the immoral atmosphere of the smoking car—even death."

Ida raised an eyebrow. "Death?"

Mollie smiled wanly. "If you knew the stories I've heard of how women have been abused in those cars, you'd maybe think me less dramatic. But let's turn our conversation to more pleasant topics."

After pouring them each a cup of tea in a bone-china cup that Ida was terrified of breaking, Mollie asked, "Do you know I actually had people—I mean dozens of people—warn me that no man would want to marry a woman so highly educated?"

"Would you like to get married?" Ida asked. At this point, she was now the only teacher at her school who was still single.

"I would," Mollie said evenly. "Eventually. If it is not indiscreet of me to say, it's my understanding that this summer we are dating brothers. I have been going out with John Alexander. And you have been seeing Albert. Mind you, I'm mostly dating John to make my former beau jealous. But he is a dashing divertissement."

Ida just smiled and vowed to look up the word—*divertissement*—in her dictionary later.

Ida thought this was what it must be like to be so rich. It wasn't just the beautiful house and the servants and the gorgeous clothes. This is what a pocketful of money must feel like in the heart—the way Mollie seemed to fear no societal boundary or convention.

"I will host a dinner and a musical soiree next week. I will be sure to invite you."

Mollie stood, indicating that their time together was over. Ida was surprised to see from the commanding clock in the entry hall that they had been talking for more than two hours.

That night, Ida wrote in her journal:

> She is the first woman of my age I've met who is similarly inspired with the same desires and ambitions. I benefited so greatly from this meeting. I only wish I'd known her long ago.

Chapter Thirty-Five

Better Clever Than Good

A few days later, Ida received another visit from the young manservant from the Church household. She answered the door, and another envelope with the beautiful handwriting was handed to her:

Mademoiselle Ida B. Wells

"Thank you," she said. "And shall you return in an hour's time for the response?"

He smiled. "Oh, longer this time. I thought I might try to get a haircut on Beale Street."

"You do that," she said approvingly. "Tell me your name."

"George."

Ida sighed. The same as her youngest brother.

"And tell me where you're from."

"You wouldn't know it."

"Try me."

"It's Shelby, Mississippi, ma'am."

"Oh, I know it. I had my first teaching job there."

"Well, I'll be. Maybe you remember my older sister, Henrietta."

"I do."

"She's studying to be a teacher herself now."

"Well, that's very good to hear."

Ida had not always had a lot of confidence in her teaching ability, so it pleased her to hear of former students thriving. She opened the letter and read it with a wide smile on her face:

Dear Ida,

Come and dine with us on Friday next. You'll meet new friends and pass the evening with a few old and valued friends. I will make no mention of their names here, but you have my word that it will be quite the gathering and it will give you great joy to see them.

After dinner, we propose a party of music and cards. Expect a late night with carriages to carry all the ladies safely home. Pray let me have a favorable reply.

Believe me to be yours and sincerely,
Mollie Church

When George returned, Ida handed him her letter, which read:

My dear Mollie,

I hasten to reply to your wonderful invitation, which reached me this morning. I am most happy to accept it. My only regret is that I am not musical and cannot offer any assistance in the evening's entertainment. I can say that I am quite good at cards and will be delighted to give our friends, old and new, a game worth remembering.

Late nights are my favorite nights and I am impatiently looking forward to the treat of your fine company.

With thanks, your most obliged,
Ida B. Wells

On the appointed evening, Ida proudly laid out a dress that she'd been saving for a special occasion: a reddish-purple silk visiting dress with ivory pintuckings that she'd purchased at Menken's. She appreciated the way the dress flattered her figure as she brushed her hair into a tidy chignon.

She strolled down Lauderdale Street and, upon approaching the Church home, was pleased to see that the door was opened by the same young man who had delivered her invitation.

"Good evening, George," she said, handing him her cloak.

"Good evening, Miss Wells," he said gallantly.

In the parlor, Ida greeted Mollie, who was wearing a beautiful marine-blue silk frock with a diamond pin at the collar.

She said her hellos to the guests she knew—Virginia Broughton, Julia Hooks, and Patrick Guignon—and took her seat next to Albert Alexander. His brother, John, was seated next to Mollie and was staring at their host with the wide-eyed wonder of a man who could not believe his luck.

Dinner was served, and everything was something Ida had

never tasted before. To start with there was New Orleans–style chicken gumbo, served in the same bone-china teacups in which she'd had tea. Then there was braised beef with a kind of wide noodle that Ida loved. This was served with a side of mushrooms on toast, which Ida did not love.

Dessert was a white dome with dark brown markings. Everyone at the table exchanged glances. Ida was glad to see she was not the country rube in the room.

"This," Mollie said dramatically, "is Baked Alaska. It was invented at Delmonico's, the chicest restaurant in New York, where my poor mother, my father's first wife, lives. Ladies, if you can help it, never become a first wife. The second wife takes everything, including your man. But back to dessert. It is ice cream and cake covered by meringue, which has been finished with a fire torch!"

As the cook passed out slices of the Baked Alaska, a lively conversation was underway.

"So, I have a question for the gentlemen in the room," Mollie said flirtatiously. "Are there some women—I count myself and my new friend, Ida, in this category—who are too educated and accomplished to be marriage material?"

"No such thing!" Ida jumped in. "When there is so much to learn, how could one ever consider herself 'too educated'?"

"I have a question about the definition of *accomplished*," Albert said, addressing Mollie. "I think it is wrong to underestimate the effort it takes for a woman to sustain a strong marriage and a home where her family thrives. To me that is an accomplishment."

Mollie and Ida exchanged glances, though the other women in the room seemed to swoon at Albert's pro-wife and promotherhood statement.

"Now a question for the ladies at the table," Mollie said. "Would you rather be known to be clever or to be good?"

"Good," Julia said quickly.

"Oh, certainly, good, as it is the path of godliness, is it not?" Virginia added.

"What would *you* say, Mollie?" Ida asked.

"I would say that to be good in such a world as ours requires one to be clever," Mollie said decisively. "And what about you, Ida?"

Ida said, "I would say that in every community, there is at least one woman—or two or three—who is a wonder at inhabiting the countenance of goodness. But everyone knows that these women are, at the heart of things, wicked gossips and capable of the most withering comments."

There was mumbling in the room then, and Mollie raised a hand. "No naming names, please. We mustn't turn this gathering into a scandal. Ida, please continue."

"I think one's goodness is a private matter," Ida said softly. "It is between you and God, who knows all. But a new century is coming, and the world we as Black people will inhabit for generations to come is being built *right now.* Our people and our nation need women who will apply whatever talents they might have to the business of equality and justice, and to the real work of forming a more perfect union."

"Elect that woman to office!" Mollie said.

"Well, first we must get the vote," Ida said softly.

1889

Chapter Thirty-Six

Educated Romeos

In March of 1889, Ida traveled to Washington, DC, to attend the National Colored Press Association meeting. The meeting was held at the Metropolitan AME Church. Ida stood for a second, admiring the redbrick Gothic building that seemed more like a castle than a church.

"It is something, isn't it," Thomas Fortune said. "Built just three years ago, by all Black craftsmen. Did you hear what happened to Jesse Duke?" Thomas asked her.

Ida had not. She knew of Duke, editor of the *Montgomery Herald*. But she had never met him in person.

"He wrote an editorial questioning a lynching. It was a rape charge, but Duke insisted that everyone in town knew that the relationship between the Black man and the white woman was consensual.

"I've got it right here. You should read it," Fortune said. "Check this out."

Ida read Duke's words:

> There's a secret to this thing and we greatly suspect it is the growing appreciation of the white Juliet for the colored Romeo as he becomes more and more intelligent and refined.

Ida gasped. "He wrote that?"

"He did," Fortune said. "He was out of town when it was published, but a white mob stormed his house. They broke every window in the place while his wife and children hid, shivering with fear."

"Have mercy," Ida said.

Ida wondered if interracial relationships would be safe and accepted in their country. Maybe a hundred years past Emancipation, a young Black person and a young white one could look at each other and notice the crinkle around their eyes or the way they laughed. But at this moment, in 1889, it seemed like the past was still too close. History, Ida thought, was like a thin layer of powder that covered their skin, all of them, Black and white. And that powder, the dynamite residue of all that was wicked and unbearable about slavery, would not, could not, be washed off. It was with them and on them, wherever they might go.

Nobody loved love like Ida. But it seemed to her that anytime a white person claimed to love a Black person, pain and punishment for her people seemed to quickly follow.

That night, in the boarding house where she was staying, Ida wrote a fiery editorial that she planned to send off to the *Christian Index*, insisting that Black people must be prepared to defend themselves. What was there to do but fight back against the violent attacks and lynchings that were becoming increasingly commonplace? "God expects us to defend ourselves," she wrote. "When we fail to do so, we only have ourselves to blame."

The speaker the next morning was John Mitchell Jr. Just twenty-two, he was the editor and publisher of a weekly called the *Richmond Planet.* His hair was elegantly coiffed and his mustache was groomed impeccably. Only the roundness of his caramel-brown cheeks gave the hint that he was still growing out of his baby fat. His navy-blue suit and ascot-style tie looked like they were made for him.

"I stand before you today," Mitchell said. "With the promise that there is only one line of coverage that demands our collective attention. It is not the mighty men who sit in Congress and the Senate. It is not the train lines that are transforming our cities and bringing industry and opportunity in their steam engines. The story we cannot take our eye off is lynching. This is a list of the more than two hundred lynching victims that the *Richmond Planet* has composed over the last two years."

He paused, then said, "If my esteemed colleagues will allow me, I will read all two hundred names. Let us offer a prayer for the souls of these victims in this hallowed house of the Lord. May their memory incite us to action:

"John Simms, seventeen, Annapolis, Maryland, alleged assault of a white woman.

"William Keemer, twenty-three, Greenfield, Indiana, accused of sexually assaulting a white woman.

"Howard Cooper, fifteen, Baltimore, Maryland, accused of assaulting a white woman.

"Simeon Garnett, twenty-one, Oxford, Ohio, accused of assaulting a white woman.

"Orion Anderson, fourteen, Leesburg, Virginia, hung on the charge of 'scaring a teenage white girl.' "

As he read the names, the charges, and the ages of the slain men, Ida began to cry and could not stop.

"My brothers and sisters," Mitchell called out to the crowd. "Are you starting to see a *theme* in the charges against these men? Are you starting to see a *pattern* in the way that they are dragged from their homes and holding cells and murdered with cruelty as if their killing were no more than the shooting of a clay pigeon for sport?"

That night, Ida wrote in her journal: "My eyes filled with tears as I thought of the *Richmond Planet*'s list of unfortunates. They had no requiem, save the night and no memorial service to mourn their sad and troubled fate. No record of the time and place of their death. Save this is extant and like many a brave union soldier their bodies lie in many an unknown and unhonored spot."

She felt that it was critical that journalists and law makers begin to separate the crime of lynching from the falsehoods of sexual violence and assault used to justify mob violence. It would take courage to keep calling out the ugly truth. She wondered what it would cost her in the long run. Would she ever get married and have a family of her own? She hoped so. She longed for it more than she dared say out loud to even her dearest friends. But the career she had begun building as a journalist was now almost ten years old. She had written that "the way to right wrongs is to turn the light of truth upon them," and that was the work she meant to do for as long as she drew breath.

Chapter Thirty-Seven

Mr. President, Will You Help Us?

The National Colored Press Association meeting had been organized in Washington, DC, to coincide with the inauguration of President Benjamin Harrison. Although none of the Black press had been invited to the inauguration, Ida woke early that day and dressed. John Mitchell had formed a Committee on Outrages, which Ida had joined, to address the growing lynching epidemic. Ida and the fellow members had prepared an antilynching petition that they planned to present to the president, who had agreed to meet with them.

She was going to meet the president of the United States. If only her parents were alive so she could share the news. They would have been so proud of her. As Ida got older, what family she had on this earth cared little for her accomplishments outside of what monetary assistance she could provide. As for Aunt Fanny, the closest Ida had to a parent, Ida was pretty sure that woman would never forgive her for leaving Visalia. It did not matter how Ida made a living as long as a check arrived every month.

At the appointed hour, six members of the Committee on Outrages, including Ida and John Mitchell, walked over to the Library of Congress.

Mitchell told the group that, while it was an honor to meet the president, they had also played a role in his election. They were voting members of his constituency: "Harrison beat Grover Cleveland, and it was down to the Black vote—and he knows it."

It was agreed that it would be best that, on his first day in office, President Harrison not be seen meeting a contingent of radical Black journalists in public. The library was closed for the inauguration, and their privacy could be ensured.

Ida had never met Daniel Murray, the Black man who had been kissed as a boy on the forehead by Lincoln and had risen to become one of the custodians of the most important library in the country, but she had read about his career highs and the doings of his family in the *Washington Bee.*

He introduced himself and said, "Miss Ida B. Wells, it's my hope that we have a book of yours someday in this collection."

Ida was flattered. In her early days in Memphis, books had been so hard to come by. One of the reasons she fell for Isaiah Graham, she was sure of it, was that he had such a huge private collection of books.

"How many works are housed here?"

"We estimate it will be more than a million volumes by the end of 1890, and twice that amount by the end of the century."

Ida could hardly believe it. How many lifetimes would you

need to read a million books? She wished that she might have the chance to find out.

When President Benjamin Harrison entered the room, accompanied by a phalanx of trusted aides, he greeted each of them with a hearty handshake, including Ida, the only woman in the group.

Harrison was slighter than Ida expected. He was just five foot six, and seemed—to Ida—to be rather shy.

He gestured to the committee to sit.

John Mitchell handed him the anti-lynching petition.

Harrison looked around at the table and said, "I have had a deep respect for your people and the necessary protections of your rights as American citizens since I was a little boy. Back in Ohio, I discovered a fugitive slave eating walnuts in my grandfather's orchard but I said not a word about his presence, only whispering to him that I prayed he would find his way to freedom."

Ida had to will herself not to roll her eyes. She looked over at John Mitchell, and she could see he was struggling in the same manner.

"On that petition, sir," Mitchell began, "are the names of over two hundred lynched, the vast majority of which we believe are falsely accused."

"Lynching has become a way of halting Black progress in the South," Ida said passionately. "Our boys, and sometimes even our women, are murdered brutally by mobs who have made such killings a sport. Mr. President, will you help us?"

"I am a president, not a monarch," Harrison said. "But I assure you that my words when I was running for office remain my bond and pledge. I would not be willing myself to purchase the presidency for a compact of silence upon this question. I will take the matter to Congress and push with all my might."

An aide whispered in his ear, and the president stood. "Gentlemen and ma'am, it has been my great pleasure to meet you all. As you can imagine, my inauguration day schedule goes from morning to night, and I have already spent more time than intended. You may write to me and be assured that you will always get a response. I am aware that slavery and all of its subsequent ills are our shame, not yours."

He shook hands with the members of the committee again, then turned to Daniel Murray.

"I suspect that we'll be seeing a lot of each other," President Harrison said.

"Yes, sir," Murray demurred. "The library's collection grows by the thousands each year. If you need a book, let us know, and we will have it for you within a day's time at the most."

When the president and his aides had left, Murray turned to the group, "What you expected?"

"Just about," Mitchell said.

"It was an audience with the newly elected president of the United States," Thomas Fortune noted. "I've never met the president before."

"It is a start," Ida said.

"But how many more will die while our feet are stuck, as if in cement, in the starting blocks?" John Mitchell asked.

Chapter Thirty-Eight

The Memphis Free Speech

After church one Sunday, Reverend F. Nightingale asked Ida to stay behind for a conversation in the rectory. "Ida, we are ready for the *Free Speech* to reach the next level of journalism. We'd like you to come in as editor."

Ida was pleased. She had begun to believe that becoming an editor of a newspaper was the next logical step. She could author editorials under the pen name Iola indefinitely, but she wanted to be more than a voice. Men like T. Thomas Fortune and Calvin Chase, editor of the *Washington Bee*, had real power.

But as the Black press paid next to nothing, Ida knew that a figurehead post would add to her work without easing the financial woes that plagued her.

"How many papers do you sell every week?"

"Well, as you know, Beale Street Baptist isn't just the largest church in Memphis, we are the largest in the state."

“Figures, Reverend Nightingale,” Ida asked politely. “We are discussing business, and I would like the figures.”

“Well, we sell five hundred papers a week every Sunday after church alone,” he said. “We can also usually count on additional revenue of two hundred dollars a month that we receive in advertising from white businesses.”

Ida always believed that her greatest currency was her good name. Now she needed to see what that might translate into financially.

“I’d like to come in as a third owner of the paper,” Ida said. “I’ll be editor and co-owner.”

Reverend Nightingale guffawed. Her boldness only affirmed the wisdom of his decision. She was Ida the Indefatigable, and that was the kind of firepower he needed on his side. But he was going to make her work for it.

“And what are you offering in exchange for such a hefty stake in our enterprise,” he asked.

Ida thought for a second and then answered evenly: “My good name. Just two weeks ago, as you well know, I was part of the committee of journalists sent to meet with President Harrison on the crisis of lynching.”

She handed him a press clipping from the *New York Age*, in which Thomas Fortune had written about her:

> She has become famous as one of the few women who handle a goose quill with diamond point as easily as any man in newspaper work. If Iola was a man she would be a humming independent in politics. She has plenty of nerve and is sharp as a steel trap.

Ida knew that Fortune meant if she were a man, she could run for office as an independent and win, but she had no interest in the machinations of politics. She believed deeply in the words she herself had written: "The people must know before they can act, and there is no educator to compare with the press."

Nightingale handed the clip back to her.

"Oh, I am familiar with your admirers," he said. "It extends across the nation. Although you have your detractors, as you well know."

Ida looked at him coolly, "If you would like, I can give you a few days to think about it."

"No need," Nightingale said. "No need. You are the finest journalist in Memphis—man or woman—and ultimately that is what this whole endeavor is about. Giving our people the information they need so we might save the gates of our democracy, together."

Chapter Thirty-Nine

Pretty or Smart, but Not Both

Ida's feet hurt. Her head and her back were aching, too, but when she closed the door to her tiny, simple room, it was her feet that demanded her attention. Her knees seemed to buckle as she collapsed onto the bed, and she was grateful that she need not stand for one second more.

She started her days in the dark—working on lesson plans for school and editorials for the *Christian Index* and the *Free Speech.* Sunrise meant waking Lily, who earned extra pocket money by running errands for the married women in town, and sorting her for the day. By 8 AM, Ida was at the Kortrecht School. At this point, she could teach fourth grade with her eyes closed, but the children were never the same, and the urgency to do right by them, to equip them to become foot soldiers in the effort for race and equality, only became more dire as each year wore on.

After school, she went to the *Free Speech* office to lay out the paper as well as to chase down advertising revenue and delinquent subscribers. On the weekends, she rode the rails for the Afro-American League, a civil rights organization founded by Thomas Fortune and other prominent men in the community. In the past six weeks alone, she had visited Chicago, Milwaukee, and Philadelphia.

It would help, she told herself, if she could see the fruits of all this labor. If, from one month to the next, she earned more money for her writing, more praise for her work as a teacher, more advertisers and subscribers for the paper.

She knew it was a *better* paper than the one she had been handed when she became editor. She had seen to it that they were quicker with the news, and she carefully proofread every page so it published without the typos and grammatical errors that had plagued its pages before.

On the one-year anniversary of her editorship, Thomas Fortune had written that the *Free Speech* had become "a stunningly good paper." The praise had pleased her, for the *New York Age* set the standard for all the Black newspapers. But the compliments for her work as editor and her ever-popular editorials did not shorten her days or soothe the toll that all that work and travel took on her body. She fell into bed at midnight, knowing she had just five hours before the call of 5 AM woke her up and all the toil began again.

The next week, Ida opened the *New York Age* to find a withering cartoon. It was of three dogs, each representing the biggest Black newspapers in the country. The one that was labeled the leader of the pack had the head of Thomas Fortune. He loomed, large and majestic, over two tiny yapping pups. One of the little dogs bore a head and face that were the spitting image of Ida, right down to her sweeping updo and familiar bun. And if that were not enough, in the same issue, there was a drawing of a woman dressed in men's clothing and a quote that said, "If only I were a man."

Ida closed the paper and tried not to cry. Just weeks before, Fortune had praised her as an editor. He had not penned these cartoons, but as editor, he had approved and printed them. Her as a yappy little dog. Her as a woman who only hoped to be a man.

Ida had been sitting in the New Century House, having a cup of coffee and reading a book, when she heard a voice behind her say, "Did you hear? Isaiah Graham has married."

She turned to see Danielle Whittier, a teacher from another school in the district.

"Excuse me, not to intrude," Ida said. "But what did you say?"

The woman smiled. "Isaiah Graham, that old fuddy-duddy, has found a wife. No one knows who she is and where she came from, but they are most certainly wed."

Ida took the news harder than she expected. Walking down Beale Street, trying not to cry, she wondered if Isaiah had ever loved her. The way he was married so swiftly to some girl she had never heard of suggested otherwise.

It steamed her the way he had demanded declarations of affection, begged for kisses, and occupied her time for years without ever once hinting at any real possibility of marriage.

When she got home, she went straight to her room and sat on her bed. She needed to think. The anger she had felt upon first hearing the news had settled into a kind of cloudy melancholy. She did not love Isaiah, and a life with him would have been a small life, with Memphis as a fenced-in garden instead of a gateway to the world.

Ida had no doubt that their marriage, like their courtship, would have been filled with pointless bickering and petty annoyances that they could not avoid because it would have been the inevitable outcome of two people being so poorly suited.

She decided then to think back to the good, early days of their courtship, when his energetic affections and good looks amused her and how he lent her books and took her on long strolls when she was still so new to Memphis.

She opened her diary and wrote, "Mr. G. was married very unexpectedly last week. I wish him joy." And in the truest part of her heart, she meant it.

The campaign against her only continued. The *Cleveland Gazette* wrote, "Iola makes the mistake of trying to be pretty as well as smart." The journalist begrudgingly noted that her writing was as powerful as that of the titans of women in letters, George Eliot and Harriet Beecher Stowe, but warned that neither of these women was known for her beauty. They were "not paragons by any means."

The illustrations got more and more savage and the editorials got more pointed. Ida needed to decide. Was she on the path to marriage and life in polite society, or did she want to compete with the men to be one of the voices of her generation? The men who drew the cartoons and wrote the editorials hoped that she would choose marriage and soon. As the *Washington Bee* opined, "Iola will never get a husband so long as she lets those editors make her hideous."

1891

Chapter Forty

You See, People Forget You

On the morning of October 28, 1891, Ida woke with a chill. It was the day of Mollie Church's wedding, and it promised to be the social event of the season. The elite of Memphis would be there, as would many of the local and national leaders whom Ida had tussled with on and off the page, including former Senator Blanche K. Bruce. Ida was not invited.

Ida had loved the time she spent with Mollie and had hoped they would become friends. The fact that they were not—despite Ida's accomplishments and the joy of their early meetings—made Ida feel out of sync.

Across town, at 362 Lauderdale Street, in the Church mansion, Mollie Church was sleeping in. The wedding was at six. She was not concerned about the dress, the ceremony, the food, or the guests. Her father and his third wife had seen to all those details—so much so that she felt, as many an educated daughter of the Industrial Age had felt before and would feel after—that the wedding was more for her parents' benefit than her own.

Ida walked to the offices of the *Free Speech*, determined to let work take the place of the hurt she felt at being left out of Mollie Church's wedding celebrations. She had also fallen out with many of her teacher friends, and just months before, because of her fiery—and admittedly, sometimes loose-cannon—editorials, the school board had terminated her contract. And there was a new Black women's organization, the Coterie Migratory Club. Julia Hooks was the founding president, but Ida was not, despite her prominence as a journalist, even invited to join, much less be an elected leader.

She let herself into the office and was relieved to find that her business partner, J. L. Fleming, was not in the office. Ida had bought out their third partner, Reverend Nightingale, and moved the *Free Speech*'s office to Beale Street. Sitting in the quiet of the office, she wondered what Mollie Church was wearing on her wedding day.

After their first meetings, Mollie had taken off for Europe. News came back to Ida of Mollie's adventures through Tommie Moss and Julia Hooks, who received letters from her.

One letter explained that Mollie had spent some time in Paris, where she felt frustrated by how rote her French was in practice. She could translate exercises on the page but when Parisians spoke to her in French, meaning eluded her. Another letter explained that Paris was, alas, expensive, even for the daughter of the richest Black man in the South. Mollie moved on to Lausanne, Switzerland. There she lived with a family, enrolled in a French course, and woke daily to a view of the Alps.

Julia Hooks reported to Ida that in Lausanne, Mollie was indulging in daily hikes during the day, and at night, she had exquisite meals and treated herself to rich local chocolate. Reading from one of Mollie's letters, Julia had said, "Mollie says, 'God guided me. What happiness for me.'"

Ida knew that Mollie Church was considered an "old bride." Mollie was twenty-eight, and Ida had just turned twenty-nine. She wished she had been invited to the wedding so they could have shared a laugh about getting married when they were good and ready. Mollie had, in total, spent two years in Europe—France, Switzerland, Italy, and Germany.

Ida wondered if she would ever make it across the Atlantic. She had no rich father. She did not know who she might marry, but she hoped to marry a man of purpose, someone dedicated to uplifting the race—and this was important—someone who would not prevent her from continuing her career as a journalist. Chances were that person would not be let's-sail-across-the-sea rich. But she would be happy if they did good work and they were good to each other. In the meantime, as she traveled within the US, she continued to enjoy meeting the eligible men of color in each town.

She would ask Tommie Moss the next day about the wedding. Tommie had fulfilled his dream of becoming a federal letter carrier, a job that carried with it a great salary and no small amount of prestige. He had started the People's Grocery, a collective grocery in a suburb of Memphis, that he was the president of. His two business partners ran the grocery store in the day while Tommie worked. Ida always joked that she should add Tommie to the payroll as a reporter because whatever news there was to be had, he made sure Ida got wind of it first.

As she left and locked the door to the office, Ida wondered

what the wedding guests were dining on. Surely there would be champagne, and fine oysters. That was going to be her wedding gift to Mollie Church—a pair of silver oyster forks. Ida had seen a gorgeous pair at Menken's and even set aside the funds for it. But her invitation to the wedding never came.

What Ida didn't know and what never entered the letters Mollie sent to her friends back home in Memphis was that Mollie had tried to break things off with Robert Terrell. She had received an invitation to become the registrar of Oberlin College and had truly wanted the position. It wouldn't be until later, when they were both much older women, that Ida would learn that on the day of her wedding Mollie Church was mourning her freedom and her ambitions and wondering how she was going to make her life—as an educated Black woman—count. Which is to say she wasn't thinking about Ida at all.

1892

Chapter Forty-One

Losing Tommie

It started with a game of marbles in a predominantly Black suburb of Memphis called the Curve, because it was there that the streetcar line made a sharp curve. A Black boy, Armour Harris, was playing marbles with a white boy, Cornelius Hurst. When Armour won the match, Cornelius started a fight. Which he also lost. Cornelius's father came and then proceeded to flog the young Armour Harris. Neighborhood Black men including the shopkeepers of Tommie's store, the People's Grocery, jumped in to protect the young boy.

Ida was in her home state of Mississippi on what had been a successful promotional tour of the *Free Speech*. A bar association meeting in Greenville yielded so many subscriptions that Ida had to carry a bag full of silver dollars directly to the bank. As she would reminisce, "I was the daughter of Mississippi and my father had been a master mason. So, it's no wonder that I came out of the meeting with paid subscriptions from every delegate." As a lovely bonus, the acclaimed Princess of the Press was feted at dinners and teas, where she was introduced to the most eligible young bachelors in town.

But back home in Memphis, unbeknownst to Ida, tensions were mounting. After the fights in the Curve, Tommie Moss and his partners heard that an edict had been ordered—a mob of whites would be coming to loot and raid the People's Grocery.

This, Tommie knew, was not about marbles. For as long as anyone could remember, there had been only one grocery store in the Curve—one owned and operated by William Barrett, a white man. The People's Grocery was run by Tommie and Calvin McDowell, both men who were beloved in their churches and lodges. It quickly became the most popular store in the area.

Hearing that they had been targeted, Tommie and Calvin went to the authorities for protection and were told that because the Curve sat outside of city limits, the police could offer no assistance. Taking matters into their own hands, they posted armed guards at the front and back of the store.

On Saturday night, the People's Grocery was attacked by a crew of armed men. The guards retaliated, and three white men were wounded; the rest fled.

That Sunday, a white paper ran a headline declaring that the People's Grocery was a "low dive in which drinking and gambling were carried on, a resort of thieves and thugs." That day, more than one hundred Black men in Memphis, from all walks of life, were arrested and thrown in jail on charges of "possible association with the People's Grocery."

Fearing the worst, especially if one of the wounded white men died, a group of Black men guarded the jail for the first two nights. Lynchings often began with dragging prisoners from the jail before formal charges were filed or any sort of trial could begin. The citizens' militia hoped to protect their friends and neighbors from such a fate.

On Tuesday, it was announced that the three white men who had been wounded were stable and would make a full recovery. The men who guarded the prison left their post, confident that their peers would be released soon.

Under the shadow of night, a group of white men were allowed into the jail. They took the three men who had been targeted the whole time—Thomas Moss, Calvin McDowell, and Will Stewart, the three men named as co-owners of the People's Grocery. The captured men were carried to a railroad yard a mile outside of town, where they were murdered and mutilated.

The *Memphis Commercial Appeal*, one of the white newspapers, reported that "Tom Moss begged for his life, for the sake of his wife and child, and his unborn baby." They also published that Moss's last words were, "Tell my people to go West—there is no justice for them here."

When Ida read the news, her body crumpled as if the Almighty Himself had balled her up like a sheet of paper, marred with errors, and thrown her away.

Her first thought was: *Not Tommie.*

Not Tommie.

Not Tommie.

She, Julia, Fanny, Mollie, Isaiah, and Tommie were part of the first generation of young people born free or damn near free, and this she could say without hesitation: Tommie was the best of them. Humble and hardworking, focused. A man who had fused his heart and mind into an engine that moved with unrelenting speed toward progress. Not just for himself, never just for himself. But for his family, his friends, his people in this new city, Memphis, that he proudly called home.

It seemed anathema to her that a man who was destined to sit at the table with the next generation of Black American leaders would not live to see the century that was coming, the century when they would make their freedom a consecrated reality in all the ways that mattered. It was as if Edison had invented the lightbulb but never lived to see New York City shine like day in the darkness of night. To see, touch, feel, progress had been Tommie's birthright. Now that was stolen from him, forever.

Ida did not sleep the night she received the news of the lynching at the Curve. She knew that this death was not a Sherlock Holmes mystery for her to solve, and that solving it would not breathe life back into the three young men who had been murdered. But her journalistic mind needed to shape the story—bad news, the worst news—she needed to lay it all out in her mind. She took a deep breath and asked herself, *What do I know about mob violence?* She knew that lynching was not a random, natural disaster like a hurricane or a tornado, taking out anything in its path. It was targeted and strategic, murder as retribution for the losses of the Civil War, a tactic for reminding Black Americans that for them, the bells of freedom did not resolutely ring.

Fear stilled her and she saw it with a kind of clarity that she wished she hadn't. If she were the Devil, if her aim were to bring Black Memphis to its knees, she would end the life of the best and the brightest. Not "Not Tommie." But "Of course Tommie."

Chapter Forty-Two

On the Rails

As she prepared to return to Memphis, Ida's heart went out to Tommie's wife, Betty. How was she going to carry this grief? Every marriage had two sides; you could see only the face a couple showed in public. But from what she had observed, Tommie and Betty appeared to be more than man and wife; they seemed to be partners, and outside of the declared commitment to each other, there was, it seemed to Ida, a vibrant world of ideas between them. She observed it as they strolled down Beale Street talking animatedly or in the way their eyes never left each other as they twirled around the dance floor. Tommie would say something and Betty's smile would get just a bit wider, or she would point something out and the lines around his eyes would crinkle in amusement.

Ida vowed to continue to be a friend to Betty. They would all have to find a way to love her and their children through this loss. Tommie would not live to see the year 1900. But his wife and children should, and the good Lord willing, they would carry his gift of vision and strength of character into the new century.

Ida turned her attention back to the *Memphis Commercial*

Appeal. How had the white newspapers been able to publish, with such quickness, so vivid an account of the lynching, down to Tommie's last words?

"It's clear that the reporter was either at the lynching or interviewed the lynchers," she told Sallie Dogan, an old friend who was hosting her in Natchez. "Yet the identities of the killers have not been revealed, and no arrest warrants have been issued."

But the violence did not end with the murders of the three men. Another mob made their way out to the Curve. As witnesses would later tell Ida, "They ate and drank, celebrated, throughout the store. Then the looters carried out what they could carry." Creditors closed the store, and days later, anything salvageable in stock was sold at auction. The buyer was William Barrett, the white shop owner.

As soon as she got home, she penned an editorial, inspired by Tommie's last words:

> The city of Memphis has demonstrated that neither character nor standing avails the Negro if he dares to protect himself against the white man or become his rival. There is nothing we can do about the lynching, as we are outnumbered and without arms. The white mob could help itself to ammunition without pay, but the order was rigidly enforced against the selling of guns to Negroes. There is therefore, only one thing we can do; save our money and leave a town which will neither protect our lives and property, nor give us a fair trial in the courts, but takes us out and murders us in cold blood when accused by white persons.

Ida walked down a nearly empty Beale Street to the office of the *Free Speech.* Her independence—which she so prized—felt like loneliness. For Ida, this was always the pinhole in her heart, the murmur of fear and abject loneliness that would from time to time grab ahold of her and refuse to let go.

She stood for a second on Beale Street in the hopes of gathering her breath. Air pushed in and out of the pinhole. *Whoosh. I am alone. Whoosh. I am alone.* It was fact, not fiction. Her eyes filled with tears as she thought of Tommie's death. *I am alone,* she thought, *but I am alive. I am strong, and I can make a difference.* This was also true.

The lynching at the Curve shook the Black elite. They had all known Thomas Moss, Calvin McDowell, and Will Stewart—none of the usual charges that the mobs tried to use to justify their violence would hold. Everyone knew these men and knew their only crime was to have started and run a successful business.

Memphis had been, as Ida called it, one of the "queen cities of the South." But the brutal act of terrorism had marred the hope, possibility, and beauty that had made the riverside town feel like home. There had not been a lynching in Memphis since immediately after the Civil War. The safety the Black community had felt in a city they thought had been too educated, too sophisticated, too successful for such gruesome behavior was gone. Ida's editorial and the haunting specter of Tommie's last words had an immediate and colossal effect.

Some folks went back to the towns where they had been born. Others traveled to kin, impromptu visitations meant to gather their broken hearts and plan for next steps. Northern cities beckoned—New York, Chicago, and the Black mecca, Washington, DC, home base of the Black elite. But there were only so many government posts, places in law firms, and trade and union jobs to go around. Those who fled Memphis wanted to be sure that their next move—even if sideways—could be a long play. Otherwise, what had it all been for?

It did not help that the white press in Memphis doubled down on praising the lynching. The *Appeal-Avalanche* wrote:

> There was no whooping, not even loud talking, no cursing, in fact, nothing boisterous. Everything was done decently and in order. The vengeance was sharp, swift and sure but administered with due regard to the fact that people were asleep around the jail. They did not know until the morning papers that the avengers swooped down last night and sent the murderous souls of the ringleader in the Curve riot to eternity.

At the *Free Speech*, Ida kept the heat on with her editorials, and the Black press followed suit. No lynching had received such widespread national attention. In Chicago, Ferdinand L. Barnett, editor of the *Conservator*, wrote that "Memphis was a powerful reminder that 'the American flag is not a protection to citizens at home but a dirty, disheveled rag.'"

In the *Kansas American Citizen*, editor C. H. J. Taylor urged the white citizens of Memphis to prosecute the murderers of the People's Grocery proprietors. That step toward justice, he maintained, would assure the nation that "God is not dead, that religion is not a mockery and that all of your churches should not be burned to the ground."

Ida's campaign was working. It had been six weeks since

the lynching, and in that short time, two whole congregations had fled Memphis. Reverend Countee and Reverend Brinkley took their flocks and fled. Properties were sold, and those that could not be sold or rented were abandoned. The music shops of Memphis had to find storage for all the returned pianos and instruments that the Black elite could not take with them as they ran.

In a rare show of deference to the Black community, the Memphis city court commissioners had set forth a weak statement that the lynching had been "ill-advised" and that a year's allowance was being set aside to Tommie's widow, Betty Moss.

Ida was sitting in the office of the *Free Speech* when she received a visit from Richard Clarke and Andrew Shapp, the superintendent and treasurer of the City Railway Company.

She invited the men in and gestured for them to sit in the two chairs on the other side of her desk.

"Miss Wells," Clarke began, "your people aren't riding the streetcars. There has been a marked drop-off, and it has hurt our business terribly."

"Is that so?" Ida replied.

"Perhaps it's a fear of the electric streetcars," Shapp added.

Ida knew this was some foolishness, as the electric streetcars had been running for more than six months, and if there was one thing she knew about her "people," they embraced progress.

"We want the people to know that there is no danger on the rails and that any employee who does not treat our Black patrons with respect will be punished," Shapp said. He put his feet up on Ida's desk as he spoke. He was oblivious, it seemed, to the disrespect that showing her his worn-out shoe soles conveyed.

"Punished severely," Clarke added, tapping Shapp's legs in an indication that the man should take his feet off of Ida's desk, which he did.

Ida sighed. "Well, how long has this slump been going on?" she asked.

"About six weeks," Clarke said softly.

Ida stood up then. "Well, it was just six weeks ago that the lynching at the Curve took place."

The men's faces reddened.

"But the streetcar company had nothing to do with the lynching," said Clarke plaintively. "It's owned by a Northern company."

"And run by Southern lynchers," Ida snappily replied. "We have learned that every white man of any standing in town knew of the plan and consented, tacitly or implicitly, to the lynching of our boys. Did you know Tom Moss?"

"Yes, I did," Clarke replied.

"A finer, cleaner man never walked the streets of Memphis," Ida said, trying to calm the *whoosh* of air that swept in and out of the hole in her heart. "He was well-liked, a favorite with everybody. And yet he was murdered in cold blood."

The men looked at each other. Ida suspected Clarke was about to offer his condolences but then thought better of it.

"Well," he said, breezing past Ida's accusations. "We hope you can do what you can for us." The arrogance. God help her hold her tongue.

Clarke stood then, and Shapp followed his lead.

"And if you hear of any disrespect from any rail employees," Shapp said, offering again the one card he'd come prepared to play, "let us know and we will remedy it."

The men tipped their hats to Ida, a sign of respect she knew they didn't show all Black women, and then they exited.

After they left, Ida wrote up the entire conversation for the *Free Speech.* That Sunday, she visited the remaining Black churches and urged them to continue what had become a very effective boycott.

Ida herself talked about moving. Oklahoma had become a territory in 1890, and some of the Memphis population moved west in hopes of finding more freedom.

"Maybe we should take the *Free Speech* there," Ida said to Fleming, who did own half the paper. "We can't stay in Memphis. It isn't safe."

Fleming said, "I don't have any people in Oklahoma, and I don't see myself as a pioneer man."

Ida didn't have the money to buy him out, so she let the matter go.

The following week, Ida left for Philadelphia. She had been invited to give a keynote address at the AME convention there, months before the lynching. When the train pulled out of the Memphis station, she felt a lightness of spirit she did not expect. The lynching had happened. Her grief was still clawing at her heart. But she was, physically, leaving the scene of the crime, and she understood deeply why so many had left town and so quickly.

Chapter Forty-Three

Forced to Leave Memphis

When Ida's train arrived in Jersey City from Philadelphia, Thomas Fortune was waiting for her at the station.

"Ida B. Wells, it's taken all this time to get you to New York City," he said. "And by the look of things, we may just be able to convince you to stay."

Ida shook her head, confused. "I'm sure I don't know what you mean."

"Then I take it you haven't seen the morning papers."

"I have not."

He walked her to a bench in the pretty train station. From there, Ida could see the Statue of Liberty and the skyline of New York City glimmering across the Hudson.

Thomas Fortune said, "They're coming for you, Ida. Listen to this." He then read aloud from the white newspaper in Memphis, the *Commercial Appeal*: "Those Negroes who are attempting to make the lynching of individuals of their race a means for arousing the worst passions of their kind are playing with a dangerous sentiment. The fact that a Black scoundrel is allowed to live and utter such loathsome and repulsive calumnies is evidence of the wonderful patience of Southern whites."

Another local paper, the *Memphis Scimitar*, made even-less-veiled threats, these aimed at Fleming stating that it was "the duty" of white citizens to "tie the wretch who utters such calumnies to a stake at the intersection of Main and Madison streets and brand him in the forehead with a hot iron and perform upon him a surgical operation with a pair of tailor's shears."

Fleming, it turns out, had been warned of the mob's intent by a white Republican. But as the newspaper report in Ida's hands explained, the crowds had destroyed the offices of the *Free Speech*—smashing the press and all the furniture. A note at the site warned that anyone who dared attempt to publish even a single issue of the paper would be hunted down and killed.

Ida couldn't believe it. It was only luck or fate that she hadn't been sitting in that office when the mob arrived. It was where she spent most of her days and, increasingly, many of her nights. It had been her calling but also, she hoped, a means of securing her future. The paper had, shortly before the lynching, begun to turn a profit that more than covered the loss of her wages as a schoolteacher. But apart from the loss of the paper and the money, there was the real fact that she was on a list now. She and Fleming. The mob was coming and wanted to do to them what it had done to Tommie Moss and his business partners. Thank God her friends had gotten Lily out of town. The plan was for her sister to return to their aunt in California.

Ida went with Fortune to his home, unable to contemplate

the idea that her beloved paper—in which she'd invested every dollar she'd ever made—was gone.

At Thomas's home, the telegrams arrived quickly:

> IDA, YOUR HOME IS WATCHED TWENTY-FOUR HOURS A DAY. BE CAREFUL.

> IDA, EVERY BLACK PERSON YOU KNOW IS BEING QUESTIONED. THEY MEAN TO FIND YOU.

> MEN ARE POSTED AT THE TRAIN STATION. THE MOBS WILL KNOW THE MOMENT YOU ARRIVE.

> THE PLAN IS TO LYNCH YOU IN FRONT OF THE COURTHOUSE.

> WE ARE HIDING YOUR SISTER LILY. NO ONE SEEMS TO BE LOOKING FOR HER. DON'T WORRY. SHE IS SAFE.

Thomas said, "I've heard that there is a group of Black men who have assembled. They have vowed to lay down their lives to protect you, should you wish to return."

Ida closed her eyes and tried to breathe; it seemed like her body had been drained of air.

"I know who they are," she said finally. "They call themselves the Tennessee Rifles, and Tommie Moss had been a part of them before he was murdered."

"Do you want to go home?" Thomas said. "If you do, these men are your best shot getting back to Memphis and getting out alive."

Ida sighed. Part of her wanted to go home, for her books, her photographs, her clothing, her journal, what she might be able to salvage from the *Free Press* offices. But she could picture their faces, these young men who were willing to risk it all to protect her. And for what?

"I can't bear the thought of it," she said. "I can't bear the thought of more Memphis lives senselessly lost. More young women burying their husbands. More children growing up without a father."

She would stay in New York and make a new plan.

Chapter Forty-Four

The Truth About Lynching

Ida, now an exile in New York, turned her attention to a long editorial that both she and Thomas Fortune hoped would be the definitive investigative report about lynching.

The same bullheadedness, impatience, and penchant for brutal honesty that made Ida a difficult fit for polite society were the very same qualities that made her the person you wanted by your side in hard times.

For years, the Black elite of Memphis had heard the dogs barking at the perimeter of their genteel lives. They had hoped that their fine homes, impeccable manners, good jobs, and shiny degrees would protect them from the red terror that was mauling a bloody, jagged path through the South.

Three men murdered without hesitation or repercussions, solely for the crime of being successful businessmen. No one who knew them, loved them, respected them, prayed with them, or had shared a laugh with them on the porch of the People's Grocery would ever be the same.

But Ida was more than heartbroken. She was angry. She saw a connection to a string of crimes she had been keeping track of in her journal since she was twenty-two.

Tommie Moss had been her friend even when friends, for Ida, had been hard to come by. This was not an isolated crime. This was an evil that oozed from the unhealed wounds of the Civil War and Reconstruction. It was about money, race, and power. She was going to take her reporter's notebook, get the facts, and then tell the world about it. Tommie Moss had been her *friend*, and fear would not keep her from pursuing the truth.

Sitting in the office of the *New York Age*, Ida felt tired deep in her bones. "I am so used to the quick editorial or the short dispatch. How am I going to gather *years* of reporting into one powerful piece?"

Thomas said, "You're drowning in your notebooks. Put them down. Let's talk it out. What do we know?"

Thomas sat at the edge of the desk, opposite the one he'd generously assigned her. "When did the practice of lynching begin?"

Ida picked up her notebook. "In the 1830s, lynching began as a practice of brutal punishment—thirty-nine lashes on bare skin with a whip, until the skin broke and a man was bent and bloodied. Back then, it was used as a disciplinary action for a man of any color who had been accused and found guilty of a crime. It picked up after the Civil War as a means of extrajudicial punishment for men, Black, white, and others, accused but not convicted of crimes."

"Okay, good," Thomas said. "Start there. How did it grow into the form of terrorism we know now?"

"In the early 1880s, more and more Blacks moved from the countryside to the cities. Proportionately, the number of Blacks lynched began to surpass the number of whites."

"That's important," he said. "Write that down. We're making an outline for more than a newspaper article, Ida. This investigation could blow the lid off the whole thing. Mob violence relies on certain things to operate as blatantly and brutally as it does: misconception about the crimes and the victims, secrecy, and a seemingly random pattern of violence. But what we're aiming to do is show that it's a system of violence and intimidation that is being dispensed in a calculated fashion because it is *very* effective. This is front-page news, Ida."

Ida looked up at Thomas and smiled. She missed Memphis. She missed Tommie Moss and life before the lynching at the Curve. But there was a reason that the *New York Age* was considered one of the top newspapers in the country, Black or white: Thomas Fortune had a fine mind and the vision to execute stories more complex than Ida had ever published in the *Free Speech.*

"Thank you, Thomas," she said, taking notes as quickly as she could.

"Let's keep going," he said. "Why was this mob violence allowed to continue unchecked?"

"Because after Reconstruction, ex-Confederates were able to consolidate judicial power on the state level, and the Republicans' protections of Black people, from Lincoln's era, fell away as newer, less sympathetic white Republicans began to take office."

He went out to get them sandwiches for lunch.

"Now give me the numbers," he said.

"Well, the *Chicago Tribune* reported that there were seven

hundred twenty-eight lynchings in the last ten years—most of them Black men."

"What else do we know?"

"The numbers go up year by year. There have been two hundred lynchings this year alone, and it's only June."

On June 25, the *New York Age* published Ida's opus in a seven-column spread called "The Truth About Lynching." Thomas Fortune ordered a ten-thousand-copy printing of the issue, betting—correctly—that white and Black readers in New York and across the nation had never read anything like it. Ida's article changed American history.

Ida did not use her beloved pen name, Iola, in the article. She signed it simply, "Exiled."

Chapter Forty-Five

Brave Woman!

It was October 5, 1892, and Ida was about to give the most important speech of her life.

A group of 250 women from all over New York City had organized an evening in Ida's honor. New York's Lyric Hall was chosen as the venue, and from the moment she opened the doors to the majestic auditorium, Ida felt uncharacteristically nervous.

Her pen name, Iola, was spelled out on the hall stage with gas jets. Ushers wore silk badges that had "Iola" embroidered on them in colorful threads. The program for the evening's entertainment was designed to look like copies of the *Free Speech.*

The crowd of hundreds included Ida's former beau, Charles Morris, who was now married to Annie Sprague, granddaughter of the Great Man, Frederick Douglass. Prominent women such as Josephine St. Pierre Ruffin and Frances Ellen Watkins Harper were also in attendance.

Upon being introduced, Ida was presented with a purse

holding five hundred dollars' worth of gold coins and a gold brooch in the shape of a pen.

Ida took to the stage and told the story of the lynching at the Curve and the reporting that she had dedicated herself to. But as she told the story of how Tommie and his business partners had been murdered, so clearly and without question, for starting a business that became more successful than their white counterparts', she could feel the tears flooding her eyes.

I cannot cry. I cannot cry! she told herself. She *never* cried in the line of duty. Not when she was reporting a story and heard the most horrific details of a lynching. Not when she recounted such stories on the page or to her editors. Never when she gave speeches. It was vital that she be seen as a serious journalist, not a sentimental sop. And yet here the tears were. More than five hundred people in the audience, and this was the moment that her grief demanded release.

When she realized that she could not hold back the tears, she turned from the audience, signaled to the hosts what she needed, and was brought a handkerchief. She dabbed her eyes, took a deep breath, and read the rest of her speech.

It was, in the end, a rousing success. The applause went on for what seemed an age. Papers across the country raved about the speech given by Iola, and the *Washington Bee* declared it to be "one of the finest testimonials ever rendered by an Afro-American."

At the end of the month, Ida published her editorial from the *New York Age* in a pamphlet called *Southern Horrors: Lynch Law in All Its Phases.*

Ida had gotten the attention of Frederick Douglass.

The next week, in the office, Thomas Fortune slapped the

latest copy of the *New York Age* on her desk. "Read this," he said with a wide smile.

In an editorial, Douglass wrote about *Southern Horrors*:

> There has been no word equal to it in its convincing power. I have spoken, but my words are feeble in comparison.

Ida flushed. "He doesn't mean it!"

Thomas smirked. "Oh that's part of Old Man Eloquent's charm. He likes to be humble and self-deprecating. Keep reading."

Douglass concluded by writing:

> You have given us what we know and testify from actual knowledge. Brave woman! You have done your people and mine a service which can never be weighed or measured.

Ida put the paper down. She had never felt so seen, or vindicated, in her life.

Chapter Forty-Six

Cedar Hill

Ida arrived in Washington by train, and when the horse-drawn carriage pulled up in front of the Douglass home in Anacostia, she let out a low whistle that made the driver chuckle.

"It's something, isn't it," the older gentleman said as he helped her out of the cab. "I was born in Alabama, lived the first twenty years of my life as a slave. Never thought I'd live to see a Black man live in a house like this. But God had another plan for us, young lady. Whenever it seems that there is nothing but darkness and despair, remember that God always has another plan."

Ida nodded and pressed a silver coin into the man's gloved hand. "Thank you, sir," Ida said. "I'm in the midst of some tough times myself and am grateful for the encouragement."

She stood for a second and gazed at the house as the carriage clip-clopped away. Cedar Hill, the home of Frederick Douglass. She was to be a guest here for the weekend. The words didn't seem to belong together. For surely she had not ascended such heights as to be invited into the home of one of the greatest Americans to have ever lived.

She picked up her bag, packed with two carefully cleaned and pressed dresses, her journal, and the novel she was reading. In her left hand, she clutched the telegram containing the invitation, just in case, in some wild unlikelihood, she was turned away at the door.

"Courage!" she whispered to herself as she made her way up the hill to the house—was *mansion* the right word?—which rose mightily from beneath a canopy of trees.

At the door, Ida was greeted by Helen Pitts Douglass, the Great Man's second wife, a white woman, which Ida knew was the talk among some circles of the Black upper classes.

Ida smiled broadly and reached out to shake the woman's hand. "I'm most delighted by this kind invitation," she said. There was no reason not to be polite. Regardless of her race, Helen Douglass was the lady of this house.

Helen smiled sweetly and said, "Here, let me give you a quick tour."

They stood in the vast entryway, where a painting of Douglass took pride of place.

"Such majesty," Ida said admiringly.

"It's the only portrait he has ever sat for," Helen explained. "Artists around the world have copied his likeness, and as you know, there are many photographs. But this is the only painting done with him as a model."

Ida stared at the painting. It depicted Douglass as a younger man, his hair a wooly white mane but his beard a salt-and-pepper mix of black and white. He was dressed in a crisp white shirt, a black bowtie, a black wool vest, and a black overcoat. The background of the painting was dark, but it had a kind of glow to it, as if the artist wanted the viewer to know that this was no mere man; he was a chosen hero, anointed even.

"Frederick purchased Cedar Hill with nine acres, but he was able to purchase an additional six acres as they became available, and now the property sits on fifteen acres total."

"What a blessing," Ida said softly, thinking of how many Black Americans had worked the land and how many still did. Yet she knew that precious few Black Americans owned one acre, much less fifteen.

"The house originally had fourteen rooms. Now there are twenty-one. The kitchen wing is new, and the attic was converted into a suite of extra bedrooms."

"Now Helen!" a deep voice boomed from the top of the central staircase. "Are you trying to put me out of work? You know I do the tours around here."

He was so regal, so king-like, with his tall stature, finely cut suit, and mane of white hair, Ida had to fight the urge to curtsy.

"Mr. Douglass," she said, bowing her head ever so slightly, "I am honored to make your acquaintance."

"As I am by your presence," he said. "The one and only Iola. Or will you go by the name Exiled indefinitely?"

Ida shook her head. "I imagine I'll keep using Iola."

"I was just telling Helen that Ida B. Wells is more than a journalist," Douglass said. "She's a fighter. I read your columns, and I am reminded of my own fiery youth. We have that in common—the ability to use words to throw blows."

Ida smiled. The idea that she had anything in common—anything at all—with Frederick Douglass was dizzying.

Down a long hallway, Ida could see well-dressed young men and women going to and fro, in a busy choreography of domestic tasks.

"Leave your bag here," Douglass said. "Come, let us see the grounds."

As they stepped out of the house, Douglass grabbed a silver-tipped walking stick from a stand near the front door.

"Follow me," he said.

Ida trailed behind him onto the front porch, and together they took in the majestic view.

"If you look to the right, you can see the Capitol. Even when I'm resting, I want to keep an eye on our elected officials."

Ida nodded. "My father loved the Declaration of Independence," she said. "He had us all memorize the sentence: 'We hold these truths to be self-evident, that all men are created equal, that they are endowed by their Creator with certain unalienable rights, that among these are Life, Liberty and the pursuit of Happiness.' He said it was more of a prayer than a promise for Black Americans, but it was a prayer we must never stop believing in."

Douglass gave her the full blast of his gaze then, and Ida felt that more than looking at her, he was looking through her as if to determine the true fiber of her character.

"Oh, you were *well* raised," Douglass said warmly. "Not that anyone who has ever read your writing could ever have doubted it. But my dear, hear me when I say, the Declaration of Independence is the ringbolt to the chain of our nation's destiny. We are in a storm now; we've been navigating a raging ocean that has threatened our destruction since our arrival on these rocky shores. But trust in me, the words of the founding fathers are the compass to the freedom and equality we seek."

Ida took a deep breath in. "I believe you are right, sir."

"And if you disagree with me, then you can tell me that too."

Ida nodded.

As they descended into the grounds, Ida saw two little girls playing croquet.

"My granddaughter Hattie and her friend Eveline," Douglass said.

He opened the door to a small stone building. "This is my study. That desk belonged to Charles Sumner, the great senator from Massachusetts. It was given to me upon his death, by his widow." He walked over to the library of books in his study and said, "Have you read Charles Dickens, child?"

"I have," Ida said.

"Do you remember Mr. Jarndyce?"

"I do."

"He had a little study, a refuge of books and papers where he could 'come and growl.' That was my inspiration," he said.

He paused then, and Ida could tell he was on the verge of making a kind of confession. "Mine is a full life," he said, his voice both grateful and weary. "But one full of chaos and a seemingly never-ending stream of obligations. When I am feeling out of sorts, this is where I come and growl."

Ida nodded. "It makes sense. Every lion needs its lair."

Douglass laughed. "So says the lioness."

Ida blushed. If only it were so.

As they walked, Ida didn't mention that she had, at one time, been impossibly besotted with the husband of Douglass's granddaughter, the charming and handsome Charles S. Morris. She did not say that in the end, Charles had made it abundantly clear that he did not want a lioness for a wife, or a princess of the press, for that matter.

He pointed to a vast bed of plantings and a grove of tall trees and said, "Come spring, this will be abloom with strawberries and persimmon. Let us walk on."

They continued walking as the house faded in the distance behind them.

"You are fighting an ugly battle in taking on lynching," he said. "But do not let the machinations of man distract you from the wonders of the world that God has made. In these grounds alone, there are more than a hundred species growing: wild rose and jasmine, Kentucky bluegrass, trumpet honeysuckle, and grape hyacinth. I collect specimens and press them into my books. They remind me that outside the conflict of race, there is much beauty to enjoy—and it is for us as much as for anyone."

Ida took in the beauty that was Cedar Hill and wondered if a life like this might ever be possible for her. Marriage. Children. Grandchildren. What a thought! A home where she and her loved ones could spend their summers playing croquet and eating berries straight off the vine. She was thirty, and sadly, at the present moment, there were no prospects that thrilled her.

Still, she could not be living life all wrong. She was at Cedar Hill, at the personal invitation of Frederick Douglass. He had praised her, more than once. And beyond any expectation on her part, he seemed to be enjoying her company.

At the end of the long path, there was a clearing in the woods where they could no longer see the city around them, or the sprawling family home, or any building for that matter. They were surrounded by trees—the kind of older-than-time trees that Ida knew had been there before she was born and would be there long after she had drawn her last breath.

There were two stumps that had been shaved clean. Douglass sat on one and gestured for Ida to sit on the other, next to him.

He pointed to the sky, and Ida took in how, in between the branches, white clouds floated across the blue sky as if they were in a painting that could move and change, ever so subtly, second by second.

She wanted to say something erudite or charming. She wanted to say, *My oh my, the wonder of it all,* or simply once again, *Thank you.* But she did not want to ruin the moment with words that might fall short of their task.

He seemed to understand her hesitation, because he put his hand on her shoulder and patted it. Then he removed it and clasped his hands, as if in prayer, on his lap.

Then he smiled at her and said, "Let us be silent for a while and listen to nature."

Chapter Forty-Seven

Dinner at the Station

In Philadelphia, Ida found the home of William Still easily. The three-story brick townhouse at 244 South Twelfth Street was impressive. She knocked on the door and was greeted by William's wife, Letitia.

"Welcome, Ida," Letitia said. "Hurry in before you catch your death of cold."

In the living room, William Still rose. He wore a crisp white shirt and a dark brown tweed vest and pants.

"Good afternoon, Mr. Still," Ida said. "It was so kind of you and your wife to offer me lodging as I attend the AME conference."

"Nonsense, my child," William said warmly. "How are you going along since those monsters ran you out of Memphis?"

Ida flinched. It was hard to believe that it had been eight months since the lynching at the Curve. There were days when she did not know how she found the fortitude to keep going.

But she knew she had no right to complain. It was said that William Still, now in his seventies, had personally helped more than eight hundred men, women, and children escape from slavery. He had written about how he and others had made Philadelphia the hub of the Underground Railroad, but he took little credit for himself. He was not an orator like Frederick Douglass or a newspaperman like Thomas Fortune, but you ask anyone to tell you who the father of the Underground Railroad was, and they would tell you, William Still.

He was a quiet man with a head for business. She'd heard of his vast real estate holdings and how the investment he'd made in coal right after the war had paid off beyond his wildest imaginings. Ida wanted to ask him questions that had nothing to do with his professional dealings. She could only imagine the tales he could tell of narrow escapes and feats of unprecedented bravery in the dead of the Philadelphia night. But she knew from experience, because she had pressed Frederick Douglass on the matter at Cedar Hill, that these older Black men had no interest in revisiting their battles for emancipation. They wrote books about it, but they had no wish to relive it. As the fireplace roared and their loved ones gathered close around them, they had no desire to poison the sweet air of freedom in their homes with the horrors they had endured in their youth. So Ida did not ask.

At dinner that night, there were several guests at dinner—William and his wife, Letitia; the poet and abolitionist Frances Ellen Watkins Harper; William's son William Jr. and his new wife, Elizabeth; and the Stills' daughter, Frances Ellen Still, named after their longtime family friend. Also in attendance at dinner was Catherine Impey, a Quaker woman from England.

Seated next to Ida, Catherine said, "You know I begged an invitation to dinner tonight so that I could meet you."

William Still shook his head and said, "Begging was not necessary, but she did ask to make your acquaintance. To save the lady from having to boast about herself, let me tell you that Miss Impey is the founding editor of a very influential journal in England called *Anti-Caste*. She campaigns for the rights of our brothers and sisters in India, who suffer terribly under the oppression of British colonial rule. But she is also concerned about the cause of Black American rights."

"That I am," Miss Impey said.

"Ida, you are young," William continued, "so you may not fully know, but the Quakers around the world provided unending support during the years we were fighting for emancipation. It was the Quakers who—in 1783—long before an old man like me was even born, formed the first anti-slavery society in England."

Catherine Impey turned to Ida and said, "Two years ago, my dear friend Albion Tourgée sent me a picture postcard of a man hanging from a tree in Clanton, Alabama."

Ida shuddered. The souvenirs people were beginning to make of lynchings, as if it were a sport, terrified her.

"I put that photo on the cover of *Anti-Caste*, and do you know what happened next?"

Ida did not.

"British society was in arms that I would choose to cover my journal with such a brutal and abhorrent drawing."

Catherine Impey had the whole table's attention. It was not every day that a group of Black Americans heard how citizens in another country reacted to the grim reality that was creeping into their day-to-day lives.

"Ida," Catherine Impey said her name with a slight *L* at the end, so it sounded like "Ida-l."

"Ida," Catherine said again, "I told them, 'I'll have you know that is not a drawing, it is a photograph. That is journalistic proof of the atrocities that are happening right now in America.'"

Ida was uncharacteristically quiet that dinner. Partly because she was tired of talking. She had been traveling, and lecturing, for weeks. There had been an unsuccessful speaking engagement in Washington, DC, where she appeared at the invitation of Frederick Douglass but found the auditorium empty except for the Great Man and a few of his relatives. And she would travel next to Boston, at the invitation of Josephine St. Pierre Ruffin to speak to the Women's Department at Wesleyan Hall.

That night after dinner in the Still home, she thought of her siblings. Her sister Lily had returned to California, and she hardly kept in touch with her brothers. George was married, A. J. seemed determined to live a life of intemperance and vice. He'd written to Ida of his gambling habit, saying that she must not chide him to stop gambling as it "takes time to break up a habit that has been forming for years." He'd signed that letter "Your wild and reckless brother."

She wrote in her diary, "I am so thankful and more than delighted with my success so far and pray for it to continue. But I seem to be a failure so far as my own brother is concerned, for I speak harshly or indifferently or repulsively to him before I think of the consequences. God help me be more careful and watchful over my manners and bearing toward him. Let not my own brothers perish while I am laboring to save others!"

Chapter Forty-Eight

Keep My Name Out of Your Mouth

Ida had been gone from Memphis for the better part of the year, but her editorials in the *New York Age* and her successful speaking tours in the North were the talk of both white and Black Memphis.

That year, the *Memphis Commercial*, the biggest white paper, gained a new editor in Edward Ward Carmack. He was a Tennessee-born lawyer with aspirations for a political career on the national stage. In 1884, he won a seat in the Tennessee House of Representatives, but he quickly realized that the press was a far more powerful perch to skewer his rivals than the halls of the state legislature. When he took over the *Memphis Commercial*, he set his sights on the person he considered to be the biggest threat to the old ways of the South—Ida.

On December 15, 1892, with little regard to journalistic ethics, Carmack published an all-out attack on Ida—he called her a "wench" and "the mistress of a scoundrel," referring to J. L. Fleming, her business partner on the *Memphis Free Speech.* He claimed she was a swindler whose fundraising efforts were meant to enrich only herself. He finished the editorial by calling her a "Black harlot" whose only true aim was to "marry a white husband."

Ida was in Brooklyn when she received the copy of the paper, with its vile, outrageous claims and her photograph on the front page. She sat in her room at 395 Gold Street, and it felt as if the walls were closing in on her. She knew Carmack was ruthless: His paper never missed an opportunity to take a shot at her. But this was more than a shot—it was a reputational execution by firing squad.

She wanted to cry. She wanted to crawl back into her bed, pull the covers over her head, and sob until she could cry no more. But then she thought of Carmack, of his haughty glare in the photo that ran of him in every edition of the paper and how he'd tried to hack her life, her work, and her good name to pieces. She thought of how he must have smirked under that enormous walrus mustache when he called her a "Black harlot," and she could not give him the ransom that her tears would represent.

She wanted to go back to bed. Instead, she got dressed and went to the office of the *New York Age.* Thomas Fortune would know what to do.

Ida walked into the office of the *Age,* where a half dozen newspapermen were quietly at work.

Thomas stood to greet her and said only, "This won't stand. As God is my witness, this won't stand."

He led her to his desk, and she sat across from him. She tried to look brave but she felt anything but. "What can I do?" she asked, defeated.

Thomas shook his head. "This is not a *you* problem, Ida. This is a *we* problem. In attacking you, Carmack is seeking to bring down all Black women. I've been getting telegrams all morning."

He explained that the *New York Age* would run a front-page editorial in Ida's defense. He showed her the headline he'd been working on:

MEMPHIS MISCREANTS FAIL AT SILENCING IDA B. WELLS

She smiled for the first time all day. "It's a good headline, Thomas." It was such a good word, *miscreant.*

"I've already heard from the *Topeka Weekly Call* and John Mitchell of the *Richmond Planet.* Let me read you Mitchell's telegram: 'The Black press must and will defend our own. Tell Miss Wells that she need feel in no way embarrassed or cast down.'"

Ida remembered accompanying John Mitchell in Washington, DC, when they met with President Harrison.

Josephine St. Pierre Ruffin in Boston wrote, "The Women's Era Club stands with Ida B. Wells, whose purity of purpose and character is an example to us all."

All throughout the day, more telegrams arrived, and Ida began to wonder if she ought not to make a bolder retaliation.

"Thomas," she began, "Carmack will not be chastened by the ire of the Black press, although all of this work is essential to repairing the damage done to my reputation. Perhaps I should sue him—for slander. Make him pay where the struggling South feels it the most—in his pocket."

Ida wrote first to Albion Tourgée, a white lawyer who had gained national attention for the case of Homer Plessy, a mixed-race man who had been thrown out of the first-class section of a Louisiana train and sued the railroad company. The case had made it all the way to the US Supreme Court.

Tourgée wrote back to Ida right away.

> *Dear Miss Wells,*
>
> *Thank you ever so much for your letter. The case of your own railroad suit was cited in our briefs for Plessy. Sadly, I am so consumed with that case that I cannot take yours on at the moment. But I can offer you some guidance on how to proceed.*
>
> *I think there is an opportunity for you to win damages, of a not inconsequential amount, if you can prove your character is unassailable. As a single woman, you bear the burden of proof. This is unfortunate, but we must speak plainly if we are to move strategically and with power. The newspaper will imply that you were the mistress of your former business partner at the Memphis Free Speech, J. L. Fleming. You must be able to prove that not only is this not so, but that you have not had relationships of an improper nature with any man.*
>
> *I would like to suggest that you enlist the services of a lawyer that I hold in high esteem, Ferdinand Barnett of Chicago. He will keep me*

informed of the details of your case, and I will offer any insight and assistance that I can.

May justice be served.

Yours most sincerely,
Albion Tourgée

Ida wrote to Ferdinand Barnett, who had, of course, heard of her and, with Tourgée's recommendation, was more than happy to take the case on. In a letter to Tourgée, Barnett wrote:

Dear Albion,

I have been in touch with Miss Wells. I have the strongest faith that the libelous article is wholly without foundation.

She has given me a number of people to contact in Memphis and admits that, over the years, she has fallen out with some of them—in particular, Thomas Cassells and the Settles, Josiah and Therese.

I already hold an increased admiration for Miss Wells in being so forthright. If her record was assailable, she would not send me to her enemies—especially as they are my friends.

I will keep you informed as I make my own investigations.

Yours respectfully,
Ferdinand Barnett

Ferdinand Barnett then wrote to Ida. The day she received the letter at her home on Gold Street, she felt a long-lost sense of excitement at seeing her name rendered in the elegant swirl of his handwriting. She made herself a cup of tea, then took her time in opening the envelope.

Dear Miss Wells,

I have been in touch with a number of friends and colleagues in Memphis. You should rest easy in the knowledge that among your former circle of neighbors and friends, you are regarded highly—there is nothing but fondness for your warmth, wit, and loyalty. To a one, the citizens of Memphis feel nothing but the deepest pride in your work as a journalist and your tireless efforts against lynching.

It is the opinion of all surveyed that since your exile from Memphis has denied your enemies the ability to do you physical harm, they have turned to the papers in a vain attempt to damage you to whatever extent is within their limited means.

Having been involved in a legal suit before, you know that this undertaking will certainly take months, if not years. But I am writing to say that I am willing to take the battle on and will fight with you and for you, should you decide to pursue the case. Carmack is a dastardly piece of work, and it would be my pleasure to toil in the effort for him to get the comeuppance he so sorely deserves.

Yours with esteem,
Ferdinand Barnett

Ida appreciated so much about the letter. Mr. Barnett was, of course, right, that a lawsuit would be long and potentially costly. But she had more stature than she did when she took on the railroad company. Perhaps this time she would prevail. But she also could not help but notice the chivalry that was woven throughout his letter. She read the words again: *I am willing…to fight with you and for you.* That was something. And then the way he had described her reputation among the Memphis set: *There is nothing but fondness for your warmth, wit, and loyalty.* "Oh, Mr. Barnett," she whispered to herself as she unfolded the letter to reread one more time, "you are the picture of charm."

1893

Chapter Forty-Nine

Freedom's Eve

January 3, 1893, found Ida again at Cedar Hill. Frederick Douglass had written to her, saying, "The holidays are over but the pantry is still overflowing from all the food that was cooked. Why don't you come and stay a night or two?"

In the kitchen, Ida helped Helen Douglass lay out a feast for dinner. There were collard greens cooked with succulent bits of pork, sweet potato yams, corn bread, and hoppin' John, a one-pot meal of rice and peas. For dessert, there was molasses pie with cinnamon-spiced syrup.

As he prepared to say a blessing for the meal, Douglass said, "It's hard to believe it's thirty years almost to the day since Abraham Lincoln signed the Emancipation Proclamation."

Ida could see the tears filling his eyes as he continued, "I remember how the night before, December 31, 1862, all across the country, when they could, as they could, our people gathered to worship on a night that came to be known as Freedom's Eve."

"Dear Lord," the Great Man prayed, "we thank you for the

blessings of thirty years of freedom, for the generations that sit at this table, and for the strength and wisdom to take on all the work that still lies ahead."

As soon as grace was over, a lively conversation began around the table, mostly centered around which dish to dig into first.

Ida said, "Miss Helen, would you mind passing the collards? I need all the luck I can get."

"Well, speaking of good fortune," Douglass said, "I received this letter. It was sent to your address in Brooklyn, then forwarded to me. It arrived yesterday morning, so it is excellent timing that you are here today."

He handed her an envelope and then said, "I also received a letter from Catherine Impey. Let me read you what she has said to me."

> *Dear Friends in the Pursuit of Justice and Equality,*
>
> *My dear and esteemed Mr. Douglass, it feels too long since I have seen you last. As I mentioned in my previous letter, I was thrilled to meet Miss Ida B. Wells at the home of William Still in Philadelphia when I was there, recently, visiting American relatives.*
>
> *Since that trip, I have joined forces with a Scottish writer and activist named Isabella Fyvie Mayo, who has agreed to finance a trip to England for Miss Wells.*
>
> *We have sent this invitation to her address in Brooklyn, with the understanding that such a trip would be difficult for you to undertake at this time.*
>
> *If Miss Wells is unable to come, could you recommend another bright light who might make the trip instead?*

With the deepest respect and
the hopes of conveying
Our profound solidarity,
Catherine Impey

Ida could hardly believe it.

"What do you think, child?" Douglass asked.

Ida knew that in 1845, Douglass had embarked on an ambitious nineteen-month trip through the United Kingdom, where he spoke on the evils of slavery and sold copies of his book. He had been just twenty-eight years old, but that trip had galvanized the international abolitionist effort and would have a long-lasting effect on emancipation efforts back home.

Now Ida was being invited to tour the UK, to follow in Douglass's footsteps, and it felt like more than an opportunity: It meant that she had his approval and he viewed her as worthy of his endorsement, which many Black male leaders wanted but had not received.

Ida, who had never been abroad, whispered, "I would love to go."

In her diary that night, she wrote, "For nearly a year I have been in the North, hoping to spread the truth and get the moral support for my demand that those accused of crimes be given a fair trial and punished by law instead of a mob."

Ida wrote that, when Frederick Douglass read the invitation for her to travel to England to take the cause to a global audience, "It seemed like an open door in a stone wall."

Chapter Fifty

To England

They called them the greyhounds of the Atlantic, these steamships that sailed, with unprecedented speed, from New York to Liverpool. Older ships took weeks to make the journey, but these new vessels had cut that time down to a matter of days.

Ida boarded the *Teutonic*, with a very Ida-esque mixture of enthusiasm, confidence, and just a smidge of arrogance. She had heard tales of those who had spent the entire voyage doubled over, sick to their stomach. But she had judged the tellers of such tales to be weak sorts. She would be, she was sure of it, different.

Ida was pleased to see that her roommate in the stateroom was a tall, attractive, smartly dressed Black woman.

"I'm Georgia," the woman said warmly.

"I am Ida B. Wells."

"The famed lady journalist," Georgia said. "I hope someday to earn some acclaim in my field as well. If the records do not lie, then I am the first Black woman to become a licensed surgeon in Tennessee."

Ida was impressed and said so. "What a marvelous feat. So, you are actually Dr. Georgia."

"Yes, Dr. Georgia E. L. Patton."

The two women walked to the deck of the ship and sat side by side looking out at the ocean.

"I am going to England to promote the anti-lynching campaign," Ida explained. "I am traveling at the behest of a remarkable woman named Catherine Impey—she says that it is not merely a matter of race—which is too tangled up in our recent and shameful history of inhumane and bloodied deeds. Miss Impey prefers to speak of caste—which she believes more powerfully confronts the artificial structures of society constructed to benefit the rich and powerful. She says it is not just American and British, or Black and white. You can see it all around the world."

"Well, when I get to Africa, I will report what I learn about caste," Georgia said. "I am merely passing through England. I am on my way to Liberia."

Ida had actually never met a woman who had visited the continent of Africa, and she found herself fascinated by Georgia and her bravery in traveling so far into a world unknown by most Americans.

"What takes you there?" she asked.

"Since I was a little girl, it has been my goal to be a medical missionary. I have no real desire to convert people to my religion. But if I can offer my services, as a doctor, for some time, I think that is certainly something the Lord would want me to do."

"Amen," Ida said.

"Are you afraid of being on the ocean?" Georgia asked.

Ida looked at Georgia levelly. "I make it a practice not to fear anyone or anything but the Lord."

"My father told me I should remember the ancestors as I make this passage," Georgia said. "He said, 'There will come a time on the boat when you lose sight of the shore and you are days away from seeing land. That is the moment, when there's nothing around you but water, that you might grasp just a bit of the strength and hope that it took for our people to survive the journey on the slave ships.'"

"Let us say a prayer, then, for the ancestors," Ida said, taking her new friend's hand in her own.

The two young women held hands, bowed their heads, and prayed.

The next day, Ida woke up feeling fine. "No seasickness!" she declared triumphantly. "I think I will get through this journey with no problems at all."

Georgia Patton was more cautious. "I think we're going to need to take this day by day."

Before she left New York, Ida had mailed a letter to Ferdinand Barnett. She'd written:

> *Dear Mr. Barnett,*
>
> *I am writing to thank you, with the most sincerity, for your kind offer to represent me in suing, for slander, the Memphis Commercial.*
>
> *Through my burgeoning friendship with Mr. Frederick Douglass, I have received the kind invitation to travel to England and tell the world about the horrors of lynching and our campaign to stop this wave of mob violence that gets worse every year.*

I believe it is best for me to turn my full attention to this work so as to make Mr. Douglass proud in his recommendations of me and to gain some real traction in our work. White Americans do not always listen to the pleas of Black Americans. But when British abolitionists sounded the alarm on the horrors of slavery, it made a difference in this country and the wheels of justice began to turn. Perhaps I can, in some small way, reanimate that fine grind once more.

When you receive this letter, I will be on the ocean. I hope you will understand my decision and that I will get an opportunity to thank you for your sage counsel and faith in me at a moment when I sorely needed it. I hope to visit Chicago later this year.

Ever, Mr. Barnett,
and faithfully,
Ida B. Wells

On the second day of their journey, Ida woke up sick to her stomach and dizzy. "It's come for me," she whispered from the lower berth of the stateroom. "Seasick."

Her companion nodded. "Me too."

The women had the stateroom to themselves and lay on the lower berths, staring at each other. When they were too weak to stand, they laughed at their sorry state. "The glamour of transatlantic travel," Ida joked.

Day four was no better. By day five, Ida, who slept with her head turned toward a tin bucket, asked Georgia, "Is there such a word as *seasicker*?"

Georgia laughed. "If it is accurate, the terminology serves."

The sixth day was the worst; Ida declared herself "sea*sickest*."

But the ship's doctor finally made his way to their cabin that day, and Ida declared, "I think I swallowed half the contents of his medicine chest."

The next day, which was their seventh at sea, both Ida and Georgia were able to eat a little bread. Ida wrote a few letters to friends, dramatically embellishing how the journey had nearly killed her and her companion both.

On the eighth day, the ship stopped at Queenstown, Ireland. Ida mailed her letters to the States. A telegram from Miss Catherine Impey was waiting for her:

> COME TO MY HOME IN SOMERSET WHEN YOU LAND. OUR BEST CARRIAGE AND ALL OUR GREAT AFFECTIONS WILL AWAIT YOU IN LIVERPOOL.

The boat approached Liverpool that night, but it was too late to make a landing. Ida woke early the next morning and made her way to the deck. She thought about all that she had left behind and the fight against terrorism that had brought her to these shores. It was not enough that slavery had filled the American coffers for centuries and given this baby nation the might to stand as an equal among all the Old World powers. But now the weak, greedy, and morally bankrupt among them were turning two hundred years of race privilege into a sadistic sport. Black people were being targeted in the most brutal fashion, their bodies hung up as trophies for their wives, children, and neighbors to ponder and hate. *Lucky England*, Ida thought. That nation had just one Jack the Ripper. America had thousands.

Chapter Fifty-One

The Anti-Caste Society

After Ida and Georgia had said their goodbyes, Ida met her benefactor, Catherine Impey, and then traveled to the home of Mrs. Isabella Fyvie Mayo in Aberdeen, Scotland.

As Ida arrived at the large townhouse, she was greeted by Isabella, a tall woman with dark, wavy hair and an elegant profile. She reminded Ida of the ballet dancers she'd seen in a performance when she was in New York. She moved with a kind of slow grace that was underpinned with a tremendous strength.

"Come in, come in, welcome to our home," Isabella said.

Ida smiled.

"Let me introduce you to our other guests: Dr. George Ferdinands, who hails from Ceylon and is studying a medical course at the University of Aberdeen, and Andrew Hahn, a music teacher from Berlin."

Over the next few days, Ida, Isabella, Andrew, and George worked day and night to mail out ten thousand copies of the *Anti-Caste* newspaper, all in anticipation of Ida's speaking tour.

In the afternoons, Isabella invited members of the press to meet Ida. *Society*, a popular London magazine, noted:

> **A very interesting young lady is about to visit London in the hopes of arousing sympathy for the Blacks whose treatment in the United States is not seldom fiendishly cruel. Miss Ida Wells is an American Negro lady who is fortunate enough to have secured as an ally Mrs. Isabella Fyvie Mayo, one of our cleverest writers of sound and useful literature. Miss Wells has opened her campaign in Aberdeen with a drawing room meeting at Mrs. Mayo's home.**

The next Saturday, Isabella took Ida by carriage to her first big speaking event.

"This will be good practice for you," she said. "This gathering is called the Pleasant Saturday Evening Meeting."

"And how many will be in attendance?"

"Fifteen hundred men."

"That seems like an awful lot," Ida said, thinking of how one hundred people gathered at the Lyceum made it seem like the building was packed to the rafters.

As the room filled, Ida could feel her left knee begin to shake beyond control.

"All shall be well," Isabella said, placing a reassuring hand on the errant limb. "They don't call it 'the Pleasant Evening Meeting' for nothing."

Ida took a deep breath and said a quiet prayer to herself.

"You've been allotted fifteen minutes," Isabella said. "It will go by in a flash."

Ida stood and spoke. "Ours has been a hard row since the days of the Civil War. There have been Jim Crow laws, ballot-box intimidation is rampant, and there are many white Americans who would sooner take our lives than allow us to exercise our constitutional right to vote. And the violence against us is growing state by state, year by year.

"In Mississippi, where I hail from, a Black man, who claimed to have killed a white man in self-defense, stood trial. The report read that, 'on the day of the preliminary examination, a crowd of twenty colored men were in attendance at the trial, all unarmed, when like a Texas cyclone, a gang of fifty cutthroats with Winchester rifles, rode into town, surrounded the courthouse and opened fire on all of the colored men, killing ten outright, wounding mortally three and severely wounding six. Only one was able to escape the massacre.'"

She put her papers down. When Ida was finished, there was a quiet thrum of applause, and even tears from some of the men.

Ida stepped off the stage and glanced at the clock. "I spoke for twenty-five minutes. I should apologize to the host."

Isabella said, "No need. Truth and honesty cannot be bound by time."

After that night, Ida's schedule was packed. On the following Friday afternoon, she spoke at the Bible Society Rooms on St. Andrews Square. On Saturday, there was a drawing room meeting at the Free Church Manse. More engagements followed, at the YMCA on St. Andrew Street and the Friends Meeting House in Glasgow.

Leaving Scotland, Ida met again with Catherine Impey and traveled throughout Newcastle, Birmingham, and Manchester, all with the idea of a big finish to the tour in London.

In Manchester, Ida was the guest of Mr. William Axon, the editor of the *Guardian*, who invited Ida and Catherine Impey to dinner at his home.

"I hope you will not mind," Mrs. Axon said. "We are vegetarians."

"I do not mind at all," Ida said. "Miss Impey is also a vegetarian, though she always has meat on offer for visitors and guests."

William Axon looked shocked, "I would no more offer you meat than I would offer you alcohol or tobacco. Our choice to not eat meat is a spiritual one to honor all living beings."

Catherine said, "I do not think such beliefs are as widely prevalent in the United States as they are here."

Ida confirmed that they were not.

Demurring to her hosts, she said no more but found the entire meal hard to take: She was served plate after plate of vegetables boiled to within an inch of their ripped-from-the-garden lives, without an iota of seasoning.

Alas, temperance has come for me, she thought, resolving to think of the whole meal as penance for past sins.

Back in Aberdeen, Ida found Isabella Mayo to be in a state of near rage.

"Oh dear," Ida said as she entered the house. "What in heaven is wrong?"

"Follow me to the library," Isabella whispered in a tone that was tinged with anger.

Ida did as she was asked.

"May I count upon your discretion?" Isabella asked.

"Yes, always," Ida said.

She held a letter up. "This is a letter from Catherine Impey to *my* esteemed house guest, Dr. George Ferdinands."

Ida was intrigued.

"In the letter, she claims to return the feelings she says she has suspected the good doctor has been trying to hide for some time. She then goes on to wildly assert that she thinks Dr. Ferdinands has not declared his affection because of the limitations placed upon him as a man of darker hue."

"Really?" Ida said.

"But this is the maddest thing of all," Isabella said, clutching at her desk to steady herself. "She has apparently written to *her* family asking for their permission to marry. This permission has, without any *actual* input from the dear doctor, been granted. She writes—and I quote—'Let us be married and show the world that caste is the devil's work and in the eyes of the Lord, all brothers and sisters are equal.' "

Ida sighed. "This is quite a revelation. What does Dr. Ferdinands have to say about the matter?"

"He *never* sought such a connection with that woman," Isabella said, furious.

She went on to explain that she was breaking all ties with Catherine Impey and would destroy every remaining copy of the *Anti-Caste* newspaper, as it had their names side by side and such an alliance no longer existed.

"You have a choice to make, Ida," Isabella said. "You can continue to work with me—or choose to work with a woman of debatable morals and judgment."

That night, Ida could hardly sleep. Her UK tour had been such a success. She agreed that Catherine Impey had made several wild leaps in the letter, as Isabella described it. But she also hadn't examined the letter—and even if she had, she could not punish Catherine for being a fool for love. That was not, Ida felt, either her desire or her place.

The next morning she told Isabella of her decision and begged her to make amends with the woman with whom she'd done so much good work for the cause of anti-racism.

Stone-faced, her formerly garrulous host said simply, "I shall arrange for you to be on the next train to Somersetshire."

Ida soon learned just how powerful Isabella Mayo was. The timing of her visit to London had been particularly planned to coincide with Parliament, but Isabella Mayo had written to block Catherine Impey's introductions at the most important meetings. A few weeks later, having only arranged a few small engagements, Ida sailed home from Southampton. She never saw Isabella Mayo again.

Chapter Fifty-Two

Home to America

On the ship home from England, Ida found herself in better health than on the passage over. There wasn't the joy in having a woman like Dr. Georgia Patton share her stateroom, but other surprises awaited her.

While sitting on the deck, Ida was approached by an elegantly dressed young white woman.

"Hello, I'm Ada Dell Collins," the woman said, with what Ida recognized to be a London accent. "Are you traveling alone?"

"I am," Ida explained.

"And what brought you to England?" Ada said, taking a seat in the deck chair next to Ida.

"I was the guest of Catherine Impey, head of the Anti-Caste Society."

Ada clasped her gloved hands together. "How wonderful! I know Catherine Impey well. My husband and I are on our way to Chicago for the World's Fair."

Ida nodded. "That is my destination as well. I may well move to Chicago."

It was such a short sentence that the brevity and finality of it surprised her. It was true. Thomas Fortune had tried to convince her to stay in New York, but it was so big, and as welcoming as the Black elite there had been to her, she felt overwhelmed by the size and pace of it. She felt like she was always out of breath in New York, and she could barely hear herself think as she tried to read and write.

She had loved living in Memphis, loved how you could connect with anyone and everyone just by strolling down Beale Street. The pace of it was slower, and the size of it made it feel like home. But the lynching at the Curve had ruined what they had all so carefully built in Memphis. It might one day be that place again, but not for her. Her friends who had remained said that Black citizens of that once-prized small city were still randomly approached by whites who asked, "Have you heard from Ida B. Wells? Do you think she might come through and visit? She must miss Memphis." She did miss Memphis, but she also realized that those who sought to make an example by lynching her still quivered for revenge.

Chicago was bigger than Memphis but smaller than New York. Ida had old friends there and had made new friends, like Ferdinand Barnett, the editor of the *Conservator*, who after offering to represent her in the slander trial had so kindly offered her a column and a job.

"Miss Ida, did you hear me?" Ada said, looking puzzled.

Ida had been so lost in thought that she had not.

"I'm so sorry," Ida said. "When I look out at the sea like this, I am prone to daydreaming."

Ada smiled. "I understand. The Atlantic is a wonder to

behold. I asked if you would like to join me and my party for dinner tonight."

"I would love to," Ida said softly. She had dined with many white Brits in the company of Catherine Impey, but this was an American ship, and she wasn't sure how the sight of her at a table of white guests would go over.

She smiled to herself and thought, *I guess we will find out.*

The meal lasted for hours, and at the end of it, Ida marveled that this was one of the first times she had met "members of the white race who saw no reason why they should not extend to me the courtesy they would offer any lady of their own race."

She noted that the Americans in the dining room seemed bewildered that the Brits could sit so comfortably with a woman who looked like Ida.

When Ida arrived in Chicago, she was surprised to see how much press—both in the Black and white newspapers—was devoted to commentary on her trip to England. The *Indianapolis Freeman*, a Black paper, called her "the modern Joan of the race"—equating her with Joan of Arc.

But the *Memphis Appeal Avalanche*, a white newspaper, called her trip to England "yet another deplorable low in a career of triumphant mendacity."

More insults were hurled from the *Atlanta Constitution*, the *Macon Telegraph*, and the *Washington City Post.*

Ida reckoned that criticism of her speaking out against lynching only underscored the importance of the crisis. "I know the work has done great good," she told Ferdinand Barnett as they sat side by side in the office of the *Conservator*, "if by no other sign than the abuse it has brought me from the white press."

"Keep doing that good work, Ida," Ferdinand said. "Come work at the *Conservator* with me."

Ida said she would think about it, but she had spent the whole journey back by steamship, from Liverpool to New York, considering the possibility. She knew that the answer would be yes.

Chapter Fifty-Three

Making a Home in Chicago

More than twenty million people from forty-seven countries were expected to attend the World's Fair in Chicago, called the Columbian Exhibition to celebrate the four hundredth anniversary of Columbus's arrival in the New World.

It was three months before the fair was to begin, and Ida, ever the newspaperwoman, told her editor, Ferdinand, "That's a lot of eyeballs."

He nodded. "Do you propose setting up a stand to sell the *Conservator*?"

Ida shook her head. "No, but what if we produced a pamphlet about the horrors of lynching—had it translated into six different languages—get people like Frederick Douglass and Albion Tourgée to write for it? It could go a long way toward getting some anti-lynching laws passed."

Ferdinand knew that some people found Ida hard to take. She was nothing if not outspoken. And ambitious. And relentless. America had shaken off their ties to British royalty more than a century before, but in both Black and white society, Victorian ideals still prevailed. Women should be pure, chaste, and modest. They should show their worth by their etiquette and their morals, and their beauty if they were lucky enough to possess it. Ida was beautiful, she held to Christian ideals, and if she'd had the will, she could have joined the ranks of upper-class Black women who longed simply for the Victorian ideal that had been denied them for so long—to be put on the pedestals of virtuosity and femininity. But that was not Ida.

He also knew something about breaking the mold. He had been the third Black person admitted to the bar in Illinois. His late wife, God rest her soul, had been the first Black woman to graduate from the University of Michigan. He believed with every fiber of his being that you did not make a place in a world that had never seen the likes of you without winding up for the pitch. You could not change this same world without valuing justice and a bigger purpose over the safety and sanctity of your little patch of woods. The longer he spent working with Ida, the more he saw this in her too. In both her efforts at the paper and in her character as a woman.

He asked how much publishing such a pamphlet would cost, knowing that she would not have proposed the project without working out the budget. Ida had gotten savvier about money since her schoolteacher days. There was still never enough, but she earned, spent, and saved with the purpose of a wiser woman than she had been.

"Five thousand dollars, ideally, and on the back page, we could have an ad for subscriptions to the *Conservator*."

But by summer, the funds to publish the pamphlet had not been raised.

The World's Fair proclaimed August 25, 1893, a "Jubilee Day" in honor of Black American citizens. Black Americans had been shut out of almost every level of planning and presentation of the fair. From President Harrison down to the executive committee of the fair, the fear was that America would not be seen as a paradigm of freedom, achievement, and ingenuity. Any discussion of racism would hurt the quest to make Chicago's World's Fair a calling card to the global community for the future of America as a force to be reckoned with in the Gilded Age and the century to come.

Jubilee Day was meant to appease Black protestors, but Ida, Ferdinand Barnett, and several prominent Black Chicagoans boycotted the event as a token, empty gesture. They told Douglass that he shouldn't give his planned speech and that, if he did, they would not attend. Frederick Douglass, in contrast, thought it was too big a stage to turn down. Douglass had just turned seventy-five. Ida lacked his patience or his strategic tactics.

The day of the Great Man's speech, Ida felt out of sorts. "Maybe I should follow Mr. Douglass's example more closely," she told herself. "He may appear at times conciliatory, but he is a master at getting things done."

Arriving at the fairgrounds that morning, Douglass saw that the main element of the so-called celebration of Black culture was that watermelon vendors had been set up across the fairgrounds. Offended, he turned around and went back to the residence he was staying in.

However, he returned that afternoon, just after two, as he

had been told that a crowd of Black and white visitors had gathered to hear him speak.

Perhaps it was the insult of the watermelon vendors, perhaps it was that the venue was hot, but when he stepped up to the podium, many noted that Douglass seemed older than he had ever had before. He'd had a mane of shockingly white hair for decades, but he always seemed more like a venerable lion than an old man. Yet as he approached the podium, he seemed to be trembling, holding the sides of the lectern as if it was holding him up rather than his own legs. His voice, those present observed, had a tremble to it they hadn't expected.

Some of the whites in the audience began to taunt the Great Man. In their heckling, Douglass found himself again. He straightened to his full height, threw his notes on the floor, and began to speak in the powerful, thunderous voice that had made him one of the most beloved speakers of his generation.

"Men talk of the Negro problem," he began. "There is no Negro problem. The *problem* is whether the American people have honor enough, patriotism enough, to live up to their Constitution. We Negroes love our country. We fought for it. We ask only that we be treated as well as those who fought against it."

Douglass spoke for more than thirty minutes, and when he was done, many knew that the age of the man and the setting—the World's Fair!—made this an experience that was likely never to be repeated in their lifetime. The applause, from both Black and white audience members, was deafening.

Reporters rushed from the room to file the story: Douglass, the old lion, had risen once again to remind America of the words of their founding fathers and all the ways the nation continued to fall short of their ideals. As for the hecklers, one reporter wrote that Douglass's sonorous voice and high-toned speech had drowned them out the way "an organ would a pennywhistle."

Ida heard news of the speech before the print on the afternoon papers was dry. Knowing that she had wronged the Great Man by boycotting his event, she dressed quickly and took a trolley directly to the Haitian pavilion, where Douglass was still receiving well-wishers.

"May I speak to you privately, sir?" Ida said.

"But of course," Douglass replied. The slight smile on his face showed that he knew an apology was on deck.

Ida was stubborn, but she had learned since her Memphis days that, while she could not always control her temper or insouciance, she should aim to make amends as soon as humanly possible.

"I was wrong to miss your speech," Ida began. "I blame my youth and inexperience. That I might presume to know better than you how to advance our cause was folly. Please accept my apology."

"Oh, I forgave you the moment you came into this place with your head down and that scared little expression on your face," Douglass said, letting out a booming laugh at the memory of it. "Ida B. Wells cowers rarely, and I knew before you said a single word that your attempts to patch things up would be sincere."

"I am so sad to have missed your speech," Ida said softly.

Douglass puffed out his chest and said, "Ha! It was a *very* good speech. But that is done. There is the business of the anti-lynching pamphlet you wish to publish."

"I failed to raise the funds, sir," Ida said, disappointed in herself.

"Let's have lunch on Wednesday. Where will you be?"

"At the Clark Street office of the *Conservator*," Ida said.

Douglass smiled and said, "I'll pick you up there."

Douglass showed up at the newspaper office, nattily dressed, and the men and women in the newsroom made their best attempts not to stare.

Ida greeted him, and he made the rounds of the office, shaking the hands of the young journalists who worked for the *Conservator* and giving a warm hello to Ferdinand, whom Douglass knew well.

"Shall we go?" he said finally, guiding Ida to the door.

"Where should we have lunch?" Ida asked as they stepped out into the heat of a Chicago summer day.

Douglass looked across the street. "How about that place? Boston Oyster House."

Ida hesitated. "They don't serve Black people there."

Douglass laughed. "Where you see a limitation, I see an opportunity. Come, that's exactly where we should go."

Ida smiled. "I'm game."

The two luminaries sauntered into the restaurant, Ida trying to project as much confidence as she could muster.

They stood at the front for a long moment, but no waiter would seat them. The white waiters walked around them as if they were invisible. But the white patrons of the restaurant stared at them so boldly, it was clear that they were anything but invisible.

Taking matters into his own hands, Douglass selected a table. He pulled out a chair for Ida and saw to it that she was comfortably settled. Then he took the seat opposite her.

In a short while, the owner of the restaurant came out and, recognizing Douglass, greeted him warmly.

Before Ida knew it, she and Douglass were surrounded by a bevy of servers who had clearly been instructed to see to their every need.

"It is almost *too* much attention," Ida whispered.

"Ida," Douglass said to her, loudly, so that everyone who was within listening distance could hear him. "And I thought you said they didn't serve us here."

Chapter Fifty-Four

What We Want the World to Know About America

A few weeks later, with Frederick Douglass's help, Ida's dream of an anti-lynching pamphlet to distribute at the World's Fair had come true. The Clark Street offices were filled with thousands of copies of Ida's pamphlet entitled *The Reason Why the Colored American Is Not in the World's Columbian Exposition—the Afro-American's Contribution to Columbian Literature.*

Ferdinand, who was realizing that he'd become quite fond of Ida, had decided it wasn't worth it to tell her that the title of the pamphlet, besides barely fitting on the cover of the little book, was really quite a mouthful.

"I fell short of the budget I hoped to raise, but we got it done," Ida said proudly. "Look, we were able to publish in English and pay to have it translated into French and German. Imagine the way this will advance our global cause when visitors take the pamphlet home to Paris, Berlin, and Vienna."

"Ida the Unstoppable," Ferdinand said admiringly. He thought that he was doing a commendable job of pretending that his interest in her was strictly professional. But he did not know if she saw the growing affection in his eyes or, if she did, how she would acknowledge it.

"We shall distribute it from the Haitian pavilion for the rest of the fair," Ida said proudly. "And we will mail copies for free, to anyone who sends in the three cents' postage."

The pamphlet began with an introduction from the Great Man, ready to tell the many visitors to the World's Fair the unvarnished truth about the precarious state of race and the democracy at the turn of the century. Douglass wrote:

> We would like, for instance, to tell our visitors... that two hundred and sixty years of progress and enlightenment have banished barbarism and race hate from the United States, that the old things of slavery have entirely passed away, and that all things pertaining to the colored people have become new...
>
> That the statement of human rights contained in its glorious Declaration of Independence, including the right to life, liberty and the pursuit of happiness is not an empty boast nor a mere rhetorical flourish...
>
> But unhappily, nothing of all this can be said, without qualification and without flagrant disregard for the truth.

Douglass was followed by essays about the convict lease system, which falsely imprisoned men—and increasingly children—then let them "work off" their sentences for white southerners. The essays sought to explain how these imprisonments were thinly veiled attempts to replace the lost free labor of slavery.

Ida contributed a piece called "Lynch Law." In addition to her carefully collected data and interviews, she shared the results of one of her recent investigations. Lee Walker had been lynched in Ida's beloved city of Memphis.

What Ida wanted the world to know was that lynching was not a crowd driven out of control in the moment. Her proof? Ten hours before Walker was murdered, Ida had received a telegram from one of the Memphis daily newspapers. The telegram assured her that Lee Walker would die that night. Then the newspaper cheekily asked, did Ida—who had never returned to Memphis—want to come down and report the story herself?

"It must be scary," Ferdinand said, sitting at the edge of her desk. "The way they target you personally."

"It is... troubling," Ida admitted.

"The amazing thing is that most of these white southerners have never seen you in person," Ferdinand said. "I wonder what they might think if they knew the woman they were all so afraid of was only four foot ten in stockinged feet."

Ida raised an eyebrow. "I am a full five feet tall."

Ferdinand tsk-tsked. "In your shoes, maybe. You are the very definition of what Shakespeare meant when he wrote, 'Though she be little, she be fierce.'"

Walking home to the boardinghouse where she was staying, Ida ran the conversation over in her head. *I do believe that Ferdinand Barnett was flirting with me tonight.*

She hoped her instincts were right. It would be nice to have a new romance to balance out all that was hard and ugly in her work.

The following week, as they closed up the office, Ferdinand asked if he could take Ida out to dinner. She had never dated an older man, had never considered it. But she had wondered if there might be a chance for romance with the widower. She had noted the care he took with his clothes, his quiet confidence, the way he smiled subtly, the corners of his mouth turning up in amusement. His manner was the polar opposite of the showy grin that so many men thought was charming but Ida found to be wholly unappealing.

Ferdinand was different from the others who had come so close to capturing her heart—Isaiah Graham, Louis Brown, Charles S. Morris. That Charles Morris, what a heartbreaker. But all that felt like such a long time ago, before the sky had darkened and the world had sent her tumbling from Memphis as if she had been ejected from a dream. A time when she went for strolls down Beale Street and coffee at the New Central House, when she bought dresses on credit at Menken's and danced the quadrille all night. She had never dated an older man, but now—she had to admit it—she was older too.

For their first date, he took her to a fish fry at a park on the south side of the city.

"Well, this is surprising," she said as he laid out a picnic blanket and handed her a plate of fried fish and a napkin so large it could double as a scarf.

"Why is that?" he asked, with that slightly amused smile.

"You're always so formal, with your impeccable suits and perfect diction," she said. "I'm from Holly Springs, Mississippi, so I'm quite comfortable at a Friday night fish fry. I didn't think this was your crowd."

She pointed to the men playing cards and the musicians playing vibrant tunes as couples danced informally on the grass.

"Well, I think one thing you'll discover that we have in common, Miss Wells, is that neither one of us likes to be put in a box," he said.

"That is true," she said, biting into her sandwich. "This is, by the way, delicious."

"A good time is a good time, whether it's in the ballroom, at the barbershop, or out here in the park with our people," Ferdinand said. "And if I am not too forward for saying it, a good time is made better anytime I can spend time with you."

Ida flushed. *So here it is,* she thought, with a smile. *I guess we're courting.*

Chapter Fifty-Five

The Ida B. Wells Club

Ida made sure she was early for tea at the home of Mary Jane Richardson Jones. It was a big, imposing home, with a white stone facade and a dark metal roof. An elaborate carving of an angel had been placed high above the arched doorway, and Ida knew, even before meeting the woman of the house, that she was about to have an encounter unlike any other.

A maid wearing a formal black dress with a crisp white apron let Ida into the house and escorted her to the sitting room, where Mrs. Jones was waiting.

Mary Jane Jones was Chicago royalty. She and her husband were one of the few Black families that had come to the city before the Great Fire of 1871.

She looked like royalty, dressed in a pale cream velvet dress and sitting by a roaring fire. Her hair was in a loose chignon, and girlish tendrils framed her face. Ida was glad she had dressed carefully for the occasion, wearing a lavender and cream checked jacket with a matching skirt.

"I have heard a lot about you, young woman," Mrs. Jones

said in a voice that sounded as sweet as a Southern sunset on the Mississippi, all honey with just a touch of whiskey. "Frederick Douglass wrote to tell me that from Memphis to New York to Great Britain, wherever you go, you make our people proud."

The maid returned with a silver tea set and placed it between the two women. Mrs. Jones poured a cup for Ida and one for herself. Then she gestured to the plate and said, "You must have one of these cookies. They are all the rage in Paris and the only sweets I eat. They are called *cigarettes russes*, and they are nothing but finely crafted butter, egg whites, flour, and sugar, but it took my cook, Elizabeth, almost a year to master the recipe."

Ida tried one of the cookies, which indeed looked like a cigarette. "Oh my stars," she said. It was, quite possibly, the most delicious thing she'd ever eaten.

Mrs. Jones smiled. "I *meant* what I said. Heavenly. So, tell me, now you have come to Chicago, do you intend to make this city your home?"

Ida thought of Ferdinand and where their courting might lead. She liked him, she liked their work together, and she liked Chicago. The East Coast cities she knew—Boston, New York, Washington—were run by powerful Black families who had been doing things their way for a very long time.

Chicago was different. The city was growing, and Ida thought perhaps she might grow with it. It felt like a place where she could lead and shape things, where she wouldn't be expected to merely fall in with the old guard. Which is not to say that Chicago had no gatekeepers. As far as she could tell, Mrs. Jones was the universal key to the city. With her approval, you might do just about anything.

"I take it you have come to ask for my blessing on some sort of enterprise, and I would be most happy to give it, but first let me tell you my story. It matters to me that my new acquaintances understand my journey from the source, not merely what is rumored in the streets."

Ida nodded. She, herself, was no fan of secondhand yarns.

"Like you, I have ties to Memphis. I was born there," Mrs. Jones began. "When I was still a child, my family moved to Alton. In 1841, when I was twenty-one, I married John Jones, a freeman from North Carolina."

Ida nodded and sipped her tea.

"John Jones was a big man, with dark, curly hair and an easy smile," she continued. "He made a promise to me on our wedding day that he would dedicate his life to two things—working hard to give me all the good things he believed I deserved, and that he would work just as hard to topple slavery so that all Black people could have the freedom they deserved.

"We arrived in Chicago in the spring of 1845, eight years after the city was incorporated. We had three dollars to our name. I pawned my father's watch to cover our first two months' rent. We spent that time teaching ourselves to read and write. John used to say that 'reading makes a free man.'

"Life was good to us. John opened a tailoring business, which thrived. There were one hundred fifty Blacks living in Chicago at that time, and we knew all of them. We bought our first home in 1850, and it became the second stop on Chicago's Underground Railroad.

"My husband's tailoring business grew into a business so successful that he had more than two dozen tailors working across four floors of a building that he owned, not rented.

But our real business was freedom. We helped hundreds flee to Canada, and I kept in touch with all those families by letter, making sure that all was well on the other side.

"We were married for nearly forty years, and when my husband died, he left us a fortune that meant I would never want for anything again in this life. But more than the money, he left me the satisfaction of knowing that we had built a life together in service of a dream that was bigger than the two of us."

"Ma'am, you have had the most extraordinary life," Ida said.

"I know it," Mrs. Jones said. "That's why I wanted to tell it to you, so you might know my character and not just the rumors of my wealth and power. I hear you have been seeing Ferdinand Barnett. I expect he will propose."

"Well, ma'am, he has not proposed."

"He will," Mrs. Jones said reassuringly. "I've known that man nearly all his life, and I can tell that you have his heart. After his wife died, he didn't think he had any love left to give away. But you have captured his heart."

"From your lips to God's ears," Ida said softly.

Ida had never met a woman like Mary Jane Jones. She wondered if she might someday occupy the elder woman's chair. Did she flatter herself with such thoughts of power, wealth, and influence? Could it be that she might become one of the legends of the city, braced by accomplishment, gifted with hard-earned wealth, and possessing of the rarest of things, a beauty that did not fade but only deepened like the patina of the fine silver tray that sat between them?

Ida said, "As you may know, a movement of women's clubs is afoot in the nation. In Washington, the descendants of the founding fathers have organized as the Daughters of the American Revolution. In Boston, Josephine St. Pierre Ruffin has founded the Women's Era Club, which is an outgrowth of her wonderful newspaper by and about Black women. These aren't merely opportunities for women to socialize but for us to be a voice in the community and do the kind of work that you and your husband prized so greatly."

"I am intrigued," her host said. "What is your plan?"

"As you know, the men of our community have opened a clubhouse on Dearborn Street called the Tourgée Club. They have designated Thursdays as ladies' day and have offered us the space for meetings. It is my aim to charter a club for Black women there."

"How can I help?"

"Will you, Mrs. Jones, serve as our first chair?" Ida asked plaintively. "Every Black woman in Chicago would jump at the opportunity to join an organization with you in the leadership ranks. Will you consider it?"

Mary Jane Jones smiled. "I will do more than consider it. I will say yes, right now."

From the moment it was chartered, the club was a success, and each week, women poured into the Tourgée Club to hear guest speakers, plan fundraisers, and discuss how they might weigh in on the issues of the day. Whenever friends from England visited Chicago, Ida invited them to the club. One week, the women spent a rousing afternoon with W. T. Stead, the editor of the *Review of Reviews* and a man who came to be known as the most "famous journalist in the British Empire."

The organization, with Mary Jane Jones as its chair, voted to rename itself the Ida B. Wells club, in honor of their founding president, but also as an acknowledgment that Ida's name was synonymous with the kind of social justice work they wanted to support. As Ida would later write, "the most prominent women in church and secret society, schoolteachers, housewives and high school girls crowded our meetings until we had over three hundred enrolled and many new ones at every meeting."

1894

Chapter Fifty-Six

Ida Abroad

On this trip, Ida stayed in an elegant Georgian townhouse on Bloomsbury Square in London. Her host was Peter Clayden, the editor of the *London Daily News.* When she looked out the window, she could see into the former home of Charles Dickens. London had made its mark on her, as she wrote, with "the charm of antiquity and historic association about every part of the city."

She traveled with the imprimatur of the press as well. William Penn Nixon, a white editor of considerable influence, had hired her to write a regular column for his Chicago newspaper, the *Inter-Ocean.* As far as Ida knew, she was the first Black American to file a regular column to a major American newspaper as a foreign correspondent. The column was called Ida B. Wells Abroad.

The Clayden home was only a five-minute walk from the British Museum, but although she passed it every day, Ida had little time for sightseeing. The days were packed with meetings, speeches, interviews with the press, and working on her column.

It was a spring day in April when Keir Hardie met Ida in front of St. Pancras Church near Bloomsbury Square.

Ida had been introduced to Hardie by Catherine Impey, and he had agreed to bring her to Parliament as his guest. Hardie was a labor activist, Scottish born, and now represented the neighborhood of West Ham as their member of Parliament. Ida knew that MPs were like the congressmen and senators back home.

As they walked, he said, "I should warn you, I don't dress like the other MPs."

Ida could only imagine, taking in Hardie's dark tweed suit, workman's cap, and red tie.

When they arrived in Parliament, she could see that Keir Hardie was quite the contrast to the other MPs, who were all dressed in long black coats, starched wing collars, and silk top hats.

Hardie escorted Ida to what was called the gallery for women.

In the balcony, above the Parliamentary floor, the women were allowed to sit and listen to the proceedings, but the "women's gallery" had a screen so the women would not be a distraction to the elected officials, who were, of course, all men.

"I apologize for the screen," Hardie said.

Ida shook her head, remembering the high galleries of the opera house in Memphis. She sat enthralled there for hours as the MPs debated the issues of the day.

She could hear Hardie say, "Any man earning more than a thousand pounds a year should pay a higher rate of income tax. That income would provide funding for us to create pensions so that our elderly do not have to work themselves into the grave and poor children can receive free schooling."

Ida wanted to applaud and nearly did, but the woman seated

next to her put a gloved hand on hers and whispered ever so quietly, "Don't."

After Parliament, Keir Hardie took Ida out to tea. They sat on the terrace of a restaurant on the Thames, and he interviewed her for his newspaper, the *Labor Leader.*

In the weeks that followed, Ida gave dozens of speeches. She told her audiences about the lynching of her friend Tommie and shared data about how lynching was growing as a tool of control, terrorism, and perverse entertainment in an embittered South.

"You are, in this great nation, uniquely poised to help us," Ida told her audiences abroad. "White Americans will not listen to Black citizens. But they will unquestionably heed the voice of the British people."

At each city, Ida found that Ferdinand had a letter waiting for her.

> *Dear Ida,*
>
> *The work you do in the world is vital, but I also know it is exhausting. I hope when you return to the States and Chicago that you will take at least a little time to rest. I know that you were angry at yourself for being moved to tears at the gala in your honor in Brooklyn. But you must allow yourself to feel.*
>
> *You are, despite the breadth of your accomplishments, still young. Strong emotions are arrows in the quiver of youth. Embrace them all—the sadness, the fury, the fear, and the confusion. They shall all be tempered by your courage and intelligence.*

Most affectionately and
kindly yours,
Ferdinand

Ida folded the sheet of paper and held it to her heart, thinking of all the many miles Ferdinand's words had traveled to reach her. *Say what you want about my older man*, she thought. *But he knows how to write a beautiful love letter.* She wrote to him that night.

Dear Ferdinand,

The city of London, or at least the residential portions that I have visited, is a collection of squares. In the middle of each square is a gated garden, and only those who live on the square are granted the treasure that is the key to the garden.

Inside, a world of delights awaits the residents—there are tennis courts and lush, verdant lawns where children play. Ladies read in the shade of trees that have not been tinged with blood on their leaves. Men promenade down gravel paths and do not fear for their safety or reputation.

It seems to me as I walk around these gardens that this is what I am trying to convey in my speeches. We as Blacks in America live a life of precarious so-called freedom. Our men, women, and children, regardless of class or education, are perpetually in danger of the life-threatening rise of terror that lynch law has wrought upon us.

White Americans have the keys to a garden where, so often, they live lives of security and unsuspecting frivolity. We live in the shadows and alleyways. I will not rest until we, too, find what is our God-given right of humanity and a place in the sun.

Yours forever,
Ida

Ida traveled then from London to Liverpool, where in a week's time she would take a ship back to New York, and from there a train back to Chicago. One afternoon, Ida walked around Liverpool with her new friend Charles Aked, the young pastor of Pembroke Chapel, and his wife, Ann. The three of them were just thirty. They were, they felt, both old enough and young enough to change the world.

Charles told Ida that he had visited the World's Fair in Chicago. "I read your account of the lynching of C. J. Miller while sitting in the shadow of the *Statue of the Republic,* the giant sculpture that was the centerpiece of the World's Fair, and wondering how it could be that ending slavery had not led a straight path to peace and equality."

As they walked, he added, "We are still so young, and yet I fear the specter of slavery will overshadow our entire lifetime."

Ida nodded, not wanting it to be true, but knowing how brutal the South had been in its retaliation for Emancipation.

"Liverpool was known as the Gateway to the British Empire," Charles explained. "It was here that the cotton markets thrived. Half of the slave ships that brought slaves to the Americas were built here."

Ida was shocked. "But slavery ended here decades before it did in the US."

"It is true," Ann Aked noted. "And William Gladstone, Liverpool's most beloved native son, came from a family whose wealth was built on the slave trade. But he made the shift from Tory to Liberal. He's been shifting the government toward a more egalitarian agenda. But the work of dismantling caste has hardly begun."

Liverpool's history notwithstanding, Ida marveled at how freely she moved through England—no hiding in the back of opera houses, invitations to dine side by side with the most elite white citizens every night. It was not perfect. She was not naive. She knew she was an invited guest of some renown from abroad, but the freedom she felt poured into her a quiet kind of joy at being alive, the kind she had not felt since before Tommie's lynching had blown her life in Memphis apart.

In her next column, she wrote:

> It is like being born into another world, to be welcomed among persons of the highest order of intellectual and societal culture as if one were one of themselves.
>
> Here, a "colored" person can ride in any sort of conveyance without being insulted, stop at any hotel, or be accommodated at any restaurant one wishes without being refused with contempt. I can wander into any picture gallery, lecture room, concert hall, theater or church and receive the most courteous treatment from officers and fellow sightseers.

Chapter Fifty-Seven

The Modern Joan of the Race

Ida returned to the United States with a renewed energy and focus from her second speaking tour in Britain. She wanted every city to form an anti-lynching committee, with an executive leadership board formed of men and women, dedicated to raising awareness, pushing for legislation, and soliciting donations for the national movement. The Executive Anti-Lynching Committee would be based in Brooklyn, and they would distribute funds, including, most importantly, the hiring of professional investigators, such as the Pinkerton detective agency, to look into as many of the killings as possible and provide evidence that could be used in legal proceedings.

The *Indianapolis Freeman* had called her "the modern Joan of her race," and many believed that, among her generation, only she had taken up the mantle of Frederick Douglass's work with the ferocity and disregard for playing by the rules of polite society that the Sage of Anacostia had shown in his early years.

After a brief stop in Chicago, Ida headed east, where she gave sold-out speeches to mostly white audiences. Her biggest win came when a white senator, Henry Blair of New Hampshire, called upon Congress to set aside $25,000 to investigate lynching on a national level by professional detectives, in just the same way that Ida had specified. Blair did not credit Ida when he put the resolution forward, but she—and the Black community—took such unprecedented actions as a sign that Ida's campaign was working.

By August 1894, however, Ida was exhausted. She was only thirty-two, but there were days and nights when she felt much older. "Working for the cause will do it to you," Josephine St. Pierre Ruffin had said to her when Ida had tried to discreetly take off her shoes at a dinner in Boston. She had spent months walking the city streets and trawling the dust roads in rural towns, searching down the true stories behind every lynching. So much death. It made her heart hurt. When she first decided to take on lynching and to report the stories as Philip Bell at the *Elevator* had implored her to, to "report the facts without a tinge of personal supplication or subjectivity," she didn't expect how much of a toll the work would take on her feet or how her whole body would ache.

She wrote to her readers in the *New York Age* that she was going to take a month-long break and would return to her national speaking tour in the fall. What she didn't say was how disheartened she was by how all of her hard work to start anti-lynching committees had stalled. Her efforts at fundraising had largely failed. It seemed like people were happy to have her come and speak, offering to cover her travel expenses and, increasingly, a small speaking fee. But getting individuals and racial-justice groups to invest in her campaign was proving hard.

She had traveled back and forth to England, and traversed the East Coast: The need for rest was real. But she was also not interested in having the weight of the movement rest solely on her shoulders. As she said in one speech during this period: "There remains a part for every man, woman, and child to do in this fight for equality and justice. It must not be said that eight million people have left the work of defending the race to one person. I have the same faith that I always had in my race that when it fully knows its duty, it will perform it."

Chapter Fifty-Eight

Harbor

One afternoon in August 1894, Ferdinand said to Ida, "Let us leave work early and take a trolley-car ride. Summer will be over before we know it. We should enjoy ourselves before another Chicago winter is upon us."

Ida had no objection. She had been writing letters in an attempt to secure donations for a national anti-lynching committee, but the work of raising money was exhausting. "I'd like nothing more than to call it a day," Ida said, putting her pen down and reaching for her purse.

As they rode the streetcar, Ida and Ferdinand talked and laughed. Times were getting harder for Black people, but when they were alone, they put down talk of lynching and fighting the good fight. Ida, ever the intrepid reporter, had an ear for accents and never failed to make Ferdinand laugh with her impersonations. "I shall allow no man to belittle my soul by making me hate him," she said, in a deep, sonorous bass, with a pitch-perfect rendition of Booker T. Washington's Virginia drawl.

They were laughing so much that Ida didn't notice they had traveled all the way to the northern breakwater.

"Let us walk along the harbor," Ferdinand said, reaching for Ida's hand.

They walked together along the waterfront. The lake was so big you could not see where it ended. It reminded Ida of standing at the pier in Brooklyn or Liverpool, staring out at miles and miles of splashing waves, and the way it made her feel joyous and hopeful, as if her life still might contain oceans of possibilities.

"Oh, look at the lighthouse!" Ida said.

The Chicago Harbor Lighthouse had been constructed just the year before for the World's Fair. Ida had passed it dozens of times as she went back and forth to the fair. But she had been too busy for most of the summer to just stand and take in its beauty.

"Isn't she something?" Ida said, squeezing Ferdinand's hand. "I'm glad you brought me here."

The building was white with a red roof, and its tower stood nearly seventy feet high. The waves lapped all around it, and Ida could only imagine the feeling of safety it provided to sailors traveling through the most tempestuous of storms.

"Let's get a closer look," Ferdinand said.

As they approached the lighthouse door, a man came out.

"Ferdinand Barnett," he said, grasping his hand in a firm shake.

"Samuel Parker, I'd like to introduce you to the one and only Ida B. Wells."

"It's an honor, ma'am," he said. "I relieve the lighthouse keeper on Fridays. Would you like to come in and take a look around?"

"I would like to go all the way to the top," Ida said intrepidly.

"That can be arranged," Samuel said, inviting them in and pointing them to a spiral staircase. "Visitors aren't typically allowed in here because of the importance of protecting the navigational devices. So please don't share that you were here with anyone."

Ida and Ferdinand nodded. Ferdinand climbed the steps with a sprightly speed. But by the time she got to the top, Ida was out of breath.

"It's a long way up," Ferdinand said, reaching to help her out onto the top platform of the lighthouse.

"Oh my," she said, retrieving a handkerchief from her purse and dabbing the sweat off of her forehead. "This climb has me feeling most unladylike."

"Never," Ferdinand said. "You are the perfect picture of womanhood at all times."

Ida smiled, then looked out at the harbor.

"The city has never looked more beautiful," she said. "Everywhere you look, it is nothing but sky and sea."

Samuel said, "Enjoy the view. I need to take care of a quick matter, but I will be back to escort you down in ten minutes or so."

Ferdinand said, "Ida, I brought you to this place because I wanted to be as close to heaven as possible when I asked you this question."

Ida's heart fluttered. She was not so much shocked by the proposal as moved by the exquisite beauty of the setting and all the romance Ferdinand had poured into the planning.

"Ida B. Wells," he said, "will you marry me?"

"I will," she said softly.

He kissed her then with a passion that was more driving

than any other time he had kissed her before. She would be his wife. Their lives would be intertwined, and she would never be alone again.

"I know that to ask you to turn your attentions to being the lady of the house would not only be futile but a grievous misuse of the gifts you have to share with the world," Ferdinand said. "But I brought you here because I wanted you to know that you can and should sail away as much as you must. It is my hope that you will come to see our marriage as a lighthouse, your safe harbor in every storm."

She turned from him then and did the thing she never expected to do when a man offered his hand in marriage. She wept.

Ferdinand put his arms around her, and she rested her head on his chest.

Looking up at him, she said, "I love you, Ferdinand."

"Well," he said playfully, "this may be the first and last time I have you beat, because I loved you first."

1895

Chapter Fifty-Nine

A Radical

Ida gazed at her second publication, the *Red Record.* It was her attempt to show—literally by the numbers—how lynching was operating across the country. A more ambitious booklet than *Southern Horrors*, it reflected all she'd learned as a journalist. The work featured carefully gathered statistics, photographs, and reported accounts of crimes. It had cost Ida everything she had—in time, money, and energy. But she needed it to be a substantive work because in the near future, for a while at least, she would no longer be able to travel the country on the kind of reporting expeditions that had been the focus of her life for so long.

Ferdinand had proposed, and Ida had accepted. He had two children of his own, but he had made it clear that he wanted to have a family with Ida. She had never felt particularly called to motherhood. But Ida loved her intended, and the thought of having a child with him felt like hope. Hope that things could get better, that her children and their children might live lives where lynching felt like a far and distant thing, a ghost story of a past generation that feels frightening but a little untrue. Holding the copy of the *Red Record*, she thought of something she heard the minister say in church a few weeks before. He said, "Babies are our most powerful answer to death." His words had stayed with Ida. She didn't love babies, but Lord knows she had seen too much death.

She knew her work and the work of the many Black newspapers that had taken on the cause of lynching were having an impact. The number of lynchings had dropped by 15 percent from the previous year. The number of lynching victims accused of rape had dropped by 40 percent. The crimes were still happening, but the old excuses were no longer widely accepted. Ida was proud of that. As she wrote in the introduction to the *Red Record*, "The student of American sociology will find the year 1894 marked by a pronounced awakening of the public conscience to a system of anarchy and outlawry."

Each time a speaking engagement was offered, she felt compelled to accept. In March, she traveled to Rochester to the First Baptist Church.

Upon her arrival, she saw that the *Rochester Union and Advertiser*, the local paper, declared her a failure on the lecture circuit. She was, simply, "too radical."

The words stung partly because she knew that this was an opinion shared by many of her peers. They supported her at a distance, but Mollie Church Terrell and Josephine St. Pierre Ruffin managed to be both prominent women on the upper-class circuit and active club women. A more conservative wave had taken over the Black leadership, and there was no small amount of ambition for Black Americans to join the more prosperous ranks of the Gilded Age.

Ida did not have a fancy degree or a fancy home. She did

not throw elegant dinners and rarely attended formal functions. The work she did, reporting on lynching, giving speeches about its bloody, brutal, inner workings, was not the epitome of the Victorian ideal. It was dangerous, and messy, and always brought her to the edge of what might be called proper, ladylike behavior.

On the way home from Rochester, Ida read an article in the *Women's Era* by Rosa Dixon Bowser in which the author wrote, "Race progress is the direct outgrowth of individual success in life. The race rises as the individuals rise and the individuals rise with the race."

Ida sighed. It wasn't that she hadn't tried to rise in her fortunes. She had hoped that there would be more support from her community for her anti-lynching work. Susan B. Anthony had been gifted an eight-hundred-dollar annuity by the suffrage community for her many years of service. Ida had worked so hard, but she had so little to show for it. She needed, she wanted, to get off the lecture circuit. She needed to put the *Red Record* down. She wanted love and a home and some ease in her days.

When she arrived at the station in Chicago, Ferdinand was waiting for her, as he always was. He took her bag and kissed her on the forehead.

"Good trip?" he asked.

She just closed her eyes and lay her head against his overcoat.

Then she looked at him and said, "Enough with my Joan of the Race shenanigans. Let's set a date for the wedding. I want to be your wife. As soon as possible."

Chapter Sixty

Ida's Wedding Day

Ida had said she wanted to marry Ferdinand "as soon as possible" but soon was not in the cards. A series of postponements brought about by speaking opportunities for Ida pushed the wedding back month after month.

Ida quickly realized that part of postponing the wedding was tied to how little desire she had to plan a wedding. Luckily, the members of the Ida B. Wells Club were more than happy to step in, and a date was agreed upon—June 27, 1895. All Ida had to do was say yes or no. This church or that one. This meal for supper or that one. They made it so easy for her after a year that had been so, so hard.

The invitation read:

THE I.B.W. WOMEN'S CLUB
INVITE YOU TO THE MARRIAGE OF THEIR PRESIDENT
IDA B. WELLS
TO
FERDINAND LEE BARNETT

Bethel AME Church

Thursday, June 27, 1895

8 pm

Reception: 2465 Wabash Avenue, 8:30 pm

The weight of family was something the couple felt deeply. Ferdinand had two sons from his first marriage, and both of his parents lived with him. A few days before the wedding, Ida and Ferdinand went to the cemetery together to put flowers on his first wife's grave.

Ida saw him tear up and worried that she could never take the place of a woman who, by all accounts, had been extraordinary in life and had become saintly in death. She told him as much.

"It's not that," Ferdinand said. "It's just that for so long, I carried on my shoulders a mountain of grief. It was crippling. In those first years, I could barely get out of bed some days."

He stood from the grave and walked Ida out of the cemetery.

"I met you," he continued. "And I started to feel excitement, just for being alive, for the first time in a long time. That excitement turned into possibility, then joy, then love. Surely God has blessed me more than I deserve. But I also feel this sense of worry that if I don't hold on to a little bit of that weight, the loneliness and sadness, then she will be lost to me, forever."

Ida looked at him—this kind, lovely man she was about to marry. "I do not know exactly how you feel," she said. "But when I lost my parents, I was sixteen, more a girl than a woman. I used to think the only way to honor that loss was by protecting the cannon-size hole in my heart. But little by little I started thinking of their spirits as lights I carry in my heart, embers that warm me and guide me from the inside out."

"That is beautiful, Ida."

"I will never replace your wife," she said. "I would never seek to extinguish the flame you and your boys will carry for her, forever. Just let her be a light, Ferdinand. A light we both know that time will never diminish."

He held her then and thanked God, as he had every day since he had proposed, that Ida B. Wells would soon be his wife.

Nine hundred well-wishers crowded into the AME Bethel Church for the ceremony. The choice of the church was, in and of itself, a political statement by the couple. Bethel was architecturally stunning, but it was on the poorer side of town. Quinn Chapel, on the fancier Wabash Avenue, would have been a more expected choice for the local celebrities.

Guests came from as far away as California and New York. Ida's Memphis friends filled the pews, including Florence Cooper, Tommie Moss's sister-in-law.

Speculation as to whether Ida would *ever* marry had been a recurring topic of editorials in the Black newspapers. The *Women's Era* had written in an editorial that verged on catty:

> **The public has become so interested in the unique career of Miss Wells that her determination to marry a man while still married to a cause will be a topic of national interest and comment.**

But the day had come, and the afternoon edition of the *New York Times* carried the news of the wedding on its front page:

> **Miss Ida B. Wells, the colored woman who gained international publicity by her anti-lynching lectures**

> in England, was married in Bethel Church tonight to Ferdinand L. Barnett, a local colored attorney of prominence who is the publisher of the *Conservator* and president of the Illinois Anti-Lynching League.

The wedding was supposed to start at 8 PM, but the crowds outside the church were all intent on greeting the couple. Ida would later remark, "The streets were so packed with humanity that it was almost impossible for the carriage bearing the wedding bridal party to reach the church door."

Finally, when it was confirmed that the bride and groom were indeed in the building, the organ began to play a favorite hymn, "Call Me Thine Own," followed by the wedding march. A flower girl with a basket of fresh petals began the procession. Ida's sisters, Lily and Annie, followed, dressed in lemon crepe dresses and crisp white gloves. The groomsmen were the staff of the *Conservator*, and the best man was the paper's editor, R. P. Bird. The bride, thirty-two, wore a white satin gown trimmed with chiffon and orange blossoms. The groom, forty-three, wore a crisp, new suit and a lovestruck sweet smile.

As she walked down the aisle, Ida remembered advice that Frederick Douglass had given her when he first met Ferdinand. "Be careful with each other," he said. "So you can be a force for good together." It saddened her that he had died just months before her wedding day. What it would have meant to have him in the church to bless the union. He had been, in ways big and small, the closest thing to a father figure she'd had since her own father had passed.

When they finally made it to the altar, Ida looked at Ferdinand and felt the weight of all their particular histories as a foundation to their union. When Ida had been a young teacher, she watched her peers get married. At twenty-two, twenty-three, twenty-four—they had been old enough for the institution, but were still very young people, like dolls come to life, learning how to play house.

Ida believed that what she and Ferdinand shared was a grown-up love—with equal parts passion and practicality. They had both been bruised and battered by the world. Ida's anti-lynching campaign meant that she had come face-to-face, a hundred times or more, with the kind of sadistic violence and devastating cruelty that she would seriously consider giving up a limb to unsee and unknow.

Ferdinand had also, in his own way, reckoned with death up close. Unable to save his young wife, he had undertaken the mission of saving the world, or as much of it as he could from his perch as a lawyer and newspaper publisher in Chicago.

Like soldiers coming home from a war, they had shown each other their wounds without shame or fear of rejection. In the days of their courting, the joy they found in each other's company made them believe that, while they were each fractured in places, they were not at all broken beyond repair. They knew the worst about each other and still decided there was plenty left to love.

So when the minister declared them man and wife and the church cried out, "Amen! Amen!" Ida looked up at Ferdinand and whispered, "Okay, husband."

In response he said, "Okay, you little wisp of a thing."

Because when they said, "I do," what they meant was, "I got you."

It was a promise they would both keep all of their days, no matter what life threw at them: I got you. I got you. I got you.

Coda
LOVE

The new century brought with it—for Ida and for the nation—a two-steps-forward, one-step-back march toward civil rights. Ida and Ferdinand had four children—Charles Aked, named after the British progressive minister who had been her host in Liverpool and became a dear friend; Herman; then Ida Bell Jr.; and Alfreda Marguerita.

Along with raising four children, without household help, Ida became the editor of the *Conservator* and continued as president of the Ida B. Wells Club, the largest Black women's organization outside New York and Washington, DC. She was so often underpaid and exhausted, but wherever she saw a need for the community, she moved to fill it. When, for example, she realized that there were no proper kindergartens for Black children in Chicago, she worked with young graduates of the teachers' colleges to fund and found the first one.

Yet she was constantly criticized for prioritizing family alongside her civic work. Upon visiting the home of Susan B. Anthony with her young son Charles, the great women's rights leader called Ida "distracted" by motherhood. Anthony even went so far as to say that, while she thought the institution of marriage was fine for *some* women, Ida had chosen poorly in deciding to become a wife because Anthony believed that Ida "had a special call for special work." For Ida, the backhanded compliment about her being "special" was hurtful. She noted that not only had Anthony never married, she also lived off a generous allowance provided to her by donors—the kind of rich financial support that Ida never had.

In 1895, a book called *The College of Life* named Ida as one of the four most important race leaders of the next generation, the heirs to Frederick Douglass. But as the new century approached, she would find herself ostracized by the Black elite. When the National Association of Colored Women's Clubs held their convention in Chicago, Mary Church Terrell, the organization's president, did not invite Ida to be part of the program. In her autobiography, Ida called this "a staggering blow."

By the early 1900s, she sometimes found herself pushed to the sidelines. She was part of the "founding forty," whose work led to the founding of the National Association for the Advancement of Colored People, also known as the NAACP. But she would play no leadership role in the organization and was passed over for the editorship of the organization's publication, the *Crisis*, in favor of W. E. B. Du Bois, who was fresh off of publishing his groundbreaking book *The Souls of Black Folk*.

Ida pushed on. In 1913, she founded the Alpha Suffrage Club with two white women suffragists, Virginia Brooks and Belle Squire. It was the first suffrage club for Black women in Chicago.

Later that year, the day before the presidential inauguration of Woodrow Wilson, Alice Paul planned a suffrage parade down Pennsylvania Avenue. Ida arrived in Washington with a delegation of sixty-two from Illinois. The organizers of the march, fearful of offending their southern contingent, decided that Black women should march in the back.

Ida discussed the matter with a reporter from the *Chicago Tribune.* Fighting back tears, she said, "If the Illinois women do not take a stand now in this great democratic parade, then the colored women are lost. When I was asked to come down here, I was asked to march with the other women of our state and I intend to do so or not take part in the parade at all."

The next day, five thousand women lined up along Pennsylvania Avenue. The Illinois contingent arrived, but Ida was nowhere to be found. The march began, and out of the crowd, Ida walked up to her states' delegation and took her place next to her white Alpha Suffrage Club friends, Virginia and Belle. While many were shocked, no one questioned her or dared to stop her. The March 5 issue of the *Tribune* featured a huge photo of the three women—Ida, Virginia, and Belle—smiling, arm in arm, with suffrage sashes across their dresses.

She was fifty-eight when women got the vote, and immediately set about using that power to change the political landscape in Chicago. For years, the people of Chicago had sought to elect a Black candidate to city government. As she told the *Chicago Defender,* "The men have made several attempts to elect an alderman. They failed but we, the women, will succeed."

Ida organized a group of one hundred members of the Alpha Suffrage Club to work on the campaign of an aspiring alderman that she called "our young giant, Oscar De Priest." At Ida and her teams' urging, "club women and church women" showed up and out at the poll, many of them casting a vote for the first time. With the support of Ida and her crew, De Priest won his election by a stunning 25 percent margin.

In 1928, Ida began writing her autobiography, *Crusade for Justice.* In it, she described her path to journalism—her anti-lynching campaign, her encounters with the great men and women of her era. She tried to capture how she had been called to push past fear into bravery because she refused to let lynching carry on, unchecked, in the shadows: "I'd rather go down in history as the one lone Negro who dared to tell the government that it had done a dastardly thing than to save my skin by taking back what I have said."

What she didn't write about in her autobiography was her early Memphis days—the dreams she had of being a novelist and what great friends books had been to her throughout her life. She wrote little about her love for Shakespeare and how she thrilled to perform theatrical monologues in costume at the Lyceum.

She didn't think it was important to write about her horseback riding adventures and how she loved beautiful clothes, almost to a fault. She didn't mention how nights at the opera and twirling around elegant ballrooms brought her so much happiness.

We live life forward and understand it backward. Surely Ida understood by the gray-haired days of her life that her innocence was stolen from her twice. Once, when she was sixteen, when the yellow fever epidemic took both of her parents and made her an orphan with four younger siblings in her charge. And then again at twenty-nine, when Tommie Moss was lynched at the Curve and a whole city was robbed of joy and hope and faith as life as they knew it changed forever.

Even as she aged and weakened, she dreamed that her legacy might be the generations of Black men and women who would one day build upon the base she had built—first in Memphis, then in Chicago.

In the end, Ida wished she could have left her children more: more money, more security, more of a standing among the Black elite. But the century was still young and the story of her people was still unwritten.

Sometimes, when she closed her eyes, she could imagine being twenty-five again. Tommie Moss would be selling bread and fruit at the People's Grocery. There would be dances and games of checkers and Parcheesi. Memphis might still be the New City, and the dreams she and her friends had might be, similarly, still new.

She could not hide the way it hurt—all the ways in which she was left out and diminished by her own people. Jane Austen once said, "I do not want people to be very agreeable as it saves me the trouble of liking them a great deal." Ida thought she knew something of what the author might mean. Ida believed in community—and the nation. But individuals, with rare exception, so often disappointed her.

At twenty-three, she told the *Memphis Appeal* that she might be a journalist, a physician, or an actress. She made good on the dream of being a journalist, and the light she shone saved lives and reinforced the tenet that journalism, the gathering of data, the relentless pursuit of facts, was a powerful weapon against injustice.

She was not, as it turned out, much of an actress. She rarely hid her impatience, her rage, her frustration, or her pride. She was too strong for proper society and just mighty enough to do the dirty work of investigating the systemic practice of murder as a form of retaliation when so many of her Victorian peers would decry the issue but not put themselves in harm's way. Hers was not an age of girl power and womanism. She did not know that it was her daughter, and then her granddaughter, and then her granddaughter's daughter, who would fight for her legacy. She could not have imagined the scores of journalists—men and women, Black and white and others—who would claim her as foremother, ancestor, and inspiration.

In 2020, she was awarded a posthumous Pulitzer Prize for "her outstanding and courageous reporting on the horrific and vicious violence against African Americans during the era of lynching."

On March 29, 2022, President Joe Biden and Vice President Kamala Harris signed the Emmett Till Antilynching Act into law. More than one hundred years after Ida and lawyers and activists like Thomas Cassells first proposed it. Ida's great-granddaughter Michelle Duster spoke at the ceremony on Ida's behalf.

Ida B. Wells did the best she could with what she had, and then she took the scraps of resources, energy, and insight that were left at the end of each backbreaking day and did more. She did it for the people because that was how Jim and Lizzie Wells had taught her to show up. She did it because she was, as Susan B. Anthony said, a woman with a special calling and the gifts, grit, and grace to accomplish what had never been done before. But from her earliest days in Holly Springs to her halcyon days in Memphis to the house of political power she built in Chicago, the thing that fueled her and focused her was always, always love.

Author's Note

This book owes the greatest debt to writer and historian Paula Giddings, who changed my life not once, but twice. The first time was when I read *When and Where I Enter: The Impact of Black Women on Race and Sex in America* in college, and I remember just weeping throughout, overwhelmed by the depth and complexity of a history I'd never been taught. That was my introduction to Ida. Then Professor Giddings published *Ida: A Sword Among Lions: Ida B. Wells and the Campaign Against Lynching,* and I knew that I would love Ida forever. Several other books influenced this novel—you'll see them in the Sources and Further Reading section—but *A Sword Among Lions* is chief among them.

Ida began to come alive for me when I read *The Memphis Diary of Ida B. Wells: An Intimate Portrait of the Activist as a Young Woman,* edited by Miriam DeCosta-Wills. It was Ida, in her own words, talking about things she would gloss over decades later in her autobiography: love letters and pretty dresses, parties, friendships, her early ambitions, and her love of opera and the theater.

I should say that this is not so much a biography of Ida B. Wells as a novelistic snapshot of the young woman she was and the formidable investigative journalist and activist she would become. I didn't focus on every aspect of Ida's life, but I leaned into the relationships and moments that fascinated me—her working relationship with T. Thomas Fortune, her friendship with Frederick Douglass, her romances, and her writing career, as well as the time she spent abroad in England. During her second trip to England, she wrote a series of columns called Ida Abroad, and they can be found in a volume edited by Ida's formidable great-granddaughter, the writer Michelle Duster.

Throughout, it is helpful to remember that this is a work of fiction inspired by a dizzying array of facts. The diary, which primarily covers Ida's early years as a teacher—1885 through 1887—informed the first part of this novel, though I have taken a good deal of creative license with the time line as well as the creation and expansion of characters in her Memphis community. Ida's life was jam-packed with events, people, and romantic suitors; I've played with time so that we can get to know and become invested in a handful of them rather than wade through a deluge of names.

I quote from *The Memphis Diary* throughout this novel; however, I wrote all the letters. For inspiration, I pored through dozens of Victorian love letters and read a number of articles about the conventions of correspondence in the late nineteenth century. A book called *Searching the Heart: Women, Men, and Romantic Love in Nineteenth-Century America*, by Karen Lystra, helped me understand why the love letters Ida sent and received were so important to her.

There are also several quotes from Ida's own autobiography, *Crusade for Justice: The Autobiography of Ida B. Wells.* It didn't make sense to rewrite her when she had captured the dialogue so perfectly.

A few other details worth mentioning: As far as I know, Lewis Latimer never went to Memphis, and he and Ida may have never met. But once I realized they were contemporaries, I felt compelled to bring them together.

Similarly, it is unclear whether W. E. B. Du Bois and Ida corresponded in those early years, but as he was a student and an editor at the *Fisk Herald*, where she published work, I imagined a scenario where they might have connected earlier than their known twentieth-century interactions.

Finally, the Fisk Jubilee Singers were actually in Australia during the summer of 1887 while Ida was at the National Education Association in Topeka, but I felt that the historic interracial conference of teachers needed a song, so I teleported the choir into the novel.

It is easy to admire Ida B. Wells-Barnett as a champion of social justice. When she was posthumously awarded a Pulitzer Prize in 2020, the committee cited "her outstanding and courageous reporting on the horrific and vicious violence against African Americans during the era of lynching." But I wanted to write a novel about the Ida that I found in her diary, in all her brave, determined, witty, joy-filled, loving complexity. It's my deepest hope that this book is the breath of life for Ida the young woman versus Ida, the icon, in the same way that the Memphis Lyceum and steeping herself in theater and literature was a "breath of life" for Ida all those years ago.

Acknowledgments

I've dreamed of writing a historical novel for a very long time. I'm grateful to my coach, Caroline Kim Oh, who always says, "I keep receipts on your dreams." Thank you for pulling focus and for helping me, week by week, organize the time and space to do the work.

I love working with my editor, Margaret Raymo. Merci for saying yes to me and Ida. Thanks to the team at Little, Brown Books for Young Readers, including Roddyna Saint-Paul, Jake Regier, and Patrick Hulse, and to the copy editor, Logan Hill, and the amazing proofreaders, Lara Stelmaszyk and Carla Jablonski. Thank you for all your good catches.

I'm so grateful to Kimberly Witherspoon, Jessica Mileo, and my agents at Anonymous Content, Kassie Evashevski and Emma Gobillot.

Rachel Bowie and Nate Barksdale provided invaluable research and close reads. My mom, Cecilia Ortega, is an amazing first reader and an eagle-eyed copy editor. Gracias a ti, Mom. The Paris Bash WhatsApp group is such a lifeline; they can be counted on for cheers, outrage, and so much joy.

Jason and Flora Clampet make everything possible. You are the contours of my heart.

Finally, I want to thank Ida B. Wells for the bravery, tenacity, talent, and vision it took for her to craft such a big, powerful life. My novel captures only a fraction of it. The years I have spent in the company of Ida's words and her writing have been some of the most joyful of my life.

I loved writing this book. I hope you've enjoyed reading it.

Notable Figures

In her lifetime, Ida interacted with dozens of important figures. I've included here short biographies of twelve of the ones who play significant roles in this book.

J. Dallas Bowser

James Dallas Bowser was a prominent figure in the fight for equality and opportunity after Reconstruction. A high school principal and active member of the Republican Party in Kansas City, Missouri, he joined the *Gate City Press* in 1880, and under his leadership, it became one of the most influential African American papers in the nation. He was an early supporter of Ida's work and tried to get her to move to Kansas City to be both a teacher and an editor at his paper, which published her writing often. As Irvine Garland Penn wrote in *The Afro-American Press and Its Editors,* "Mr. Bowser pursues a line of duty in his writings as editor which he regards as right, without fear or favor." Penn also noted that Bowser was a "fierce antagonist of quacks, humbugs, and political mountebanks."

Blanche K. Bruce

Born enslaved and educated at Oberlin, Blanche Kelso Bruce became the first African American to serve a full term in the US Senate, serving for Mississippi from 1875 to 1881. He was part of a rare wave of Black elected officials following the Civil

War. It's estimated that two thousand Black citizens held office in the nation during Reconstruction, serving at all levels: local, state, and federal. When Rutherford B. Hayes removed federal troops from the South, protections for Black Americans vanished almost overnight and states began to implement what would become Jim Crow laws, which severely restricted Black Americans' right to vote. Bruce held several public offices, including Register of the Treasury, after his term in the Senate. In Washington, DC, Bruce was considered one of the most influential members of the Black elite. Ida was not a fan. In 1892, she chastised Bruce and his cohort of elected officials for doing too little for their people, writing, "A few big offices and the control of a little Federal patronage is not sufficient recompense for the lives lost, the blood shed, and the rights denied the race." Of Bruce, in particular, she stated in an editorial that he had "never uttered a protest, sought to arouse public sentiment against such outrages nor exerted himself for his people at any time save when he wanted their votes to save his job."

Robert Church

Robert Reed Church, of Memphis, was known in his lifetime as the first Black millionaire in the South. His mother, Emmeline, was Black, and his father, Captain Charles B. Church, was a white steamship owner. After his mother's death, Church worked as a steward on his father's ship, meeting many of the prominent white southerners who would help him in his future endeavors. He would go on to own a number of businesses on Beale Street. Helping African Americans gain access to entrepreneurship and homeownership was one of the tenets of his activism, and once, despite knowing Ida only on reputation, he responded to a letter she sent with a substantial cash loan. In 1906, he became cofounder and president of Solvent Savings Bank, the first Black-owned bank in Memphis. He was married three times and was the father of Mary Church Terrell, who would go on to become a prominent activist in her own right.

Frederick Douglass

Few individuals left as big a mark on the United States in the nineteenth century as Frederick Douglass. Born enslaved, he gained renown as a gifted orator and powerful writer, and his books, speeches, and deft political strategy played a critical role in the abolition of slavery. He joined the abolitionist movement in 1841, right around the time that photography became prominent in everyday life in America. Douglass believed that photography, in its verisimilitude, was a powerful combatant to centuries of illustrated racist stereotypes and caricatures. He is often referred to as the most photographed American of the nineteenth century.

Douglass was also a prominent supporter of women's rights. He was one of the thirty-two men to sign the Declaration of Sentiments at the Seneca Falls Convention, the first women's rights convention, in 1848. The last speech he gave, more than forty years later, was in support of women's voting rights.

Beginning in 1845, Douglass spent nineteen months in England, bringing the case against slavery to a global audience. And it was his influence that led to Ida being invited to England to make the case against lynching, first in 1893 and then again in 1894. The friendship between Ida and Douglass came at a critical time in her young career. But Ida was meaningful to Douglass as well. As David Blight writes in *Frederick Douglass:*

Prophet of Freedom, "Sometime in the summer of 1892, he finally met Ida B. Wells, striking up an activist friendship that would animate his remaining years." Ida always gave as good as she got, and as Blight explains, "From their first encounter, she saw Douglass as a heroic model, but one she felt safe in criticizing as well as adoring."

W. E. B. Du Bois

William Edward Burghardt Du Bois was one of the most important public intellectuals of the first half of the twentieth century. Born in 1868 in Great Barrington, Massachusetts, he did his undergraduate work at Fisk University, in Tennessee, where he worked as an editor for the *Fisk Herald*, one of the many publications Ida wrote for. He went on to become the first Black person to be awarded a doctorate at Harvard. In 1903, he published an essay called "The Talented Tenth," in which he posited that "the Negro race, like all races, is going to be saved by its exceptional men." While Du Bois's activism placed him in opposition to the conservative Booker T. Washington, he increasingly found Ida to be too radical in both her writing and her public stances. He was the editor of the NAACP's *Crisis* and the author of a number of important works, including *The Souls of Black Folk.*

T. Thomas Fortune

Timothy Thomas Fortune was the editor of a New York newspaper that was called the *Freeman* when Ida first began writing for it and later became the *New York Age.* Although never formally educated, he trained at newspapers in Florida, where he grew up. In New York, he gained a nationwide reputation as a gifted editor who had no tolerance for the rumor-mongering and sensationalism that were often used to sell papers at a time when a glut of publications made profitability challenging. By the time of his death, he was known as the dean of African American journalism. He was instrumental in Ida's career, seeing her talent early and encouraging her transition from early essays such as "Woman's Mission" to the powerful piece that began her investigative reporting career, "The Truth About Lynching."

Keir Hardie

James Keir Hardie was born in Scotland to parents who were so poor that he was forced to begin working to help feed the family at the age of seven. He worked at a bakery, as a messenger, and in a shipyard. By the age of ten, he was the main source of income for his family, and he took a job in a mine, opening and closing the ventilation doors. As a teenager, determined not to spend his life in mines, he taught himself to read and write and joined a well-respected local church, the Evangelical Union. The public speaking he did on behalf of the church and the temperance movement eventually led him to London, where he became a prominent spokesperson for working-class people. In 1892, he became the first member of the Labour Party to win a seat in Parliament. In 1894, during Ida's second visit to England, he invited her to Parliament as his guest. More than a hundred years later, the labor movement continues to be a major force in UK politics.

Catherine Impey

Catherine Impey was born in 1847, on an apple farm in Somerset, England, to a distinguished Quaker family. In 1888, she founded *Anti-Caste*, Britain's first publication focused on the battle against racism. As she was close to her American Quaker relatives in Philadelphia, Impey decided that the journal would focus on both the struggle of African Americans in the United States as well as people who suffered subjugation because of race across the British Empire, particularly in India. With nearly two thousand copies in print each month, *Anti-Caste* brought to the forefront issues that many of the leading papers failed to cover. Encouraged by Frederick Douglass, Impey invited Ida to England in 1893 and again in 1894.

Lewis Latimer

Lewis Howard Latimer was born in 1848 to enslaved parents who escaped to freedom. An early job at a patent firm helped him hone his skills for mechanical drawing. It was at that firm that he began to develop his first inventions: a bathroom unit that could operate on railroad cars and an early prototype of the modern air conditioner. In 1876, while working with Alexander Graham Bell, Latimer used his skills as a draftsman to draw the blueprints for Bell's patent of the telephone. Four years later, Latimer joined the US Electric Lighting Company. There, he developed a carbon filament that made the light-bulb prototypes of that era longer lasting and more affordable. He then joined Thomas Edison at the Edison Electric Light Company in 1880 as both an engineer and a member of the legal team working on patents.

Mary Jane Richardson Jones

In her autobiography, Ida refers to Mary Jane Richardson Jones by her husband's name, Mrs. John Jones. But the woman herself led an extraordinary life. She was an active operative on the Underground Railroad during the Civil War, and she became president of the Colored Ladies' Freedmen's Aid Society of Chicago. This organization helped raise money and supplies for the families of Black soldiers during the war. After her husband's death, Jones became a leader in the Black women's club movement, helping Ida found the first club in Chicago (which would quickly rename itself the Ida B. Wells Club). She also took up the mantle of suffrage, organizing with Ida, Susan B. Anthony, and Carrie Chapman Catt. Jones died in 1910, just ten years before American women would win the right to vote.

William Still

In his time, William Still was heralded as the father of the Underground Railroad, but today he is far less known than his contemporaries, such as Frederick Douglass and Harriet Tubman. Still began his career as a clerk at the Pennsylvania Anti-Slavery Society; later, he and his wife made their home an important stop on the Underground Railroad. But Still's prominence in the movement came not from giving speeches like Douglass or Tubman but from maintaining a powerful clandestine network that went from Philadelphia to New York and New Jersey, through New England, and across Canada, helping Black people to freedom. Having found his own long-lost brother early in his work, Still kept careful records of who traveled the railroad and where, with the goal of being able to unite families that slavery had brutally torn apart.

After the Civil War, Still built one of the largest real estate holdings of a Black man in the United States and took on numerous philanthropic efforts. His 1872 book, *The Underground*

Railroad Records, details the stories of more than six hundred people he personally helped to freedom.

Mary Church Terrell

Mary Church Terrell (Mollie to her friends) was born in Memphis, the eldest daughter of Robert Church. She studied French, German, and Latin at Oberlin College, where she became one of the first Black women in the nation to graduate with a four-year bachelor's degree instead of the two-year diploma often called "the ladies' degree." Along with her classmate and lifelong friend Anna Julia Cooper, Church Terrell went on to earn a master's degree at Oberlin. They are believed to be two of the first Black women to earn graduate degrees in the United States. After graduating, she embarked on a two-year tour of Europe, traveling to France, Switzerland, Italy, and Germany and studying languages. While there, she wrote in her diary in French or German, depending on which country she was in.

She and Ida would come to differ in their strategies. Church Terrell believed that the path to ending racial discrimination lay in education and achievement, similar to Du Bois's thoughts about the Talented Tenth. Her phrase "lifting as we climb" became, and remains, the slogan for the National Association for Colored Women. Church Terrell was president of that organization for five years and became an active leader in women's suffrage. She continued her activism in her adopted hometown of Washington, DC, into her eighties, organizing and winning landmark cases against segregation.

Sources and Further Reading

This book focuses on the first thirty-three years of Ida's life, from her early twenties as she established herself as a teacher and journalist through her move to Chicago, her leadership as an editor of the Chicago Conservator, *and her marriage to the* Conservator's *founder, Ferdinand Lee Barnett. Here are some of the books I found most helpful in learning about Ida and her era.*

Bay, Mia. *To Tell the Truth Freely: The Life of Ida B. Wells.* New York: Hill and Wang, 2009.

Blight, David W. *Frederick Douglass, Prophet of Freedom.* New York: Simon and Schuster, 2018.

Duster, Michelle. *Ida B., the Queen: The Extraordinary Life and Legacy of Ida B. Wells.* New York: One Signal / Atria, 2021.

Duster, Michelle, ed. *Ida from Abroad: The Timeless Writings of Ida B. Wells from England in 1894.* Chicago: Benjamin Williams, 2010.

Gatewood, Willard B. *Aristocrats of Color: The Black Elite, 1880–1920.* Fayetteville: University of Arkansas Press, 2000.

Giddings, Paula J. *Ida: A Sword Among Lions: Ida B. Wells and the Campaign Against Lynching.* New York: Amistad, 2009.

Giddings, Paula J. *When and Where I Enter: The Impact of Black Women on Race and Sex in America.* New York: William Morrow, 1984.

Loewenberg, Bert James, and Ruth Bogin, eds. *Black Women in Nineteenth-Century American Life: Their Words, Their Thoughts, Their Feelings.* University Park: Pennsylvania State University Press, 1976.

Lystra, Karen. *Searching the Heart: Women, Men, and Romantic Love in Nineteenth-Century America.* New York: Oxford University Press, 1989.

Parker, Alison M. *Unceasing Militant: The Life of Mary Church Terrell.* Chapel Hill: University of North Carolina Press, 2020.

Taylor, Elizabeth Dowling. *The Original Black Elite: Daniel Murray and the Story of a Forgotten Era*. New York: Amistad, 2017.

Wells-Barnett, Ida B. *A Red Record: Tabulated Statistics and Alleged Causes of Lynchings in the United States.* Chicago: Donohue and Henneberry, 1894.

Wells-Barnett, Ida B. *Crusade for Justice: The Autobiography of Ida B. Wells.* Edited by Alfreda M. Duster. Chicago: University of Chicago Press, 2020.

Wells-Barnett, Ida B. *The Light of Truth: Writings of an Anti-Lynching Crusader.* Edited by Mia Bay. New York: Penguin, 2014.

Wells-Barnett, Ida B. *The Memphis Diary of Ida B. Wells: An Intimate Portrait of the Activist as a Young Woman.* Edited by Miriam DeCosta-Willis. Boston: Beacon, 1995